Fantasies of Science, Romance, and the Weird

Fantasies of Science, Romance, and the Weird

Robert W. Chambers

Volume 1

Coachwhip Publications
Landisville, Pennsylvania

Fantasies of Science, Romance, and the Weird by Robert W. Chambers, Volume 1
Copyright © 2009 Coachwhip Publications

ISBN 1-930585-78-0
ISBN-13 978-1-930585-78-2

Cover: Butterfly © Oliver Lenz

Coachwhipbooks.com

CONTENTS

The Harbor-Master

I

Because it all seems so improbable—so horribly impossible to me now, sitting here safe and sane in my own library—I hesitate to record an episode which already appears to me less horrible than grotesque. Yet, unless this story is written now, I know I shall never have the courage to tell the truth about the matter—not from fear of ridicule, but because I myself shall soon cease to credit what I now know to be true. Yet scarcely a month has elapsed since I heard the stealthy purring of what I believed to be the shoaling under-tow—scarcely a month ago, with my own eyes, I saw that which, even now, I am beginning to believe never existed. As for the harbor-master—and the blow I am now striking at the old order of things—But of that I shall not speak now, or later; I shall try to tell the story simply and truthfully, and let my friends testify as to my probity and the publishers of this book corroborate them.

On the 29th of February I resigned my position under the government and left Washington to accept an offer from Professor Farrago—whose name he kindly permits me to use—and on the first day of April I entered upon my new and congenial duties as general superintendent of the water-fowl department connected with the Zoological Gardens then in course of erection at Bronx Park, New York.

For a week I followed the routine, examining the new foundations, studying the architect's plans, following the surveyors through the Bronx thickets, suggesting arrangements for water-courses and pools destined to be included in the enclosures for swans, geese, pelicans, herons, and such of the waders and swimmers as we might expect to acclimate in Bronx Park.

It was at that time the policy of the trustees and officers of the Zoological Gardens neither to employ collectors nor to send out expeditions in search of specimens. The society decided to depend upon voluntary contributions, and I was always busy, part of the day, in dictating answers to correspondents who wrote offering their services as hunters of big game, collectors of all sorts of fauna, trappers, snarers, and also to those who offered specimens for sale, usually at exorbitant rates.

To the proprietors of five-legged kittens, mangy lynxes, moth-eaten coyotes, and dancing bears I returned courteous but uncompromising refusals—of course, first submitting all such letters, together with my replies, to Professor Farrago.

One day towards the end of May, however, just as I was leaving Bronx Park to return to town, Professor Lesard, of the reptilian department, called out to me that Professor Farrago wanted to see me a moment; so I put my pipe into my pocket again and retraced my steps to the temporary, wooden building occupied by Professor Farrago, general superintendent of the Zoological Gardens. The professor, who was sitting at his desk before a pile of letters and replies submitted for approval by me, pushed his glasses down and looked over them at me with a whimsical smile that suggested amusement, impatience, annoyance, and perhaps a faint trace of apology.

"Now, here's a letter," he said, with a deliberate gesture towards a sheet of paper impaled on a file— "a letter that I suppose you remember." He disengaged the sheet of paper and handed it to me.

"Oh yes," I replied, with a shrug; "of course the man is mistaken—or—"

"Or what?" demanded Professor Farrago, tranquilly, wiping his glasses.

"—Or a liar," I replied.

After a silence he leaned back in his chair and bade me read the letter to him again, and I did so with a contemptuous tolerance for the writer, who must have been either a very innocent victim or a very stupid swindler.

I said as much to Professor Farrago, but, to my surprise, he appeared to waver.

"I suppose," he said, with his near-sighted, embarrassed smile, "that nine hundred and ninety-nine men in a thousand would throw that letter aside and condemn the writer as a liar or a fool?"

"In my opinion," said I, "he's one or the other."

"He isn't—in mine," said the professor, placidly.

"What!" I exclaimed. "Here is a man living all alone on a strip of rock and sand between the wilderness and the sea, who wants you to send somebody to take charge of a bird that doesn't exist!"

"How do you know," asked Professor Farrago, "that the bird in question does not exist?"

"It is generally accepted," I replied, sarcastically, "that the great auk has been extinct for years. Therefore I may be pardoned for doubting that our correspondent possesses a pair of them alive."

"Oh, you young fellows," said the professor, smiling wearily, "you embark on a theory for destinations that don't exist."

He leaned back in his chair, his amused eyes searching space for the imagery that made him smile.

"Like swimming squirrels, you navigate with the help of Heaven and a stiff breeze, but you never land where you hope to—do you?"

Rather red in the face, I said: "Don't you believe the great auk to be extinct?"

"Audubon saw the great auk."

"Who has seen a single specimen since?"

"Nobody—except our correspondent here," he replied, laughing.

I laughed, too, considering the interview at an end, but the professor went on, coolly:

"Whatever it is that our correspondent has—and I am daring to believe that it is the great auk itself—I want you to secure it for the society."

When my astonishment subsided my first conscious sentiment was one of pity. Clearly, Professor Farrago was on the verge of dotage—ah, what a loss to the world!

I believe now that Professor Farrago perfectly interpreted my thoughts, but he betrayed neither resentment nor impatience. I drew a chair up beside his desk—there was nothing to do but to obey, and this fool's errand was none of my conceiving.

Together we made out a list of articles necessary for me and itemized the expenses I might incur, and I set a date for my return, allowing no margin for a successful termination to the expedition.

"Never mind that," said the professor. "What I want you to do is to get those birds here safely. Now, how many men will you take?"

"None," I replied, bluntly; "it's a useless expense, unless there is something to bring back. If there is I'll wire you, you may be sure."

"Very well," said Professor Farrago, good-humoredly, "you shall have all the assistance you may require. Can you leave to-night?"

The old gentleman was certainly prompt. I nodded, half-sulkily, aware of his amusement.

"So," I said, picking up my hat, "I am to start north to find a place called Black Harbor, where there is a man named Halyard who possesses, among other household utensils, two extinct great auks—"

We were both laughing by this time. I asked him why on earth he credited the assertion of a man he had never before heard of.

"I suppose," he replied, with the same half-apologetic, half-humorous smile, "it is instinct. I feel, somehow, that this man Halyard has got an auk—perhaps two. I can't get away from the idea that we are on the eve of acquiring the rarest of living creatures. It's odd for a scientist to talk as I do; doubtless you're shocked—admit it, now!"

But I was not shocked; on the contrary, I was conscious that the same strange hope that Professor Farrago cherished was beginning, in spite of me, to stir my pulses, too.

"If he has—" I began, then stopped.

The professor and I looked hard at each other in silence.

"Go on," he said, encouragingly.

But I had nothing more to say, for the prospect of beholding with my own eyes a living specimen of the great auk produced a series of conflicting emotions within me which rendered speech profanely superfluous.

As I took my leave Professor Farrago came to the door of the temporary, wooden office and handed me the letter written by the man Halyard. I folded it and put it into my pocket, as Halyard might require it for my own identification.

"How much does he want for the pair?" I asked.

"Ten thousand dollars. Don't demur—if the birds are really—"

"I know," I said, hastily, not daring to hope too much.

"One thing more," said Professor Farrago, gravely; "you know, in that last paragraph of his letter, Halyard speaks of something else in the way of specimens—an undiscovered species of amphibious biped—just read that paragraph again, will you?"

I drew the letter from my pocket and read as he directed:

"When you have seen the two living specimens of the great auk, and have satisfied yourself that I tell the truth, you may be wise enough to listen without prejudice to a statement I shall make concerning the existence of the strangest creature ever fashioned. I will merely say, at this time, that the creature referred to is an amphibious biped and inhabits the ocean near this coast. More I cannot say, for I personally have not seen the animal, but I have a witness who has, and there are many who affirm that they have seen the creature.

"You will naturally say that my statement amounts to nothing; but when your representative arrives, if he be free from prejudice, I expect his reports to you concerning this sea-biped will confirm the solemn statements of a witness I know to be unimpeachable.

"Yours truly,
"Burton Halyard.
"Black Harbor"

"Well," I said, after a moment's thought, "here goes for the wild-goose chase."

"Wild auk, you mean," said Professor Farrago, shaking hands with me. "You will start to-night, won't you?"

"Yes, but Heaven knows how I'm ever going to land in this man Halyard's door-yard. Good-bye!"

"About that sea-biped—" began Professor Farrago, shyly.

"Oh, don't!" I said; "I can swallow the auks, feathers and claws, but if this fellow Halyard is hinting he's seen an amphibious creature resembling a man—"

"—Or a woman," said the professor, cautiously.

I retired, disgusted, my faith shaken in the mental vigor of Professor Farrago.

II

The three days' voyage by boat and rail was irksome. I bought my kit at Sainte Croix, on the Central Pacific Railroad, and on June 1st I began the last stage of my journey via the Sainte Isole broad-gauge, arriving in the wilderness by daylight. A tedious forced march by blazed trail, freshly spotted on the wrong side, of course, brought me to the northern terminus of the rusty, narrow-gauge lumber railway which runs from the heart of the hushed pine wilderness to the sea.

Already a long train of battered flat-cars, piled with sluice-props and roughly hewn sleepers, was moving slowly off into the brooding forest gloom, when I came in sight of the track; but I developed a gratifying and unexpected burst of speed, shouting all the while. The train stopped; I swung myself aboard the last car, where a pleasant young fellow was sitting on the rear brake, chewing spruce and reading a letter.

"Come aboard, sir," he said, looking up with a smile; "I guess you're the man in a hurry."

"I'm looking for a man named Halyard," I said, dropping rifle and knapsack on the fresh-cut, fragrant pile of pine. "Are you Halyard?"

"No, I'm Francis Lee, bossing the mica pit at Port-of-Waves," he replied, "but this letter is from Halyard, asking me to look out for a man in a hurry from Bronx Park, New York."

"I'm that man," said I, filling my pipe and offering him a share of the weed of peace, and we sat side by side smoking very amiably, until a signal from the locomotive sent him forward and I was left alone, lounging at ease, head pillowed on both arms, watching the blue sky flying through the branches overhead.

Long before we came in sight of the ocean I smelled it; the fresh, salt aroma stole into my senses, drowsy with the heated odor of pine and hemlock, and I sat up, peering ahead into the dusky sea of pines.

Fresher and fresher came the wind from the sea, in puffs, in mild, sweet breezes, in steady, freshening currents, blowing the feathery crowns of the pines, setting the balsam's blue tufts rocking.

Lee wandered back over the long line of flats, balancing himself nonchalantly as the cars swung around a sharp curve, where water dripped from a newly propped sluice that suddenly emerged from the depths of the forest to run parallel to the railroad track.

"Built it this spring," he said, surveying his handiwork, which seemed to undulate as the cars swept past. "It runs to the cove—or ought to—" He stopped abruptly with a thoughtful glance at me.

"So you're going over to Halyard's?" he continued, as though answering a question asked by himself.

I nodded.

"You've never been there—of course?"

"No," I said, "and I'm not likely to go again."

I would have told him why I was going if I had not already begun to feel ashamed of my idiotic errand.

"I guess you're going to look at those birds of his," continued Lee, placidly.

"I guess I am," I said, sulkily, glancing askance to see whether he was smiling.

But he only asked me, quite seriously, whether a great auk was really a very rare bird; and I told him that the last one ever seen had been found dead off Labrador in January, 1870. Then I asked him whether these birds of Halyard's were really great auks, and he replied, somewhat indifferently, that he supposed they were—at least, nobody had ever before seen such birds near Port-of-Waves.

"There's something else," he said, running a pine-sliver through his pipe-stem— "something that interests us all here more than auks, big or little. I suppose I might as well speak of it, as you are bound to hear about it sooner or later."

He hesitated, and I could see that he was embarrassed, searching for the exact words to convey his meaning.

"If," said I, "you have anything in this region more important to science than the great auk, I should be very glad to know about it."

Perhaps there was the faintest tinge of sarcasm in my voice, for he shot a sharp glance at me and then turned slightly. After a moment, however, he put his pipe into his pocket, laid hold of the brake with both hands, vaulted to his perch aloft, and glanced down at me.

"Did you ever hear of the harbor-master?" he asked, maliciously.

"Which harbor-master?" I inquired.

"You'll know before long," he observed, with a satisfied glance into perspective.

This rather extraordinary observation puzzled me. I waited for him to resume, and, as he did not, I asked him what he meant.

"If I knew," he said, "I'd tell you. But, come to think of it, I'd be a fool to go into details with a scientific man. You'll hear about the harbor-master—perhaps you will see the harbor-master. In that event I should be glad to converse with you on the subject."

I could not help laughing at his prim and precise manner, and, after a moment, he also laughed, saying:

"It hurts a man's vanity to know he knows a thing that somebody else knows he doesn't know. I'm damned if I say another word about the harbor-master until you've been to Halyard's!"

"A harbor-master," I persisted, "is an official who superintends the mooring of ships—isn't he?"

But he refused to be tempted into conversation, and we lounged silently on the lumber until a long, thin whistle from the locomotive and a rush of stinging salt-wind brought us to our feet. Through the trees I could see the bluish-black ocean, stretching out beyond black headlands to meet the clouds; a great wind was roaring among the trees as the train slowly came to a stand-still on the edge of the primeval forest.

Lee jumped to the ground and aided me with my rifle and pack, and then the train began to back away along a curved side-track which, Lee said, led to the mica-pit and company stores.

"Now what will you do?" he asked, pleasantly. "I can give you a good dinner and a decent bed to-night if you like—and I'm sure

Mrs. Lee would be very glad to have you stop with us as long as you choose."

I thanked him, but said that I was anxious to reach Halyard's before dark, and he very kindly led me along the cliffs and pointed out the path.

"This man Halyard," he said, "is an invalid. He lives at a cove called Black Harbor, and all his truck goes through to him over the company's road. We receive it here, and send a pack-mule through once a month. I've met him; he's a bad-tempered hypochondriac, a cynic at heart, and a man whose word is never doubted. If he says he has a great auk, you may be satisfied he has."

My heart was beating with excitement at the prospect; I looked out across the wooded headlands and tangled stretches of dune and hollow, trying to realize what it might mean to me, to Professor Farrago, to the world, if I should lead back to New York a live auk.

"He's a crank," said Lee; "frankly, I don't like him. If you find it unpleasant there, come back to us."

"Does Halyard live alone?" I asked.

"Yes—except for a professional trained nurse—poor thing!"

"A man?"

"No," said Lee, disgustedly.

Presently he gave me a peculiar glance; hesitated, and finally said: "Ask Halyard to tell you about his nurse and—the harbor-master. Good-bye—I'm due at the quarry. Come and stay with us whenever you care to; you will find a welcome at Port-of-Waves."

We shook hands and parted on the cliff, he turning back into the forest along the railway, I starting northward, pack slung, rifle over my shoulder. Once I met a group of quarrymen, faces burned brick-red, scarred hands swinging as they walked. And, as I passed them with a nod, turning, I saw that they also had turned to look after me, and I caught a word or two of their conversation, whirled back to me on the sea-wind. They were speaking of the harbor-master.

III

Towards sunset I came out on a sheer granite cliff where the sea-birds were whirling and clamoring, and the great breakers dashed, rolling in double-thundered reverberations on the sun-dyed, crimson sands below the rock.

Across the half-moon of beach towered another cliff, and, behind this, I saw a column of smoke rising in the still air. It certainly came from Halyard's chimney, although the opposite cliff prevented me from seeing the house itself.

I rested a moment to refill my pipe, then resumed rifle and pack, and cautiously started to skirt the cliffs. I had descended half-way towards the beech, and was examining the cliff opposite, when something on the very top of the rock arrested my attention—a man darkly outlined against the sky. The next moment, however, I knew it could not be a man, for the object suddenly glided over the face of the cliff and slid down the sheer, smooth face like a lizard. Before I could get a square look at it, the thing crawled into the surf—or, at least, it seemed to—but the whole episode occurred so suddenly, so unexpectedly, that I was not sure I had seen anything at all.

However, I was curious enough to climb the cliff on the land side and make my way towards the spot where I imagined I saw the man. Of course, there was nothing there—not a trace of a human being, I mean. Something had been there—a sea-otter, possibly—for the remains of a freshly killed fish lay on the rock, eaten to the back-bone and tail.

The next moment, below me, I saw the house, a freshly painted, trim, flimsy structure, modern, and very much out of harmony with the splendid savagery surrounding it. It struck a nasty, cheap note in the noble, gray monotony of headland and sea.

The descent was easy enough. I crossed the crescent beach, hard as pink marble, and found a little trodden path among the rocks, that led to the front porch of the house.

There were two people on the porch—I heard their voices before I saw them—and when I set my foot upon the wooden steps, I saw one of them, a woman, rise from her chair and step hastily towards me.

"Come back!" cried the other, a man with a smooth-shaven, deeply lined face, and a pair of angry, blue eyes; and the woman stepped back quietly, acknowledging my lifted hat with a silent inclination.

The man, who was reclining in an invalid's rolling-chair, clapped both large, pale hands to the wheels and pushed himself out along the porch. He had shawls pinned about him, an untidy, drab-colored hat on his head, and, when he looked down at me, he scowled.

"I know who you are," he said, in his acid voice; "you're one of the Zoological men from Bronx Park. You look like it, anyway."

"It is easy to recognize you from your reputation," I replied, irritated at his discourtesy.

"Really," he replied, with something between a sneer and a laugh, "I'm obliged for your frankness. You're after my great auks, are you not?"

"Nothing else would have tempted me into this place," I replied, sincerely.

"Thank Heaven for that," he said. "Sit down a moment; you've interrupted us." Then, turning to the young woman, who wore the neat gown and tiny cap of a professional nurse, he bade her resume what she had been saying. She did so, with deprecating glance at me, which made the old man sneer again.

"It happened so suddenly," she said, in her low voice, "that I had no chance to get back. The boat was drifting in the cove; I sat in the stern, reading, both oars shipped, and the tiller swinging. Then I heard a scratching under the boat, but thought it might be seaweed—and, next moment, came those soft thumpings, like the sound of a big fish rubbing its nose against a float."

Halyard clutched the wheels of his chair and stared at the girl in grim displeasure.

"Didn't you know enough to be frightened?" he demanded.

"No—not then," she said, coloring faintly; "but when, after a few moments, I looked up and saw the harbor-master running up and down the beach, I was horribly frightened."

"Really?" said Halyard, sarcastically; "it was about time." Then, turning to me, he rasped out: "And that young lady was obliged to row all the way to Port-of-Waves and call to Lee's quarrymen to take her boat in."

Completely mystified, I looked from Halyard to the girl, not in the least comprehending what all this meant.

"That will do," said Halyard, ungraciously, which curt phrase was apparently the usual dismissal for the nurse.

She rose, and I rose, and she passed me with an inclination, stepping noiselessly into the house.

"I want beef-tea!" bawled Halyard after her; then he gave me an unamiable glance.

"I was a well-bred man," he sneered; "I'm a Harvard graduate, too, but I live as I like, and I do what I like, and I say what I like."

"You certainly are not reticent," I said, disgusted.

"Why should I be?" he rasped; "I pay that young woman for my irritability; it's a bargain between us."

"In your domestic affairs," I said, "there is nothing that interests me. I came to see those auks."

"You probably believe them to be razor-billed auks," he said, contemptuously. "But they're not; they're great auks."

I suggested that he permit me to examine them, and he replied, indifferently, that they were in a pen in his backyard, and that I was free to step around the house when I cared to.

I laid my rifle and pack on the veranda, and hastened off with mixed emotions, among which hope no longer predominated. No man in his senses would keep two such precious prizes in a pen in his backyard, I argued, and I was perfectly prepared to find anything from a puffin to a penguin in that pen.

I shall never forget, as long as I live, my stupor of amazement when I came to the wire-covered enclosure. Not only were there two great auks in the pen, alive, breathing, squatting in bulky majesty on their seaweed bed, but one of them was gravely contemplating two newly hatched chicks, all hill and feet, which nestled sedately at the edge of a puddle of salt-water, where some small fish were swimming. For a while excitement blinded, nay, deafened me. I tried to realize that I was gazing upon the last individuals of an all but extinct race—the sole survivors of the gigantic auk, which, for thirty years, has been accounted an extinct creature.

I believe that I did not move muscle nor limb until the sun had gone down and the crowding darkness blurred my straining eyes and blotted the great, silent, bright-eyed birds from sight.

Even then I could not tear myself away from the enclosure; I listened to the strange, drowsy note of the male bird, the fainter responses of the female, the thin plaints of the chicks, huddling under her breast; I heard their flipper-like, embryotic wings beating sleepily as the birds stretched and yawned their beaks and clacked them, preparing for slumber.

"If you please," came a soft voice from the door, "Mr. Halyard awaits your company to dinner."

IV

I dined well—or, rather, I might have enjoyed my dinner if Mr. Halyard had been eliminated; and the feast consisted exclusively of a joint of beef, the pretty nurse, and myself. She was exceedingly attractive—with a disturbing fashion of lowering her head and raising her dark eyes when spoken to. As for Halyard, he was unspeakable, bundled up in his snuffy shawls, and making uncouth noises over his gruel. But it is only just to say that his table was worth sitting down to and his wine was sound as a bell.

"Yah!" he snapped, "I'm sick of this cursed soup—and I'll trouble you to fill my glass—"

"It is dangerous for you to touch claret," said the pretty nurse.

"I might as well die at dinner as anywhere," he observed.

"Certainly," said I, cheerfully passing the decanter, but he did not appear overpleased with the attention.

"I can't smoke, either," he snarled, hitching the shawls around until he looked like Richard the Third.

However, he was good enough to shove a box of cigars at me, and I took one and stood up, as the pretty nurse slipped past and vanished into the little parlor beyond.

We sat there for a while without speaking. He picked irritably at the bread-crumbs on the cloth, never glancing in my direction; and I, tired from my long foot-tour, lay back in my chair, silently appreciating one of the best cigars I ever smoked.

"Well," he rasped out at length, "what do you think of my auks—and my veracity?"

I told him that both were unimpeachable.

"Didn't they call me a swindler down there at your museum?" he demanded.

I admitted that I had heard the term applied. Then I made a clean breast of the matter, telling him that it was I who had doubted; that my chief, Professor Farrago, had sent me against my will, and that I was ready and glad to admit that he, Mr. Halyard, was a benefactor of the human race.

"Bosh!" he said. "What good does a confounded wobbly, bandy-toed bird do to the human race?"

But he was pleased, nevertheless; and presently he asked me, not unamiably, to punish his claret again.

"I'm done for," he said; "good things to eat and drink are no good to me. Some day I'll get mad enough to have a fit, and then—"

He paused to yawn.

"Then," he continued, "that little nurse of mine will drink up my claret and go back to civilization, where people are polite."

Somehow or other, in spite of the fact that Halyard was an old pig, what he said touched me. There was certainly not much left in life for him—as he regarded life.

"I'm going to leave her this house," he said, arranging his shawls. "She doesn't know it. I'm going to leave her my money, too. She doesn't know that. Good Lord! What kind of a woman can she be to stand my bad temper for a few dollars a month!"

"I think," said I, "that it's partly because she's poor, partly because she's sorry for you."

He looked up with a ghastly smile.

"You think she really is sorry?"

Before I could answer he went on: "I'm no mawkish sentimentalist, and I won't allow anybody to be sorry for me—do you hear?"

"Oh, I'm not sorry for you!" I said, hastily, and, for the first time since I had seen him, he laughed heartily, without a sneer.

We both seemed to feel better after that; I drank his wine and smoked his cigars, and he appeared to take a certain grim pleasure in watching me.

"There's no fool like a young fool," he observed, presently.

As I had no doubt he referred to me, I paid him no attention.

After fidgeting with his shawls, he gave me an oblique scowl and asked me my age.

"Twenty-four," I replied.

"Sort of a tadpole, aren't you?" he said.

As I took no offence, he repeated the remark.

"Oh, come," said I, "there's no use in trying to irritate me. I see through you; a row acts like a cocktail on you—but you'll have to stick to gruel in my company."

"I call that impudence!" he rasped out, wrathfully.

"I don't care what you call it," I replied, undisturbed, "I am not going to be worried by you. Anyway," I ended, "it is my opinion that you could be very good company if you chose."

The proposition appeared to take his breath away—at least, he said nothing more; and I finished my cigar in peace and tossed the stump into a saucer.

"Now," said I, "what price do you set upon your birds, Mr. Halyard?"

"Ten thousand dollars," he snapped, with an evil smile.

"You will receive a certified check when the birds are delivered," I said, quietly.

"You don't mean to say you agree to that outrageous bargain—and I won't take a cent less, either—Good Lord!—haven't you any spirit left?" he cried, half rising from his pile of shawls.

His piteous eagerness for a dispute sent me into laughter impossible to control, and he eyed me, mouth open, animosity rising visibly.

Then he seized the wheels of his invalid chair and trundled away, too mad to speak; and I strolled out into the parlor, still laughing.

The pretty nurse was there, sewing under a hanging lamp.

"If I am not indiscreet—" I began.

"Indiscretion is the better part of valor," said she, dropping her head but raising her eyes.

So I sat down with a frivolous smile peculiar to the appreciated.

"Doubtless," said I, "you are hemming a 'kerchief."

"Doubtless I am not," she said; "this is a night-cap for Mr. Hal-yard."

A mental vision of Halyard in a night-cap, very mad, nearly set me laughing again.

"Like the King of Yvetot, he wears his crown in bed," I said, flippantly.

"The King of Yvetot might have made that remark," she observed, re-threading her needle.

It is unpleasant to be reproved. How large and red and hot a man's ears feel.

To cool them, I strolled out to the porch; and, after a while, the pretty nurse came out, too, and sat down in a chair not far away. She probably regretted her lost opportunity to be flirted with.

"I have so little company—it is a great relief to see somebody from the world," she said. "If you can be agreeable, I wish you would."

The idea that she had come out to see me was so agreeable that I remained speechless until she said: "Do tell me what people are doing in New York."

So I seated myself on the steps and talked about the portion of the world inhabited by me, while she sat sewing in the dull light that straggled out from the parlor windows.

She had a certain coquetry of her own, using the usual methods with an individuality that was certainly fetching. For instance, when she lost her needle—and, another time, when we both, on hands and knees, hunted for her thimble.

However, directions for these pastimes may be found in contemporary classics.

I was as entertaining as I could be—perhaps not quite as entertaining as a young man usually thinks he is.

However, we got on very well together until I asked her tenderly who the harbor-master might be, whom they all discussed so mysteriously.

"I do not care to speak about it," she said, with a primness of which I had not suspected her capable.

Of course I could scarcely pursue the subject after that—and, indeed, I did not intend to—so I began to tell her how I fancied I had seen a man on the cliff that afternoon, and how the creature slid over the sheer rock like a snake.

To my amazement, she asked me to kindly discontinue the account of my adventures, in an icy tone, which left no room for protest.

"It was only a sea-otter," I tried to explain, thinking perhaps she did not care for snake stories.

But the explanation did not appear to interest her, and I was mortified to observe that my impression upon her was anything but pleasant.

"She doesn't seem to like me and my stories," thought I, "but she is too young, perhaps, to appreciate them."

So I forgave her—for she was even prettier than I had thought her at first—and I took my leave, saying that Mr. Halyard would doubtless direct me to my room.

Halyard was in his library, cleaning a revolver, when I entered.

"Your room is next to mine, " he said; "pleasant dreams, and kindly refrain from snoring."

"May I venture an absurd hope that you will do the same!" I replied, politely.

That maddened him, so I hastily withdrew.

I had been asleep for at least two hours when a movement by my bedside and a light in my eyes awakened me. I sat bolt upright in bed, blinking at Halyard, who, clad in a dressing-gown and wearing a night-cap, had wheeled himself into my room with one hand, while with the other he solemnly waved a candle over my head.

"I'm so cursed lonely," he said— "come, there's a good fellow— talk to me in your own original, impudent way."

I objected strenuously, but he looked so worn and thin, so lonely and bad-tempered, so lovelessly grotesque, that I got out of bed and passed a spongeful of cold water over my head.

Then I returned to bed and propped the pillows up for a back-rest, ready to quarrel with him if it might bring some little pleasure into his morbid existence.

"No," he said, amiably, "I'm too worried to quarrel, but I'm much obliged for your kindly offer. I want to tell you something."

"What?" I asked, suspiciously.

"I want to ask you if you ever saw a man with gills like a fish?"

"Gills?" I repeated.

"Yes, gills! Did you?"

"No," I replied, angrily, "and neither did you."

"No, I never did," he said, in a curiously placid voice, "but there's a man with gills like a fish who lives in the ocean out there. Oh, you needn't look that way—nobody ever thinks of doubting my word, and I tell you that there's a man—or a thing that looks like a man—as big as you are, too—all slate-colored—with nasty red gills like a fish!—and I've a witness to prove what I say!"

"Who?" I asked, sarcastically.

"The witness? My nurse."

"Oh! She saw a slate-colored man with gills?"

"Yes, she did. So did Francis Lee, superintendent of the Mica Quarry Company at Port-of-Waves. So have a dozen men who work in the quarry. Oh, you needn't laugh, young man. It's an old story here, and anybody can tell you about the harbor-master."

"The harbor-master!" I exclaimed.

"Yes, that slate-colored thing with gills, that looks like a man—and—by Heaven! is a man—that's the harbor-master. Ask any quarryman at Port-of-Waves what it is that comes purring around their boats at the wharf and unties painters and changes the mooring of every cat-boat in the cove at night! Ask Francis Lee what it was he saw running and leaping up and down the shoal at sunset last Friday! Ask anybody along the coast what sort of a thing moves about the cliffs like a man and slides over them into the sea like an otter—"

"I saw it do that!" I burst out.

"Oh, did you? Well, what was it?"

Something kept me silent, although a dozen explanations flew to my lips.

After a pause, Halyard said: "You saw the harbor-master, that's what you saw!"

I looked at him without a word.

"Don't mistake me," he said, pettishly; "I don't think that the harbor-master is a spirit or a sprite or a hobgoblin, or any sort of damned rot. Neither do I believe it to be an optical illusion."

"What do you think it is?" I asked.

"I think it's a man—I think it's a branch of the human race—that's what I think. Let me tell you something: the deepest spot in the Atlantic Ocean is a trifle over five miles deep—and I suppose you know that this place lies only about a quarter of a mile off this headland. The British exploring vessel, *Gull*, Captain Marotte, discovered and sounded it, I believe. Anyway, it's there, and it's my belief that the profound depths are inhabited by the remnants of the last race of amphibious human beings!"

This was childish; I did not bother to reply.

"Believe it or not, as you will," he said, angrily; "one thing I know, and that is this: the harbor-master has taken to hanging around my cove, and he is attracted by my nurse! I won't have it! I'll blow his fishy gills out of his head if I ever get a shot at him! I don't care whether it's homicide or not—anyway, it's a new kind of murder and it attracts me!"

I gazed at him incredulously, but he was working himself into a passion, and I did not choose to say what I thought.

"Yes, this slate-colored thing with gills goes purring and grinning and spitting about after my nurse—when she walks, when she rows, when she sits on the beach! Gad! It drives me nearly frantic. I won't tolerate it, I tell you!"

"No," said I, "I wouldn't either." And I rolled over in bed convulsed with laughter.

The next moment I heard my door slam. I smothered my mirth and rose to close the window, for the land-wind blew cold from the forest, and a drizzle was sweeping the carpet as far as my bed.

That luminous glare which sometimes lingers after the stars go out, threw a trembling, nebulous radiance over sand and cove. I heard the seething currents under the breakers' softened thunder—louder than I ever heard it. Then, as I closed my window, lingering for a last look at the crawling tide, I saw a man standing, ankle-deep, in the surf, all alone there in the night. But—was it a man? For the figure suddenly began running over the beach on all fours like a beetle, waving its limbs like feelers. Before I could throw open the window again it darted into the surf, and, when I leaned out into the chilling drizzle, I saw nothing save the flat ebb crawling on the coast—I heard nothing save the purring of bubbles on seething sands.

V

It took me a week to perfect my arrangements for transporting the great auks, by water, to Port-of-Waves, where a lumber schooner was to be sent from Petite Sainte Isole, chartered by me for a voyage to New York.

I had constructed a cage made of osiers, in which my auks were to squat until they arrived at Bronx Park. My telegrams to Professor Farrago were brief. One merely said "Victory!" Another explained that I wanted no assistance; and a third read: "Schooner chartered. Arrive New York July 1st. Send furniture-van to foot of Bluff Street."

My week as a guest of Mr. Halyard proved interesting. I wrangled with that invalid to his heart's content, I worked all day on my osier cage, I hunted the thimble in the moonlight with the pretty nurse. We sometimes found it.

As for the thing they called the harbor-master, I saw it a dozen times, but always either at night or so far away and so close to the sea that of course no trace of it remained when I reached the spot, rifle in hand.

I had quite made up my mind that the so-called harbor-master was a demented darky—wandered from, Heaven knows where—perhaps shipwrecked and gone mad from his sufferings. Still, it was far from pleasant to know that the creature was strongly attracted by the pretty nurse.

She, however, persisted in regarding the harbor-master as a sea-creature; she earnestly affirmed that it had gills, like a fish's gills, that it had a soft, fleshy hole for a mouth, and its eyes were luminous and lidless and fixed.

"Besides," she said, with a shudder, "it's all slate color, like a porpoise, and it looks as wet as a sheet of india-rubber in a dissecting-room."

The day before I was to set sail with my auks in a cat-boat bound for Port-of-Waves, Halyard trundled up to me in his chair and announced his intention of going with me.

"Going where?" I asked.

"To Port-of-Waves and then to New York," he replied, tranquilly.

I was doubtful, and my lack of cordiality hurt his feelings.

"Oh, of course, if you need the sea-voyage—" I began.

"I don't; I need you," he said, savagely; "I need the stimulus of our daily quarrel. I never disagreed so pleasantly with anybody in my life; it agrees with me; I am a hundred per cent. better than I was last week."

I was inclined to resent this, but something in the deep-lined face of the invalid softened me. Besides, I had taken a hearty liking to the old pig.

"I don't want any mawkish sentiment about it," he said, observing me closely; "I won't permit anybody to feel sorry for me—do you understand?"

"I'll trouble you to use a different tone in addressing me," I replied, hotly; "I'll feel sorry for you if I choose to!" And our usual quarrel proceeded, to his deep satisfaction.

By six o'clock next evening I had Halyard's luggage stowed away in the cat-boat, and the pretty nurse's effects corded down, with the newly hatched auk-chicks in a hat-box on top. She and I placed the osier cage aboard, securing it firmly, and then, throwing table-cloths over the auks' heads, we led those simple and dignified birds down the path and across the plank at the little wooden pier. Together we locked up the house, while Halyard stormed at us both and wheeled himself furiously up and down the beach below. At the last moment she forgot her thimble. But we found it, I forget where.

"Come on!" shouted Halyard, waving his shawls furiously; "what the devil are you about up there?"

He received our explanation with a sniff, and we trundled him aboard without further ceremony.

"Don't run me across the plank like a steamer trunk!" he shouted, as I shot him dexterously into the cock-pit. But the wind was dying away, and I had no time to dispute with him then.

The sun was setting above the pine-clad ridge as our sail flapped and partly filled, and I cast off, and began a long tack, east by south, to avoid the spouting rocks on our starboard bow.

The sea-birds rose in clouds as we swung across the shoal, the black surf-ducks scuttered out to sea, the gulls tossed their sun-tipped wings in the ocean, riding the rollers like bits of froth.

Already we were sailing slowly out across that great hole in the ocean, five miles deep, the most profound sounding ever taken in the Atlantic. The presence of great heights or great depths, seen or unseen, always impresses the human mind—perhaps oppresses it. We were very silent; the sunlight stain on cliff and beach deepened to crimson, then faded into sombre purple bloom that lingered long after the rose-tint died out in the zenith.

Our progress was slow; at times, although the sail filled with the rising land breeze, we scarcely seemed to move at all.

"Of course," said the pretty nurse, "we couldn't be aground in the deepest hole in the Atlantic."

"Scarcely," said Halyard, sarcastically, "unless we're grounded on a whale."

"What's that soft thumping?" I asked. "Have we run afoul of a barrel or log?"

It was almost too dark to see, but I leaned over the rail and swept the water with my hand.

Instantly something smooth glided under it, like the back of a great fish, and I jerked my hand back to the tiller. At the same moment the whole surface of the water seemed to begin to purr, with a sound like the breaking of froth in a champagne-glass.

"What's the matter with you?" asked Halyard, sharply.

"A fish came up under my hand," I said; "a porpoise or some-thing—"

With a low cry, the pretty nurse clasped my arm in both her hands.

"Listen!" she whispered. "It's purring around the boat."

"What the devil's purring?" shouted Halyard. "I won't have anything purring around me!"

At that moment, to my amazement, I saw that the boat had stopped entirely, although the sail was full and the small pennant fluttered from the mast-head. Something, too, was tugging at the rudder, twisting and jerking it until the tiller strained and creaked in my hand. All at once it snapped; the tiller swung useless and the boat whirled around, heeling in the stiffening wind, and drove shoreward.

It was then that I, ducking to escape the boom, caught a glimpse of something ahead—something that a sudden wave seemed to toss on deck and leave there, wet and flapping—a man with round, fixed, fishy eyes, and soft, slaty skin.

But the horror of the thing were the two gills that swelled and relaxed spasmodically, emitting a rasping, purring sound—two gasping, blood-red gills, all fluted and scolloped and distended.

Frozen with amazement and repugnance, I stared at the creature; I felt the hair stirring on my head and the icy sweat on my forehead.

"It's the harbor-master!" screamed Halyard.

The harbor-master had gathered himself into a wet lump, squatting motionless in the bows under the mast; his lidless eyes were phosphorescent, like the eyes of living codfish. After a while I felt that either fright or disgust was going to strangle me where I sat, but it was only the arms of the pretty nurse clasped around me in a frenzy of terror.

There was not a fire-arm aboard that we could get at. Halyard's hand crept backward where a steel-shod boat-hook lay, and I also made a clutch at it. The next moment I had it in my hand, and staggered forward, but the boat was already tumbling shoreward among the breakers, and the next I knew the harbor-master ran at me like a colossal rat, just as the boat rolled over and over through the surf, spilling freight and passengers among the sea-weed-covered rocks.

When I came to myself I was thrashing about knee-deep in a rocky pool, blinded by the water and half suffocated, while under my feet, like a stranded porpoise, the harbor-master made the water boil in his efforts to upset me. But his limbs seemed soft and boneless; he had no nails, no teeth, and he bounced and thumped and flapped and splashed like a fish, while I rained blows on him with the boat-hook that sounded like blows on a football. And all the while his gills were blowing out and frothing, and purring, and his lidless eyes looked into mine, until, nauseated and trembling, I dragged myself back to the beach, where already the pretty nurse alternately wrung her hands and her petticoats in ornamental despair.

Beyond the cove, Halyard was bobbing up and down, afloat in his invalid's chair, trying to steer shoreward. He was the maddest man I ever saw.

"Have you killed that rubber-headed thing yet?" he roared.

"I can't kill it," I shouted, breathlessly. "I might as well try to kill a football!"

"Can't you punch a hole in it?" he bawled. "If I can only get at him—"

His words were drowned in a thunderous splashing, a roar of great, broad flippers beating the sea, and I saw the gigantic forms of my two great auks, followed by their chicks, blundering past in a shower of spray, driving headlong out into the ocean.

"Oh, Lord!" I said. "I can't stand that," and, for the first time in my life, I fainted peacefully—and appropriately—at the feet of the pretty nurse.

It is within the range of possibility that this story may be doubted. It doesn't matter; nothing can add to the despair of a man who has lost two great auks.

As for Halyard, nothing affects him—except his involuntary sea-bath, and that did him so much good that he writes me from the South that he's going on a walking-tour through Switzerland—if I'll join him. I might have joined him if he had not married the pretty nurse. I wonder whether—But, of course, this is no place for speculation.

In regard to the harbor-master, you may believe it or not, as you choose. But if you hear of any great auks being found, kindly throw a table-cloth over their heads and notify the authorities at the new Zoological Gardens in Bronx Park, New York. The reward is ten thousand dollars.

I

Before I proceed any further, common decency requires me to reassure my readers concerning my intentions, which, Heaven knows, are far from flippant.

To separate fact from fancy has always been difficult for me, but now that I have had the honor to be chosen secretary of the Zoological Gardens in Bronx Park, I realize keenly that unless I give up writing fiction nobody will believe what I write about science. Therefore it is to a serious and unimaginative public that I shall hereafter address myself; and I do it in the modest confidence that I shall neither be distrusted nor doubted, although unfortunately I still write in that irrational style which suggests covert frivolity, and for which I am undergoing a course of treatment in English literature at Columbia College. Now, having promised to avoid originality and confine myself to facts, I shall tell what I have to tell concerning the dingue, the mammoth, and—*something else.*

For some weeks it had been rumored that Professor Farrago, president of the Bronx Park Zoological Society, would resign, to accept an enormous salary as manager of Barnum & Bailey's circus. He was now with the circus in London, and had promised to cable his decision before the day was over.

I hoped he would decide to remain with us. I was his secretary and particular favorite, and I viewed, without enthusiasm, the advent of a new president, who might shake us all out of our congenial and carefully excavated ruts. However, it was plain that the trustees of the society expected the resignation of Professor Farrago, for they had been in secret session all day, considering the names of possible candidates to fill Professor Farrago's large, old-fashioned shoes. These preparations worried me, for I could scarcely expect another chief as kind and considerate as Professor Leonidas Farrago.

That afternoon in June I left my office in the Administration Building in Bronx Park and strolled out under the trees for a breath of air. But the heat of the sun soon drove me to seek shelter under a little square arbor, a shady retreat covered with purple wistaria and honeysuckle. As I entered the arbor I noticed that there were three other people seated there—an elderly lady with masculine features and short hair, a younger lady sitting beside her, and, farther away, a rough-looking young man reading a book.

For a moment I had an indistinct impression of having met the elder lady somewhere, and under circumstances not entirely agreeable, but beyond a stony and indifferent glance she paid no attention to me. As for the younger lady, she did not look at me at all. She was very young, with pretty eyes, a mass of silky brown hair, and a skin as fresh as a rose which had just been rained on.

With that delicacy peculiar to lonely scientific bachelors, I modestly sat down beside the rough young man, although there was more room beside the younger lady. "Some lazy loafer reading a penny dreadful," I thought, glancing at him, then at the title of his book. Hearing me beside him, he turned around and blinked over his shabby shoulder, and the movement uncovered the page he had been silently conning. The volume in his hands was Darwin's famous monograph on the monodactyl.

He noticed the astonishment on my face and smiled uneasily, shifting the short clay pipe in his mouth.

"I guess," he observed, "that this here book is too much for me, mister."

"It's rather technical," I replied, smiling.

"Yes," he said, in vague admiration; "it's fierce, ain't it?"

After a silence I asked him if he would tell me why he had chosen Darwin as a literary pastime.

"Well," he said, placidly, "I was tryin' to read about annermals, but I'm up against a word-slinger this time all right. Now here's a gum-twister," and he painfully spelled out m-o-n-o-d-a-c-t-y-l, breathing hard all the while.

"Monodactyl," I said, "means a single-toed creature."

He turned the page with alacrity. "Is that the beast he's talkin' about?" he asked.

The illustration he pointed out was a wood-cut representing Darwin's reconstruction of the dingue from the fossil bones in the British Museum. It was a well-executed wood-cut, showing a dingue in the foreground and, to give scale, a mammoth in the middle distance.

"Yes," I replied, "that is the dingue."

"I've seen one," he observed, calmly.

I smiled and explained that the dingue had been extinct for some thousands of years.

"Oh, I guess not," he replied, with cool optimism. Then he placed a grimy forefinger on the mammoth.

"I've seen them things, too," he remarked.

Again I patiently pointed out his error, and suggested that he referred to the elephant.

"Elephant be blowed!" he replied, scornfully. "I guess I know what I seen. An' I seen that there thing you call a dingue, too."

Not wishing to prolong a futile discussion, I remained silent. After a moment he wheeled around, removing his pipe from his hard mouth.

"Did you ever hear tell of Graham's Glacier?" he demanded.

"Certainly," I replied, astonished; "it's the southernmost glacier in British America."

"Right," he said. "And did you ever hear tell of the Hudson Mountings, mister?"

"Yes," I replied.

"What's behind 'em?" he snapped out.

"Nobody knows," I answered. "They are considered impassable."

"They ain't, though," he said, doggedly; "I've been behind 'em."

"Really!" I replied, tiring of his yarn.

"Ya-as, reely," he repeated, sullenly. Then he began to fumble and search through the pages of his book until he found what he wanted. "Mister," he said, "jest read that out loud, please."

The passage he indicated was the famous chapter beginning:

"Is the mammoth extinct? Is the dingue extinct? Probably. And yet the aborigines of British America maintain the contrary. Probably both the mammoth and the dingue are extinct; but until expeditions have penetrated and explored not only the unknown region in Alaska but also that hidden tableland beyond the Graham Glacier and the Hudson Mountains, it will not be possible to definitely announce the total extinction of either the mammoth or the dingue."

When I had read it, slowly, for his benefit, he brought his hand down smartly on one knee and nodded rapidly.

"Mister," he said, "that gent knows a thing or two, and don't you forget it!" Then he demanded, abruptly, how I knew he hadn't been behind the Graham Glacier.

I explained.

"Shucks!" he said; "there's a road five miles wide inter that there table-land. Mister, I ain't been in New York long; I come inter port a week ago on the *Arctic Belle*, whaler. I was in the Hudson range when that there Graham Glacier bust up—"

"What!" I exclaimed.

"Didn't you know it?" he asked. "Well, mebbe it ain't in the papers, but it busted all right—blowed up by a earthquake an' volcano combine. An', mister, it was oreful. My, how I did run!"

"Do you mean to tell me that some convulsion of the earth has shattered the Graham Glacier?" I asked.

"Convulsions? Ya-as, an' fits, too," he said, sulkily. "The hull blame thing dropped inter a hole. An' say, mister, home an' mother is good enough fur me now."

I stared at him stupidly.

"Once," he said, "I ketched pelts fur them sharps at Hudson Bay, like any yaller husky, but the things I seen arter that convulsion-fit—the *things I seen behind the Hudson Mountings*—don't make me hanker arter no life on the pe-rarie wild, lemme tell yer. I may be a Mother Carey chicken, but this chicken has got enough."

After a long silence I picked up his book again and pointed at the picture of the mammoth.

"What color is it?" I asked.

"Kinder red an' brown," he answered, promptly. "It's woolly, too."

Astounded, I pointed to the dingue.

"One-toed," he said, quickly; "makes a noise like a bell when scutterin' about."

Intensely excited, I laid my hand on his arm. "My society will give you a thousand dollars," I said, "if you pilot me inside the Hudson table-land and show me either a mammoth or a dingue!"

He looked me calmly in the eye.

"Mister," he said, slowly, "have you got a million for to squander on me?"

"No," I said, suspiciously.

"Because," he went on, "it wouldn't be enough. Home an' mother suits me now."

He picked up his book and rose. In vain I asked his name and address; in vain I begged him to dine with me—to become my honored guest.

"Nit," he said, shortly, and shambled off down the path.

But I was not going to lose him like that. I rose and deliberately started to stalk him. It was easy. He shuffled along, pulling on his pipe, and I after him.

It was growing a little dark, although the sun still reddened the tops of the maples. Afraid of losing him in the falling dusk, I once more approached him and laid my hand upon his ragged sleeve.

"Look here," he cried, wheeling about, "I want you to quit follerin' me. Don't I tell you money can't make me go back to them mountings!" And as I attempted to speak, he suddenly tore off his cap and pointed to his head. His hair was white as snow.

"That's what come of monkeyin' inter your cursed mountings," he shouted, fiercely. "There's things in there what no Christian oughter see. Lemme alone er I'll bust yer. "

He shambled on, doubled fists swinging by his side. The next moment, setting my teeth obstinately, I followed him and caught him by the park gate. At my hail he whirled around with a snarl, but I grabbed him by the throat and backed him violently against the park wall.

"You invaluable ruffian," I said, "now you listen to me. I live in that big stone building, and I'll give you a thousand dollars to take me behind the Graham Glacier. Think it over and call on me when you are in a pleasanter frame of mind. If you don't come by noon to-morrow I'll go to the Graham Glacier without you."

He was attempting to kick me all the time, but I managed to avoid him, and when I had finished I gave him a shove which almost loosened his spinal column. He went reeling out across the sidewalk, and when he had recovered his breath and his balance he danced with displeasure and displayed a vocabulary that astonished me. However, he kept his distance.

As I turned back into the park, satisfied that he would not follow, the first person I saw was the elderly, stony-faced lady of the wistaria arbor advancing on tiptoe. Behind her came the younger lady with cheeks like a rose that had been rained on.

Instantly it occurred to me that they had followed us, and at the same moment I knew who the stony-faced lady was. Angry, but polite, I lifted my hat and saluted her, and she, probably furious at having been caught tiptoeing after me, cut me dead. The younger lady passed me with face averted, but even in the dusk I could see the tip of one little ear turn scarlet.

Walking on hurriedly, I entered the Administration Building, and found Professor Lesard, of the reptilian department, preparing to leave.

"Don't you do it," I said, sharply; "I've got exciting news."

"I'm only going to the theatre," he replied. "It's a good show—Adam and Eve; there's a snake in it, you know. It's in my line."

"I can't help it," I said; and I told him briefly what had occurred in the arbor.

"But that's not all," I continued, savagely. "Those women followed us, and who do you think one of them turned out to be? Well, it was Professor Smawl, of Barnard College, and I'll bet every pair of boots I own that she starts for the Graham Glacier within a week. Idiot that I was!" I exclaimed, smiting my head with both hands. "I never recognized her until I saw her tiptoeing and craning her neck to listen. Now she knows about the glacier; she heard every word that young ruffian said, and she'll go to the glacier if it's only to forestall me."

Professor Lesard looked anxious. He knew that Miss Smawl, professor of natural history at Barnard College, had long desired an appointment at the Bronx Park gardens. It was even said she had a chance of succeeding Professor Farrago as president, but that, of course, must have been a joke. However, she haunted the gardens, annoying the keepers by persistently poking the animals with her umbrella. On one occasion she sent us word that she desired to enter the tigers' enclosure for the purpose of making experiments in hypnotism. Professor Farrago was absent, but I took it upon myself to send back word that I feared the tigers might injure her. The miserable small boy who took my message informed her that I was afraid she might injure the tigers, and the unpleasant incident almost cost me my position.

"I am quite convinced," said I to Professor Lesard, "that Miss Smawl is perfectly capable of abusing the information she overheard, and of starting herself to explore a region that, by all the laws of decency, justice, and prior claim, belongs to me."

"Well," said Lesard, with a peculiar laugh, "it's not certain whether you can go at all."

"Professor Farrago will authorize me," I said, confidently.

"Professor Farrago has resigned," said Lesard. It was a bolt from a clear sky.

"Good Heavens!" I blurted out. "What will become of the rest of us, then?"

"I don't know," he replied. "The trustees are holding a meeting over in the Administration Building to elect a new president for us. It depends on the new president what becomes of us."

"Lesard," I said, hoarsely, "you don't suppose that they could possibly elect Miss Smawl as our president, do you?"

He looked at me askance and bit his cigar.

"I'd be in a nice position, wouldn't I?" said I, anxiously.

"The lady would probably make you walk the plank for that tiger business," he replied.

"But I didn't do it," I protested, with sickly eagerness. "Besides, I explained to her—"

He said nothing, and I stared at him, appalled by the possibility of reporting to Professor Smawl for instructions next morning.

"See here, Lesard," I said, nervously, "I wish you would step over to the Administration Building and ask the trustees if I may prepare for this expedition. Will you?"

He glanced at me sympathetically. It was quite natural for me to wish to secure my position before the new president was elected—especially as there was a chance of the new president being Miss Smawl.

"You are quite right," he said; "the Graham Glacier would be the safest place for you if our next president is to be the Lady of the Tigers." And he started across the park puffing his cigar.

I sat down on the doorstep to wait for his return, not at all charmed with the prospect. It made me furious, too, to see my ambition nipped with the frost of a possible veto from Miss Smawl.

"If she is elected," thought I, "there is nothing for me but to resign—to avoid the inconvenience of being shown the door. Oh, I wish I had allowed her to hypnotize the tigers!"

Thoughts of crime flitted through my mind. Miss Smawl would not remain president—or anything else very long—if she persisted in her desire for the tigers. And then when she called for help I would pretend not to hear.

Aroused from criminal meditation by the return of Professor Lesard, I jumped up and peered into his perplexed eyes. "They've elected a president," he said, "but they won't tell us who the president is until tomorrow."

"You don't think—" I stammered.

"I don't know. But I know this: the new president sanctions the expedition to the Graham Glacier, and directs you to choose an assistant and begin preparations for four people."

Overjoyed, I seized his hand and said, "Hurray!" in a voice weak with emotion. "The old dragon isn't elected this time," I added, triumphantly.

"By-the-way," he said, "who was the other dragon with her in the park this evening?"

I described her in a more modulated voice.

"Whew!" observed Professor Lesard, "that must be her assistant, Professor Dorothy Van Twiller! She's the prettiest blue-stocking in town."

With this curious remark my confrère followed me into my room and wrote down the list of articles I dictated to him. The list included a complete camping equipment for myself and three other men.

"Am I one of those other men?" inquired Lesard, with an unhappy smile.

Before I could reply my door was shoved open and a figure appeared at the threshold, cap in hand.

"What do you want?" I asked, sternly; but my heart was beating high with triumph.

The figure shuffled; then came a subdued voice:

"Mister, I guess I'll go back to the Graham Glacier along with you. I'm Billy Spike, an' it kinder scares me to go back to them Hudson Mountains, but somehow, mister, when you choked me and kinder walked me off on my ear, why, mister, I kinder took to you like."

There was absolute silence for a minute; then he said:

"So if you go, I guess I'll go, too, mister."

"For a thousand dollars?"

"Fur nawthin'," he muttered— "or what you like."

"All right, Billy," I said, briskly; "just look over those rifles and ammunition and see that everything's sound."

He slowly lifted his tough young face and gave me a doglike glance. They were hard eyes, but there was gratitude in them.

"You'll get your throat slit," whispered Lesard.

"Not while Billy's with me," I replied, cheerfully.

Late that night, as I was preparing for pleasant dreams, a knock came on my door and a telegraph-messenger handed me a note, which I read, shivering in my bare feet, although the thermometer marked eighty Fahrenheit:

> "You will immediately leave for the Hudson Mountains via Wellman Bay, Labrador, there to await further instructions. Equipment for yourself and one assistant will include following articles" [here began a list of camping utensils, scientific paraphernalia, and provisions]. "The steamer *Penguin* sails at five o'clock to-morrow morning. Kindly find yourself on board at that hour. Any excuse for not complying with these orders will be accepted as your resignation.
> "Susan Smawl,
> "President, Bronx Zoological Society."

"Lesard!" I shouted, trembling with fury.

He appeared at his door, chastely draped in pajamas, and he read the insolent letter with terrified alacrity.

"What are you going to do—resign?" he asked, much frightened.

"Do!" I snarled, grinding my teeth; "I'm going—that's what I'm going to do!"

"But—but you can't get ready and catch that steamer, too," he stammered.

He did not know me.

II

And so it came about that one calm evening towards the end of June, William Spike and I went into camp under the southerly shelter of that vast granite wall called the Hudson Mountains, there to await the promised "further instructions."

It had been a tiresome trip by steamer to Anticosti, from there by schooner to Widgeon Bay, then down the coast and up the Cape Clear River to Port Porpoise. There we bought three pack-mules and started due north on the Great Fur Trail. The second day out we passed Fort Boise, the last outpost of civilization, and on the sixth day we were travelling eastward under the granite mountain parapets.

On the evening of the sixth day out from Fort Boise we went into camp for the last time before entering the unknown land.

I could see it already through my field-glasses, and while William was building the fire I climbed up among the rocks above and sat down, glasses levelled, to study the prospect.

There was nothing either extraordinary or forbidding in the landscape which stretched out beyond; to the right the solid palisade of granite cut off the view; to the left the palisade continued, an endless barrier of sheer cliffs crowned with pine and hemlock. But the interesting section of the landscape lay almost directly in front of me—a rent in the mountain-wall through which appeared to run a level, arid plain, miles wide, and as smooth and even as a highroad.

There could be no doubt concerning the significance of that rent in the solid mountain-wall; and, moreover, it was exactly as William

Spike had described it. However, I called to him and he came up from the smoky camp-fire, axe on shoulder.

"Yep," he said, squatting beside me; "the Graham Glacier used to meander through that there hole, but somethin' went wrong with the earth's in'ards an' there was a bust-up."

"And you saw it, William?" I said, with a sigh of envy.

"Hey? Seen it? Sure I seen it! I was to Spoutin' Springs, twenty mile west, with a bale o' blue fox an' otter pelt. Fust I knew them geysers begun for to groan egregious like, an' I seen the caribou gallopin' hell-bent south. 'This climate,' sez I, 'is too bracin' for me,' so I struck a back trail an' landed onto a hill. Then them geysers blowed up, one arter the next, an' I heard somethin' kinder cave in between here an' China. I disremember things what happened. Somethin' throwed me down, but I couldn't stay there, for the blamed ground was runnin' like a river—all wavy-like, an' the sky hit me on the back o' me head."

"And then?" I urged, in that new excitement which every repetition of the story revived. I had heard it all twenty times since we left New York, but mere repetition could not apparently satisfy me.

"Then," continued William, "the whole world kinder went off like a fire-cracker, an' I come too, an' ran like—"

"I know," said I, cutting him short, for I had become wearied of the invariable profanity which lent a lurid ending to his narrative.

"After that," I continued, "you went through the rent in the mountains?"

"Sure."

"And you saw a dingue and a creature that resembled a mammoth?"

"Sure," he repeated, sulkily.

"And you saw something else?" I always asked this question; it fascinated me to see the sullen fright flicker in William's eyes, and the mechanical backward glance, as though what he had seen might still be behind him.

He had never answered this third question but once, and that time he fairly snarled in my face as he growled: "I seen what no Christian oughter see."

So when I repeated: "And you saw something else, William?" he gave me a wicked, frightened leer, and shuffled off to feed the mules. Flattery, entreaties, threats left him unmoved; he never told me what the third thing was that he had seen behind the Hudson Mountains.

William had retired to mix up with his mules; I resumed my binoculars and my silent inspection of the great, smooth path left by the Graham Glacier when something or other exploded that vast mass of ice into vapor.

The arid plain wound out from the unknown country like a river, and I thought then, and think now, that when the glacier was blown into vapor the vapor descended in the most terrific rain the world has ever seen, and poured through the newly blasted mountain-gateway, sweeping the earth to bed-rock. To corroborate this theory, miles to the southward I could see the debris winding out across the land towards Wellman Bay, but as the terminal moraine of the vanished glacier formerly ended there I could not be certain that my theory was correct. Owing to the formation of the mountains I could not see more than half a mile into the unknown country. What I could see appeared to be nothing but the continuation of the glacier's path, scored out by the cloud-burst, and swept as smooth as a floor.

Sitting there, my heart beating heavily with excitement, I looked through the evening glow at the endless, pine-crowned mountain-wall with its giant's gateway pierced for me! And I thought of all the explorers and the unknown heroes—trappers, Indians, humble naturalists, perhaps—who had attempted to scale that sheer barricade and had died there or failed, beaten back from those eternal cliffs. Eternal? No! For the Eternal Himself had struck the rock, and it had sprung asunder, thundering obedience.

In the still evening air the smoke from the fire below mounted in a straight, slender pillar, like the smoke from those ancient altars builded before the first blood had been shed on earth.

The evening wind stirred the pines; a tiny spring brook made thin harmony among the rocks; a murmur came from the quiet camp. It was William adjuring his mules. In the deepening twilight I descended the hillock, stepping cautiously among the rocks.

Then, suddenly, as I stood outside the reddening ring of fire-light, far in the depths of the unknown country, far behind the mountain-wall, a sound grew on the quiet air. William heard it and turned his face to the mountains. The sound faded to a vibration which was felt, not heard. Then once more I began to divine a vibration in the air, gathering in distant volume until it became a sound, lasting the space of a spoken word, fading to vibration, then silence.

Was it a cry?

I looked at William inquiringly. He had quietly fainted away.

I got him to the little brook and poked his head into the icy water, and after a while he sat up pluckily.

To an indignant question he replied: "Naw, I ain't a-cussin' you. Lemme be or I'll have fits."

"Was it that sound that scared you?" I asked.

"Ya-as," he replied with a dauntless shiver.

"Was it the voice of the mammoth?" I persisted, excitedly. "Speak, William, or I'll drag you about and kick you!"

He replied that it was neither a mammoth nor a dingue, and added a strong request for privacy, which I was obliged to grant, as I could not torture another word out of him.

I slept little that night; the exciting proximity of the unknown land was too much for me. But although I lay awake for hours, I heard nothing except the tinkle of water among the rocks and the plover calling from some hidden marsh. At daybreak I shot a ptarmigan which had walked into camp, and the shot set the echoes yelling among the mountains.

William, sullen and heavy-eyed, dressed the bird, and we broiled it for breakfast.

Neither he nor I alluded to the sound we had heard the night before; he boiled water and cleaned up the mess-kit, and I pottered about among the rocks for another ptarmigan. Wearying of this, presently, I returned to the mules and William, and sat down for a smoke.

"It strikes me," I said, "that our instructions to 'await further orders' are idiotic. How are we to receive 'further orders' here?"

William did not know.

"You don't suppose," said I, in sudden disgust, "that Miss Smawl believes there is a summer hotel and daily mail service in the Hudson Mountains?"

William thought perhaps she did suppose something of the sort.

It irritated me beyond measure to find myself at last on the very border of the unknown country, and yet checked, held back, by the irresponsible orders of a maiden lady named Smawl. However, my salary depended upon the whim of that maiden lady, and although I fussed and fumed and glared at the mountains through my glasses, I realized that I could not stir without the permission of Miss Smawl. At times this grotesque situation became almost unbearable, and I often went away by myself and indulged in fantasies, firing my gun off and pretending I had hit Miss Smawl by mistake. At such moments I would imagine I was free at last to plunge into the strange country, and I would squat on a rock and dream of bagging my first mammoth.

The time passed heavily; the tension increased with each new day. I shot ptarmigan and kept our table supplied with brook-trout. William chopped wood, conversed with his mules, and cooked very badly.

"See here," I said, one morning; "we have been in camp a week to-day, and I can't stand your cooking another minute!"

William, who was washing a saucepan, looked up and begged me sarcastically to accept the cordon bleu. But I know only how to cook eggs, and there were no eggs within some hundred miles.

To get the flavor of the breakfast out of my mouth I walked up to my favorite hillock and sat down for a smoke. The next moment, however, I was on my feet, cheering excitedly and shouting for William.

"Here come 'further instructions' at last!" I cried, pointing to the southward, where two dots on the grassy plain were imperceptibly moving in our direction.

"People on mules," said William, without enthusiasm.

"They must be messengers for us!" I cried, in chaste joy. "Three cheers for the northward trail, William, and the mischief take Miss— Well, never mind now," I added.

"On them approachin' mules," observed William, "there is wimmen."

I stared at him for a second, then attempted to strike him. He dodged wearily and repeated his incredible remark: "Ya-as, there is—wimmen—two female ladies onto them there mules."

"Bring me my glasses!" I said, hoarsely; "bring me those glasses, William, because I shall destroy you if you don't!"

Somewhat awed by my calm fury, he hastened back to camp and returned with the binoculars. It was a breathless moment. I adjusted the lenses with a steady hand and raised them.

Now, of all unexpected sights my fate may reserve for me in the future, I trust—nay, I know—that none can ever prove as unwelcome as the sight I perceived through my binoculars. For upon the backs of those distant mules were two women, and the first one was Miss Smawl!

Upon her head she wore a helmet, from which fluttered a green veil. Otherwise she was clothed in tweeds; and at moments she beat upon her mule with a thick umbrella.

Surfeited with the sickening spectacle, I sat down on a rock and tried to cry.

"I told yer so," observed William; but I was too tired to attack him.

When the caravan rode into camp I was myself again, smilingly prepared for the worst, and I advanced, cap in hand, followed furtively by William.

"Welcome," I said, violently injecting joy into my voice. "Welcome, Professor Smawl, to the Hudson Mountains!"

"Kindly take my mule," she said, climbing down to mother earth.

"William," I said, with dignity, "take the lady's mule."

Miss Smawl gave me a stolid glance, then made directly for the camp-fire, where a kettle of game-broth simmered over the coals. The last I saw of her she was smelling of it, and I turned my back and advanced towards the second lady pilgrim, prepared to be civil until snubbed.

Now, it is quite certain that never before had William Spike or I beheld so much feminine loveliness in one human body on the back of a mule. She was clad in the daintiest of shooting-kilts, yet there was nothing mannish about her except the way she rode the mule, and that only accentuated her adorable femininity.

I remembered what Professor Lesard had said about blue stockings—but Miss Dorothy Van Twiller's were gray, turned over at the tops, and disappearing into canvas spats buckled across a pair of slim shooting-boots.

"Welcome," said I, attempting to restrain a too violent cordiality. "Welcome, Professor Van Twiller, to the Hudson Mountains."

"Thank you," she replied, accepting my assistance very sweetly; "it is a pleasure to meet a human being again."

I glanced at Miss Smawl. She was eating game-broth, but she resembled a human being in a general way.

"I should very much like to wash my hands," said Professor Van Twiller, drawing the buckskin gloves from her slim fingers.

I brought towels and soap and conducted her to the brook.

She called to Professor Smawl to join her, and her voice was crystalline; Professor Smawl declined, and her voice was batrachian.

"She is so hungry!" observed Miss Van Twiller. "I am very thankful we are here at last, for we've had a horrid time. You see, we neither of us know how to cook."

I wondered what they would say to William's cooking, but I held my peace and retired, leaving the little brook to mirror the sweetest face that was ever bathed in water.

III

That afternoon our expedition, in two sections, moved forward. The first section comprised myself and all the mules; the second section was commanded by Professor Smawl, followed by Professor Van Twiller, armed with a tiny shot-gun. William, loaded down with the ladies' toilet articles, skulked in the rear. I say skulked; there was no other word for it.

"So you're a guide, are you?" observed Professor Smawl when William, cap in hand, had approached her with well-meant advice. "The woods are full of lazy guides. Pick up those Gladstone bags! I'll do the guiding for this expedition."

Made cautious by William's humiliation, I associated with the mules exclusively. Nevertheless, Professor Smawl had her hard eyes on me, and I realized she meant mischief.

The encounter took place just as I, driving the five mules, entered the great mountain gateway, thrilled with anticipation which almost amounted to foreboding. As I was about to set foot across the imaginary frontier which divided the world from the unknown land, Professor Smawl hailed me and I halted until she came up.

"As commander of this expedition," she said, somewhat out of breath, "I desire to be the first living creature who has ever set foot behind the Graham Glacier. Kindly step aside, young sir!"

"Madam," said I, rigid with disappointment, "my guide, William Spike, entered that unknown land a year ago."

"He *says* he did," sneered Professor Smawl.

"As you like," I replied; "but it is scarcely generous to forestall the person whose stupidity gave you the clew to this unexplored region."

"You mean yourself?" she asked, with a stony stare.

"I do," said I, firmly.

Her little, hard eyes grew harder, and she clutched her umbrella until the steel ribs crackled.

"Young man," she said, insolently; "if I could have gotten rid of you I should have done so the day I was appointed president. But Professor Farrago refused to resign unless your position was assured, subject, of course, to your good behavior. Frankly, I don't like you, and I consider your views on science ridiculous, and if an opportunity presents itself I will be most happy to request your resignation. Kindly collect your mules and follow me."

Mortified beyond measure, I collected my mules and followed my president into the strange country behind the Hudson Mountains—I who had aspired to lead, compelled to follow in the rear, driving mules.

The journey was monotonous at first, but we shortly ascended a ridge from which we could see, stretching out below us, the wilderness where, save the feet of William Spike, no human feet had passed.

As for me, tingling with enthusiasm, I forgot my chagrin, I forgot the gross injustice, I forgot my mules.

"Excelsior!" I cried, running up and down the ridge in uncontrollable excitement at the sublime spectacle of forest, mountain, and valley all set with little lakes.

"Excelsior!" repeated an excited voice at my side, and Professor Van Twiller sprang to the ridge beside me, her eyes bright as stars.

Exalted, inspired by the mysterious beauty of the view, we clasped hands and ran up and down the grassy ridge.

"That will do," said Professor Smawl, coldly, as we raced about like a pair of distracted kittens. The chilling voice broke the spell; I dropped Professor Van Twiller's hand and sat down on a bowlder, aching with wrath.

Late that afternoon we halted beside a tiny lake, deep in the unknown wilderness, where purple and scarlet bergamot choked the shores and the spruce-partridge strutted fearlessly under our very feet. Here we pitched our two tents. The afternoon sun slanted through the pines; the lake glittered; acres of golden brake perfumed the forest silence, broken only at rare intervals by the distant thunder of a partridge drumming.

Professor Smawl ate heavily and retired to her tent to lie torpid until evening. William drove the unloaded mules into an intervale full of sun-cured, fragrant grasses; I sat down beside Professor Van Twiller.

The wilderness is electric. Once within the influence of its currents, human beings become positively or negatively charged, violently attracting or repelling each other.

"There is something the matter with this air," said Professor Van Twiller. "It makes me feel as though I were desperately enamoured of the entire human race."

She leaned back against a pine, smiling vaguely, and crossing one knee over the other.

Now I am not bold by temperament, and, normally, I fear ladies. Therefore it surprised me to hear myself begin a frivolous *causerie*, replying to her pretty epigrams with epigrams of my own, advancing to the borderland of badinage, fearlessly conducting her and myself over that delicate frontier to meet upon the terrain of undisguised flirtation.

It was clear that she was out for a holiday. The seriousness and restraints of twenty-two years she had left behind her in the civilized world, and now, with a shrug of her young shoulders, she unloosened her burden of reticence, dignity, and responsibility and let the whole load fall with a discreet thud.

"Even hares go mad in March," she said, seriously. "I know you intend to flirt with me—and I don't care. Anyway, there's nothing else to do, is there?"

"Suppose," said I, solemnly, "I should take you behind that big tree and attempt to kiss you!"

The prospect did not appear to appall her, so I looked around with that sneaking yet conciliatory caution peculiar to young men who are novices in the art. Before I had satisfied myself that neither William nor the mules were observing us, Professor Van Twiller rose to her feet and took a short step backward.

"Let's set traps for a dingue," she said, "will you?"

I looked at the big tree, undecided. "Come on," she said; "I'll show you how." And away we went into the woods, she leading, her kilts flashing through the golden half-light.

Now I had not the faintest notion how to trap the dingue, but Professor Van Twiller asserted that it formerly fed on the tender tips of the spruce, quoting Darwin as her authority.

So we gathered a bushel of spruce-tips, piled them on the bank of a little stream, then built a miniature stockade around the bait, a foot high. I roofed this with hemlock, then laboriously whittled out and adjusted a swinging shutter for the entrance, setting it on springy twigs.

"The dingue, you know, was supposed to live in the water," she said, kneeling beside me over our trap.

I took her little hand and thanked her for the information.

"Doubtless," she said, enthusiastically, "a dingue will come out of the lake to-night to feed on our spruce-tips. Then," she added, "we've got him."

"True!" I said, earnestly, and pressed her fingers very gently.

Her face was turned a little away; I don't remember what she said; I don't remember that she said anything. A faint rose-tint stole over her cheek. A few moments later she said: "You must not do that again."

It was quite late when we strolled back to camp. Long before we came in sight of the twin tents we heard a deep voice bawling our names. It was Professor Smawl, and she pounced upon Dorothy and drove her ignominiously into the tent.

"As for you," she said, in hollow tones, " you may explain your conduct at once, or place your resignation at my disposal."

But somehow or other I appeared to be temporarily lost to shame, and I only smiled at my infuriated president, and entered my own tent with a step that was distinctly frolicsome.

"Billy," said I to William Spike, who regarded me morosely from the depths of the tent, "I'm going out to bag a mammoth to-morrow, so kindly clean my elephant-gun and bring an axe to chop out the tusks."

That night Professor Smawl complained bitterly of the cooking, but as neither Dorothy nor I knew how to improve it, she revenged herself on us by eating everything on the table and retiring to bed, taking Dorothy with her. I could not sleep very well; the mosquitoes were intrusive, and Professor Smawl dreamed she was a pack of wolves and yelped in her sleep.

"Bird, ain't she?" said William, roused from slumber by her weird noises.

Dorothy, much frightened, crawled out of her tent, where her blanket-mate still dreamed dyspeptically, and William and I made her comfortable by the camp-fire.

It takes a pretty girl to look pretty half asleep in a blanket.

"Are you sure you are quite well?" I asked her.

To make sure, I tested her pulse. For an hour it varied more or less, but without alarming either of us. Then she went back to bed and I sat alone by the campfire.

Towards midnight I suddenly began to feel that strange, distant vibration that I had once before felt. As before, the vibration grew on the still air, increasing in volume until it became a sound, then died out into silence. I rose and stole into my tent.

William, white as death, lay in his corner, weeping in his sleep.

I roused him remorselessly, and he sat up scowling, but refused to tell me what he had been dreaming.

"Was it about that third thing you saw—" I began. But he snarled up at me like a startled animal, and I was obliged to go to bed and toss about and speculate.

The next morning it rained. Dorothy and I visited our dingue-trap but found nothing in it. We were inclined, however, to stay out in the rain behind a big tree, but Professor Smawl vetoed that proposition and sent me off to supply the larder with fresh meat.

I returned, mad and wet, with a dozen partridges and a white hare—brown at that season—and William cooked them vilely.

"I can taste the feathers!" said Professor Smawl, indignantly.

"There is no accounting for taste," I said, with a polite gesture of deprecation; "personally, I find feathers unpalatable."

"You may hand in your resignation this evening!" cried Professor Smawl, in hollow tones of passion.

I passed her the pancakes with a cheerful smile, and flippantly pressed the hand next me. Unexpectedly it proved to be William's sticky fist, and Dorothy and I laughed until her tears ran into Professor Smawl's coffee-cup—an accident which kindled her wrath to red heat, and she requested my resignation five times during the evening.

The next day it rained again, more or less. Professor Smawl complained of the cooking, demanded my resignation, and finally marched out to explore, lugging the reluctant William with her. Dorothy and I sat down behind the largest tree we could find.

I don't remember what we were saying when a peculiar sound interrupted us, and we listened earnestly.

It was like a bell in the woods, ding-dong! ding-dong! ding-dong!—a low, mellow, golden harmony, coming nearer, then stopping.

I clasped Dorothy in my arms in my excitement.

"It is the note of the dingue!" I whispered, "and that explains its name, handed down from remote ages along with the names of the behemoth and the coney. It was because of its bell-like cry that it was named! Darling!" I cried, forgetting our short acquaintance, "we have made a discovery that the whole world will ring with!"

Hand in hand we tiptoed through the forest to our trap. There was something in it that took fright at our approach and rushed panic-stricken round and round the interior of the trap, uttering its alarm-note, which sounded like the jangling of a whole string of bells.

I seized the strangely beautiful creature; it neither attempted to bite nor scratch, but crouched in my arms, trembling and eying me.

Delighted with the lovely, tame animal, we bore it tenderly back to the camp and placed it on my blanket. Hand in hand we stood before it, awed by the sight of this beast, so long believed to be extinct.

"It is too good to be true," sighed Dorothy, clasping her white hands under her chin and gazing at the dingue in rapture.

"Yes," said I, solemnly, "you and I, my child, are face to face with the fabled dingue—*Dingus solitarius!* Let us continue to gaze at it, reverently, prayerfully, humbly—"

Dorothy yawned—probably with excitement.

We were still mutely adoring the dingue when Professor Smawl burst into the tent at a hand-gallop, bawling hoarsely for her kodak and note-book.

Dorothy seized her triumphantly by the arm and pointed at the dingue, which appeared to be frightened to death.

"What!" cried Professor Smawl, scornfully; "*that* a dingue? Rubbish!"

"Madam," I said, firmly, "it is a dingue! It's a monodactyl! See! It has but a single toe!"

"Bosh!" she retorted; "it's got four!"

"Four!" I repeated, blankly.

"Yes; one on each foot!"

"Of course," I said; "you didn't suppose a monodactyl meant a beast with one leg and one toe!"

But she laughed hatefully and declared it was a woodchuck.

We squabbled for a while until I saw the significance of her attitude. The unfortunate woman wished to find a dingue first and be accredited with the discovery.

I lifted the dingue in both hands and shook the creature gently, until the chiming ding-dong of its protestations filled our ears like sweet bells jangled out of tune.

Pale with rage at this final proof of the dingue's identity, she seized her camera and note-book.

"I haven't any time to waste over that musical woodchuck!" she shouted, and bounced out of the tent.

"What have you discovered, dear?" cried Dorothy, running after her.

"A mammoth!" bawled Professor Smawl, triumphantly; "and I'm going to photograph him!"

Neither Dorothy nor I believed her. We watched the flight of the infatuated woman in silence.

And now, at last, the tragic shadow falls over my paper as I write. I was never passionately attached to Professor Smawl, yet I would gladly refrain from chronicling the episode that must follow if, as I have hitherto attempted, I succeed in sticking to the unornamented truth.

I have said that neither Dorothy nor I believed her. I don't know why, unless it was that we had not yet made up our minds to believe that the mammoth still existed on earth. So, when Professor Smawl disappeared in the forest, scuttling through the underbrush like a demoralized hen, we viewed her flight with unconcern. There was a large tree in the neighborhood—a pleasant shelter in case of rain. So we sat down behind it, although the sun was shining fiercely.

It was one of those peaceful afternoons in the wilderness when the whole forest dreams, and the shadows are asleep and every little leaflet takes a nap. Under the still tree-tops the dappled sunlight, motionless, soaked the sod; the forest-flies no longer whirled in circles, but sat sunning their wings on slender twig-tips. The heat was sweet and spicy; the sun drew out the delicate essence of gum and sap, warming volatile juices until they exhaled through the aromatic bark.

The sun went down into the wilderness; the forest stirred in its sleep; a fish splashed in the lake. The spell was broken. Presently the wind began to rise somewhere far away in the unknown land. I heard it coming, nearer, nearer—a brisk wind that grew heavier and blew harder as it neared us—a gale that swept distant branches—a furious gale that set limbs clashing and cracking, nearer and nearer. Crack! and the gale grew to a hurricane, trampling trees like dead twigs! Crack! Crackle! Crash! Crash!

Was it the wind?

With the roaring in my ears I sprang up, staring into the forest vista, and at the same instant, out of the crashing forest, sped Professor Smawl, skirts tucked up, thin legs flying like bicycle-spokes.

I shouted, but the crashing drowned my voice. Then all at once the solid earth began to shake, and with the rush and roar of a tornado a gigantic living thing burst out of the forest before our eyes—a vast shadowy bulk that rocked and rolled along, mowing down trees in its course.

Two great crescents of ivory curved from its head; its back swept through the tossing tree-tops. Once it bellowed like a gun fired from a high bastion.

The apparition passed with the noise of thunder rolling on towards the ends of the earth. Crack! crash went the trees, the tempest swept away in a rolling volley of reports, distant, more distant, until, long after the tumult had deadened, then ceased, the stunned forest echoed with the fall of mangled branches slowly dropping.

That evening an agitated young couple sat close together in the deserted camp, calling timidly at intervals for Professor Smawl and William Spike. I say timidly, because it is correct; we did not care to have a mammoth respond to our calls. The lurking echoes across the lake answered our cries; the full moon came up over the forest to look at us. We were not much to look at. Dorothy was moistening my shoulder with unfeigned tears, and I, afraid to light the fire, sat hunched up under the common blanket, wildly examining the darkness around us.

Chilled to the spinal marrow, I watched the gray lights whiten in the east. A single bird awoke in the wilderness. I saw the nearer trees looming in the mist, and the silver fog rolling on the lake.

All night long the darkness had vibrated with the strange monotone which I had heard the first night, camping at the gate of the unknown land. My brain seemed to echo that subtle harmony which rings in the auricular labyrinth after sound has ceased.

There are ghosts of sound which return to haunt long after sound is dead. It was these voiceless spectres of a voice long dead that stirred the transparent silence, intoning toneless tones.

I think I make myself clear.

It was an uncanny night; morning whitened the east; gray daylight stole into the woods, blotting the shadows to paler tints. It was nearly mid-day before the sun became visible through the fine-spun web of mist—a pale spot of gilt in the zenith.

By this pallid light I labored to strike the two empty tents, gather up our equipments and pack them on our five mules. Dorothy aided me bravely, whimpering when I spoke of Professor Smawl and William Spike, but abating nothing of her industry until we had the mules loaded and I was ready to drive them, Heaven knows whither.

"Where shall we go?" quavered Dorothy, sitting on a log with the dingue in her lap.

One thing was certain; this mammoth-ridden land was no place for women, and I told her so.

We placed the dingue in a basket and tied it around the leading mule's neck. Immediately the dingue, alarmed, began dingling like a cow-bell. It acted like a charm on the other mules, and they gravely filed off after their leader, following the bell. Dorothy and I, hand in hand, brought up the rear.

I shall never forget that scene in the forest—the gray arch of the heavens swimming in mist through which the sun peered shiftily, the tall pines wavering through the fog, the preoccupied mules marching single file, the foggy bell-note of the gentle dingue in its swinging basket, and Dorothy, limp kilts dripping with dew, plodding through the white dusk.

We followed the terrible tornado-path which the mammoth had left in its wake, but there were no traces of its human victims— neither one jot of Professor Smawl nor one solitary tittle of William Spike.

And now I would be glad to end this chapter if I could; I would gladly leave myself as I was, there in the misty forest, with an arm encircling the slender body of my little companion, and the mules moving in a monotonous line, and the dingue discreetly jingling— but again that menacing shadow falls across my page, and truth bids me tell all, and I, the slave of accuracy, must remember my vows as the dauntless disciple of truth.

Towards sunset—or that pale parody of sunset which set the forest swimming in a ghastly, colorless haze—the mammoth's trail of ruin brought us suddenly out of the trees to the shore of a great sheet of water. It was a desolate spot; northward a chaos of sombre peaks rose, piled up like thunder-clouds along the horizon; east and south the darkening wilderness spread like a pall. Westward, crawling out into the mist from our very feet, the gray waste of water moved under the dull sky, and flat waves slapped the squatting rocks, heavy with slime.

And now I understood why the trail of the mammoth continued straight into the lake, for on either hand black, filthy tamarack swamps lay under ghostly sheets of mist. I strove to creep out into the bog, seeking a footing, but the swamp quaked and the smooth surface trembled like jelly in a bowl. A stick thrust into the slime sank into unknown depths.

Vaguely alarmed, I gained the firm land again and looked around, believing there was no road open but the desolate trail we had traversed. But I was in error; already the leading mule was wading out into the water, and the others, one by one, followed.

How wide the lake might be we could not tell, because the band of fog hung across the water like a curtain. Yet out into this flat, shallow void our mules went steadily, slop! slop! slop! in single file. Already they were growing indistinct in the fog, so I bade Dorothy hasten and take off her shoes and stockings.

She was ready before I was, I having to unlace my shooting-boots, and she stepped out into the water, kilts fluttering, moving her white feet cautiously. In a moment I was beside her, and we waded forward, sounding the shallow water with our poles.

When the water had risen to Dorothy's knees I hesitated, alarmed. But when we attempted to retrace our steps we could not find the shore again, for the blank mist shrouded everything, and the water deepened at every step.

I halted and listened for the mules. Far away in the fog I heard a dull splashing, receding as I listened. After a while all sound died away, and a slow horror stole over me—a horror that froze the little net-work of veins in every limb. A step to the right and the water rose to my knees; a step to the left and the cold, thin circle of the flood chilled my breast. Suddenly Dorothy screamed, and the next moment a far cry answered—a far, sweet cry that seemed to come from the sky, like the rushing harmony of the world's swift winds. Then the curtain of fog before us lighted up from behind; shadows moved on the misty screen, outlines of trees and grassy shores, and tiny birds flying. Thrown on the vapory curtain, in silhouette, a man and a woman passed under the lovely trees, arms about each other's necks; near them the shadows of five mules grazed peacefully; a dingue gambolled close by.

"It is a mirage!" I muttered, but my voice made no sound. Slowly the light behind the fog died out; the vapor around us turned to rose, then dissolved, while mile on mile of a limitless sea spread away till, like a quick line pencilled at a stroke, the horizon cut sky and sea in half, and before us lay an ocean from which towered a mountain of snow—or a gigantic berg of milky ice—for it was moving.

"Good Heavens," I shrieked; "it is alive!"

At the sound of my crazed cry the mountain of snow became a pillar, towering to the clouds, and a wave of golden glory drenched the figure to its knees! Figure? Yes—for a colossal arm shot across the sky, then curved back in exquisite grace to a head of awful beauty—a woman's head, with eyes like the blue lake of heaven—ay, a woman's splendid form, upright from the sky to the earth, knee-deep in the sea. The evening clouds drifted across her brow; her shimmering hair lighted the world beneath with sunset. Then, shading her white brow with one hand, she bent, and with the other hand dipped in the sea, she sent a wave rolling at us. Straight out of the horizon it sped—a ripple that grew to a wave, then to a furious breaker which caught us up in a whirl of foam, bearing us onward, faster, faster, swiftly flying, through leagues of spray until consciousness ceased and all was blank.

Yet ere my senses fled I heard again that strange cry—that sweet, thrilling harmony rushing out over the foaming waters, filling earth and sky with its soundless vibrations.

And I knew it was the hail of the Spirit of the North warning us back to life again.

Looking back, now, over the days that passed before we staggered into the Hudson Bay outpost at Gravel Cove, I am inclined to believe that neither Dorothy nor I were clothed entirely in our proper minds—or, if we were, our minds, no doubt, must have been in the same condition as our clothing. I remember shooting ptarmigan, and that we ate them; flashes of memory recall the steady downpour of rain through the endless twilight of shaggy forests; dim days on the foggy tundra, mud-holes from which the wild ducks rose in thousands; then the stunted hemlocks, then the forest again. And I do not even recall the moment when, at last, stumbling into the smooth path left by the Graham Glacier, we crawled through the mountain-wall, out of the unknown land, and once more into a world protected by the Lord Almighty.

A hunting-party of Elbon Indians brought us in to the post, and everybody was most kind—that I remember, just before going into several weeks of unpleasant delirium mercifully mitigated with unconsciousness.

Curiously enough, Professor Van Twiller was not very much battered, physically, for I had carried her for days, pickaback. But the awful experience had produced a shock which resulted in a nervous condition that lasted so long after she returned to New York that the wealthy and eminent specialist who attended her in- sisted upon taking her to the Riviera and marrying her. I some- times wonder—but, as I have said, such reflections have no place in these austere pages.

However, anybody, I fancy, is at liberty to speculate upon the fate of the late Professor Smawl and William Spike, and upon the mules and the gentle dingue. Personally, I am convinced that the suggestive silhouettes I saw on that ghastly curtain of fog were cast by beatified beings in some earthly paradise—a mirage of bliss of which we caught but the colorless shadow-shapes floating 'twixt sea and sky.

At all events, neither Professor Smawl nor her William Spike ever returned; no exploring expedition has found a trace of mule or lady, of William or the dingue. The new expedition to be orga- nized by Barnard College may penetrate still farther. I suppose that, when the time comes, I shall be expected to volunteer. But Professor Van Twiller is married, and William and Professor Smawl ought to be, and altogether, considering the mammoth and that gigantic and splendid apparition that bent from the zenith to the ocean and sent a tidal-wave rolling from the palm of one white hand—I say, taking all these various matters under consideration, I think I shall de- cide to remain in New York and continue writing for the scientific periodicals. Besides, the mortifying experience at the Paris Exposition has dampened even my perennially youthful enthusiasm. And as for the late expedition to Florida, Heaven knows I am ready to repeat it—nay, I am already forming a plan for the rescue—but though I am prepared to encounter any danger for the sake of my beloved superior, Professor Farrago, I do not feel inclined to commit indiscretions in order to pry into secrets which, as I regard it, concern Professor Smawl and William Spike alone.

But all this is, in a measure, premature. What I now have to relate is the recital of an eye-witness to that most astonishing scandal which occurred during the recent exposition in Paris.

Is the Ux Extinct?

I

When the delegates were appointed to the International Scientific Congress at the Paris Exposition of 1900, how little did anybody imagine that the great conference would end in the most gigantic scandal that ever stirred two continents?

Yet, had it not been for the pair of American newspapers published in Paris, this scandal would never have been aired, for the continental press is so well muzzled that when it bites its teeth merely meet in the empty atmosphere with a discreet snap.

But to the Yankee nothing excepting the Monroe Doctrine is sacred, and the unsopped watch-dogs of the press bite right and left, unmuzzled. The biter bites—it is his profession—and that ends the affair; the bitee is bitten, and, in the deplorable argot of the hour, "it is up to him."

So now that the scandal has been well aired and hung out to dry in the teeth of decency and the four winds, and as all the details have been cheerfully and grossly exaggerated, it is, perhaps, the proper moment for the truth to be written by the only person whose knowledge of all the facts in the affair entitles him to speak for himself as well as for those honorable ladies and gentlemen whose names and titles have been so mercilessly criticised.

These, then, are the simple facts:

The International Scientific Congress, now adjourned *sine die*, met at nine o'clock in the morning, May 3, 1900, in the Tasmanian Pavilion of the Paris Exposition. There were present the most famous scientists of Great Britain, France, Germany, Russia, Italy, Switzerland, and the United States.

His Royal Highness the Crown-Prince of Monaco presided.

It is not necessary, now, to repeat the details of that preliminary meeting. It is sufficient to say that committees representing the various known sciences were named and appointed by the Prince of Monaco, who had been unanimously elected permanent chairman of the conference. It is the composition of a single committee that concerns us now, and that committee, representing the science which treats of bird life, was made up as follows:

Chairman—His Royal Highness the Crown-Prince of Monaco. Members—Sir Peter Grebe, Great Britain; Baron de Becasse, France; his Royal Highness King Christian, of Finland; the Countess d'Alzette, of Belgium; and I, from the United States, representing the Smithsonian Institution and the Bronx Park Zoological Society of New York.

This, then, was the composition of that now notorious ornithological committee, a modest, earnest, self-effacing little band of workers, bound together—in the beginning—by those ties of mutual respect and esteem which unite all laborers in the vineyard of science.

From the first meeting of our committee, science, the great leveller, left no artificial barriers of rank or title standing between us. We were enthusiasts in our love for ornithology; we found new inspiration in the democracy of our common interests.

As for me, I chatted with my fellows, feeling no restraint myself and perceiving none. The King of Finland and I discussed his latest monograph on the speckled titmouse, and I was glad to agree with the King in all his theories concerning the nesting habits of that important bird.

Sir Peter Grebe, a large, red gentleman in tweeds, read us some notes he had made on the domestic hen and her reasons for running ahead of a horse and wagon instead of stepping aside to let the disturbing vehicle pass.

The Crown-Prince of Monaco took issue with Sir Peter; so did the Baron de Becasse; and we were entertained by a friendly and marvellously interesting three-cornered dispute, shared in by three of the most profound thinkers of the century.

I shall never forget the brilliancy of that argument, nor the modest, good-humored retorts which gave us all a glimpse into depths of erudition which impressed us profoundly and set the seal on the bonds which held us so closely together.

Alas, that the seal should ever have been broken! Alas, that the glittering apple of discord should have been flung into our midst!— no, not flung, but gently rolled under our noses by the gloved fingers of the lovely Countess d'Alzette.

"Messieurs," said the fair Countess, when all present, excepting she and I, had touched upon or indicated the subjects which they had prepared to present to the congress— "messieurs mes confrères, I have been requested by our distinguished chairman, the Crown-Prince of Monaco, to submit to your judgment the subject which, by favor of the King of the Belgians, I have prepared to present to the International Scientific Congress."

She made a pretty courtesy as she named her own sovereign, and we all rose out of respect to that most austere and moral ruler the King of Belgium.

"But," she said, with a charming smile of depreciation, "I am very, very much afraid that the subject which I have chosen may not meet with your approval, gentlemen." She stood there in her dainty Parisian gown and bonnet, shaking her pretty head uncertainly, a smile on her lips, her small, gloved fingers interlocked.

"Oh, I know how dreadful it would be if this great congress should be compelled to listen to any hoax like that which Monsieur de Rougemont imposed on the British Royal Society," she said, gravely; "and because the subject of my paper is as strange as the strangest phenomenon alleged to have been noted by Monsieur de Rougemont, I hesitate—"

She glanced at the silent listeners around her. Sir Peter's red face had hardened; the King of Finland frowned slightly; the Crown-Prince of Monaco and Baron de Becasse wore anxious smiles. But when her violet eyes met mine I gave her a glance of encouragement, and that glance, I am forced to confess, was not dictated by scientific approval, but by something that never entirely dries up in the mustiest and dustiest of savants—the old Adam implanted in us all.

Now, I knew perfectly well what her subject must be; so did every man present. For it was no secret that his Majesty of Belgium had been swindled by some natives in Tasmania, and had paid a very large sum of money for a skin of that gigantic bird, the ux, which has been so often reported to exist among the inaccessible peaks of the Tasmanian Mountains. Needless, perhaps, to say that the skin proved a fraud, being nothing more than a Barnum contrivance made up out of the skins of a dozen ostriches and cassowaries, and most cleverly put together by Chinese workmen; at least, such was the report made on it by Sir Peter Grebe, who had been sent by the British Society to Antwerp to examine the acquisition. Needless, also, perhaps, to say that King Leopold, of Belgium, stoutly maintained that the skin of the ux was genuine from beak to claw.

For six months there had been a most serious difference of opinion among European ornithologists concerning the famous ux in the Antwerp Museum; and this difference had promised to result in an open quarrel between a few Belgian savants on one side and all Europe and Great Britain on the other.

Scientists have a deep-rooted horror of anything that touches on charlatanism; the taint of trickery not only alarms them, but drives them away from any suspicious subject, and usually ruins, scientifically speaking, the person who has introduced the subject for discussion.

Therefore, it took no little courage for the Countess d'Alzette to touch, with her dainty gloves, a subject which every scientist in Europe, with scarcely an exception, had pronounced fraudulent and unworthy of investigation. And to bring it before the great International Congress required more courage still; for the person who could face, in executive session, the most brilliant intellects in the world, and openly profess faith in a Barnumized bird skin, either had no scientific reputation to lose or was possessed of a bravery far above that of the savants who composed the audience.

Now, when the pretty Countess caught a flash of encouragement in my glance she turned rosy with gratification and surprise. Clearly, she had not expected to find a single ally in the entire congress. Her quick smile of gratitude touched me, and made me ashamed, too, for I had encouraged her out of the pure love of mischief, hoping to hear the whole matter threshed before the congress and so have it settled once for all. It was a thoughtless thing to do on my part. I should have remembered the consequences to the Countess if it were proven that she had been championing a fraud. The ruffled dignity of the congress would never forgive her; her scientific career would practically be at an end, because her theories and observations could no longer command respect or even the attention of those who knew that she herself had once been deceived by a palpable fraud.

I looked at her guiltily, already ashamed of myself for encouraging her to her destruction. How lovely and innocent she appeared, standing there reading her notes in a low, clear voice, fresh as a child's, with now and then a delicious upward sweep of her long, dark lashes.

With a start I came to my senses and bestowed a pinch on myself. This was neither the time nor the place to sentimentalize over a girlish beauty whose small, Parisian head was crammed full of foolish, brave theories concerning an imposition which her aged sovereign had been unable to detect.

I saw the gathering frown on the King of Finland's dark face; I saw Sir Peter Grebe grow redder and redder, and press his thick lips together to control the angry "Bosh!" which need not have been uttered to have been understood. The Baron de Becasse wore a painfully neutral smile, which froze his face into a quaint gargoyle; the Crown-Prince of Monaco looked at his polished finger-nails with a startled yet abstracted resignation. Clearly the young Countess had not a sympathizer in the committee.

Something—perhaps it was the latent chivalry which exists imbedded in us all, perhaps it was pity, perhaps a glimmering dawn of belief in the ux skin—set my thoughts working very quickly.

The Countess d'Alzette finished her notes, then glanced around with a deprecating smile, which died out on her lips when she perceived the silent and stony hostility of her fellow-scientists. A quick expression of alarm came into her lovely eyes. Would they vote against giving her a hearing before the congress? It required a unanimous vote to reject a subject. She turned her eyes on me.

I rose, red as fire, my head humming with a chaos of ideas all disordered and vague, yet whirling along in a single, resistless current.

I had come to the congress prepared to deliver a monograph on the great auk; but now the subject went overboard as the birds themselves had, and I found myself pleading with the committee to give the Countess a hearing on the ux.

"Why not?" I exclaimed, warmly. "It is established beyond question that the ux does exist in Tasmania. Wallace saw several uxen, through his telescope, walking about upon the inaccessible heights of the Tasmanian Mountains. Darwin acknowledged that the bird exists; Professor Farrago has published a pamphlet containing an accumulation of all data bearing upon the ux. Why should not Madame la Comtesse be heard by the entire congress?"

I looked at Sir Peter Grebe.

"Have you seen this alleged bird skin in the Antwerp Museum?" he asked, perspiring with indignation.

"Yes, I have," said I. "It has been patched up, but how are we to know that the skin did not require patching? I have not found that ostrich skin has been used. It is true that the Tasmanians may have shot the bird to pieces and mended the skin with bits of cassowary hide here and there. But the greater part of the skin, and the beak and claws, are, in my estimation, well worth the serious attention of savants. To pronounce them fraudulent is, in my opinion, rash and premature."

I mopped my brow; I was in for it now. I had thrown in my reputation with the reputation of the Countess.

The displeasure and astonishment of my confrères was unmistakable. In the midst of a strained silence I moved that a vote be taken upon the advisability of a hearing before the congress on the subject of the ux. After a pause the young Countess, pale and determined, seconded my motion. The result of the balloting was a foregone conclusion; the Countess had one vote—she herself refraining from voting—and the subject was entered on the committee-book as acceptable and a date set for the hearing before the International Congress.

The effect of this vote on our little committee was most marked. Constraint took the place of cordiality, polite reserve replaced that guileless and open-hearted courtesy with which our proceedings had begun.

With icy politeness, the Crown-Prince of Monaco asked me to state the subject of the paper I proposed to read before the congress, and I replied quietly that, as I was partly responsible for advocating the discussion of the ux, I proposed to associate myself with the Countess d'Alzette in that matter—if Madame la Comtesse would accept the offer of a brother savant.

"Indeed I will," she said, impulsively, her blue eyes soft with gratitude.

"Very well," observed Sir Peter Grebe, swallowing his indignation and waddling off towards the door; "I shall resign my position on this committee—yes, I will, I tell you!"—as the King of Finland laid a fatherly hand on Sir Peter's sleeve— "I'll not be made responsible for this damn—"

He choked, sputtered, then bowed to the horrified Countess, asking pardon, and declaring that he yielded to nobody in respect for the gentler sex. And he retired with the Baron de Becasse.

Rut out in the hallway I heard him explode. "Confound it! This is no place for petticoats, Baron! And as for that Yankee ornithologist, he's hung himself with the Countess's corset-string—yes, he has! Don't tell me, Baron! The young idiot was all right until the Countess looked at him, I tell you. Gad! how she crumpled him up with those blue eyes of hers! What the devil do women come into such committees for? Eh? It's an outrage, I tell you! Why, the whole world will jeer at us if we sit and listen to her monograph on that fraudulent bird!"

The young Countess, who was writing near the window, could not have heard this outburst; but I heard it, and so did King Christian and the Crown-Prince of Monaco.

"Lord," thought I, "the Countess and I are in the frying-pan this time. I'll do what I can to keep us both out of the fire."

When the King and the Crown-Prince had made their adieux to the Countess, and she had responded, pale and serious, they came over to where I was standing, looking out on the Seine.

"Though we must differ from you," said the King, kindly, "we wish you all success in this dangerous undertaking."

I thanked him.

"You are a young man to risk a reputation already established," remarked the Crown-Prince; then added: "You are braver than I.

Ridicule is a barrier to all knowledge, and, though we know that, we seekers after truth always bring up short at that barrier and dismount, not daring to put our hobbies to the fence."

"One can but come a cropper," said I.

"And risk staking our hobbies? No, no, that would make us ridiculous; and ridicule kills in Europe."

"It's somewhat deadly in America, too," I said, smiling.

"The more honor to you," said the Crown-Prince, gravely.

"Oh, I am not the only one," I answered, lightly. "There is my confrère, Professor Hyssop, who studies apparitions and braves a contempt and ridicule which none of us would dare challenge. We Yankees are learning slowly. Some day we will find the lost key to the future while Europe is sneering at those who are trying to pick the lock."

When King Christian, of Finland, and the Crown-Prince of Monaco had taken their hats and sticks and departed, I glanced across the room at the young Countess, who was now working rapidly on a type-writer, apparently quite oblivious of my presence.

I looked out of the window again, and my gaze wandered over the exposition grounds. Gilt and scarlet and azure the palaces rose in every direction, under a wilderness of fluttering flags. Towers, minarets, turrets, golden spires cut the blue sky; in the west the gaunt Eiffel Tower sprawled across the glittering Esplanade; behind it rose the solid golden dome of the Emperor's tomb, gilded once more by the Almighty's sun, to amuse the living rabble while the dead slumbered in his imperial crypt, himself now but a relic for the amusement of the people whom he had despised. O tempora! O mores! O Napoleon!

Down under my window, in the asphalted court, the King of Finland was entering his beautiful victoria. An adjutant, wearing a cocked hat and brilliant uniform, mounted the box beside the green-and-gold coachman; the two postilions straightened up in their saddles; the four horses danced. Then, when the Crown-Prince of Monaco had taken a seat beside the King, the carriage rolled away, and far down the quay I watched it until the flutter of the green-and-white plumes in the adjutant's cocked hat was all I could see of vanishing royalty.

I was still musing there by the window, listening to the click and ringing of the type-writer, when I suddenly became aware that the clicking had ceased, and, turning, I saw the young Countess standing beside me.

"Thank you for your chivalrous impulse to help me," she said, frankly, holding out her bare hand.

I bent over it.

"I had not realized how desperate my case was," she said, with a smile. "I supposed that they would at least give me a hearing. How can I thank you for your brave vote in my favor?"

"By giving me your confidence in this matter," said I, gravely. "If we are to win, we must work together and work hard, madame. We are entering a struggle, not only to prove the genuineness of a bird skin and the existence of a bird which neither of us has ever seen, but also a struggle which will either make us famous forever or render it impossible for either of us ever again to face a scientific audience."

"I know it," she said, quietly. "And I understand all the better how gallant a gentleman I have had the fortune to enlist in my cause. Believe me, had I not absolute confidence in my ability to prove the existence of the ux I should not, selfish as I am, have accepted your chivalrous offer to stand or fall with me"

The subtle emotion in her voice touched a responsive chord in me. I looked at her earnestly; she raised her beautiful eyes to mine.

"Will you help me?" she asked.

Would I help her? Faith, I'd pass the balance of my life turning flip-flaps to please her. I did not attempt to undeceive myself; I realized that the lightning had struck me—that I was desperately in love with the young Countess from the tip of her bonnet to the toe of her small, polished shoe. I was curiously cool about it, too, although my heart gave a thump that nigh choked me, and I felt myself going red from temple to chin.

If the Countess d'Alzette noticed it she gave no sign, unless the pink tint under her eyes, deepening, was a subtle signal of understanding to the signal in my eyes.

"Suppose," she said, "that I failed, before the congress, to prove my theory? Suppose my investigations resulted in the exposure of a fraud and my name was held up to ridicule before all Europe? What would become of you, monsieur?"

I was silent.

"You are already celebrated as the discoverer of the mammoth and the great auk," she persisted. "You are young, enthusiastic, renowned, and you have a future before you that anybody in the world might envy."

I said nothing.

"And yet," she said, softly, "you risk all because you will not leave a young woman friendless among her confrères. It is not wise, monsieur; it is gallant and generous and impulsive, but it is not wisdom. Don Quixote rides no more in Europe, my friend."

"He stays at home—seventy million of him—in America," said I.

After a moment she said, "I believe you, monsieur."

"It is true enough," I said, with a laugh. "We are the only people who tilt at windmills these days—we and our cousins, the British, who taught us."

I bowed gayly, and added:

"With your colors to wear, I shall have the honor of breaking a lance against the biggest windmill in the world."

"You mean the Citadel of Science," she said, smiling

"And its rock-ribbed respectability," I replied.

She looked at me thoughtfully, rolling and unrolling the scroll in her hands. Then she sighed, smiled, and brightened, handing me the scroll. "Read it carefully," she said; "it is an outline of the policy I suggest that we follow. You will be surprised at some of the statements. Yet every word is the truth. And, monsieur, your reward for the devotion you have offered will be no greater than you deserve, when you find yourself doubly famous for our joint monograph on the ux. Without your vote in the committee I should have been denied a hearing, even though I produced proofs to support my theory. I appreciate that; I do most truly appreciate the courage which prompted you to defend a woman at the risk of your own ruin. Come to me this evening at nine. I hold for you in store a surprise and pleasure which you do not dream of."

"Ah, but I do," I said, slowly, under the spell of her delicate beauty and enthusiasm.

"How can you?" she said, laughing. "You don't know what awaits you at nine this evening?"

"You," I said, fascinated.

The color swept her face; she dropped me a deep courtesy.

"At nine, then," she said. "No. 8 Rue d'Alouette."

I bowed, took my hat, gloves, and stick, and attended her to her carriage below.

Long after the blue-and-black victoria had whirled away down the crowded quay I stood looking after it, mazed in the web of that ancient enchantment whose spell fell over the first man in Eden, and whose sorcery shall not fail till the last man returns his soul.

II

I lunched at my lodgings on the Quai Malthus, and I had but little appetite, having fed upon such an unexpected variety of emotions during the morning.

Now, although I was already heels over head in love, I do not believe that loss of appetite was the result of that alone. I was slowly beginning to realize what my recent attitude might cost me, not only in an utter collapse of my scientific career, and the consequent material ruin which was likely to follow, but in the loss of all my friends at home. The Zoological Society of Bronx Park and the Smithsonian Institution of Washington had sent me as their trusted delegate, leaving it entirely to me to choose the subject on which I was to speak before the International Congress. What, then, would be their attitude when they learned that I had chosen to uphold the dangerous theory of the existence of the ux.

Would they repudiate me and send another delegate to replace me? Would they merely wash their hands of me and let me go to my own destruction?

"I will know soon enough," thought I, "for this morning's proceedings will have been cabled to New York ere now, and read at the breakfast-tables of every old, moss-grown naturalist in America before I see the Countess d'Alzette this evening." And I drew from my pocket the roll of paper which she had given me, and, lighting a cigar, lay back in my chair to read it.

The manuscript had been beautifully type-written, and I had no trouble in following her brief, clear account of the circumstances under which the notorious ux-skin had been obtained. As for the story itself, it was somewhat fishy, but I manfully swallowed my growing nervousness and comforted myself with the belief of Darwin in the existence of the ux, and the subsequent testimony of Wallace, who simply stated what he had seen through his telescope, and then left it to others to identify the enormous birds he described as he had observed them stalking about on the snowy peaks of the Tasmanian Alps.

My own knowledge of the ux was confined to a single circumstance. When, in 1897, I had gone to Tasmania with Professor Farrago, to make a report on the availability of the so-called "Tasmanian devil," as a substitute for the mongoose in the West Indies, I of course heard a great deal of talk among the natives concerning the birds which they affirmed haunted the summits of the mountains.

Our time in Tasmania was too limited to admit of an exploration then. But although we were perfectly aware that the summits of the Tasmanian Alps are inaccessible, we certainly should have attempted to gain them had not the time set for our departure arrived before we had completed the investigation for which we were sent.

One relic, however, I carried away with me. It was a single greenish bronzed feather, found high up in the mountains by a native, and sold to me for a somewhat large sum of money.

Darwin believed the ux to be covered with greenish plumage; Wallace was too far away to observe the color of the great birds; but all the natives of Tasmania unite in affirming that the plumage of the ux is green.

It was not only the color of this feather that made me an eager purchaser, it was the extraordinary length and size. I knew of no living bird large enough to wear such a feather. As for the color, that might have been tampered with before I bought it, and, indeed, testing it later, I found on the fronds traces of sulphate of copper. But the same thing has been found in the feathers of certain birds whose color is metallic green, and it has been proven that such birds pick up and swallow shining bits of copper pyrites.

Why should not the ux do the same thing?

Still, my only reason for believing in the existence of the bird was this single feather. I had easily proved that it belonged to no known species of bird. I also proved it to be similar to the tail-feathers of the ux-skin in Antwerp. But the feathers on the Antwerp specimen were gray, and the longest of them was but three feet in length, while my huge, bronze-green feather measured eleven feet from tip to tip.

One might account for it supposing the Antwerp skin to be that of a young bird, or of a moulting bird, or perhaps of a different sex from the bird whose feather I had secured.

Still, these ideas were not proven. Nothing concerning the birds had been proven. I had but a single fact to lean on, and that was that the feather I possessed could not have belonged to any known species of bird. Nobody but myself knew of the existence of this feather. And now I meant to cable to Bronx Park for it, and to place this evidence at the disposal of the beautiful Countess d'Alzette.

My cigar had gone out, as I sat musing, and I relighted it and resumed my reading of the type-written notes, lazily, even a trifle sceptically, for all the evidence that she had been able to collect to substantiate her theory of the existence of the ux was not half as important as the evidence I was to produce in the shape of that enormous green feather.

I came to the last paragraph, smoking serenely, and leaning back comfortably, one leg crossed over the other. Then, suddenly, my attention became riveted on the words under my eyes. Could I have read them aright? Could I believe what I read in ever-grow-ing astonishment which culminated in an excitement that stirred the very hair on my head?

"The ux exists. There is no longer room for doubt. Ocu-lar proof I can now offer in the shape of five living eggs of this gigantic bird. All measures have been taken to hatch these eggs; they are now in the vast incubator. It is my plan to have them hatch, one by one, under the very eyes of the International Congress. It will be the greatest triumph that science has witnessed since the discovery of the New World.

[Signed] Susanne D'Alzette.

"Either," I cried out, in uncontrollable excitement— "either that girl is mad or she is the cleverest woman on earth."

After a moment I added:

"In either event I am going to marry her."

III

That evening, a few minutes before nine o'clock, I descended from a cab in front of No. 8 Rue d'Alouette, and was ushered into a pretty reception-room by an irreproachable servant, who disappeared directly with my card.

In a few moments the young Countess came in, exquisite in her silvery dinner-gown, eyes bright, white arms extended in a charming, impulsive welcome. The touch of her silky fingers thrilled me; I was dumb under the enchantment of her beauty; and I think she understood my silence, for her blue eyes became troubled and the happy parting of her lips changed to a pensive curve.

Presently I began to tell her about my bronzed-green feather; at my first word she looked up brightly, almost gratefully, I fancied; and in another moment we were deep in eager discussion of the subject which had first drawn us together.

What evidence I possessed to sustain our theory concerning the existence of the ux I hastened to reveal; then, heart beating excitedly, I asked her about the eggs and where they were at present, and whether she believed it possible to bring them to Paris—all these questions in the same breath—which brought a happy light into her eyes and a delicious ripple of laughter to her lips.

"Why, of course it is possible to bring the eggs here," she cried. "Am I sure? Parbleu! The eggs are already here, monsieur!"

"Here!" I exclaimed. "In Paris?"

"In Paris? Mais oui; and in my own house—*this very house*, monsieur. Come, you shall behold them with your own eyes!"

Her eyes were brilliant with excitement; impulsively she stretched out her rosy hand. I took it; and she led me quickly back through the drawing-room, through the dining-room, across the butler's pantry, and into a long, dark hallway. We were almost running now—I keeping tight hold of her soft little hand, she, raising her gown a trifle, hurrying down the hallway, silken petticoats rustling like a silk banner in the wind. A turn to the right brought us to the cellar-stairs; down we hastened, and then across the cemented floor towards a long, glass-fronted shelf, pierced with steam-pipes.

"A match," she whispered, breathlessly.

I struck a wax match and touched it to the gas-burner overhead.

Never, never can I forget what that flood of gas-light revealed. In a row stood five large, glass-mounted incubators; behind the glass doors lay, in dormant majesty, five enormous eggs. The eggs were pale-green—lighter, somewhat, than robins' eggs, but not as pale as herons' eggs. Each egg appeared to be larger than a large hogshead, and was partly embedded in bales of cotton-wool.

Five little silver thermometers inside the glass doors indicated a temperature of 95° Fahrenheit. I noticed that there was an automatic arrangement connected with the pipes which regulated the temperature.

I was too deeply moved for words. Speech seemed superfluous as we stood there, hand in hand, contemplating those gigantic, pale-green eggs.

There is something in a silent egg which moves one's deeper emotions—something solemn in its embryotic inertia, something awesome in its featureless immobility.

I know of nothing on earth which is so totally lacking in expression as an egg. The great desert Sphinx, brooding through its veil of sand, has not that tremendous and meaningless dignity which wraps the colorless oval effort of a single domestic hen.

I held the hand of the young Countess very tightly. Her fingers closed slightly.

Then and there, in the solemn presence of those emotionless eggs, I placed my arm around her supple waist and kissed her.

She said nothing. Presently she stooped to observe the thermometer. Naturally, it registered 95° Fahrenheit.

"Susanne," I said, softly.

"Oh, we must go up-stairs," she whispered, breathlessly; and, picking up her silken skirts, she fled up the cellar-stairs.

I turned out the gas, with that instinct of economy which early wastefulness has implanted in me, and followed the Countess

Suzanne through the suite of rooms and into the small reception-hall where she had first received me.

She was sitting on a low divan, head bent, slowly turning a sapphire ring on her finger, round and round.

I looked at her romantically, and then—

"Please don't," she said.

The correct reply to this is:

"Why not?"—very tenderly spoken.

"Because," she replied, which was also the correct and regular answer.

"Suzanne," I said, slowly and passionately.

She turned the sapphire ring on her finger. Presently she tired of this, so I lifted her passive hand very gently and continued turning the sapphire ring on her finger, slowly, to harmonize with the cadence of our unspoken thoughts.

Towards midnight I went home, walking with great care through a new street in Paris, paved exclusively with rose-colored blocks of air.

IV

At nine o'clock in the evening, July 31, 1900, the International Congress was to assemble in the great lecture-hall of the Belgian Scientific Pavilion, which adjourned the Tasmanian Pavilion, to hear the Countess Suzanne d'Alzette read her paper on the ux.

That morning the Countess and I, with five furniture vans, had transported the five great incubators to the platform of the lecture-hall, and had engaged an army of plumbers and gas-fitters to make the steam-heating connections necessary to maintain in the incubators a temperature of 100° Fahrenheit.

A heavy green curtain hid the stage from the body of the lecture-hall. Behind this curtain the five enormous eggs reposed, each in its incubator.

The Countess Suzanne was excited and calm by turns, her cheeks were pink, her lips scarlet, her eyes bright as blue planets at midnight. Without faltering, she rehearsed her discourse before me, reading from her type-written manuscript in a clear voice, in which I could scarcely discern a tremor. Then we went through the dumb show of exhibiting the uxen eggs to a frantically applauding audience; she responded to countless supposititious encores, I leading her out repeatedly before the green curtain to face the great, damp, darkened auditorium.

Then, in response to repeated imaginary recalls, she rehearsed the extemporaneous speech, thanking the distinguished audience for their patience in listening to an unknown confrère, and confessing her obligations to me (here I appeared and bowed in self-abasement) for my faith in her and my aid in securing for her a public hearing before the most highly educated audience in the world.

After that we retired behind the curtain to sit on an empty box and eat sandwiches and watch the last lingering plumbers pasting up the steam connections with a pot of molten lead.

The plumbers were Americans, brought to Paris to make repairs on the American buildings during the exposition, and we conversed with them affably as they pottered about, plumber-like, poking under the flooring with lighted candles, rubbing their thumbs up and down musty old pipes, and prying up planks in dark corners.

They informed us that they were union men and that they hoped we were too. And I replied that union was certainly my ultimate purpose, at which the young Countess smiled dreamily at vacancy.

We did not dare leave the incubators. The plumbers lingered on, hour after hour, while we sat and watched the little silver thermometers, and waited.

It was time for the Countess Suzanne to dress, and still the plumbers had not finished; so I sent a messenger for her maid, to bring her trunk to the lecture-hall, and I despatched another messenger to my lodgings for my evening clothes and fresh linen.

There were several dressing-rooms off the stage. Here, about six o'clock, the Countess retired with her maid, to dress, leaving me to watch the plumbers and the thermometers.

When the Countess Suzanne returned, radiant and lovely in an evening gown of black lace, I gave her the roses I had brought for her and hurried off to dress in my turn, leaving her to watch the thermometers.

I was not absent more than half an hour, but when I returned I found the Countess anxiously conversing with the plumbers and pointing despairingly at the thermometers, which now registered only 95°.

"You must keep up the temperature!" I said. "Those eggs are due to hatch within a few hours. What's the trouble with the heat?"

The plumber did not know, but thought the connections were defective.

"But that's why we called you in!" exclaimed the Countess. "Can't you fix things securely?"

"Oh, we'll fix things, lady," replied the plumber, condescendingly, and he ambled away to rub his thumb up and down a pipe.

As we alone were unable to move and handle the enormous eggs, the Countess, whose sweet character was a stranger to vindictiveness or petty resentment, had written to the members of the ornithological committee, revealing the marvellous fortune which had crowned her efforts in the search for evidence to sustain her theory concerning the ux, and inviting these gentlemen to aid her in displaying the great eggs to the assembled congress.

This she had done the night previous. Every one of the gentlemen invited had come post-haste to her "hotel," to view the eggs with their own sceptical and astonished eyes; and the fair young Countess and I tasted our first triumph in her cellar, whither we conducted Sir Peter Grebe, the Crown-Prince of Monaco, Baron de Becasse, and his Majesty King Christian of Finland.

Scepticism and incredulity gave place to excitement and unbounded enthusiasm. The old King embraced the Countess; Baron de Becasse attempted to kiss me; Sir Peter Grebe made a handsome apology for his folly and vowed that he would do open penance for his sins. The poor Crown-Prince, who was of a nervous temperament, sat on the cellar-stairs and wept like a child.

His grief at his own pig-headedness touched us all profoundly.

So it happened that these gentlemen were coming tonight to give their aid to us in moving the priceless eggs, and lend their countenance and enthusiastic support to the young Countess in her maiden effort.

Sir Peter Grebe arrived first, all covered with orders and decorations, and greeted us affectionately, calling the Countess the

"sweetest lass in France," and me his undutiful Yankee cousin who
had landed feet foremost at the expense of the British Empire.

The King of Finland, the Crown-Prince, and Baron de Becasse
arrived together, a composite mass of medals, sashes, and academy palms. To see them moving boxes about, straightening chairs,
and pulling out rugs reminded me of those golden-embroidered
gentlemen who run out into the arena and roll up carpets after the
acrobats have finished their turn in the Nouveau Cirque.

I was aiding the King of Finland to move a heavy keg of nails,
when the Countess called out to me in alarm, saying that the thermometers had dropped to 80° Fahrenheit. I spoke sharply to the plumbers, who were standing in a circle behind the dressing-rooms; but
they answered sullenly that they could do no more work that day.

Indignant and alarmed, I ordered them to come out to the stage,
and, after some hesitation, they filed out, a sulky, silent lot of workmen, with their tools already gathered up and tied in their kits. At
once I noticed that a new man had appeared among them—a red-
faced, stocky man wearing a frock-coat and a shiny silk hat.

"Who is the master-workman here?" I asked.

"I am," said a man in blue overalls.

"Well," said I, "why don't you fix those steam-fittings?"

There was a silence. The man in the silk hat smirked.

"Well?" said I.

"Come, come, that's all right," said the man in the silk hat.
"These men know their business without you tellin' them."

"Who are you?" I demanded, sharply.

"Oh, I'm just a walkin' delegate," he replied, with a sneer.
"There's a strike in New York and I come over here to tie this here
exposition up. See?"

"You mean to say you won't let these men finish their work?" I
asked, thunderstruck.

"That's about it, young man," he said, coolly.

Furious, I glanced at my watch, then at the thermometers,
which now registered only 75°. Already I could hear the first-comers
of the audience arriving in the body of the hall. Already a stage-
hand was turning up the footlights and dragging chairs and tables
hither and thither.

"What will you take to stay and attend to those steam-pipes?" I demanded, desperately.

"It can't be done nohow," observed the man in the silk hat. "That New York strike is good for a month yet." Then, turning to the workmen, he nodded and, to my horror, the whole gang filed out after him, turning deaf ears to my entreaties and threats.

There was a deathly silence, then Sir Peter exploded into a vivid shower of words. The Countess, pale as a ghost, gave me a heart-breaking look. The Crown-Prince wept.

"Great Heaven!" I cried; "the thermometers have fallen to 70°!"

The King of Finland sat down on a chair and pressed his hands over his eyes. Baron de Becasse ran round and round, uttering subdued and plaintive screams; Sir Peter swore steadily.

"Gentlemen," I cried, desperately, "we must save those eggs! They are on the very eve of hatching! Who will volunteer?"

"To do what?" moaned the Crown-Prince.

"I'll show you," I exclaimed, running to the incubators and beckoning to the Baron to aid me.

In a moment we had rolled out the great egg, made a nest on the stage floor with the bales of cotton-wool, and placed the egg in it. One after another we rolled out the remaining eggs, building for each its nest of cotton; and at last the five enormous eggs lay there in a row behind the green curtain.

"Now," said I, excitedly, to the King, "you must get up on that egg and try to keep it warm."

The King began to protest, but I would take no denial, and presently his Majesty was perched up on the great egg, gazing foolishly about at the others, who were now all climbing up on their allotted eggs.

"Great Heaven!" muttered the King, as Sir Peter settled down comfortably on his egg, "I am willing to give life and fortune for the sake of science, but I can't bear to hatch out eggs like a bird!"

The Crown-Prince was now sitting patiently beside the Baron de Becasse.

"I feel in my bones," he murmured, "that I'm about to hatch something. Can't you hear a tapping on the shell of your egg, Baron?"

"Parbleu!" replied the Baron. "The shell is moving under me."

It certainly was; for, the next moment, the Baron fell into his egg with a crash and a muffled shriek, and floundered out, dripping, yellow as a canary.

"N'importe!" he cried, excitedly. "Allons! Save the eggs! Hurrah! Vive la science!" And he scrambled up on the fourth egg and sat there, arms folded, sublime courage transfiguring him from head to foot.

We all gave him a cheer, which was hushed as the stage-manager ran in, warning us that the audience was already assembled and in place.

"You're not going to raise the curtain while we're sitting, are you?" demanded the King of Finland, anxiously.

"No, no," I said; "sit tight, your Majesty. Courage, gentlemen! Our vindication is at hand!"

The Countess glanced at me with startled eyes; I took her hand, saluted it respectfully, and then quietly led her before the curtain, facing an ocean of upturned faces across the flaring footlights.

She stood a moment to acknowledge the somewhat ragged applause, a calm smile on her lips. All her courage had returned; I saw that at once.

Very quietly she touched her lips to the *eau-sucrée*, laid her manuscript on the table, raised her beautiful head, and began:

"That the ux is a living bird I am here before you to prove—"

A sharp report behind the curtain drowned her voice. She paled; the audience rose amid cries of excitement.

"What was it?" she asked, faintly.

"Sir Peter has hatched out his egg," I whispered. "Hark! There goes another egg!" And I ran behind the curtain.

Such a scene as I beheld was never dreamed of on land or sea. Two enormous young uxen, all over gigantic pin-feathers, were wandering stupidly about. Mounted on one was Sir Peter Grebe, eyes starting from his apoplectic visage; on the other, clinging to the bird's neck, hung the Baron de Becasse.

Before I could move, the two remaining eggs burst, and a pair of huge, scrawny fledgelings rose among the debris, bearing off on their backs the King and Crown-Prince.

"Help!" said the King of Finland, faintly. "I'm falling off!"

I sprang to his aid, but tripped on the curtain-spring. The next instant the green curtain shot up, and there revealed to that vast and distinguished audience, roamed four enormous chicks, bearing on their backs the most respected and exclusive aristocracy of Europe.

The Countess Suzanne turned with a little shriek of horror, then sat down in her chair, laid her lovely head on the table, and very quietly fainted away, unconscious of the frantic cheers which went roaring to the roof.

This, then, is the *true* history of the famous exposition scandal. And, as I have said, had it not been for the presence in that audience of two American reporters nobody would have known what all the world now knows—nobody would have read of the marvellous feats of bareback riding indulged in by the King of Finland—nobody would have read how Sir Peter Grebe steered his mount safely past the footlights only to come to grief over the prompter's box.

But this *is* scandal. And, as for the charming Countess Suzanne d'Alzette, the public has heard all that it is entitled to hear, and much that it is not entitled to hear.

However, on second thoughts, perhaps the public is entitled to hear a little more. I will therefore say this much—the shock of astonishment which stunned me when the curtain flew up, revealing the King-bestridden uxen, was nothing to the awful blow which smote me when the Count d'Alzette leaped from the orchestra, over the footlights, and bore away with him the fainting form of his wife, the lovely Countess d'Alzette.

I sometimes wonder—but, as I have repeatedly observed, this dull and pedantic narrative of fact is no vehicle for sentimental soliloquy. It is, then, merely sufficient to say that I took the earliest steamer for kinder shores, spurred on to haste by a venomous cablegram from the Smithsonian, repudiating me, and by another from Bronx Park, ordering me to spend the winter in some inexpensive, poisonous, and unobtrusive spot, and make a collection of isopods. The island of Java appeared to me to be as poisonously unobtrusive and inexpensive a region as I had ever heard of; a steamer sailed from Antwerp for Batavia in twenty-four hours. Therefore, as I say, I took the night-train for Brussels, and the steamer from Antwerp the following evening.

Of my uneventful voyage, of the happy and successful quest, there is little to relate. The Javanese are frolicsome and hospitable. There was a girl there with features that were as delicate as though chiselled out of palest amber, and I remember she wore a most wonderful jewelled, helmet-like head-dress, and jingling bangles on her ankles, and when she danced she made most graceful and poetic gestures with her supple wrists—but that has nothing to do with isopods, absolutely nothing.

Letters from home came occasionally. Professor Farrago had returned to the Bronx and had been re-elected to the high office he had so nobly held when I first became associated with him.

Through his kindness and by his advice I remained for several years in the Far East, until a letter from him arrived recalling me and also announcing his own hurried and sudden departure for Florida. He also mentioned my promotion to the office of subcurator of department; so I started on my homeward voyage very much pleased with the world, and arrived in New York on April 1, 1904, ready for a rest to which I believed myself entitled. And the first thing that they handed me was a letter from Professor Farrago, summoning me South.

THE SPHYX

I

The letter that started me—I was going to say startled me, but only imaginative people are startled—the letter, then, that started me from Bronx Park to the South I print without the permission of my superior, Professor Farrago. I have not obtained his permission, for the somewhat exciting reason that nobody knows where he is. Publicity being now recognized as the annihilator of mysteries, a benevolent purpose alone inspires me to publish a letter so strange, so pathetically remarkable, in view of what has recently occurred.

As I say, I had only just returned from Java with a valuable collection of undescribed isopods—an order of edriophthalmous crustaceans with seven free thoracic somites furnished with fourteen legs—and I beg my reader's pardon, but my reader will see the necessity for the author's absolute accuracy in insisting on detail, because the story that follows is a dangerous story for a scientist to tell, in view of the vast amount of nonsense and fiction in circulation masquerading as stories of scientific adventure.

I was, therefore, anticipating a delightful summer's work with pen and microscope, when on April 1st I received the following extraordinary letter from Professor Farrago:

"In Camp, Little Sprite Lake,
"Everglades, Florida, March 15, 1902.
"My Dear Mr. Gilland,—On receipt of this communication you will immediately secure for me the following articles:
"One complete outfit of woman's clothing.
"One camera.

83

"One light steel cage, large enough for you to stand in,

"One stenographer (male sex).

"One five-pound steel tank, with siphon and hose attachment.

"One rifle and ammunition.

"Three ounces rosium oxyde.

"One ounce chlorate strontium.

"You will then, within twenty-four hours, set out with the stenographer and the supplies mentioned and join me in camp on Little Sprite Lake. This order is formal and admits of no delay. You will appreciate the necessity of absolute and unquestioning obedience when I tell you that I am practically on the brink of the most astonishing discovery recorded in natural history since Monsieur Zani discovered the purple-spotted zoombok in Nyanza; and that I depend upon you and your zeal and fidelity for success.

"I dare not, lest my letter fall into unscrupulous hands, convey to you more than a hint of what lies before us in these uncharted solitudes of the Everglades.

"You must read between the lines when I say that because one can see through a sheet of glass, the glass is none the less solid and palpable. One can see through it—if that is also seeing it, but one can nevertheless hold it and feel it and receive from it sensations of cold or heat according to its temperature.

"Certain jellyfish are absolutely transparent when in the water, and one can only know of their presence by accidental contact, not by sight.

"*Have you ever thought that possibly there might exist larger and more highly organized creatures transparent to eyesight, yet palpable to touch?*

"Little Sprite Lake is the jumping-off place; beyond lie the Everglades, the outskirts of which are haunted by the Seminoles, the interior of *which have never been visited by man, as far as we know.*

"As you are aware, no general survey of Florida has yet been made; there exist no maps of the Everglades south of

Okeechobee; even Little Sprite Lake is but a vague blot on our maps. We know, of course, that south of the eleven thousand square miles of fresh water which is called Lake Okeechobee the Everglades form a vast, delta-like projection of thousands and thousands of square miles. Darkest Africa is no longer a mystery; but the Everglades to-day remain the sombre secret of our continent. And, to-day, this unknown expanse of swamps, barrens, forests, and lagoons is greater than in the days of De Soto, because the entire region has been slowly rising.

"All this, my dear sir, you already know, and I ask your indulgence for recalling the facts to your memory. I do it for this reason—the search for *what I am seeking* may lead us to utter destruction; and therefore my formal orders to you should be modified to this extent:—do you volunteer? If you volunteer, my orders remain; if not, turn this letter over to Mr. Kingsley, who will find for me the companion I require.

"In the event of your coming, you must break your journey at False Cape and ask for an old man named Slunk. He will give you a packet; you will give him a dollar, and drive on to Cape Canaveral, and you will do what is to be done there. From there to Fort Kissimmee, to Okeechobee, traversing the lake to the Rita River, where I have marked the trail to Little Sprite.

"At Little Sprite I shall await you; beyond that point a merciful Providence alone can know what awaits us.

"Yours fraternally,

Farrago.

"P.S.—I think that you had better make your will, and suggest the same idea to the stenographer who is to accompany you. F."

And that was the letter I received while seated comfortably on the floor of my work-room, surrounded by innocent isopods, all patiently awaiting scientific investigation.

And this is what I did: Within twenty-four hours I had assembled the supplies required—the cage, the woman's clothing,
tank, arms and ammunition, and the chemicals; I had secured ac-
commodations, for that evening, on the Florida, Volusia, and Fort
Lauderdale Railway as far as Citron City; and I had been inter-
viewing stenographers all day long, the result of an innocently
worded advertisement in the daily newspapers.

It was now very close to the time when I must summon a cab
and drive to the ferry; and yet I was still shy one stenographer.

I had seen scores; they simply would not listen to the proposition. "Why does a gentleman in the backwoods of Florida want a
stenographer?" they demanded; and as I had not the faintest idea,
I could only say so. I think the majority interviewed concluded I
had escaped from a State institution.

As the time for departure approached I became desperate, urg-
ing and beseeching applicants to accompany me; but neither sympathy for my instant need nor desire for salary moved them.

I waited until the last moment, hoping against hope. Then, with a
groan of despair, I seized luggage and raincoat, made for the door and
flung it open, only to find myself face to face with an attractive
young girl, apparently on the point of pressing the electric button.

"I'm sorry," I said, "but I have a train to catch."

She was noticeably attractive in her storm-coat and pretty hat,
and I really was sorry—so sorry that I added:

"I have about twenty-seven seconds to place at your service
before I go."

"Twenty will be sufficient," she replied, pleasantly. "I saw your
advertisement for a stenographer—"

"We require a man," I interposed, hastily.

"Have you engaged him?"

"N-no."

We looked at each other.

"You wouldn't accept, anyway," I began.

"How do you know?"

"You wouldn't leave town, would you?"

"Yes, if you required it."

"What? Go to Florida?"

"Y-yes—if I must."

"But think of the alligators! Think of the snakes—big, bitey snakes!"

"Gracious!" she exclaimed, eyes growing bigger.

"Indians, too!—unreconciled, sulky Seminoles! Fevers! Mud-puddles! Spiders! And only fifty dollars a week—"

"I—I'll go," she stammered.

"Go?" I repeated, grimly; "then you've exactly two and three-quarter seconds left for preparations."

Instinctively she raised her little gloved hand and patted her hair. "I'm ready," she said, unsteadily.

"One extra second to make your will," I added, stunned by her self-possession.

"I—I have nothing to leave—nobody to leave it to," she said, smiling; "I am ready."

I took that extra second myself for a lightning course in reflection upon effects and consequences.

"It's silly, it's probably murder," I said, "but you're engaged! Now we must run for it!"

And that is how I came to engage the services of Miss Helen Barrison as stenographer.

II

At noon on the second day I disembarked from the train at Citron City with all paraphernalia—cage, chemicals, arsenal, and stenographer; an accumulation of very dusty impedimenta—all but the stenographer. By three o'clock our hotel livery-rig was speeding along the beach at False Cape towards the tall light-house looming above the dunes.

The abode of a gentleman named Slunk was my goal. I sat brooding in the rickety carriage, still dazed by the rapidity of my flight from New York; the stenographer sat beside me, blue eyes bright with excitement, fair hair blowing in the sea-wind.

Our railway companionship had been of the slightest, also absolutely formal; for I was too absorbed in conjecturing the meaning of this journey to be more than absent-mindedly civil; and she, I fancy, had had time for repentance and perhaps for a little fright, though I could discover traces of neither.

I remember she left the train at some city or other where we were held for an hour; and out of the car-window I saw her returning with a brand-new grip-sack.

She must have bought clothes, for she continued to remain cool and fresh in her summer shirt-waists and short outing skirt; and she looked immaculate now, sitting there beside me, the trace of a smile curving her red mouth.

"I'm looking for a personage named Slunk," I observed.

After a moment's silent consideration of the Atlantic Ocean she said, "When do my duties begin, Mr. Gilland?"

"The Lord alone knows," I replied, grimly. "Are you repenting of your bargain?"

"I am quite happy," she said, serenely.

Remorse smote me that I had consented to engage this frail, pink-and-ivory biped for an enterprise which lay outside the suburbs of Manhattan. I glanced guiltily at my victim; she sat there, the incarnation of New York piquancy—a translated denizen of the metropolis—a slender spirit of the back offices of sky-scrapers. Why had I lured her hither?—here where the heavy, lavender-tinted breakers thundered on a lost coast; here where above the dune-jungles vultures soared, and snowy-headed eagles, hulking along the sands, tore dead fish and yelped at us as we passed.

Strange waters, strange skies—a strange, lost land aquiver under an exotic sun; and there she sat with her wise eyes of a child, unconcerned, watching the world in perfect confidence.

"May I pay a little compliment to your pluck?" I asked, amused.

"Certainly," she said, smiling as the maid of Manhattan alone knows how to smile—shyly, inquiringly—with a lingering hint of laughter in the curled lips' corners. Then her sensitive features fell a trifle. "Not pluck," she said, "but necessity. I had no chance to choose, no time to wait. My last dollar, Mr. Gilland, is in my purse!"

With a gay little gesture she drew it from her shirtfront, then, smiling, sat turning it over and over in her lap.

The sun fell on her hands, gilding the smooth skin with the first tint of sunburn. Under the corners of her eyes above the rounded

cheeks a pink stain lay like the first ripening flush on a wild strawberry. That, too, was the mark left by the caress of wind and sun. I
had had no idea she was so pretty.

"I think we'll enjoy this adventure," I said; "don't you?"

"I try to make the best of things," she said, gazing off into the
horizon haze. "Look," she added; "is that a man?"

A spot far away on the beach caught my eye. At first I thought
it was a pelican—and small wonder, too, for the dumpy, waddling,
goose-necked individual who loomed up resembled a heavy bot-
tomed bird more than a human being.

"Do you suppose that could be Mr. Slunk?" asked the stenographer, as our vehicle drew nearer.

He looked as though his name ought to be Slunk; he was digging coquina clams, and he dug with a pecking motion like a water-
turkey mastering a mullet too big for it.

His name was Slunk; he admitted it when I accused him. Our
negro driver drew rein, and I descended to the sand and gazed on
Mr. Slunk.

He was, as I have said, not impressive, even with the tremendous background of sky and ocean.

"I've come something over a thousand miles to see you," I said,
reluctant to admit that I had come as far to see such a specimen of
human architecture.

A weather-beaten grin stretched the skin that covered his face,
and he shoved a hairy paw into the pockets of his overalls, digging
deeply into profound depths. First he brought to light a twist of
South Carolina tobacco, which he leisurely inserted in his mouth—
not, apparently, for pleasure, but merely to get rid of it.

The second object excavated from the overalls was a small
packet addressed to me. This he handed to me; I gravely handed him
a silver dollar; he went back to his clam-digging, and I entered the
carriage and drove on. All had been carried out according to the
letter of my instructions so far, and my spirits brightened.

"If you don't mind I'll read my instructions," I said, in high
good-humor.

"Pray do not hesitate," she said, smiling in sympathy.

So I opened the little packet and read:

"Drive to Cape Canaveral along the beach. You will find
a gang of men at work on a government breakwater. The
superintendent is Mr. Rowan. Show him this letter.
                              "Farrago."

Rather disappointed—for I had been expecting to find in the
packet some key to the interesting mystery which had sent Professor Farrago into the Everglades—I thrust the missive into my
pocket and resumed a study of the immediate landscape. It had
not changed as we progressed: ocean, sand, low dunes crowned
with impenetrable tangles of wild bay, sparkleberry, and live oak,
with here and there a weather-twisted palmetto sprawling, and here
and there the battered blades of cactus and Spanish-bayonet thrust
menacingly forward; and over all the vultures, sailing, sailing—
some mere circling motes lost in the blue above, some sheering
the earth so close that their swiftly sweeping shadows slanted continually across our road.

"I detest a buzzard," I said, aloud.

"I thought they were crows," she confessed.

"Carrion-crows—yes.

  'The carrion-crows
   Sing, Caw! caw!'

—only they don't," I added, my song putting me in good-humor
once more. And I glanced askance at the pretty stenographer.

"It is a pleasure to be employed by agreeable people," she said,
innocently.

"Oh, I can be much more agreeable than that," I said.

"Is Professor Farrago—amusing?" she asked.

"Well—oh, certainly—but not in—in the way I am."

Suddenly it flashed upon me that my superior was a confirmed
hater of unmarried women. I had clean forgotten it; and now the
full import of what I had done scared me silent.

"Is anything the matter?" asked Miss Barrison.

"No—not yet," I said, ominously.

How on earth could I have overlooked that well-known fact.

The hurry and anxiety, the stress of instant preparation and departure, had clean driven it from my absent-minded head.

Jogging on over the sand, I sat silent, cudgelling my brains for a solution of the disastrous predicament I had gotten into. I pictured the astonished rage of my superior—my probable dismissal from employment—perhaps the general overturning and smash-up of the entire expedition.

A distant, dark object on the beach concentrated my distracted thoughts; it must be the breakwater at Cape Canaveral. And it was the breakwater, swarming with negro workmen, who were swinging great blocks of coquina into cemented beds, singing and whistling at their labor.

I forgot my predicament when I saw a thin white man in sun-helmet and khaki directing the work from the beach; and as our horses plodded up, I stepped out and hailed him by name.

"Yes, my name is Rowan," he said, instantly, turning to meet me. His sharp, clear eyes included the vehicle and the stenographer, and he lifted his helmet, then looked squarely at me.

"My name is Gilland," I said, dropping my voice and stepping nearer. "I have just come from Bronx Park, New York."

He bowed, waiting for something more from me; so I presented my credentials.

His formal manner changed at once. "Come over here and let us talk a bit," he said, cordially—then hesitated, glancing at Miss Barrison— "if your wife would excuse us—"

The pretty stenographer colored, and I dryly set Mr. Rowan right—which appeared to disturb him more than his mistake.

"Pardon me, Mr. Gilland, but you do not propose to take this young girl into the Everglades, do you?"

"That's what I had proposed to do," I said, brusquely.

Perfectly aware that I resented his inquiry, he cast a perplexed and troubled glance at her, then slowly led the way to a great block of sun-warmed coquina, where he sat down, motioning me to do the same.

"I see," he said, "that you don't know just where you are going or just what you are expected to do."

"No, I don't," I said.

"Well, I'll tell you, then. You are going into the devil's own country to look for something that I fled five hundred miles to avoid."

"Is that so?" I said, uneasily.

"That is so, Mr. Gilland."

"Oh! And what is this object that I am to look for and from which you fled five hundred miles?"

"I don't know."

"You don't know what you ran away from?"

"No, sir. Perhaps if I had known I should have run a thousand miles."

We eyed one another.

"You think, then, that I'd better send Miss Barrison back to New York?" I asked.

"I certainly do. It may be murder to take her."

"Then I'll do it!" I said, nervously. "Back she goes from the first railroad station."

In a flash the thought came to me that here was a way to avoid the wrath of Professor Farrago—and a good excuse, too. He might forgive my not bringing a man as stenographer in view of my limited time; he never would forgive my presenting him with a woman.

"She must go back," I repeated; and it rather surprised me to find myself already anticipating loneliness—something that never in all my travels had I experienced before.

"By the first train," I added, firmly, disliking Mr. Rowan without any reason except that he had suddenly deprived me of my stenographer.

"What I have to tell you," he began, lighting a cigarette, the mate to which I declined, "is this: Three years ago, before I entered this contracting business, I was in the government employ as officer in the Coast Survey. Our duties took us into Florida waters; we were months at a time working on shore."

He pulled thoughtfully at his cigarette and blew a light cloud into the air. "I had leave for a month once; and like an ass I prepared to spend it in a hunting-trip among the Everglades."

He crossed his lean legs and gazed meditatively at his cigarette.

"I believe," he went on, "that we penetrated the Everglades farther than any white man who ever lived to return. There's nothing very dismal about the Everglades—the greater part, I mean. You get high and low hummock, marshes, creeks, lakes, and all that. If you get lost, you're a goner. If you acquire fever, you're as well off as the seraphim—and not a whit better. There are the usual animals there—bears (little black fellows), lynxes, deer, panthers, alligators, and a few stray crocodiles. As for snakes, of course they're there, moccasins a-plenty, some rattlers, but, after all, not as many snakes as one finds in Alabama, or even northern Florida and Georgia.

"The Seminoles won't help you—won't even talk to you. They're a sullen pack—but not murderous, as far as I know. Beyond their inner limits lie the unknown regions."

He bit the wet end from his cigarette.

"I went there," he said; "I came out as soon as I could."

"Why?"

"Well—for one thing, my companion died of fright."

"Fright? What at?"

"Well, there's something in there."

"What ?"

He fixed a penetrating gaze on me. "I don't know, Mr. Gilland."

"Did you see anything to frighten you?" I insisted.

"No, but I felt something." He dropped his cigarette and ground it into the sand viciously. "To cut it short," he said, "I am most unwillingly led to believe that there are—creatures—of some sort in the Everglades—living creatures quite as large as you or I—and that they are perfectly transparent—as transparent as a colorless jellyfish."

Instantly the veiled import of Professor Farrago's letter was made clear to me. He, too, believed that.

"It embarrasses me like the devil to say such a thing," continued Rowan, digging in the sand with his spurred heels. "It seems so—so like a whopping lie—it seems so childish and ridiculous—so cursed cheap! But I fled; and there you are. I might add," he said, indifferently, "that I have the ordinary portion of courage allotted to normal men."

"But what do you believe these—these animals to be?" I asked, fascinated.

"I don't know." An obstinate look came into his eyes. "I don't know, and I absolutely refuse to speculate for the benefit of anybody. I wouldn't do it for my friend Professor Farrago; and I'm not going to do it for you," he ended, laughing a rather grim laugh that somehow jarred me into realizing the amazing import of his story. For I did not doubt it, strange as it was—fantastic, incredible though it sounded in the ears of a scientist.

What it was that carried conviction I do not know—perhaps the fact that my superior credited it; perhaps the manner of narration. Told in quiet, commonplace phrases, by an exceedingly practical and unimaginative young man who was plainly embarrassed in the telling, the story rang out like a shout in a canon, startling because of the absolute lack of emphasis employed in the telling.

"Professor Farrago asked me to speak of this to no one except the man who should come to his assistance. He desired the first chance of clearing this—this rather perplexing matter. No doubt he didn't want exploring parties prowling about him," added Rowan, smiling. "But there's no fear of that, I fancy. I never expect to tell that story again to anybody; I shouldn't have told him, only somehow it's worried me for three years, and though I was deadly afraid of ridicule, I finally made up my mind that science ought to have a hack at it.

"When I was in New York last winter I summoned up courage and wrote Professor Farrago. He came to see me at the Holland House that same evening; I told him as much as I ever shall tell anybody. That is all, Mr. Gilland."

For a long time I sat silent, musing over the strange words. After a while I asked him whether Professor Farrago was supplied with provisions; and he said he was; that a great store of staples and tins of concentrated rations had been carried in as far as Little Sprite Lake; that Professor Farrago was now there alone, having insisted upon dismissing all those he had employed.

"There was no practical use for a guide," added Rowan, "because no cracker, no Indian, and no guide knows the region beyond the Seminole country."

I rose, thanking him and offering my hand. He took it and shook it in manly fashion, saying: "I consider Professor Farrago a very brave man; I may say the same of any man who volunteers to accompany him. Goodbye, Mr. Gilland; I most earnestly wish for your success. Professor Farrago left this letter for you."

And that was all. I climbed back into the rickety carriage, carrying my unopened letter; the negro driver cracked his whip and whistled, and the horses trotted inland over a fine shell road which was to lead us across Verbena Junction to Citron City. Half an hour later we crossed the tracks at Verbena and turned into a broad marl road. This aroused me from my deep and speculative reverie, and after a few moments I asked Miss Barrison's indulgence and read the letter from Professor Farrago which Mr. Rowan had given me:

"Dear Mr. Gilland,—You now know all I dared not write, fearing to bring a swarm of explorers about my ears in case the letter was lost, and found by unscrupulous meddlers. If you still are willing to volunteer, knowing all that I know, join me as soon as possible. If family considerations deter you from taking what perhaps is an insane risk, I shall not expect you to join me. In that event, return to New York immediately and send Kingsley.

"Yours, F."

"What the deuce is the matter with him!" I exclaimed, irritably. "I'll take any chances Kingsley does!"

Miss Barrison looked up in surprise.

"Miss Barrison," I said, plunging into the subject headfirst, "I'm extremely sorry, but I have news that forces me to believe the journey too dangerous for you to attempt, so I think that it would be much better—" The consternation in her pretty face checked me.

"I'm awfully sorry," I muttered, appalled by her silence.

"But—but you engaged me!"

"I know it—I should not have done it. I only—"

"But you did engage me, didn't you?"

"I believe that I did—er—oh, of course—"

"But a verbal contract is binding between honorable people, isn't it, Mr. Gilland?"

"Yes, but—"

"And ours was a verbal contract; and in consideration you paid me my first week's salary, and I bought shirt-waists and a short skirt and three changes of—and tooth-brushes and—"

"I know, I know," I groaned. "But I'll fix all that."

"You can't if you break your contract."

"Why not?"

"Because," she said, flushing up, "I should not accept."

"You don't understand—"

"Really I do. You are going into a dangerous country and you're afraid I'll be frightened."

"It's something like that."

"Tell me what are the dangers?"

"Alligators, big, bitey snakes—"

"Oh, you've said all that before!"

"Seminoles—"

"And that too. What else is there? Did the young man in the sun-helmet tell you of something worse?"

"Yes—much worse! Something so dreadfully horrible that—"

"What?"

"I am not at liberty to tell you, Miss Barrison," I said, striving to appear shocked.

"It would not make any difference anyway," she observed, calmly. "I'm not afraid of anything in the world."

"Yes, you are!" I said. " Listen to me; I'd be awfully glad to have you go—I—I really had no idea how I'd miss you—miss such pleasant companionship. But it is not possible—" The recollection of Professor Farrago's aversion suddenly returned. "No, no," I said, "it can't be done. I'm most unhappy over this mistake of mine; please don't look as though you were ready to cry!"

"Don't discharge me, Mr. Gilland," she said.

"I'm a brute to do it, but I must; I was a bigger brute to engage you, but I did. Don't—please don't look at me that way, Miss Barrison! As a matter of fact, I'm tender-hearted and I can't endure it."

"If you only knew what I had been through you wouldn't send me away," she said, in a low voice. "It took my last penny to clothe myself and pay for the last lesson at the college of stenography. I—

I lived on almost nothing for weeks; every respectable place was filled; I walked and walked and walked, and nobody wanted me—they all required people with experience—and how can I have experience until I begin, Mr. Gilland? I was perfectly desperate when I went to see you, knowing that you had advertised for a man—"

The slightest break in her clear voice scared me.

"I'm not going to cry," she said, striving to smile. "If I must go, I will go. I—I didn't mean to say all this—but—but I've been so—so discouraged;—and you were not very cross with me—"

Smitten with remorse, I picked up her hand and fell to patting it violently, trying to think of something to say. The exercise did not appear to stimulate my wits.

"Then—then I'm to go with you?" she asked.

"I will see," I said, weakly, "but I fear there's trouble ahead for this expedition."

"I fear there is," she agreed, in a cheerful voice. "You have a rifle and a cage in your luggage. Are you going to trap Indians and have me report their language?"

"No, I'm not going to trap Indians," I said, sharply. "They may trap us—but that's a detail. What I want to say to you is this: Professor Farrago detests unmarried women, and I forgot it when I engaged you."

"Oh, is that all?" she asked, laughing.

"Not all, but enough to cost me my position."

"How absurd! Why, there are millions of things we might do!—millions!"

"What's one of them?" I inquired.

"Why, we might pretend to be married!" Her frank and absolutely innocent delight in this suggestion was refreshing, but troubling.

"We would have to be demonstrative to make that story go," I said.

"Why? Well-bred people are not demonstrative in public," she retorted, turning a trifle pink.

"No, but in private—"

"I think there is no necessity for carrying a pleasantry into our private life," she said, in a perfectly amiable voice. "Anyway, if

Professor Farrago's feelings are to be spared, no sacrifice on the part of a mere girl could be too great," she added, gayly; "I will wear men's clothes if you wish."

"You may have to anyhow in the jungle," I said; "and as it's not an uncommon thing these days, nobody would ever take you for anything except what you are—a very wilful and plucky and persistent and—"

"And what, Mr. Gilland?"

"And attractive," I muttered.

"Thank you, Mr. Gilland."

"You're welcome," I snapped. The near whistle of a locomotive warned us, and I rose in the carriage, looking out across the sand-hills.

"That is probably our train," observed the pretty stenographer.

"Our train!"

"Yes; isn't it?"

"Then you insist—"

"Ah, no, Mr. Gilland; I only trust implicitly in my employer."

"We'll wait till we get to Citron City," I said, weakly; "then it will be time enough to discuss the situation, won't it?"

"Yes, indeed," she said, smiling; but she knew, and I already feared, that the situation no longer admitted of discussion. In a few moments more we emerged, without warning, from the scrub-crested sand-hills into the single white street of Citron City, where China-trees hung heavy with bloom, and magnolias, already set with perfumed candelabra, spread soft, checkered shadows over the marl.

The train lay at the station, oceans of heavy, black smoke lazily flowing from the locomotive; negroes were hoisting empty fruit-crates aboard the baggage-car, through the door of which I caught a glimpse of my steel cage and remaining paraphernalia, all securely crated.

"Telegram hyah foh Mistuh Gilland," remarked the operator, lounging at his window as we descended from our dusty vehicle. He had not addressed himself to anybody in particular, but I said that I was Mr. Gilland, and he produced the envelope. "Toted in from Okeechobee?" he inquired, listlessly.

"Probably; it's signed 'Farrago,' isn't it?"

"It's foh yoh, suh, I reckon," said the operator, handing it out with a yawn. Then he removed his hat and fanned his head, which was perfectly bald.

I opened the yellow envelope. "Get me a good dog with points," was the laconic message; and it irritated me to receive such idiotic instructions at such a time and in such a place. A good dog? Where the mischief could I find a dog in a town consisting of ten houses and a water-tank? I said as much to the bald-headed operator, who smiled wearily and replaced his hat: "Dawg? They's moh houn'-dawgs in Citron City than they's wood-ticks to keep them busy. I reckon a dollah 'll do a heap foh you, suh."

"Could you get me a dog for a dollar?" I asked;— "one with points?"

"Points? I sholy can, suh;—plenty of points. What kind of dawg do yoh requiah, suh?—live dawg? daid dawg? houn'-dawg? raid-dawg? hawg-dawg? coon-dawg?—"

The locomotive emitted a long, lazy, softly modulated and thoroughly Southern toot. I handed the operator a silver dollar, and he presently emerged from his office and slouched off up the street, while I walked with Miss Barrison to the station platform, where I resumed the discussion of her future movements.

"You are very young to take such a risk," I said, gravely. "Had I not better buy your ticket back to New York? The north-bound train meets this one. I suppose we are waiting for it now—" I stopped, conscious of her impatience.

Her face flushed brightly: "Yes; I think it best. I have embarrassed you too long already—"

"Don't say that!" I muttered. "I—I—shall be deadly bored without you."

"I am not an entertainer, only a stenographer," she said, curtly. "Please get me my ticket, Mr. Gilland."

She gazed at me from the car-platform; the locomotive tooted two drawling toots.

"It is for your sake," I said, avoiding her gaze as the far-off whistle of the north-bound express came floating out of the blue distance.

She did not answer; I fished out my watch, regarding it in silence, listening to the hum of the approaching train, which ought presently to bear her away into the North, where nothing could menace her except the brilliant pitfalls of a Christian civilization. But I stood there, temporizing, unable to utter a word as her train shot by us with a rush, slower, slower, and finally stopped, with a long-drawn sigh from the air-brakes.

At that instant the telegraph-operator appeared, carrying a dog by the scruff of the neck—a sad-eyed, ewe-necked dog, from the four corners of which dangled enormous, cushion-like paws. He yelped when he beheld me. Miss Barrison leaned down from the car-platform and took the animal into her arms, uttering a suppressed exclamation of pity as she lifted him.

"You have your hands full," she said to me; "I'll take him into the car for you." She mounted the steps; I followed with the valises, striving to get a good view of my acquisition over her shoulder.

"That isn't the kind of dog I wanted!" I repeated again and again, inspecting the animal as it sprawled on the floor of the car at the edge of Miss Barrison's skirt. "That dog is all voice and feet and emotion! What makes it stick up its paws like that? I don't want that dog and I'm not going to identify myself with it! Where's the operator—"

I turned towards the car-window; the operator's bald head was visible on a line with the sill, and I made motions at him. He bowed with courtly grace, as though I were thanking him.

"I'm not!" I cried, shaking my head. "I wanted a dog with points— not the kind of points that stick up all over this dog. Take him away!"

The operator's head appeared to be gliding out of my range of vision; then the windows of the north-bound train slid past, taster and faster. A melancholy grace note from the dog, a jolt, and I turned around, appalled.

"This train is going," I stammered, "and you are on it!"

Miss Barrison sprang up and started towards the door, and I sped after her.

"I can jump," she said, breathlessly, edging out to the platform; "please let me! There is time yet—if you only wouldn't hold me—so tight—"

A few moments later we walked slowly back together through the car and took seats facing one another.

Between us sat the hound-dog, a prey to melancholy unutterable.

III

It was on Sunday when I awoke to the realization that I had quitted civilization and was afloat on an unfamiliar body of water in an open boat containing—

One light steel cage,

One rifle and ammunition,

One stenographer,

Three ounces rosium oxide,

One hound-dog,

Two valises.

A playful wave slopped over the bow and I lost count; but the pretty stenographer made the inventory, while I resumed the oars, and the dog punctured the primeval silence with staccato yelps.

A few minutes later everything and everybody was accounted for; the sky was blue and the palms waved, and several species of dicky-birds tuned up as I pulled with powerful strokes out into the sunny waters of Little Sprite Lake, now within a few miles of my journey's end.

From ponds hidden in the marshes herons rose in lazily laborious flight, flapping low across the water; high in the cypress yellow-eyed ospreys bent crested heads to watch our progress; sun-baked alligators, lying heavily in the shoreward sedge, slid open, glassy eyes as we passed.

"Even the 'gators make eyes at you," I said, resting on my oars.

We were on terms of badinage.

"Who was it who shed crocodile tears at the prospect of shipping me North?" she inquired.

"Speaking of tears," I observed, "somebody is likely to shed a number when Professor Farrago is picked up."

"Pooh!" she said, and snapped her pretty, sun-tanned fingers; and I resumed the oars in time to avoid shipwreck on a large mud-bar.

She reclined in the stern, serenely occupied with the view, now and then caressing the discouraged dog, now and then patting her hair where the wind had loosened a bright strand.

"If Professor Farrago didn't expect a woman stenographer," she said, abruptly, "why did he instruct you to bring a complete outfit of woman's clothing?"

"I don't know," I said, tartly.

"But you bought them. Are they for a young woman or an old woman?"

"I don't know; I sent a messenger to a department store. I don't know what he bought."

"Didn't you look them over?"

"No. Why? I should have been no wiser. I fancy they're all right, because the bill was eighteen hundred dollars—"

The pretty stenographer sat up abruptly.

"Is that much?" I asked, uneasily. "I've always heard women's clothing was expensive. Wasn't it enough? I told the boy to order the best;—Professor Farrago always requires the very best scientific instruments, and—I listed the clothes as scientific accessories— that being the object of this expedition—*What* are you laughing at?"

When it pleased her to recover her gravity she announced her desire to inspect and repack the clothing; but I refused.

"They're for Professor Farrago," I said. "I don't know what he wants of them. I don't suppose he intends to wear 'em and caper about the jungle, but they're his. I got them because he told me to. I bought a cage, too, to fit myself, but I don't suppose he means to put me in it. Perhaps," I added, "he may invite you into it."

"Let me refold the gowns," she pleaded, persuasively. "What does a clumsy man know about packing such clothing as that? If you don't, they'll be ruined. It's a shame to drag those boxes about through mud and water!"

So we made a landing, and lifted out and unlocked the boxes. All I could see inside were mounds of lace and ribbons, and with a vague idea that Miss Barrison needed no assistance I returned to the boat and sat down to smoke until she was ready.

When she summoned me her face was flushed and her eyes bright.

"Those are certainly the most beautiful things!" she said, softly. "Why, it is like a bride's trousseau—absolutely complete—all except the bridal gown—"

"Isn't there a dress there?" I exclaimed, in alarm.

"No—not a day-dress."

"Night-dresses!" I shrieked. "He doesn't want women's night-dresses! He's a bachelor! Good Heavens! I've done it this time!"

"But—but who is to wear them?" she asked.

"How do I know? I don't know anything; I can only presume that he doesn't intend to open a department store in the Everglades. And if any lady is to wear garments in his vicinity, I assume that those garments are to be anything except diaphanous!... Please take your seat in the boat, Miss Barrison. I want to row and think."

I had had my fill of exercise and thought when, about four o'clock in the afternoon, Miss Barrison directed my attention to a point of palms jutting out into the water about a mile to the southward.

"That's Farrago!" I exclaimed, catching sight of a United States flag floating majestically from a bamboo-pole. "Give me the megaphone, if you please."

She handed me the instrument; I hailed the shore; and presently a man appeared under the palms at the water's edge.

"Hello!" I roared, trying to inject cheerfulness into the hollow bellow. "How are you, professor?"

The answer came distinctly across the water:

"*Who* is that with you?"

My lips were buried in the megaphone; I strove to speak; I only produced a ghastly, chuckling sound.

"Of course you expect to tell the truth," observed the pretty stenographer, quietly.

I removed my lips from the megaphone and looked around at her. She returned my gaze with a disturbing smile.

"I want to mitigate the blow," I said, hoarsely. "Tell me how."

"I'm sure I don't know," she said, sweetly.

"Well, *I* do!" I fairly barked, and seizing the megaphone again, I set it to my lips and roared, "My fiancée!"

"Good gracious!" exclaimed Miss Barrison, in consternation, "I thought you were going to tell the truth!"

"Don't do that or you'll upset us," I snapped— "I'm telling the truth; I've engaged myself to you; I did it mentally before I bellowed."

"But—"

"You know as well as I do what engagements mean," I said, picking up the oars and digging them deep in the blue water.

She assented uncertainly.

A few minutes more of vigorous rowing brought us to a muddy landing under a cluster of tall palmettos, where a gasoline launch lay.

Professor Farrago came down to the shore as I landed, and I walked ahead to meet him. He was the maddest man I ever saw. But I was his match, for I was desperate.

"What the devil—" he began, under his breath.

"Nonsense!" I said, deliberately. "An engaged woman is practically married already, because marriages are made in heaven."

"Good Lord!" he gasped, "are you mad, Gilland? I sent for a stenographer—"

"Miss Barrison is a stenographer," I said, calmly; and before he could recover I had presented him, and left them face to face, washing my hands of the whole affair.

Unloading the boat and carrying the luggage up under the palms, I heard her saying:

"No, I am not in the least afraid of snakes, and I am quite ready to begin my duties."

And he: "Mr. Gilland is a young man who—er—lacks practical experience."

And she: "Mr. Gilland has been most thoughtful for my comfort. The journey has been perfectly heavenly."

And he, clumsily: "Ahem!—the—er—celestial aspect of your journey has—er—doubtless been colored by—er—the prospect of your—er—approaching nuptials—"

She, hastily: "Oh, I do not think so, professor."

"Idiot!" I muttered, dragging the dog to the shore, where his yelps brought the professor hurrying.

"Is *that* the dog?" he inquired, adjusting his spectacles.

"That's the dog," I said. "He's full of points, you see?"

"Oh," mused the professor; "I thought he was full of—" He hesitated, inspecting the animal, who, nose to the ground, stood investigating a smell of some sort.

"See," I said, with enthusiasm, "he's found a scent; he's trailing it already! Now he's rolling on it!"

"He's rolling on one of our concentrated food lozenges," said the professor, dryly. "Tie him up, Mr. Gilland, and ask Mrs. Gilland to come up to camp. Your room is ready."

"Rooms," I corrected; "she isn't Mrs. Gilland yet," I added, with a forced smile.

"But you're practically married," observed the professor, "as you pointed out to me. And if she's practically Mrs. Gilland, why not say so?"

"Don't, all the same," I snarled.

"But marriages are made in—"

I cast a desperate eye upon him.

From that moment, whenever we were alone together, he made a target of me. I never had supposed him humorously vindictive; he was, and his apparently innocent mistakes almost turned my hair gray.

But to Miss Barrison he was kind and courteous, and for a time over-serious. Observing him, I could never detect the slightest symptom of dislike for her sex—a failing which common rumor had always credited him with to the verge of absolute rudeness.

On the contrary, it was perfectly plain to anybody that he liked her. There was in his manner towards her a mixture of business formality and the deferential attitude of a gentleman.

We were seated, just before sunset, outside of the hut built of palmetto logs, when Professor Farrago, addressing us both, began the explanation of our future duties.

Miss Barrison, it appeared, was to note everything said by himself, making several shorthand copies by evening. In other words, she was to report every scrap of conversation she heard while in the Everglades. And she nodded intelligently as he finished, and drew pad and pencil from the pocket of her walking-skirt, jotting down his instructions as a beginning. I could see that he was pleased.

"The reason I do this," he said, "is because I do not wish to hide anything that transpires while we are on this expedition. Only the most scrupulously minute record can satisfy me; no details are too small to merit record; I demand and I court from my fellow-scientists and from the public the fullest investigation."

He smiled slightly, turning towards me.

"You know, Mr. Gilland, how dangerous to the reputation of a scientific man is any line of investigation into the unusual. If a man once is even suspected of charlatanism, of sensationalism, of turning his attention to any phenomena not strictly within the proper pale of scientific investigation, that man is doomed to ridicule; his profession disowns him; he becomes a man without honor, without authority. Is it not so?"

"Yes," I said.

"Therefore," he resumed, thoughtfully, "as I do most firmly believe in the course I am now pursuing, whether I succeed or fail I desire a true and minute record made, hiding nothing of what may be said or done. A stenographer alone can give this to the world, while I can only supplement it with a description of events—if I live to transcribe them."

Sunk in profound reverie he sat there silent under the great, smooth palm-tree—a venerable figure in his yellow dressing-gown and carpet slippers. Seated side by side, we waited, a trifle awed. I could hear the soft breathing of the pretty stenographer beside me.

"First of all," said Professor Farrago, looking up, "I must be able to trust those who are here to aid me."

"I—I will be faithful," said the girl, in a low voice.

"I do not doubt you, my child," he said; "nor you, Gilland. And so I am going to tell you this much now—more, I hope, later."

And he sat up straight, lifting an impressive forefinger.

"Mr. Rowan, lately an officer of our Coast Survey, wrote me a letter from the Holland House in New York—a letter so strange that, on reading it, I immediately repaired to his hotel, where for hours we talked together.

"The result of that conference is this expedition.

"I have now been here two months, and I am satisfied of certain facts. First, there do exist in this unexplored wilderness certain forms of life which are solid and palpable, but transparent and practically invisible. Second, these living creatures belong to the animal kingdom, are warm-blooded vertebrates, possess powers of locomotion, but whether that of flight I am not certain. Third, they appear to possess such senses as we enjoy—smell, touch, sight, hearing, and no doubt the sense of taste. Fourth, their skin is smooth to the touch, and the temperature of the epidermis appears to approximate that of a normal human being. Fifth and last, whether bipeds or quadrupeds I do not know, though all evidence appears to confirm my theory that they walk erect. One pair of their limbs appear to terminate in a sort of foot—like a delicately shaped human foot, except that there appear to be no toes. The other pair of limbs terminate in something that, from the single instance I experienced, seemed to resemble soft but firm antennæ or, perhaps, digitated palpi—"

"Feelers!" I blurted out.

"I don't know, but I think so. Once, when I was standing in the forest, perfectly aware that creatures I could not see had stealthily surrounded me, the tension was brought to a crisis when over my face, from cheek to chin, stole a soft something, brushing the skin as delicately as a child's fingers might brush it."

"Good Lord!" I breathed.

A care-worn smile crept into his eyes. "A test for nerves, you think, Mr. Gilland? I agree with you. Nobody fears what anybody can see."

There came the slightest movement beside me.

"Are you trembling?" I asked, turning.

"I was writing," she replied, steadily. "Did my elbow touch you?"

"By-the-way," said Professor Farrago, "I fear I forgot to congratulate you upon your choice of a stenographer, Mr. Gilland."

A rosy light stole over her pale face.

"Am I to record that too?" she asked, raising her blue eyes.

"Certainly," he replied, gravely.

"But, professor," I began, a prey to increasing excitement, "do you propose to attempt the capture of one of these animals?"

"That is what the cage is for," he said. "I supposed you had guessed that."

"I had," murmured the pretty stenographer.

"I do not doubt it," said Professor Farrago, gravely.

"What are the chemicals for—and the tank and hose attachment?"

"Think, Mr. Gilland."

"I can't; I'm almost stunned by what you tell me."

He laughed. "The rosium oxide and salts of strontium are to be dumped into the tank together. They'll effervesce, of course."

"Of course," I muttered.

"And I can throw a rose-colored spray over any object by the hose attachment, can't I?"

"Yes."

"Well, I tried it on a transparent jelly-fish and it became perfectly visible and of a beautiful rose-color: and I tried it on rock-crystal, and on glass, and on pure gelatine, and all became suffused with a delicate pink glow, which lasted for hours or minutes according to the substance... Now you understand, don't you'"

"Yes; you want to see what sort of creature you have to deal with."

"Exactly; so when I've trapped it I am going to spray it." He turned half humorously towards the stenographer: "I fancy you understood long before Mr. Gilland did."

"I don't think so," she said, with a sidelong lifting of the heavy lashes; and I caught the color of her eyes for a second.

"You see how Miss Barrison spares your feelings," observed Professor Farrago, dryly. "She owes you little gratitude for bringing her here, yet she proves a generous victim."

"Oh, I am very grateful for this rarest of chances!" she said, shyly. "To be among the first in the world to discover such wonders ought to make me very grateful to the man who gave me the opportunity."

"Do you mean Mr. Gilland?" asked the professor, laughing.

I had never before seen Professor Farrago laugh such a care-free laugh; I had never suspected him of harboring even an embryo of the social graces. Dry as dust, sapless as steel, precise as the magnetic needle, he had hitherto been to me the mummified embodiment of science militant. Now, in the guise of a perfectly human and genial old gentleman, I scarcely recognized my superior of the Bronx Park society. And as a woman-hater he was a miserable failure.

"Heavens," I thought to myself, "am I becoming jealous of my revered professor's social success with a stray stenographer?" I felt mean, and I probably looked it, and I was glad that telepathy did not permit Miss Barrison to record my secret and unworthy ruminations.

The professor was saying: "These transparent creatures break off berries and fruits and branches; I have seen a flower, too, plucked from its stem by invisible digits and borne swiftly through the forest—only the flower visible, apparently speeding through the air and out of sight among the thickets.

"I have found the footprints that I described to you, usually on the edge of a stream or in the soft loam along some forest lake or lost lagoon.

"Again and again I have been conscious in the forest that unseen eyes were fixed on me, that unseen shapes were following me. Never but that one time did these invisible creatures close in around me and venture to touch me.

"They may be weak; their structure may be frail, and they may be incapable of violence or harm, but the depth of the footprints indicates a weight of at least one hundred and thirty pounds, and it certainly requires some muscular strength to break off a branch of wild guavas."

He bent his noble head, thoughtfully regarding the design on his slippers.

"What was the rifle for?" I asked.

"Defence, not aggression," he said, simply.

"And the camera?"

"A camera record is necessary in these days of bad artists."

I hesitated, glancing at Miss Barrison. She was still writing, her pretty head bent over the pad m her lap.

"And the clothing?" I asked, carelessly.

"Did you get it?" he demanded.

"Of course—" I glanced at Miss Barrison. "There's no use writing down everything, is there?"

"Everything must be recorded," said Professor Farrago, inflexibly. "What clothing did you buy?"

"I forgot the gown," I said, getting red about the ears.

"Forgot the gown!" he repeated.

"Yes—one kind of gown—the day kind. I—I got the other kind."

He was annoyed; so was I. After a moment he got up, and crossing to the log cabin, opened one of the boxes of apparel.

"Is it what you wanted?" I inquired.

"Y-es, I presume so," he replied, visibly perplexed.

"It's the best to be had," said I.

"That's quite right," he said, musingly. "We use only the best of everything at Bronx Park. It is traditional with us, you know."

Curiosity pushed me. "Well, what on earth is it for?" I broke out.

He looked at me gravely over the tops of his spectacles—a striking and inspiring figure in his yellow flannel dressing-gown and slippers.

"I shall tell you some day—perhaps," he said, mildly. "Good-night, Miss Barrison; good-night, Mr. Gilland. You will find extra blankets on your bunk—"

"What!" I cried.

"Bunks," he said, and shut the door.

IV

"There is something weird about this whole proceeding," I observed to the pretty stenographer next morning.

"These pies will be weird if you don't stop talking to me," she said, opening the doors of Professor Farrago's portable camping-oven and peeping in at the fragrant pastry.

The professor had gone off somewhere into the woods early that morning. As he was not in the habit of talking to himself, the services of Miss Barrison were not required. Before he started, however, he came to her with a request for a dozen pies, the construction of which he asked if she understood. She had been to cooking-school in more prosperous days, and she mentioned it; so at his earnest solicitation she undertook to bake for him twelve apple-pies; and she was now attempting it, assisted by advice from me.

"Are they burned?" I asked, sniffing the air.

"No, they are not burned, Mr. Gilland, but my finger is," she retorted, stepping back to examine the damage.

I offered sympathy and witch-hazel, but she would have none of my offerings, and presently returned to her pies.

"We can't eat all that pastry," I protested.

"Professor Farrago said they were not for us to eat," she said, dusting each pie with powdered sugar.

"Well, what are they for? The dog? Or are they simply *objets d'art* to adorn the shanty—"

"You annoy me," she said.

"The pies annoy me; won't you tell me what they're for?"

"I have a pretty fair idea what they're for," she observed, tossing her head. "Haven't you?"

"No. What?"

"These pies are for bait."

"To bait hooks with?" I exclaimed.

"Hooks! No, you silly man. They're for baiting the cage. He means to trap these transparent creatures in a cage baited with pie."

She laughed scornfully; inserted the burned tip of her finger in her mouth and stood looking at me defiantly like a flushed and bright-eyed school-girl.

"You think you're teasing me," she said; "but you do not realize what a singularly slow-minded young man you are. "

I stopped laughing. "How did you come to the conclusion that pies were to be used for such a purpose?" I asked.

"I deduce," she observed, with an airy wave of her disengaged hand.

"Your deductions are weird—like everything else in this vicinity. Pies to catch invisible monsters? Pooh!"

"You're not particularly complimentary, are you?" she said.

"Not particularly; but I could be, with you for my inspiration. I could even be enthusiastic—"

"About my pies?"

"No—about your eyes."

"You are very frivolous—for a scientist," she said, scornfully; "please subdue your enthusiasm and bring me some wood. This fire is almost out."

When I had brought the wood, she presented me with a pail of hot water and pointed at the dishes on the breakfast-table.

"Never!" I cried, revolted.

"Then I suppose I must do them—"

She looked pensively at her scorched finger-tip, and, pursing up her red lips, blew a gentle breath to cool it.

"I'll do the dishes," I said.

Splashing and slushing the cups and saucers about in the hot water, I reflected upon the events of the last few days. The dog, stupefied by unwonted abundance of food, lay in the sunshine, sleeping the sleep of repletion; the pretty stenographer, all rosy from her culinary exertions, was removing the pies and setting them in neat rows to cool.

"There," she said, with a sigh; "now I will dry the dishes for you... You didn't mention the fact, when you engaged me, that I was also expected to do general housework."

"I didn't engage you," I said, maliciously; "you engaged me, you know."

She regarded me disdainfully, nose uptilted.

"How thoroughly disagreeable you can be!" she said. "Dry your own dishes. I'm going for a stroll."

"May I join—"

"You may *not!* I shall go so far that you cannot possibly discover me."

I watched her forestward progress; she sauntered for about thirty yards along the lake and presently sat down in plain sight under a huge live-oak.

A few moments later I had completed my task as general bottle-washer, and I cast about for something to occupy me.

First I approached and politely caressed the satiated dog. He woke up, regarded me with dully meditative eyes, yawned, and went to sleep again. Never a flop of tail to indicate gratitude for blandishments, never the faintest symptom of canine appreciation.

Chilled by my reception, I moused about for a while, poking into boxes and bundles; then raised my head and inspected the landscape. Through the vista of trees the pink shirt-waist of the pretty stenographer glimmered like a rose blooming in the wilderness.

From whatever point I viewed the prospect that pink spot seemed to intrude; I turned my back and examined the jungle, but there it was repeated in a hundred pink blossoms among the massed thickets; I looked up into the tree-tops, where pink mosses spotted the palms; I looked out over the lake, and I saw it in my mind's eye pinker than ever. It was certainly a case of pink-eye.

"I'll go for a stroll, too; it's a free country," I muttered.

After I had strolled in a complete circle I found myself within three feet of a pink shirt-waist.

"I beg your pardon," I said; "I had no inten—"

"I thought you were never coming," she said, amiably.

"How is your finger?" I asked.

She held it up. I took it gingerly; it was smooth and faintly rosy at the tip.

"Does it hurt?" I inquired.

"Dreadfully. Your hands feel so cool—"

After a silence she said, "Thank you, that has cooled the burning."

"I am determined," said I, "to expel the fire from your finger if it takes hours and hours." And I seated myself with that intention.

For a while she talked, making innocent observations concerning the tropical foliage surrounding us. Then silence crept in between us, accentuated by the brooding stillness of the forest.

"I am afraid your hands are growing tired," she said, considerately.

I denied it.

Through the vista of palms we could see the lake, blue as a violet, sparkling with silvery sunshine. In the intense quiet the splash of leaping mullet sounded distinctly.

Once a tall crane stalked into view among the sedges; once an unseen alligator shook the silence with his deep, hollow roaring. Then the stillness of the wilderness grew more intense.

We had been sitting there for a long while without exchanging a word, dreamily watching the ripple of the azure water, when all at once there came a scurrying patter of feet through the forest, and, looking up, I beheld the hound-dog, tail between his legs, bearing down on us at lightning speed. I rose instantly.

"What is the matter with the dog?" cried the pretty stenographer. "Is he going mad, Mr. Gilland?"

"Something has scared him," I exclaimed, as the dog, eyes like lighted candles, rushed frantically between my legs and buried his head in Miss Barrison's lap.

"Poor doggy!" she said, smoothing the collapsed pup; "poor, poor little beast! Did anything scare him? Tell aunty all about it."

When a dog flees *without yelping* he's a badly frightened creature. I instinctively started back towards the camp whence the beast had fled, and before I had taken a dozen steps Miss Barrison was beside me, carrying the dog in her arms.

"I've an idea," she said, under her breath.

"What?" I asked, keeping my eyes on the camp.

"It's this: I'll wager that we find those pies gone!"

"Pies gone?" I repeated, perplexed; "what makes you think—"

"They *are* gone!" she exclaimed. "Look!"

I gaped stupidly at the rough pine table where the pies had stood in three neat rows of four each. And then, in a moment, the purport of this robbery flashed upon my senses.

"The transparent creatures!" I gasped.

"Hush!" she whispered, clinging to the trembling dog in her arms.

I listened. I could hear nothing, see nothing, yet slowly I became convinced of the presence of something unseen—something in the forest close by, watching us out of invisible eyes.

A chill, settling along my spine, crept upward to my scalp, until every separate hair wiggled to the roots. Miss Barrison was pale, but perfectly calm and self-possessed.

"Let us go in-doors," I said, as steadily as I could.

"Very well," she replied.

I held the door open; she entered with the dog; I followed, closing and barring the door, and then took my station at the window, rifle in hand.

There was not a sound in the forest. Miss Barrison laid the dog on the floor and quietly picked up her pad and pencil. Presently she was deep in a report of the phenomena, her pencil flying, leaf after leaf from the pad fluttering to the floor.

Nor did I at the window change my position of scared alertness, until I was aware of her hand gently touching my elbow to attract my attention, and her soft voice at my ear—

"You don't suppose by any chance that the dog ate those pies?"

I collected my tumultuous thoughts and turned to stare at the dog.

"Twelve pies, twelve inches each in diameter," she reflected, musingly. "One dog, twenty inches in diameter. How many times will the pies go into the dog? Let me see." She made a few figures on her pad, thought awhile, produced a tape-measure from her pocket, and, kneeling down, measured the dog.

"No," she said, looking up at me, "he couldn't contain them."

Inspired by her coolness and perfect composure, I set the rifle in the corner and opened the door. Sunlight fell in bars through the quiet woods; nothing stirred on land or water save the great, yellow-striped butterflies that fluttered and soared and floated above the flowering thickets bordering the jungle.

The heat became intense; Miss Barrison went to her room to change her gown for a lighter one; I sat down under a live-oak, eyes and ears strained for any sign of our invisible neighbors.

When she emerged in the lightest and filmiest of summer gowns, she brought the camera with her; and for a while we took pictures of each other, until we had used up all but one film.

Desiring to possess a picture of Miss Barrison and myself seated together, I tied a string to the shutter-lever and attached the other end of the string to the dog, who had resumed his interrupted slumbers. At my whistle he jumped up nervously, snapping the lever, and the picture was taken.

With such innocent and harmless pastime we whiled away the afternoon. She made twelve more apple-pies. I mounted guard over them. And we were just beginning to feel a trifle uneasy about Professor Farrago, when he appeared, tramping sturdily through the forest, green umbrella and butterfly-net under one arm, shotgun and cyanide-jar under the other, and his breast all criss-crossed with straps, from which dangled field-glasses, collecting-boxes, and botanizing-tins—an inspiring figure indeed—the embodied symbol of science indomitable, triumphant!

We hailed him with three guilty cheers; the dog woke up with a perfunctory bark—the first sound I had heard from him since he yelped his disapproval of me on the lagoon.

Miss Barrison produced three bowls full of boiling water and dropped three pellets of concentrated soup-meat into them, while I prepared coffee. And in a few moments our simple dinner was ready—the red ants had been dusted from the biscuits, the spiders chased off the baked beans, the scorpions shaken from the napkins, and we sat down at the rough, improvised table under the palms.

The professor gave us a brief but modest account of his short tour of exploration. He had brought back a new species of orchid, several undescribed beetles, and a pocketful of coontie seed. He appeared, however, to be tired and singularly depressed, and presently we learned why.

It seemed that he had gone straight to that section of the forest where he had hitherto always found signs of the transparent and invisible creatures which he had determined to capture, and he had not found a single trace of them.

"It alarms me," he said, gravely. "If they have deserted this region, it might take a lifetime to locate them again in this wilderness."

Then, very quietly, sinking her voice instinctively, as though the unseen might be at our very elbows listening, Miss Barrison recounted the curious adventure which had befallen the dog and the first batch of apple-pies.

With visible and increasing excitement the professor listened until the very end. Then he struck the table with clinched fist—a resounding blow which set the concentrated soup dancing in the bowls and scattered the biscuits and the industrious red ants in every direction.

"Eureka!" he whispered. "Miss Barrison, your deduction was not only perfectly reasonable, but brilliant. You are right; the pies are for that very purpose. I conceived the idea when I first came here. Again and again the pies that my guide made out of dried apples disappeared in a most astonishing and mysterious manner when left to cool. At length I determined to watch them every second; and did so, with the result that late one afternoon I was amazed to see a pie slowly rise from the table and move swiftly away through the air about four feet above the ground, finally disappearing into a tangle of jasmine and grape-vine.

"The apparently automatic flight of that pie solved the problem; these transparent creatures cannot resist that delicacy. Therefore I decided to bait the cage for them this very night—Look! What's the matter with that dog?"

The dog suddenly bounded into the air, alighted on all fours, ears, eyes, and muzzle concentrated on a point directly behind us.

"Good gracious! The pies!" faltered Miss Barrison, half rising from her seat; but the dog rushed madly into her skirts, scrambling for protection, and she fell back almost into my arms.

Clasping her tightly, I looked over my shoulder; the last pie was snatched from the table before my eyes and I saw it borne swiftly away by something unseen, straight into the deepening shadows of the forest.

The professor was singularly calm, even slightly ironical, as he turned to me, saying:

"Perhaps if you relinquish Miss Barrison she may be able to free herself from that dog."

I did so immediately, and she deposited the cowering dog in my arms. Her face had suddenly become pink.

I passed the dog on to Professor Farrago, dumping it viciously into his lap—a proceeding which struck me as resembling a pastime of extreme youth known as "button, button, who's got the button?"

The professor examined the animal gravely, feeling its pulse, counting its respirations, and finally inserting a tentative finger in an attempt to examine its tongue. The dog bit him.

"Ouch! It's a clear case of fright," he said, gravely. "I wanted a dog to aid me in trailing these remarkable creatures, but I think this dog of yours is useless, Gilland."

"It's given us warning of the creatures' presence twice already," I argued.

"Poor little thing," said Miss Barrison, softly; "I don't know why, but I love that dog... He has eyes like yours, Mr. Gilland—"

Exasperated, I rose from the table. "He's got eyes like holes burned in a blanket!" I said. "And if ever a flicker of intelligence lighted them I have failed to observe it."

The professor regarded me dreamily. "We ought to have more pies," he observed. "Perhaps if you carried the oven into the shanty—"

"Certainly," said Miss Barrison; "we can lock the door while I make twelve more pies."

I carried the portable camping-oven into the cabin, connected the patent asbestos chimney-pipes, and lighted the fire. And in a few minutes Miss Barrison, sleeves rolled up and pink apron pinned under her chin, was busily engaged in rolling pie-crust, while Professor Farrago measured out spices and set the dried apples to soak.

The swift Southern twilight had already veiled the forest as I stepped out of the cabin to smoke a cigar and promenade a bit and cogitate. A last trace of color lingering in the west faded out as I looked; the gray glimmer deepened into darkness, through which the white lake vapors floated in thin, wavering strata across the water.

For a while the frog's symphony dominated all other sounds, then lagoon and forest and cypress branch awoke; and through the steadily sustained tumult of woodland voices I could hear the dry bark of the fox-squirrel, the whistle of the raccoon, ducks softly quacking or whimpering as they prepared for sleep among the reeds, the soft booming of bitterns, the clattering gossip of the heronry, the Southern whippoorwill's incessant call.

At regular intervals the howling note of a lone heron echoed the strident screech of a crimson-crested crane; the horned owl's savage hunting-cry haunted the night, now near, now floating from infinite distances.

And after a while I became aware of a nearer sound, low-pitched but ceaseless—the hum of thousands of lesser living creatures blending to a steady monotone.

Then the theatrical moon came up through filmy draperies of waving Spanish moss thin as cobwebs; and far in the wilderness a cougar fell a-crying and coughing like a little child with a bad cold.

I went in after that. Miss Barrison was sitting before the oven, knees gathered in her clasped hands, languidly studying the fire. She looked up as I appeared, opened the oven-doors, sniffed the aroma, and resumed her attitude of contented indifference.

"Where is the professor?" I asked.

"He has retired. He's been talking in his sleep at moments. "

"Better take it down; that's what you're here for," I observed, closing and holding the outside door. "Ugh! there's a chill in the air. The dew is pelting down from the pines like a steady fall of rain."

"You will get fever if you roam about at night," she said. "Mercy! your coat is soaking. Sit here by the fire. "

So I pulled up a bench and sat down beside her like the traditional spider.

"Miss Muffitt," I said, "don't let me frighten you away—"

"I was going anyhow—"

"Please don't."

"Why?" she demanded, reseating herself.

"Because I like to sit beside you," I said, truthfully.

"Your avowal is startling and not to be substantiated by facts," she remarked, resting her chin on one hand and gazing into the fire.

"You mean because I went for a stroll by moonlight? I did that because you always seem to make fun of me as soon as the professor joins us."

"Make fun of you? You surely don't expect me to make eyes at you!"

There was a silence; I toasted my shins, thoughtfully.

"How is your burned finger?" I asked.

She lifted it for my inspection, and I began a protracted examination.

"What would you prescribe?" she inquired, with an absent-minded glance at the professor's closed door.

"I don't know; perhaps a slight but firm pressure of the finger-tips—"

"You tried that this afternoon."

"But the dog interrupted us—"

"Interrupted *you*. Besides—"

"What?"

"I don't think you ought to," she said.

Sitting there before the oven, side by side, hand innocently clasped in hand, we heard the drumming of the dew on the roof,

the night-wind stirring the palms, the muffled snoring of the professor, the faint whisper and crackle of the fire.

A single candle burned brightly, piling our shadows together
on the wall behind us; moonlight silvered the window-panes, over
which crawled multitudes of soft-winged moths, attracted by the
candle within.

"See their tiny eyes glow!" she whispered. "How their wings
quiver! And all for a candle-flame! Alas! alas! fire is the undoing
of us all."

She leaned forward, resting as though buried in reverie. After
a while she extended one foot a trifle and, with the point of her
shoe, carefully unlatched the oven-door. As it swung outward a
delicious fragrance filled the room.

"They're done," she said, withdrawing her hand from mine.
"Help me to lift them out."

Together we arranged the delicious pastry in rows on the bench
to cool. I opened the door for a few minutes, then closed and bolted
it again.

"Do you suppose those transparent creatures will smell the odor
and come around the cabin?" she suggested, wiping her fingers on
her handkerchief.

I walked to the window uneasily. Outside the pane the moths
crawled, some brilliant in scarlet and tan-color set with black, some
snow-white with black tracings on their wings, and bodies peacock-
blue edged with orange. The scientist in me was aroused; I called
her to the window, and she came and leaned against the sill, nose
pressed to the glass.

"I don't suppose you know that the antennæ of that silvery-
winged moth are distinctly pectinate," I said.

"Of course I do" she said. "I took my degree as D. E. at Barnard
College."

"What!" I exclaimed in astonishment. "You've been through
Barnard? You are a Doctor of Entomology ?"

"It was my undoing," she said. "The department was abolished
the year I graduated. There was no similar vacancy, even in the
Smithsonian."

She shrugged her shoulders, eyes fixed on the moths.

"I had to make my own living. I chose stenography as the quickest road to self-sustenance."

She looked up, a flush on her cheeks.

"I suppose you took me for an inferior?" she said. "But do you suppose I'd flirt with you if I was?"

She pressed her face to the pane again, murmuring that exquisite poem of Andrew Lang:

"Spooning is innocuous
    and needn't have a sequel,
But recollect, if spoon you must,
    spoon only with your equal."

Standing there, watching the moths, we became rather silent—I don't know why.

The fire in the range had gone out; the candle-flame, flaring above a saucer of melted wax, sank lower and lower.

Suddenly, as though disturbed by something inside, the moths all left the window-pane, darting off in the darkness.

"That's curious," I said.

"What's curious?" she asked, opening her eyes languidly. "Good gracious! Was that a bat that beat on the window?"

"I saw nothing," I said, disturbed. "Listen!"

A soft sound against the glass, as though invisible fingers were feeling the pane—a gentle rubbing—then a tap-tap, all but inaudible.

"Is it a bird? Can you see?" she whispered.

The candle-flame behind us flashed and expired. Moonlight flooded the pane. The sounds continued, but there was nothing there.

We understood now what it was that so gently rubbed and patted the glass outside. With one accord we noiselessly gathered up the pies and carried them into my room.

Then she walked to the door of her room, turned, held out her hand, and whispering, "Good-night! A demain, monsieur!" slipped into her room and softly closed the door.

And all night long I lay in troubled slumber beside the pies, a rifle resting on the blankets beside me, a revolver under my pillow.

And I dreamed of moths with brilliant eyes and vast silvery wings harnessed to a balloon in which Miss Barrison and I sat, arms around each other, eating slice after slice of apple-pie.

V

Dawn came—the dawn of a day that I am destined never to forget. Long, rosy streamers of light broke through the forest, shaking, quivering, like unstable beams from celestial search-lights. Mist floated upward from marsh and lake; and through it the spectral palms loomed, drooping fronds embroidered with dew.

For a while the ringing outburst of bird music dominated all; but it soon ceased with dropping notes from the crimson cardinals repeated in lengthening minor intervals; and then the spell of silence returned, broken only by the faint splash of mullet, mocking the sun with sinuous, silver flashes.

"Good-morning," said a low voice from the door as I stood encouraging the camp-fire with splinter wood and dead palmetto fans.

Fresh and sweet from her toilet as a dew-drenched rose, Miss Barrison stood there sniffing the morning air daintily, thoroughly.

"Too much perfume," she said— "too much like ylang-ylang in a department-store. Central Park smells sweeter on an April morning."

"Are you criticising the wild jasmine?" I asked.

"I'm criticising an exotic smell. Am I not permitted to comment on the tropics?"

Fishing out a cedar log from the lumber-stack, I fell to chopping it vigorously. The axe-strokes made a cheerful racket through the woods.

"Did you hear anything last night after you retired?" I asked.

"Something was at my window—something that thumped softly and seemed to be feeling all over the glass. To tell you the truth, I was silly enough to remain dressed all night."

"You don't look it," I said.

"Oh, when daylight came I had a chance," she added, laughing.

"All the same," said I, leaning on the axe and watching her, "you are about the coolest and pluckiest woman I ever knew."

"We were all in the same fix," she said, modestly.

"No, we were not. Now I'll tell you the truth—my hair stood up the greater part of the night. You are looking upon a poltroon, Miss Barrison."

"Then there was something at your window, too?"

"Something? A dozen! They were monkeying with the sashes and panes all night long, and I imagined that I could hear them breathing—as though from effort of intense eagerness. Ouch! I came as near losing my nerve as I care to. I came within an ace of hurling those cursed pies through the window at them. I'd bolt to-day if I wasn't afraid to play the coward."

"Most people are brave for that reason," she said.

The dog, who had slept under my bunk, and who had contributed to my entertainment by sighing and moaning all night, now appeared ready for business—business in his case being the operation of feeding. I presented him with a concentrated tablet, which he cautiously investigated and then rolled on.

"Nice testimonial for the people who concocted it," I said, in disgust. "I wish I had an egg."

"There are some concentrated egg tablets in the shanty," said Miss Barrison; but the idea was not attractive.

"I refuse to fry a pill for breakfast," I said, sullenly, and set the coffee-pot on the coals.

In spite of the dewy beauty of the morning, breakfast was not a cheerful function. Professor Farrago appeared, clad in sun-helmet and khaki. I had seldom seen him depressed; but he was now and his very efforts to disguise it only emphasized his visible anxiety.

His preparations for the day, too, had an ominous aspect to me. He gave his orders and we obeyed, instinctively suppressing questions. First, he and I transported all personal luggage of the company to the big electric launch—Miss Barrison's effects, his, and my own. His private papers, the stenographic reports, and all memoranda were tied up together and carried aboard.

Then, to my surprise, two weeks' concentrated rations for two and mineral water sufficient for the same period were stowed away aboard the launch. Several times he asked me whether I knew how to run the boat, and I assured him that I did.

In a short time nothing was left ashore except the bare fur-
nishings of the cabin, the female wearing-apparel, the steel cage
and chemicals which I had brought, and the twelve apple-pies—
the latter under lock and key in my room.

As the preparations came to an end, the professor's gentle melancholy seemed to deepen. Once I ventured to ask him if he was
indisposed, and he replied that he had never felt in better physical
condition.

Presently he bade me fetch the pies; and I brought them, and,
at a sign from him, placed them inside the steel cage, closing and
locking the door.

"I believe," he said, glancing from Miss Barrison to me, and
from me to the dog— "I believe that we are ready to start."

He went to the cabin and locked the door on the outside, pocketing the key.

Then he backed up to the steel cage, stooped and lifted his end
as I lifted mine, and together we started off through the forest,
bearing the cage between us as porters carry a heavy piece of luggage.

Miss Barrison came next, carrying the trousseau, the tank, hose,
and chemicals; and the dog followed her—probably not from af-
fection for us, but because he was afraid to be left alone.

We walked in silence, the professor and I keeping an instinc-
tive lookout for snakes; but we encountered nothing of that sort.
On every side, touching our shoulders, crowded the closely woven
and impenetrable tangle of the jungle; and we threaded it along a
narrow path which he, no doubt, had cut, for the machete marks
were still fresh, and the blazes on hickory, live-oak, and palm were
all wet with dripping sap, and swarming with eager, brilliant butterflies.

At times across our course flowed shallow, rapid streams of
water, clear as crystal, and most alluring to the thirsty.

"There's fever in every drop," said the professor, as I mentioned
my thirst; "take the bottled water if you mean to stay a little longer."

"Stay where?" I asked.

"On earth," he replied, tersely; and we marched on.

The beauty of the tropics is marred somewhat for me; under
all the fresh splendor of color death lurks in brilliant tints. Where

painted fruit hangs temptingly, where great, silky blossoms exhale alluring scent, where the elaps coils inlaid with scarlet, black, and saffron, where in the shadow of a palmetto frond a succession of velvety black diamonds mark the rattler's swollen length, there death is; and his invisible consort, horror, creeps where the snake whose mouth is lined with white creeps—where the tarantula squats, hairy, motionless; where a bit of living enamel fringed with orange undulates along a mossy log.

Thinking of these things, and watchful lest, unawares, terror unfold from some blossoming and leafy covert, I scarcely noticed the beauty of the glade we had entered—a long oval, cross-barred with sunshine which fell on hedges of scrub-palmetto, chin high, interlaced with golden blossoms of the jasmine. And all around, like pillars supporting a high green canopy above a throne, towered the silvery stems of palms fretted with pale, rose-tinted lichens and hung with draperies of grape-vine.

"This is the place," said Professor Farrago.

His quiet, passionless voice sounded strange to me; his words seemed strange, too, each one heavily weighted with hidden meaning.

We set the cage on the ground; he unlocked and opened the steel-barred door, and, kneeling, carefully arranged the pies along the centre of the cage.

"I have a curious presentiment," he said, "that I shall not come out of this experiment unscathed."

"Don't, for Heaven's sake, say that!" I broke out, my nerves on edge again.

"Why not?" he asked, surprised. "I am not afraid."

"Not afraid to die?" I demanded, exasperated.

"Who spoke of dying?" he inquired, mildly. "What I said was that I do not expect to come out of this affair unscathed."

I did not comprehend his meaning, but I understood the reproof conveyed.

He closed and locked the cage door again and came towards us, balancing the key across the palm of his hand.

Miss Barrison had seated herself on the leaves; I stood back as the professor sat down beside her; then, at a gesture from him, took the place he indicated on his left.

"Before we begin," he said, calmly, "there are several things you ought to know and which I have not yet told you. The first concerns the feminine wearing apparel which Mr. Gilland brought me."

He turned to Miss Barrison and asked her whether she had brought a complete outfit, and she opened the bundle on her knees and handed it to him.

"I cannot," he said, "delicately explain in so many words what use I expect to make of this apparel. Nor do I yet know whether I shall have any use at all for it. That can only be a theoretical speculation until, within a few more hours, my theory is proven or disproven—and," he said, suddenly turning on me, "my theory concerning these invisible creatures is the most extraordinary and audacious theory ever entertained by man since Columbus presumed that there must lie somewhere a hidden continent which nobody had ever seen."

He passed his hand over his protruding forehead, lost for a moment in deepest reflection. Then, "Have you ever heard of the Sphyx?" he asked.

"It seems to me that Ponce de Leon wrote of something—" I began, hesitating.

"Yes, the famous lines in the third volume which have set so many wise men guessing. You recall them:

"*And there, alas! within sound of the Fountain of Youth whose waters tint the skin till the whole body glows softly like the petal of a rose—there, alas! in the new world already blooming,* THE ETERNAL ENIGMA *I beheld, in the flesh living; yet it faded even as I looked, although I swear it lived and breathed. This is the Sphyx.*"

A silence; then I said, "Those lines are meaningless to me."

"Not to me," said Miss Barrison, softly.

The professor looked at her. "Ah, child! Ever subtler, ever surer—the Eternal Enigma is no enigma to you."

"What is the Sphyx?" I asked.

"Have you read De Soto? Or Goya?"

"Yes, both. I remember now that De Soto records the Syachas legend of the Sphyx—something about a goddess—"

"Not a goddess," said Miss Barrison, her lips touched with a smile.

"Sometimes," said the professor, gently. "And Goya said:

"*It has come to my ears while in the lands of the Syachas that the Sphyx surely lives, as bolder and more curious men than I may, God willing, prove to the world hereafter.*'"

"But what is the Sphyx?" I insisted.

"For centuries wise men and savants have asked each other that question. I have answered it for myself; I am now to prove it, I trust."

His face darkened, and again and again he stroked his heavy brow.

"If anything occurs," he said, taking my hand in his left and Miss Barrison's hand in his right, "promise me to obey my wishes. Will you?"

"Yes," we said, together.

"If I lose my life, or—or disappear, promise me on your honor to get to the electric launch as soon as possible and make all speed northward, placing my private papers, the reports of Miss Barrison, and your own reports in the hands of the authorities in Bronx Park. Don't attempt to aid me; don't delay to search for me. Do you promise?"

"Yes," we breathed together.

He looked at us solemnly. "If you fail me, you betray me," he said.

We swore obedience.

"Then let us begin," he said, and he rose and went to the steel cage. Unlocking the door, he flung it wide and stepped inside, leaving the cage door open.

"The moment a single pie is disturbed," he said to me, "I shall close the steel door from the inside, and you and Miss Barrison will then dump the rosium oxide and the strontium into the tank, clap on the lid, turn the nozzle of the hose on the cage, and spray it thoroughly. Whatever is invisible in the cage will become visible and of a faint rose color. And when the trapped creature becomes visible, hold yourselves ready to aid me as long as I am able to give you orders. After that either all will go well or all will go otherwise, and you must run for the launch." He seated himself in the cage near the open door.

I placed the steel tank near the cage, uncoiled the hose attachment, unscrewed the top, and dumped in the salts of strontium. Miss Barrison unwrapped the bottle of rosium oxide and loosened the cork. We examined this pearl-and-pink powder and shook it up so that it might run out quickly. Then Miss Barrison sat down, and presently became absorbed in a stenographic report of the proceedings up to date.

When Miss Barrison finished her report she handed me the bundle of papers. I stowed them away in my wallet, and we sat down together beside the tank.

Inside the cage Professor Farrago was seated, his spectacled eyes fixed on the row of pies. For a while, although realizing perfectly that our quarry was transparent and invisible, we unconsciously strained our eyes in quest of something stirring in the forest.

"I should think," said I, in a low voice, "that the odor of the pies might draw at least one out of the odd dozen that came rubbing up against my window last night."

"Hush! Listen!" she breathed. But we heard nothing save the snoring of the overfed dog at our feet.

"He'll give us ample notice by butting into Miss Barrison's skirts," I observed. "No need of our watching, professor."

The professor nodded. Presently he removed his spectacles and lay back against the bars, closing his eyes.

At first the forest silence seemed cheerful there in the flecked sunlight. The spotted wood-gnats gyrated merrily, chased by dragon-flies; the shy wood-birds hopped from branch to twig, peering at us in friendly inquiry; a lithe, gray squirrel, plumy tail undulating, rambled serenely around the cage, sniffing at the pastry within.

Suddenly, without apparent reason, the squirrel sprang to a tree-trunk, hung a moment on the bark, quivering all over, then dashed away into the jungle.

"Why did he act like that?" whispered Miss Barrison. And, after a moment: "How still it is! Where have the birds gone?"

In the ominous silence the dog began to whimper in his sleep and his hind legs kicked convulsively.

"He's dreaming—" I began.

The words were almost driven down my throat by the dog, who, without a yelp of warning, hurled himself at Miss Barrison and alighted on my chest, fore paws around my neck.

I cast him scornfully from me, but he scrambled back, digging like a mole to get under us.

"The transparent creatures!" whispered Miss Barrison. "Look! See that pie move!"

I sprang to my feet just as the professor, jamming on his spectacles, leaned forward and slammed the cage door.

"I've got one!" he shouted, frantically. "There's one in the cage! Turn on that hose!"

"Wait a second," said Miss Barrison, calmly, uncorking the bottle and pouring a pearly stream of rosium oxide into the tank. "Quick! It's fizzing! Screw on the top!"

In a second I had screwed the top fast, seized the hose, and directed a hissing cloud of vapor through the cage bars.

For a moment nothing was heard save the whistling rush of the perfumed spray escaping; a delicious odor of roses filled the air. Then, slowly, there in the sunshine, a misty something grew in the cage—a glistening, pearl-tinted phantom, imperceptibly taking shape in space—vague at first as a shred of lake vapor, then lengthening, rounding into flowing form, clearer, clearer.

"The Sphyx!" gasped the professor. "In the name of Heaven, play that hose!"

As he spoke the treacherous hose burst. A showery pillar of rose-colored vapor enveloped everything. Through the thickening fog for one brief instant a human form appeared like magic—a woman's form, flawless, exquisite as a statue, pure as marble. Then the swimming vapor buried it, cage, pies, and all.

We ran frantically around the cage in the obscurity, appealing for instructions and feeling for the bars. Once the professor's muffled voice was heard demanding the wearing apparel, and I groped about and found it and stuffed it through the bars of the cage.

"Do you need help?" I shouted. There was no response. Staring around through the thickening vapor of rosium rolling in clouds from the overturned tank, I heard Miss Barrison's voice calling:

"I can't move! A transparent lady is holding me!"

Blindly I rushed about, arms outstretched, and the next moment struck the door of the cage so hard that the impact almost knocked me senseless. Clutching it to steady myself, it suddenly flew open. A rush of partly visible creatures passed me like a burst of pink flames, and in the midst, borne swiftly away on the crest of the outrush, the professor passed like a bolt shot from a catapult; and his last cry came wafted back to me from the forest as I swayed there, drunk with the stupefying perfume: "Don't worry! I'm all right!"

I staggered out into the clearer air towards a figure seen dimly through swirling vapor.

"Are you hurt?" I stammered, clasping Miss Barrison in my arms.

"No—oh no," she said, wringing her hands. "But the professor! I saw him! I could not scream; I could not move! *They* had him!"

"I saw him too," I groaned. "There was not one trace of terror on his face. He was actually smiling."

Overcome at the sublime courage of the man, we wept in each other's arms.

True to our promise to Professor Farrago, we made the best of our way northward; and it was not a difficult journey by any means, the voyage in the launch across Okeechobee being perfectly simple and the trail to the nearest railroad station but a few easy miles from the landing-place.

Shocking as had been our experience, dreadful as was the calamity which had not only robbed me of a life-long friend, but had also bereaved the entire scientific world, I could not seem to feel that desperate and hopeless grief which the natural decease of a close friend might warrant. No; there remained a vague expectancy which so dominated my sorrow that at moments I became hopeful—nay, sanguine, that I should one day again behold my beloved superior in the flesh. There was something so happy in his last smile, something so artlessly pleased, that I was certain no fear of impending dissolution worried him as he disappeared into the uncharted depth of the unknown Everglades.

I think Miss Barrison agreed with me, too. She appeared to be more or less dazed, which was, of course, quite natural; and during our return voyage across Okeechobee and through the lagoons and forests beyond she was very silent.

When we reached the railroad at Portulacca, a thrifty lemon-growing ranch on the Volusia and Chinkapin Railway, the first thing I did was to present my dog to the station-agent—but I was obliged to give him five dollars before he consented to accept the dog.

However, Miss Barrison interviewed the station-master's wife, a kindly, pitiful soul, who promised to be a good mistress to the creature. We both felt better after that was off our minds; we felt better still when the north-bound train rolled leisurely into the white glare of Portulacca, and presently rolled out again, quite as leisurely, bound, thank Heaven, for that abused aggregation of sinful boroughs called New York.

Except for one young man whom I encountered in the smoker, we had the train to ourselves, a circumstance which, curiously enough, appeared to increase Miss Barrison's depression, and my own as a natural sequence. The circumstances of the taking off of Professor Farrago appeared to engross her thoughts so completely that it made me uneasy during our trip out from Little Sprite—in fact it was growing plainer to me every hour that in her brief acquaintance with that distinguished scientist she had become personally attached to him to an extent that began to worry me. Her personal indignation at the caged Sphyx flared out at unexpected intervals, and there could be no doubt that her unhappiness and resentment were becoming morbid.

I spent an hour or two in the smoking compartment, tenanted only by a single passenger and myself. He was an agreeable young man, although, in the natural acquaintanceship that we struck up, I regretted to learn that he was a writer of popular fiction, returning from Fort Worth, where he had been for the sole purpose of composing a poem on Florida.

I have always, in common with other mentally balanced savants, despised writers of fiction. All scientists harbor a natural antipathy to romance in any form, and that antipathy becomes a deep horror if fiction dares to deal flippantly with the exact sciences, or if some degraded intellect assumes the warrantless liberty of using natural history as the vehicle for silly tales.

Never but once had I been tempted to romance in any form; never but once had sentiment interfered with a passionless transfer of scientific notes to the sanctuary of the unvarnished notebook or the cloister of the juiceless monograph. Nor have I the slightest approach to that superficial and doubtful quality known as literary skill. Once, however, as I sat alone in the middle of the floor, classifying my isopods, I was not only astonished but totally unprepared to find myself repeating aloud a verse that I myself had unconsciously fashioned:

"An isopod
Is a work of God."

Never before in all my life had I made a rhyme; and it worried me for weeks, ringing in my brain day and night, confusing me, interfering with my thoughts.

I said as much to the young man, who only laughed good-naturedly and replied that it was the Creator's purpose to limit certain intellects, nobody knows why, and that it was apparent that mine had not escaped.

"There's one thing, however," he said, "that might be of some interest to you and come within the circumscribed scope of your intelligence."

"And what is that?" I asked, tartly.

"A scientific experience of mine," he said, with a careless laugh. "It's so much stranger than fiction that even Professor Bruce Stoddard, of Columbia, hesitated to credit it."

I looked at the young fellow suspiciously. His bland smile disarmed me, but I did not invite him to relate his experience, although he apparently needed only that encouragement to begin.

"Now, if I could tell it exactly as it occurred," he observed, "and a stenographer could take it down, word for word, exactly as I relate it—"

"It would give me great pleasure to do so," said a quiet voice at the door. We rose at once, removing the cigars from our lips; but

Miss Barrison bade us continue smoking, and at a gesture from her we resumed our seats after she had installed herself by the window.

"Really," she said, looking coldly at me, "I couldn't endure the solitude any longer. Isn't there anything to do on this tiresome train?"

"If you had your pad and pencil," I began, maliciously, "you might take down a matter of interest—"

She looked frankly at the young man, who laughed in that pleasant, good-tempered manner of his, and offered to tell us of his alleged scientific experience if we thought it might amuse us sufficiently to vary the dull monotony of the journey north.

"Is it fiction?" I asked, point-blank.

"It is absolute truth," he replied.

I rose and went off to find pad and pencil. When I returned Miss Barrison was laughing at a story which the young man had just finished.

"But," he ended, gravely, "I have practically decided to renounce fiction as a means of livelihood and confine myself to simple, uninteresting statistics and facts."

"I am very glad to hear you say that," I exclaimed, warmly. He bowed, looked at Miss Barrison, and asked her when he might begin his story.

"Whenever you are ready," replied Miss Barrison, smiling in a manner which I had not observed since the disappearance of Professor Farrago. I'll admit that the young fellow was superficially attractive.

A Matter of Interest

I

"Well, then," he began, modestly, "having no technical ability concerning the affair in question, and having no knowledge of either comparative anatomy or zoology, I am perhaps unfitted to tell this story. But the story is true; the episode occurred under my own eyes—within a few hours' sail of the Battery. And as I was one of the first persons to verify what has long been a theory among scientists, and, moreover, as the result of Professor Holroyd's discovery is to be placed on exhibition in Madison Square Garden on the 20th of next month, I have decided to tell you, as simply as I am able, exactly what occurred.

"I first told the story on April 1, 1903, to the editors of the *North American Review*, *The Popular Science Monthly*, the *Scientific American*, *Nature*, *Outing*, and the *Fossiliferous Magazine*. All these gentlemen rejected it; some curtly informing me that fiction had no place in their columns. When I attempted to explain that it was not fiction, the editors of these periodicals either maintained a contemptuous silence, or bluntly notified me that my literary services and opinions were not desired. But finally, when several publishers offered to take the story as fiction, I cut short all negotiations and decided to publish it myself. Where I am known at all, it is my misfortune to be known as a writer of fiction. This makes it impossible for me to receive a hearing from a scientific audience. I regret it bitterly, because now, when it is too late, I am prepared to prove certain scientific matters of interest, and to produce the proofs. In this case, however, I am fortunate, for nobody can dispute the existence of a thing when the bodily proof is exhibited as evidence.

"This is the story; and if I tell it as I write fiction, it is because I do not know how to tell it otherwise.

"I was walking along the beach below Pine Inlet, on the south shore of Long Island. The railroad and telegraph station is at West Oyster Bay. Everybody who has travelled on the Long Island Railroad knows the station, but few, perhaps, know Pine Inlet. Duck-shooters, of course, are familiar with it; but as there are no hotels there, and nothing to see except salt meadow, salt creek, and a strip of dune and sand, the summer-squatting public may probably be unaware of its existence. The local name for the place is Pine Inlet; the maps give its name as Sand Point, I believe, but anybody at West Oyster Bay can direct you to it. Captain McPeek, who keeps the West Oyster Bay House, drives duck-shooters there in winter. It lies five miles southeast from West Oyster Bay.

"I had walked over that afternoon from Captain McPeek's. There was a reason for my going to Pine Inlet—it embarrasses me to explain it, but the truth is I meditated writing an ode to the ocean. It was out of the question to write it in West Oyster Bay, with the whistle of locomotives in my ears. I knew that Pine Inlet was one of the loneliest places on the Atlantic coast; it is out of sight of everything except leagues of gray ocean. Rarely one might make out fishing-smacks drifting across the horizon. Summer squatters never visited it; sportsmen shunned it, except in winter. Therefore, as I was about to do a bit of poetry, I thought that Pine Inlet was the spot for the deed. So I went there.

"As I was strolling along the beach, biting my pencil reflectively, tremendously impressed by the solitude and the solemn thunder of the surf, a thought occurred to me—how unpleasant it would be if I suddenly stumbled on a summer boarder. As this joyless impossibility flitted across my mind, I rounded a bleak sand-dune.

"A girl stood directly in my path.

"She stared at me as though I had just crawled up out of the sea to bite her. I don't know what my own expression resembled, but I have been given to understand it was idiotic.

"Now I perceived, after a few moments, that the young lady was frightened, and I knew I ought to say something civil. So I said, 'Are there many mosquitoes here?'

"'No,' she replied, with a slight quiver in her voice; 'I have only seen one, and it was biting somebody else.'

"The conversation seemed so futile, and the young lady appeared to be more nervous than before. I had an impulse to say, 'Do not run; I have breakfasted,' for she seemed to be meditating a flight into the breakers. What I did say was: 'I did not know anybody was here. I do not intend to intrude. I come from Captain McPeek's, and I am writing an ode to the ocean.' After I had said this it seemed to ring in my ears like, 'I come from Table Mountain, and my name is Truthful James.'

"I glanced timidly at her.

"'She's thinking of the same thing,' said I to myself.

"However, the young lady seemed to be a trifle reassured. I noticed she drew a sigh of relief and looked at my shoes. She looked so long that it made me suspicious, and I also examined my shoes. They seemed to be in a fair state of repair.

"'I—I am sorry,' she said, 'but would you mind not walking on the beach?'

"This was sudden. I had intended to retire and leave the beach to her, but I did not fancy being driven away so abruptly.

"'Dear me!' she cried; 'you don't understand. I do not—I would not think for a moment of asking you to leave Pine Inlet. I merely ventured to request you to walk on the dunes. I am so afraid that your footprints may obliterate the impressions that my father is studying.'

"'Oh!' said I, looking about me as though I had been caught in the middle of a flower-bed; 'really I did not notice any impressions. Impressions of what?'

"'I don't know,' she said, smiling a little at my awkward pose. 'If you step this way in a straight line you can do no damage.'

"I did as she bade me. I suppose my movements resembled the gait of a wet peacock. Possibly they recalled the delicate manœuvres of the kangaroo. Anyway, she laughed. This seriously annoyed me. I had been at a disadvantage; I walk well enough when let alone.

"'You can scarcely expect,' said I, 'that a man absorbed in his own ideas could notice impressions on the sand. I trust I have obliterated nothing.'

"As I said this I looked back at the long line of footprints stretching away in prospective across the sand. They were my own. How large they looked! Was that what she was laughing at?

"'I wish to explain,' she said, gravely, looking at the point of her parasol 'I am very sorry to be obliged to warn you—to ask you to forego the pleasure of strolling on a beach that does not belong to me. Perhaps,' she continued, in sudden alarm, 'perhaps this beach belongs to you?'

"'The beach? Oh no,' I said.

"'But—but you were going to write poems about it?'

"'Only one—and that does not necessitate owning the beach. I have observed,' said I, frankly, 'that the people who own nothing write many poems about it.'

"She looked at me seriously.

"'I write many poems,' I added

"She laughed doubtfully.

"'Would you rather I went away?' I asked, politely. 'My family is respectable,' I added; and I told her my name.

"'Oh! Then you wrote *Culled Cowslips* and *Faded Fig-Leaves* and you imitate Maeterlinck, and you—Oh, I know lots of people that you know;' she cried, with every symptom of relief; 'and you know my brother.'

"'I am the author,' said I, coldly, 'of *Culled Cowslips*, but *Faded Fig-Leaves* was an earlier work, which I no longer recognize, and I should be grateful to you if you would be kind enough to deny that I ever imitated Maeterlinck. Possibly,' I added, 'he imitates me.'

"She was very quiet, and I saw she was sorry.

"'Never mind,' I said, magnanimously, 'you probably are not familiar with modern literature. If I knew your name I should ask permission to present myself.'

"'Why, I am Daisy Holroyd,' she said.

"'What! Jack Holroyd's little sister?'

"'Little?' she cried.

"'I didn't mean that,' said I. 'You know that your brother and I were great friends in Paris—'

"'I know,' she said, significantly.

"'Ahem! Of course,' I said, 'Jack and I were inseparable—'

"'Except when shut in separate cells,' said Miss Holroyd, coldly.

"This unfeeling allusion to the unfortunate termination of a Latin-Quarter celebration hurt me.

"'The police,' said I, 'were too officious.'

"'So Jack says,' replied Miss Holroyd, demurely.

"We had unconsciously moved on along the sandhills, side by side, as we spoke.

"'To think,' I repeated, 'that I should meet Jack's little—'

"'Please,' she said, 'you are only three years my senior.'

"She opened the sunshade and tipped it over one shoulder. It was white, and had spots and posies on it.

"'Jack sends us every new book you write,' she observed. 'I do not approve of some things you write.'

"'Modern school,' I mumbled.

"'That is no excuse,' she said, severely; 'Anthony Trollope didn't do it.'

"The foam spume from the breakers was drifting across the dunes, and the little tip-up snipe ran along the beach and teetered and whistled and spread their white-barred wings for a low, straight flight across the shingle, only to tip and run and sail on again. The salt sea-wind whistled and curled through the crested waves, blowing in perfumed puffs across thickets of sweet bay and cedar. As we passed through the crackling juicy-stemmed marsh-weed myriads of fiddler crabs raised their fore-claws in warning and backed away, rustling, through the reeds, aggressive, protesting.

"'Like millions of pygmy Ajaxes defying the lightning,' I said.

"Miss Holroyd laughed.

"'Now I never imagined that authors were clever except in print,' she said.

"She was a most extraordinary girl.

"'I suppose,' she observed, after a moment's silence— 'I suppose I am taking you to my father.'

"'Delighted!' I mumbled. 'H'm! I had the honor of meeting Professor Holroyd in Paris.'

"'Yes; he bailed you and Jack out,' said Miss Holroyd, serenely.

"The silence was too painful to last.

"'Captain McPeek is an interesting man,' I said. I spoke more loudly than I intended. I may have been nervous.

"'Yes,' said Daisy Holroyd, 'but he has a most singular hotel clerk.'

"'You mean Mr. Frisby?'

"'I do.'

"'Yes,' I admitted, 'Mr. Frisby is queer. He was once a bill-poster.'

"'I know it!' exclaimed Daisy Holroyd, with some heat. 'He ruins landscapes whenever he has an opportunity. Do you know that he has a passion for bill-posting? He has; he posts bills for the pure pleasure of it, just as you play golf, or tennis, or squash.'

"'But he's a hotel clerk now,' I said; 'nobody employs him to post bills.'

"'I know it! He does it all by himself for the pure pleasure of it. Papa has engaged him to come down here for two weeks, and I dread it,' said the girl.

"What Professor Holroyd might want of Frisby I had not the faintest notion. I suppose Miss Holroyd noticed the bewilderment in my face, for she laughed and nodded her head twice.

"'Not only Mr. Frisby, but Captain McPeek also,' she said.

"'You don't mean to say that Captain McPeek is going to close his hotel!' I exclaimed.

"My trunk was there. It contained guarantees of my respectability.

"'Oh no; his wife will keep it open,' replied the girl. 'Look! you can see papa now. He's digging.'

"'Where?' I blurted out.

"I remembered Professor Holroyd as a prim, spectacled gentleman, with close-cut, snowy beard and a clerical allure. The man I saw digging wore green goggles, a jersey, a battered sou'wester, and hip-boots of rubber. He was delving in the muck of the salt meadow, his face streaming with perspiration, his boots and jersey splashed with unpleasant-looking mud. He glanced up as we approached, shading his eyes with a sunburned hand.

"'Papa, dear,' said Miss Holroyd, 'here is Jack's friend, whom you bailed out of Mazas.'

"The introduction was startling. I turned crimson with mortification. The professor was very decent about it; he called me by name at once. Then he looked at his spade. It was clear he considered me a nuisance and wished to go on with his digging.

"'I suppose,' he said, 'you are still writing?'

"'A little,' I replied, trying not to speak sarcastically. My output had rivalled that of 'The Duchess'—in quantity, I mean.

"'I seldom read—fiction,' he said, looking restlessly at the hole in the ground.

"Miss Holroyd came to my rescue.

"'That was a charming story you wrote last,' she said. 'Papa should read it—you should, papa; it's all about a fossil.'

"We both looked narrowly at Miss Holroyd. Her smile was guileless.

"'Fossils!' repeated the professor. 'Do you care for fossils?'

"'Very much,' said I.

"Now I am not perfectly sure what my object was in lying. I looked at Daisy Holroyd's dark-fringed eyes. They were very grave.

"'Fossils,' said I, 'are my hobby.'

"I think Miss Holroyd winced a little at this. I did not care. I went on:

"'I have seldom had the opportunity to study the subject, but, as a boy, I collected flint arrowheads—'

"'Flint arrow-heads!' said the professor coldly.

"'Yes; they were the nearest things to fossils obtainable,' I replied, marvelling at my own mendacity.

"The professor looked into the hole. I also looked. I could see nothing in it. 'He's digging for fossils,' thought I to myself.

"'Perhaps,' said the professor, cautiously, 'you might wish to aid me in a little research—that is to say, if you have an inclination for fossils.' The double-entendre was not lost upon me.

"'I have read all your books so eagerly,' said I, 'that to join you, to be of service to you in any research, however difficult and trying, would be an honor and a privilege that I never dared to hope for.'

"'That,' thought I to myself, 'will do its own work.'

"But the professor was still suspicious. How could he help it, when he remembered Jack's escapades, in which my name was always blended! Doubtless he was satisfied that my influence on Jack was evil. The contrary was the case, too.

"'Fossils,' he said, worrying the edge of the excavation with his spade— 'fossils are not things to be lightly considered.'

"'No, indeed!' I protested.

"'Fossils are the most interesting as well as puzzling things in the world,' said he.

"'They are!' I cried, enthusiastically.

"'But I am not looking for fossils,' observed the professor, mildly.

"This was a facer. I looked at Daisy Holroyd. She bit her lip and fixed her eyes on the sea. Her eyes were wonderful eyes.

"'Did you think I was digging for fossils in a salt meadow?' queried the professor. 'You can have read very little about the subject. I am digging for something quite different.'

"I was silent. I knew that my face was flushed. I longed to say, 'Well, what the devil are you digging for?' but I only stared into the hole as though hypnotized.

"'Captain McPeek and Frisby ought to be here,' he said, looking first at Daisy and then across the meadows.

"I ached to ask him why he had subpœnaed Captain McPeek and Frisby.

"'They are coming,' said Daisy, shading her eyes. 'Do you see the speck on the meadows?'

"'It may be a mud-hen,' said the professor.

"'Miss Holroyd is right,' I said. 'A wagon and team and two men are coming from the north. There's a dog beside the wagon—it's that miserable yellow dog of Frisby's.'

"'Good gracious!' cried the professor, 'you don't mean to tell me that you see all that at such a distance?'

"'Why not?' I said.

"'I see nothing,' he insisted.

"'You will see that I'm right, presently,' I laughed.

"The professor removed his blue goggles and rubbed them, glancing obliquely at me.

"'Haven't you heard what extraordinary eyesight duck-shooters have?' said his daughter, looking back at her father. 'Jack says that he can tell exactly what kind of a duck is flying before most people could see anything at all in the sky.'

"'It's true,' I said; 'it comes to anybody, I fancy, who has had practice.'

"The professor regarded me with a new interest. There was inspiration in his eyes. He turned towards the ocean. For a long time he stared at the tossing waves on the beach, then he looked far out to where the horizon met the sea.

"'Are there any ducks out there?' he asked, at last.

"'Yes,' said I, scanning the sea, 'there are.'

"He produced a pair of binoculars from his coat-tail pocket, adjusted them, and raised them to his eyes. 'H'm! What sort of ducks?'

"I looked more carefully, holding both hands over my forehead.

"'Surf-ducks and widgeon. There is one bufflehead among them—no, two; the rest are coots,' I replied.

"'This,' cried the professor, 'is most astonishing. I have good eyes, but I can't see a blessed thing without these binoculars!'

"'It's not extraordinary,' said I; 'the surf-ducks and coots any novice might recognize; the widgeon and buffleheads I should not have been able to name unless they had risen from the water. It is easy to tell any duck when it is flying, even though it looks no bigger than a black pin-point.'

"But the professor insisted that it was marvellous, and he said that I might render him invaluable service if I would consent to come and camp at Pine Inlet for a few weeks.

"I looked at his daughter, but she turned her back. Her back was beautifully moulded. Her gown fitted also.

"'Camp out here?' I repeated, pretending to be unpleasantly surprised.

"'I do not think he would care to,' said Miss Holroyd, without turning.

"I had not expected that. 'Above all things,' said I, in a clear, pleasant voice, 'I like to camp out.'

"She said nothing.

"'It is not exactly camping,' said the professor. 'Come, you shall see our conservatory. Daisy, come, dear! You must put on a heavier frock; it is getting towards sundown.'

"At that moment, over a near dune, two horses' heads appeared, followed by two human heads, then a wagon, then a yellow dog.

"I turned triumphantly to the professor.

"'You are the very man I want,' he muttered— 'the very man— the very man.'

"I looked at Daisy Holroyd. She returned my glance with a defiant little smile.

"'Waal,' said Captain McPeek, driving up, 'here we be! Git out, Frisby.'

"Frisby, fat, nervous, and sentimental, hopped out of the cart.

"'Come,' said the professor, impatiently moving across the dunes. I walked with Daisy Holroyd. McPeek and Frisby followed. The yellow dog walked by himself.

II

The sun was dipping into the sea as we trudged across the meadows towards a high, dome-shaped dune covered with cedars and thickets of sweet bay. I saw no sign of habitation among the sandhills. Far as the eye could reach, nothing broke the gray line of sea and sky save the squat dunes crowned with stunted cedars.

"Then, as we rounded the base of the dune, we almost walked into the door of a house. My amazement amused Miss Holroyd, and I noticed also a touch of malice in her pretty eyes. But she said nothing, following her father into the house, with the slightest possible gesture to me.

"Was it invitation or was it menace?

"The house was merely a light wooden frame, covered with some waterproof stuff that looked like a mixture of rubber and tar. Over this—in fact, over the whole roof—was pitched an awning of heavy sail-cloth. I noticed that the house was anchored to the sand by chains, already rusted red. But this one-storied house was not the only building nestling in the south shelter of the big dune. A hundred feet away stood another structure—long, low, also built of wood. It had rows on rows of round port-holes on every side. The ports were fitted with heavy glass, hinged to swing open if necessary. A single, big double door occupied the front.

"Behind this long, low building was still another, a mere shed. Smoke rose from the sheet-iron chimney. There was somebody moving about inside the open door.

"As I stood gaping at this mushroom hamlet the professor appeared at the door and asked me to enter. I stepped in at once.

"The house was much larger than I had imagined. A straight hallway ran through the centre from east to west. On either side of this hallway were rooms, the doors swinging wide open. I counted three doors on each side; the three on the south appeared to be bedrooms.

"The professor ushered me into a room on the north side, where I found Captain McPeek and Frisby sitting at a table, upon which were drawings and sketches of articulated animals and fishes.

"'You see, McPeek,' said the professor, 'we only wanted one more man, and I think I've got him—Haven't I?' turning eagerly to me.

"'Why, yes,' I said, laughing; 'this is delightful. Am I invited to stay here?'

"'Your bedroom is the third on the south side; everything is ready. McPeek, you can bring his trunk tomorrow, can't you?' demanded the professor.

"The red-faced captain nodded, and shifted a quid.

"'Then it's all settled,' said the professor, and he drew a sigh of satisfaction. 'You see,' he said, turning to me, 'I was at my wit's end to know whom to trust. I never thought of you. Jack's out in China, and I didn't dare trust anybody in my own profession. All you care about is writing verses and stories, isn't it?'

"'I like to shoot,' I replied, mildly.

"'Just the thing!' he cried, beaming at us all in turn. 'Now I can see no reason why we should not progress rapidly. McPeek, you and Frisby must get those boxes up here before dark. Dinner will be ready before you have finished unloading. Dick, you will wish to go to your room first.'

"My name isn't Dick, but he spoke so kindly, and beamed upon me in such a fatherly manner, that I let it go. I had occasion to correct him afterwards, several times, but he always forgot the next minute. He calls me Dick to this day.

"It was dark when Professor Holroyd, his daughter, and I sat down to dinner. The room was the same in which I had noticed the drawings of beast and bird, but the round table had been extended into an oval, and neatly spread with dainty linen and silver.

"A fresh-cheeked Swedish girl appeared from a farther room, bearing the soup. The professor ladled it out, still beaming.

"'Now, this is very delightful—isn't it, Daisy?' he said.

"'Very,' said Miss Holroyd, with a tinge of irony.

"'Very,' I repeated, heartily.

"'I suppose,' said the professor, nodding mysteriously at his daughter, 'that Dick knows nothing of what we're about down here?'

"'I suppose,' said Miss Holroyd, 'that he thinks we are digging for fossils.'

"I looked at my plate. She might have spared me that.

"'Well, well,' said her father, smiling to himself, 'he shall know everything by morning. You'll be astonished, Dick, my boy.'

"'His name isn't Dick,' corrected Daisy.

"The professor said, 'Isn't it?' in an absent-minded way, and relapsed into contemplation of my necktie.

"I asked Miss Holroyd a few questions about Jack, and was informed that he had given up law and entered the consular service— as what, I did not dare ask, for I know what our consular service is.

"'In China,' said Daisy.

"'Choo Choo is the name of the city,' added her father, proudly; 'it's the terminus of the new trans-Siberian railway.'

"'It's on the Pong Ping,' said Daisy.

"'He's vice-consul,' added the professor, triumphantly.

"'He'll make a good one,' I observed. I knew Jack. I pitied his consul.

" So we chatted on about my old playmate, until Freda, the red-cheeked maid, brought coffee, and the professor lighted a cigar, with a little bow to his daughter.

"'Of course, you don't smoke,' she said to me, with a glimmer of malice in her eyes.

"'He mustn't,' interposed the professor, hastily; 'it will make his hand tremble.'

"'No, it won't,' said I, laughing; 'but my hand will shake if I don't smoke. Are you going to employ me as a draughtsman?'

"'You'll know to-morrow,' he chuckled, with a mysterious smile at his daughter. 'Daisy, give him my best cigars—put the box here on the table. We can't afford to have his hand tremble.'

"Miss Holroyd rose and crossed the hallway to her father's room, returning presently with a box of promising-looking cigars.

"'I don't think he knows what is good for him,' she said. 'He should smoke only one every day.'

"It was hard to bear. I am not vindictive, but I decided to treasure up a few of Miss Holroyd's gentle taunts. My intimacy with her brother was certainly a disadvantage to me now. Jack had apparently been talking too much, and his sister appeared to be thoroughly acquainted with my past. It was a disadvantage. I remembered her vaguely as a girl with long braids, who used to come on Sundays with her father and take tea with us in our rooms. Then she went to Germany to school, and Jack and I employed our Sunday evenings otherwise. It is true that I regarded her weekly visits as a species of infliction, but I did not think I ever showed it.

"'It is strange,' said I, 'that you did not recognize me at once, Miss Holroyd. Have I changed so greatly in five years?'

"'You wore a pointed French beard in Paris,' she said— 'a very downy one. And you never stayed to tea but twice, and then you only spoke once.'

"'Oh!' said I, blankly. 'What did I say?'

"'You asked me if I liked plums,' said Daisy, bursting into an irresistible ripple of laughter.

"I saw that I must have made the same sort of an ass of myself that most boys of eighteen do.

"It was too bad. I never thought about the future in those days. Who could have imagined that little Daisy Holroyd would have grown up into this bewildering young lady? It was really too bad. Presently the professor retired to his room, carrying with him an armful of drawings, and bidding us not to sit up late. When he closed his door Miss Holroyd turned to me.

"'Papa will work over those drawings until midnight,' she said, with a despairing smile.

"'It isn't good for him,' I said. 'What are the drawings?'

"'You may know to-morrow,' she answered, leaning forward on the table and shading her face with one hand. 'Tell me about yourself and Jack in Paris.'

"I looked at her suspiciously.

"'What! There isn't much to tell. We studied. Jack went to the law school, and I attended—er—oh, all sorts of schools.'

"'Did you? Surely you gave yourself a little recreation occasionally?'

"'Occasionally,' I nodded.

"'I am afraid you and Jack studied too hard.'

"'That may be,' said I, looking meek.

"'Especially about fossils.'

"I couldn't stand that.

"'Miss Holroyd,' I said, 'I do care for fossils. You may think that I am a humbug, but I have a perfect mania for fossils—now.'

"'Since when?'

"'About an hour ago,' I said, airily. Out of the corner of my eye I saw that she had flushed up. It pleased me.

"'You will soon tire of the experiment,' she said, with a dangerous smile.

"'Oh, I may,' I replied, indifferently.

"She drew back. The movement was scarcely perceptible, but I noticed it, and she knew I did.

"The atmosphere was vaguely hostile. One feels such mental conditions and changes instantly. I picked up a chess-board, opened it, set up the pieces with elaborate care, and began to move, first the white, then the black. Miss Holroyd watched me coldly at first, but after a dozen moves she became interested and leaned a shade nearer. I moved a black pawn forward.

"'Why do you do that?' said Daisy.

"'Because,' said I, 'the white queen threatens the pawn.'

"'It was an aggressive move,' she insisted.

"'Purely defensive,' I said. 'If her white highness will let the pawn alone, the pawn will let the queen alone.'

"Miss Holroyd rested her chin on her wrist and gazed steadily at the board. She was flushing furiously, but she held her ground.

"'If the white queen doesn't block that pawn, the pawn may become dangerous,' she said, coldly.

"I laughed, and closed up the board with a snap.

"'True,' I said, 'it might even take the queen.' After a moment's silence I asked, 'What would you do in that case, Miss Holroyd?'

"'I should resign,' she said, serenely; then, realizing what she had said, she lost her self-possession for a second, and cried: 'No, indeed! I should fight to the bitter end! I mean—'

"'What?' I asked, lingering over my revenge.

"'I mean,' she said, slowly, 'that your black pawn would never have the chance—never! I should take it immediately.'

"'I believe you would,' said I, smiling; 'so we'll call the game yours, and—the pawn captured.'

"'I don't want it,' she exclaimed. 'A pawn is worthless.'

"'Except when it's in the king row.'

"'Chess is most interesting,' she observed, sedately. She had completely recovered her self-possession. Still I saw that she now had a certain respect for my defensive powers. It was very soothing to me.

"'You know,' said I, gravely, 'that I am fonder of Jack than of anybody. That's the reason we never write each other, except to borrow things. I am afraid that when I was a young cub in France I was not an attractive personality.'

"'On the contrary,' said Daisy, smiling, 'I thought you were very big and very perfect. I had illusions. I wept often when I went home and remembered that you never took the trouble to speak to me but once.'

"'I was a cub,' I said— 'not selfish and brutal, but I didn't understand school-girls. I never had any sisters, and I didn't know what to say to very young girls. If I had imagined that you felt hurt—'

"'Oh, I did—five years ago. Afterwards I laughed at the whole thing.'

"'Laughed?' I repeated, vaguely disappointed.

"'Why, of course. I was very easily hurt when I was a child. I think I have outgrown it.'

"The soft curve of her sensitive mouth contradicted her.

"'Will you forgive me now?' I asked.

"'Yes. I had forgotten the whole thing until I met you an hour or so ago.'

"There was something that had a ring not entirely genuine in this speech. I noticed it, but forgot it the next moment.

"Presently she rose, touched her hair with the tip of one finger, and walked to the door.

"'Good-night,' she said.

"'Good-night,' said I, opening the door for her to pass.

III

"The sea was a sheet of silver tinged with pink. The tremendous arch of the sky was all shimmering and glimmering with the promise of the sun. Already the mist above, flecked with clustered clouds, flushed with rose color and dull gold. I heard the low splash of the waves breaking and curling across the beach. A wandering breeze, fresh and fragrant, blew the curtains of my window. There was the scent of sweet bay in the room, and everywhere the subtle, nameless perfume of the sea.

"When at last I stood upon the shore, the air and sea were all a-glimmer in a rosy light, deepening to crimson in the zenith. Along the beach I saw a little cove, shelving and all a-shine, where shallow waves washed with a mellow sound. Fine as dusted gold the shingle glowed, and the thin film of water rose, receded, crept up again a little higher, and again flowed back, with the low hiss of snowy foam and gilded bubbles breaking.

"I stood a little while quiet, my eyes upon the water, the invitation of the ocean in my ears, vague and sweet as the murmur of a shell. Then I looked at my bathing-suit and towels.

"'In we go!' said I, aloud. A second later the prophecy was fulfilled. I swam far out to sea, and as I swam the waters all around me turned to gold. The sun had risen.

"There is a fragrance in the sea at dawn that none can name. Whitethorn a-bloom in May, sedges a-sway, and scented rushes rustling in an inland wind recall the sea to me—I can't say why.

"Far out at sea I raised myself, swung around, dived, and set out again for shore, striking strong strokes until the flecked foam flew. And when at last I shot through the breakers, I laughed aloud and sprang upon the beach, breathless and happy. Then from the ocean came another cry, clear, joyous, and a white arm rose in the air.

"She came drifting in with the waves like a white sea-sprite, laughing at me, and I plunged into the breakers again to join her.

"Side by side we swam along the coast, just outside the breakers, until in the next cove we saw the flutter of her maid's cap-strings.

"'I will beat you to breakfast!' she cried, as I rested, watching her glide up along the beach.

"'Done!' said I— 'for a sea-shell!'

"'Done!' she called, across the water.

"I made good speed along the shore, and I was not long in dressing, but when I entered the dining-room she was there, demure, smiling, exquisite in her cool, white frock.

"'The sea-shell is yours,' said I. 'I hope I can find one with a pearl in it.'

"The professor hurried in before she could reply. He greeted me very cordially, but there was an abstracted air about him, and he called me Dick until I recognized that remonstrance was useless. He was not long over his coffee and rolls.

"'McPeek and Frisby will return with the last load, including your trunk, by early afternoon,' he said, rising and picking up his bundle of drawings. 'I haven't time to explain to you what we are doing, Dick, but Daisy will take you about and instruct you. She will give you the rifle standing in my room—it's a good Winchester. I have sent for an 'Express' for you, big enough to knock over any elephant in India. Daisy, take him through the sheds and tell him everything. Luncheon is at noon. Do you usually take luncheon, Dick?'

"'When I am permitted,' I smiled.

"'Well,' said the professor, doubtfully, 'you mustn't come back here for it. Freda can take you what you want. Is your hand unsteady after eating?'

"'Why, papa!' said Daisy. 'Do you intend to starve him?'

"We all laughed.

"The professor tucked his drawings into a capacious pocket, pulled his sea-boots up to his hips, seized a spade, and left, nodding to us as though he were thinking of something else.

"We went to the door and watched him across the salt meadows until the distant sand-dune hid him.

"'Come,' said Daisy Holroyd, 'I am going to take you to the shop.'

"She put on a broad-brimmed straw hat, a distractingly pretty combination of filmy cool stuffs, and led the way to the long, low structure that I had noticed the evening before.

"The interior was lighted by the numberless little port-holes, and I could see everything plainly. I acknowledge I was nonplussed by what I did see.

"In the centre of the shed, which must have been at least a hundred feet long, stood what I thought at first was the skeleton of an enormous whale. After a moment's silent contemplation of the thing I saw that it could not be a whale, for the frames of two gigantic, bat-like wings rose from each shoulder. Also I noticed that the animal possessed legs—four of them—with most unpleasant-looking webbed claws fully eight feet long. The bony framework of the head, too, resembled something between a crocodile and a monstrous snapping-turtle. The walls of the shanty were hung with drawings and blue prints. A man dressed in white linen was tinkering with the vertebræ of the lizard-like tail.

"'Where on earth did such a reptile come from?' I asked at length.

"'Oh, it's not real!' said Daisy, scornfully; 'it's papier-maché.'

"'I see,' said I; 'a stage prop.'

"'A what?' asked Daisy, in hurt astonishment.

"'Why, a—a sort of Siegfried dragon—a what's-his-name—er, Pfafner, or Peffer, or—'

"'If my father heard you say such things he would dislike you,' said Daisy. She looked grieved, and moved towards the door. I apologized—for what, I knew not—and we became reconciled. She ran into her father's room and brought me the rifle, a very good Winchester. She also gave me a cartridge-belt, full.

"'Now,' she smiled, 'I shall take you to your observatory, and when we arrive you are to begin your duty at once.'

"'And that duty?' I ventured, shouldering the rifle.

"'That duty is to watch the ocean. I shall then explain the whole affair—but you mustn't look at me while I speak; you must watch the sea.'

"'This,' said I, 'is hardship. I had rather go without the luncheon.'

"I do not think she was offended at my speech; still she frowned for almost three seconds.

"We passed through acres of sweet bay and spear grass, sometimes skirting thickets of twisted cedars, sometimes walking in the full glare of the morning sun, sinking into shifting sand where sun-sorched shells crackled under our feet, and sun-browned sea-weed glistened, bronzed and iridescent. Then, as we climbed a little hill, the sea-wind freshened in our faces, and lo! the ocean lay below us, far-stretching as the eye could reach, glittering, magnificent.

"Daisy sat down flat on the sand. It takes a clever girl to do that and retain the respectful deference due her from men. It takes a graceful girl to accomplish it triumphantly when a man is looking.

"'You must sit beside me,' she said—as though it would prove irksome to me.

"'Now,' she continued, 'you must watch the water while I am talking.'

"I nodded.

"'Why don't you do it, then?' she asked.

"I succeeded in wrenching my head towards the ocean, although I felt sure it would swing gradually round again in spite of me.

"'To begin with,' said Daisy Holroyd, 'there's a thing in that ocean that would astonish you if you saw it. Turn your head!'

"'I am,' I said, meekly.

"'Did you hear what I said?'

"'Yes—er—a thing in the ocean that's going to astonish me.' Visions of mermaids rose before me.

"'The thing,' said Daisy, 'is a thermosaurus!'

"I nodded vaguely, as though anticipating a delightful introduction to a nautical friend.

"'You don't seem astonished,' she said, reproachfully.

"'Why should I be?' I asked.

"'Please turn your eyes towards the water. Suppose a thermosaurus should look out of the waves!'

"'Well,' said I, 'in that case the pleasure would be mutual.'

"She frowned and bit her upper lip.

"'Do you know what a thermosaurus is?' she asked.

"'If I am to guess,' said I, 'I guess it's a jelly-fish.'

"'It's that big, ugly, horrible creature that I showed you in the shed!' cried Daisy, impatiently.

"'Eh!' I stammered.

"'Not papier-maché, either,' she continued, excitedly; 'it's a real one.'

"This was pleasant news. I glanced instinctively at my rifle and then at the ocean.

"'Well, said I at last, 'it strikes me that you and I resemble a pair of Andromedas waiting to be swallowed. This rifle won't stop a beast, a live beast, like that Nibelungen dragon of yours.'

"'Yes, it will,' she said; 'it's not an ordinary rifle.'

"Then, for the first time, I noticed, just below the magazine, a cylindrical attachment that was strange to me.

"'Now, if you will watch the sea very carefully, and will promise not to look at me,' said Daisy, 'I will try to explain.'

"She did not wait for me to promise, but went on eagerly, a sparkle of excitement in her blue eyes:

"'You know, of all the fossil remains of the great bat-like and lizard-like creatures that inhabited the earth ages and ages ago, the bones of the gigantic saurians are the most interesting. I think they used to splash about the water and fly over the land during the carboniferous period; anyway, it doesn't matter. Of course you have seen pictures of reconstructed creatures such as the ichthyosaurus, the plesiosaurus, the anthracosaurus, and the thermosaurus?'

"I nodded, trying to keep my eyes from hers.

"'And you know that the remains of the thermosaurus were first discovered and reconstructed by papa?'

"'Yes,' said I. There was no use in saying no.

"'I am glad you do. Now, papa has proved that this creature lived entirely in the Gulf Stream, emerging for occasional flights across an ocean or two. Can you imagine how he proved it?'

"'No,' said I, resolutely pointing my nose at the ocean.

"'He proved it by a minute examination of the microscopical shells found among the ribs of the thermosaurus. These shells contained little creatures that live only in the warm waters of the Gulf Stream. They were the food of the thermosaurus.'

"'It was rather slender rations for a thing like that, wasn't it? Did he ever swallow bigger food—er—men?'

"'Oh yes. Tons of fossil bones from prehistoric men are also found in the interior of the thermosaurus.'

"'Then,' said I, 'you, at least, had better go back to Captain McPeek's—'

"'Please turn around; don't be so foolish. I didn't say there was a live thermosaurus in the water, did I?'

"'Isn't there?'

"'Why, no!'

"My relief was genuine, but I thought of the rifle and looked suspiciously out to sea.

"'What's the Winchester for?' I asked.

"'Listen, and I will explain. Papa has found out—how, I do not exactly understand—that there is in the waters of the Gulf Stream the body of a thermosaurus. The creature must have been alive within a year or so. The impenetrable scale-armor that covers its body has, as far as papa knows, prevented its disintegration. We know that it is there still, or was there within a few months. Papa has reports and sworn depositions from steamer captains and seamen from a dozen different vessels, all corroborating one another in essential details. These stories, of course, get into the newspapers—sea-serpent stories—but papa knows that they confirm his theory that the huge body of this reptile is swinging along somewhere in the Gulf Stream.'

"She opened her sunshade and held it over her. I noticed that she deigned to give me the benefit of about one-eighth of it.

"'Your duty with that rifle is this: if we are fortunate enough to see the body of the thermosaurus come floating by, you are to take good aim and fire—fire rapidly every bullet in the magazine; then reload and fire again, and reload and fire as long as you have any cartridges left.'

"'A self-feeding Maxim is what I should have,' I said, with gentle sarcasm. 'Well, and suppose I make a sieve of this big lizard?'

"'Do you see these rings in the sand?' she asked.

"Sure enough, somebody had driven heavy piles deep into the sand all around us, and to the tops of these piles were attached steel rings, half buried under the spear-grass. We sat almost exactly in the centre of a circle of these rings.

"'The reason is this,' said Daisy; 'every bullet in your cartridges is steel-tipped and armor-piercing. To the base of each bullet is attached a thin wire of pallium. Pallium is that new metal, a thread of which, drawn out into finest wire, will hold a ton of iron suspended. Every bullet is fitted with minute coils of miles of this wire. When the bullet leaves the rifle it spins out this wire as a shot from a life-saver's mortar spins out and carries the life-line to a wrecked ship. The end of each coil of wire is attached to that cylinder under the magazine of your rifle. As soon as the shell is automatically ejected this wire flies out also. A bit of scarlet tape is fixed to the end, so that it will be easy to pick up. There is also a snap-clasp on the end, and this clasp fits those rings that you see in the sand. Now, when you begin firing, it is my duty to run and pick up the wire ends and attach them to the rings. Then, you see, we have the body of the thermosaurus full of bullets, every bullet anchored to the shore by tiny wires, each of which could easily hold a ton's strain.'

"I looked at her in amazement.

"'Then,' she added, calmly, 'we have captured the thermosaurus.'

"'Your father,' said I, at length, 'must have spent years of labor over this preparation.'

"'It is the work of a lifetime,' she said, simply.

"My face, I suppose, showed my misgivings.

"'It must not fail,' she added.

"'But—but we are nowhere near the Gulf Stream,' I ventured.

"Her face brightened, and she frankly held the sunshade over us both.

"'Ah, you don't know,' she said, 'what else papa has discovered. Would you believe that he has found a loop in the Gulf Stream—a genuine loop—that swings in here just outside of the breakers below? It is true! Everybody on Bong Island knows that there is a warm current off the coast, but nobody imagined it was merely a sort of backwater from the Gulf Stream that formed a great circular mill-race around the cone of a subterranean volcano, and rejoined the Gulf Stream off Cape Albatross. But it is! That is why papa bought a yacht three years ago and sailed about for two years so mysteriously. Oh, I did want to go with him so much!'

"'This,' said I, 'is most astonishing.'

"She leaned enthusiastically towards me, her lovely face aglow.

"'Isn't it?' she said; 'and to think that you and papa and I are the only people in the whole world who know this!'

"To be included in such a triology was very delightful.

"'Papa is writing the whole thing—I mean about the currents. He also has in preparation sixteen volumes on the thermosaurus. He said this morning that he was going to ask you to write the story first for some scientific magazine. He is certain that Professor Bruce Stoddard, of Columbia, will write the pamphlets necessary. This will give papa time to attend to the sixteen-volume work, which he expects to finish in three years.'

"'Let us first,' said I, laughing, 'catch our thermosaurus.'

"'We must not fail,' she said, wistfully.

"'We shall not fail,' I said, 'for I promise to sit on this sand-hill as long as I live—until a thermosaurus appears—if that is your wish, Miss Holroyd.'

"Our eyes met for an instant. She did not chide me, either, for not looking at the ocean. Her eyes were bluer, anyway.

"'I suppose,' she said, bending her head and absently pouring sand between her fingers— 'I suppose you think me a blue-stocking, or something odious?'

"'Not exactly,' I said. There was an emphasis in my voice that made her color. After a moment she laid the sunshade down, still open.

"'May I hold it?' I asked.

"She nodded almost imperceptibly.

"The ocean had turned a deep marine blue, verging on purple, that heralded a scorching afternoon. The wind died away; the odor of cedar and sweet-bay hung heavy in the air.

"In the sand at our feet an iridescent flower-beetle crawled, its metallic green-and-blue wings burning like a spark. Great gnats, with filmy, glittering wings, danced aimlessly above the young golden-rod; burnished crickets, inquisitive, timid, ran from under chips of driftwood, waved their antennæ at us, and ran back again. One by one the marbled tiger-beetles tumbled at our feet, dazed from the exertion of an aerial flight, then scrambled and ran a little way, or darted into the wire grass, where great, brilliant spiders eyed them askance from their gossamer hammocks.

"Far out at sea the white gulls floated and drifted on the water, or sailed up into the air to flap lazily for a moment and settle back among the waves. Strings of black surf-ducks passed, their strong wings tipping the surface of the water; single wandering coots whirled from the breakers into lonely flight towards the horizon.

"We lay and watched the little ring-necks running along the water's edge, now backing away from the incoming tide, now boldly wading after the undertow. The harmony of silence, the deep perfume, the mystery of waiting for that something that all await— what is it? love? death? or only the miracle of another morrow?— troubled me with vague restlessness. As sunlight casts shadows, happiness, too, throws a shadow, and the shadow is sadness.

"And so the morning wore away until Freda came with a cool-looking hamper. Then delicious cold fowl and lettuce sandwiches and champagne cup set our tongues wagging as only very young tongues can wag. Daisy went back with Freda after luncheon, leaving me a case of cigars, with a bantering smile. I dozed, half awake, keeping a partly closed eye on the ocean, where a faint gray streak showed plainly amid the azure water all around. That was the Gulf Stream loop.

"About four o'clock Frisby appeared with a bamboo shelter-tent, for which I was unaffectedly grateful.

"After he had erected it over me he stopped to chat a bit, but the conversation bored me, for he could talk of nothing but bill-posting.

"'You wouldn't ruin the landscape here, would you?' I asked.

"'Ruin it!' repeated Frisby, nervously. 'It's ruined now; there ain't a place to stick a bill.'

"'The snipe stick bills—in the sand,' I said, flippantly.

"There was no humor about Frisby. 'Do they?' he asked.

"I moved with a certain impatience.

"'Bills,' said Frisby, 'give spice an' variety to nature. They break the monotony of the everlastin' green and what-you-may-call-its.'

"I glared at him.

"'Bills,' he continued, 'are not easy to stick, lemme tell you, sir. Sign-paintin's a soft snap when it comes to bill-stickin'. Now, I guess I've stuck more bills onto New York State than ennybody.'

"'Have you?' I said, angrily.

"'Yes, siree! I always pick out the purtiest spots—kinder filled chuck full of woods and brooks and things; then I h'ist my paste-pot onto a rock, and I slather that rock with gum, and whoop she goes!'

"'Whoop what goes?'

"'The bill. I paste her onto the rock, with one swipe of the brush for the edges and a back-handed swipe for the finish—except when a bill is folded in two halves.'

"'And what do you do then?' I asked, disgusted.

"'Swipe twice,' said Frisby, with enthusiasm.

"'And you don't think it injures the landscape?'

"'Injures it!' he exclaimed, convinced that I was attempting to joke.

"I looked wearily out to sea. He also looked at the water and sighed sentimentally.

"'Floatin' buoys with bills onto 'em is a idea of mine,' he observed. 'That damn ocean is monotonous, ain't it?'

"I don't know what I might have done to Frisby—the rifle was so convenient—if his mean yellow dog had not waddled up at this juncture.

"'Hi, Davy, sic 'em!' said Frisby, expectorating upon a clam-shell and hurling it seaward. The cur watched the flight of the shell apathetically, then squatted in the sand and looked at his master.

"'Kinder lost his spirit,' said Frisby, 'ain't he? I once stuck a bill onto Davy, an' it come off, an' the paste sorter sickened him. He was hell on rats—once!'

"After a moment or two Frisby took himself off, whistling cheerfully to Davy, who followed him when he was ready. The rifle burned in my fingers.

"It was nearly six o'clock when the professor appeared, spade on shoulder, boots smeared with mud.

"'Well,' he said, 'nothing to report, Dick, my boy?'

"'Nothing, professor.'

"He wiped his shining face with his handkerchief and stared at the water. 'My calculations lead me to believe,' he said, 'that our prize may be due any day now. This theory I base upon the result of the report from the last sea-captain I saw. I cannot understand why some of these captains did not take the carcass in tow. They all say that they tried, but that the body sank before they could come within half a mile. The truth is, probably, that they did not stir a foot from their course to examine the thing.'

"'Have you ever cruised about for it?' I ventured.

"'For two years,' he said, grimly. 'It's no use; it's accident when a ship falls in with it. One captain reports it a thousand miles from where the last skipper spoke it, and always in the Gulf Stream. They think it is a different specimen every time, and the papers are teeming with sea-serpent fol-de-rol.'

"'Are you sure,' I asked, 'that it will swing into the coast on this Gulf Stream loop?'

"'I think I may say that it is certain to do so. I experimented with a dead right-whale. You may have heard of its coming ashore here last summer.'

"'I think I did,' said I, with a faint smile. The thing had poisoned the air for miles around.

"'But,' I continued, 'suppose it comes in the night?'

"He laughed.

"'There I am lucky. Every night this month, and every day, too, the current of the loop runs inland so far that even a porpoise would strand for at least twelve hours. Longer than that I have not experimented with, but I know that the shore trend of the loop runs across a long spur of the submerged volcanic mountain, and that anything heavier than a porpoise would scrape the bottom and be carried so slowly that at least twelve hours must elapse before the carcass could float again into deep water. There are chances of its stranding indefinitely, too, but I don't care to take those chances. That is why I have stationed you here, Dick.'

"He glanced again at the water, smiling to himself.

"'There is another question I want to ask,' I said, 'if you don't mind.'

"'Of course not!' he said, warmly.

"'What are you digging for?'

"'Why, simply for exercise. The doctor told me I was killing myself with my sedentary habits, so I decided to dig. I don't know a better exercise. Do you?'

"'I suppose not,' I murmured, rather red in the face. I wondered whether he'd mention fossils.

"'Did Daisy tell you why we are making our papier-maché thermosaurus?' he asked.

"I shook my head.

"'We constructed that from measurements I took from the fossil remains of the thermosaurus in the Metropolitan Museum. Professor Bruce Stoddard made the drawings. We set it up here, all ready to receive the skin of the carcass that I am expecting.'

"We had started towards home, walking slowly across the darkening dunes, shoulder to shoulder. The sand was deep, and walking was not easy.

"'I wish,' said I at last, 'that I knew why Miss Holroyd asked me not to walk on the beach. It's much less fatiguing.'

"'That,' said the professor, 'is a matter that I intend to discuss with you to-night.' He spoke gravely, almost sadly. I felt that something of unparalleled importance was soon to be revealed. So I kept very quiet, watching the ocean out of the corners of my eyes.

IV

"Dinner was ended. Daisy Holroyd lighted her father's pipe for him, and insisted on my smoking as much as I pleased. Then she sat down, and folded her hands like a good little girl, waiting for her father to make the revelation which I felt in my bones must be something out of the ordinary.

"The professor smoked for a while, gazing meditatively at his daughter; then, fixing his gray eyes on me, he said:

"'Have you ever heard of the kree—that Australian bird, half parrot, half hawk, that destroys so many sheep in New South Wales?'

"I nodded.

"'The kree kills a sheep by alighting on its back and tearing away the flesh with its hooked beak until a vital part is reached. You know that? Well, it has been discovered that the kree had pre-historic prototypes. These birds were enormous creatures, who preyed upon mammoths and mastodons, and even upon the great saurians. It has been conclusively proved that a few saurians have been killed by the ancestors of the kree, but the favorite food of these birds was undoubtedly the thermosaurus. It is believed that the birds attacked the eyes of the thermosaurus, and when, as was its habit, the mammoth creature turned on its back to claw them, they fell upon the thinner scales of its stomach armor and finally killed it. This, of course, is a theory, but we have almost absolute proofs of its correctness. Now, these two birds are known among scientists as the ekaf-bird and the ool-yllik. The names are Australian, in which country most of their remains have been unearthed. They lived during the Carboniferous period. Now, it is not generally known, but the fact is, that in 1801 Captain Ransom, of the British exploring vessel Gull, purchased from the natives of Tasmania the skin of an ekaf-bird that could not have been killed more than twenty-four hours previous to its sale. I saw this skin in the British Museum. It was labelled, "Unknown bird, probably extinct." It took me exactly a week to satisfy myself that it was actually the skin of an ekaf-bird. But that is not all, Dick,' continued the professor, excitedly. 'In 1854 Admiral Stuart, of our own navy, saw the carcass of a strange, gigantic bird floating along the southern coast of Australia. Sharks were after it, and before a boat could be lowered these miserable fish got it. But the good old admiral secured a few feathers and sent them to the Smithsonian. I saw them. They were not even labelled, but I knew that they were feathers from the ekaf-bird or its near relative, the ool-yllik.'

"I had grown so interested that I had leaned far across the table. Daisy, too, bent forward. It was only when the professor paused for a moment that I noticed how close together our heads were—Daisy's and mine. I don't think she realized it. She did not move.

"'Now comes the important part of this long discourse,' said the professor, smiling at our eagerness.

'Ever since the carcass of our derelict thermosaurus was first noticed, every captain who has seen it has also reported the presence of one or more gigantic birds in the neighborhood. These birds, at a great distance, appeared to be hovering over the carcass, but on the approach of a vessel they disappeared. Even in mid-ocean they were observed. When I heard about it I was puzzled. A month later I was satisfied that neither the ekaf-bird nor the ool-yllik was extinct. Last Monday I knew that I was right. I found forty-eight distinct impressions of the huge, seven-toed claw of the ekaf-bird on the beach here at Pine Inlet. You may imagine my excitement. I succeeded in digging up enough wet sand around one of these impressions to preserve its form. I managed to get it into a soap-box, and now it is there in my shop. The tide rose too rapidly for me to save the other footprints.'

"I shuddered at the possibility of a clumsy misstep on my part obliterating the impression of an ool-yllik.

"'That is the reason that my daughter warned you off the beach,' he said, mildly.

"'Hanging would have been too good for the vandal who destroyed such priceless prizes,' I cried out, in self-reproach.

"Daisy Holroyd turned a flushed face to mine and impulsively laid her hand on my sleeve. 'How could you know?' she said.

"'It's all right now,' said her father, emphasizing each word with a gentle tap of his pipe-bowl on the table-edge; 'don't be hard on yourself, Dick. You'll do yeoman's service yet.'

"It was nearly midnight, and still we chatted on about the thermosaurus, the ekaf-bird, and the ool-yllik, eagerly discussing the probability of the great reptile's carcass being in the vicinity. That alone seemed to explain the presence of these prehistoric birds at Pine Inlet.

"'Do they ever attack human beings?' I asked.

"The professor looked startled.

"'Gracious!' he exclaimed, 'I never thought of that. And Daisy running about out-of-doors! Dear me! It takes a scientist to be an unnatural parent!'

"His alarm was half real, half assumed; but, all the same, he glanced gravely at us both, shaking his handsome head, absorbed in thought. Daisy herself looked a little doubtful. As for me, my sensations were distinctly queer.

"'It is true,' said the professor, frowning at the wall, 'that human remains have been found associated with the bones of the ekaf-bird—I don't know how intimately. It is a matter to be taken into most serious consideration.'

"'The problem can be solved,' said I, 'in several ways. One is, to keep Miss Holroyd in the house—'

"'I shall not stay in,' cried Daisy, indignantly.

"We all laughed, and her father assured her that she should not be abused.

"'Even if I did stay in,' she said, 'one of these birds might alight on Master Dick.'

"She looked saucily at me as she spoke, but turned crimson when her father observed, quietly, 'You don't seem to think of me, Daisy!'

"'Of course I do,' she said, getting up and putting both arms around her father's neck; 'but Dick—as—as you call him—is so helpless and timid.'

"My blissful smile froze on my lips.

"'Timid!' I repeated.

"She came back to the table, making me a mocking reverence.

"'Do you think I am to be laughed at with impunity?' she said.

"'What are your other plans, Dick?" asked the professor. 'Daisy, let him alone, you little tease!'

"'One is, to haul a lot of cast-iron boilers along the dunes,' I said. 'If these birds come when the carcass floats in, and if they seem disposed to trouble us, we could crawl into the boilers and be safe.'

"'Why, that is really brilliant!' cried Daisy.

"'Be quiet, my child. Dick, the plan is sound and sensible and perfectly practical. McPeek and Frisby shall go for a dozen loads of boilers to-morrow.'

"'It will spoil the beauty of the landscape,' said Daisy, with a taunting nod to me.

"'And Frisby will probably attempt to cover them with bill-posters,' I added, laughing.

"'That,' said Daisy, 'I shall prevent, even at the cost of his life.' And she stood up, looking very determined.

"'Children, children,' protested the professor, 'go to bed—you bother me.'

"Then I turned deliberately to Miss Holroyd.

"'Good-night, Daisy,' I said.

"'Good-night, Dick,' she said, very gently.

V

The week passed quickly for me, leaving but few definite impressions. As I look back to it now I can see the long stretch of beach burning in the fierce sunlight, the endless meadows, with the glimmer of water in the distance, the dunes, the twisted cedars, the leagues of scintillating ocean, rocking, rocking, always rocking. In the starlit nights the curlew came in from the sand-bars by twos and threes; I could hear their querulous call as I lay in bed thinking. All day long the little ring-necks whistled from the shore. The plover answered them from distant, lonely inland pools. The great white gulls drifted like feathers upon the sea.

"One morning towards the end of the week, I, strolling along the dunes, came upon Frisby. He was bill-posting. I caught him red-handed.

"'This,' said I, 'must stop. Do you understand, Mr. Frisby?'

"He stepped back from his work, laying his head on one side, considering first me, then the bill that he had pasted on one of our big boilers.

"'Don't you like the color?' he asked. 'It goes well on them black boilers.'

"'Color! No, I don't like the color, either. Can't you understand that there are some people in the world who object to seeing patent-medicine advertisements scattered over a landscape?'

"'Hey?' he said, perplexed.

"'Will you kindly remove that advertisement?' I persisted.

"'Too late,' said Frisby; 'it's sot.'

"I was too disgusted to speak, but my disgust turned to anger when I perceived that, as far as the eye could reach, our boilers, lying from three to four hundred feet apart, were ablaze with yellow-and-red posters extolling the 'Eureka Liver Pill Company.'

"'It don't cost 'em nothin','' said Frisby, cheerfully; 'I done it fur the fun of it. Purty, ain't it?'

"'They are Professor Holroyd's boilers,' I said, subduing a desire to beat Frisby with my telescope. 'Wait until Miss Holroyd sees this work.'

"'Don't she like yeller and red?' he demanded, anxiously.

"'You'll find out,' said I.

"Frisby gaped at his handiwork and then at his yellow dog. After a moment he mechanically spat on a clam-shell and requested Davy to 'sic' it.

"'Can't you comprehend that you have ruined our pleasure in the landscape?' I asked, more mildly.

"'I've got some green bills,' said Frisby; 'I kin stick 'em over the yeller ones—'

"'Confound it,' said I, 'it isn't the color!'

"'Then,' observed Frisby, 'you don't like them pills. I've got some bills of the "Cropper Automobile" and a few of "Bagley, the Gents' Tailor"—'

"'Frisby,' said I, 'use them all—paste the whole collection over your dog and yourself—then walk off the cliff.'

"He sullenly unfolded a green poster, swabbed the boiler with paste, laid the upper section of the bill upon it, and plastered the whole bill down with a thwack of his brush. As I walked away I heard him muttering.

"Next day Daisy was so horrified that I promised to give Frisby an ultimatum. I found him with Freda, gazing sentimentally at his work, and I sent him back to the shop in a hurry, telling Freda at the same time that she could spend her leisure in providing Mr. Frisby with sand, soap, and a scrubbing-brush. Then I walked on to my post of observation.

"I watched until sunset. Daisy came with her father to hear my report, but there was nothing to tell, and we three walked slowly back to the house.

"In the evenings the professor worked on his volumes, the click of his type-writer sounding faintly behind his closed door. Daisy and I played chess sometimes; sometimes we played hearts. I don't remember that we ever finished a game of either—we talked too much.

"Our discussions covered every topic of interest: we argued upon politics; we skimmed over literature and music; we settled international differences; we spoke vaguely of human brotherhood. I say we slighted no subject of interest—I am wrong; we never spoke of love.

"Now, love is a matter of interest to ten people out of ten. Why it was that it did not appear to interest us is as interesting a question as love itself. We were young, alert, enthusiastic, inquiring. We eagerly absorbed theories concerning any curious phenomena in nature, as intellectual cocktails to stimulate discussion. And yet we did not discuss love. I do not say that we avoided it. No; the subject was too completely ignored for even that. And yet we found it very difficult to pass an hour separated. The professor noticed this, and laughed at us. We were not even embarrassed.

"Sunday passed in pious contemplation of the ocean. Daisy read a little in her prayer-book, and the professor threw a cloth over his type-writer and strolled up and down the sands. He may have been lost in devout abstraction; he may have been looking for foot-prints. As for me, my mind was very serene, and I was more than happy. Daisy read to me a little for my soul's sake, and the professor came up and said something cheerful. He also examined the magazine of my Winchester.

"That night, too, Daisy took her guitar to the sands and sang one or two Basque hymns. Unlike us, the Basques do not take their pleasures sadly. One of their pleasures is evidently religion.

"The big moon came up over the dunes and stared at the sea until the surface of every wave trembled with radiance. A sudden stillness fell across the world; the wind died out; the foam ran noiselessly across the beach; the cricket's rune was stilled.

"I leaned back, dropping one hand upon the sand. It touched another hand, soft and cool.

"After a while the other hand moved slightly, and I found that my own had closed above it. Presently one finger stirred a little—only a little—for our fingers were interlocked.

"On the shore the foam-froth bubbled and winked and glimmered in the moonlight. A star fell from the zenith, showering the night with incandescent dust.

"If our fingers lay interlaced beside us, her eyes were calm and serene as always, wide open, fixed upon the depths of a dark sky. And when her father rose and spoke to us, she did not withdraw her hand.

"'Is it late?' she asked, dreamily.

"'It is midnight, little daughter.'

"I stood up, still holding her hand, and aided her to rise. And when, at the door, I said good-night, she turned and looked at me for a little while in silence, then passed into her room slowly, with head still turned towards me.

"All night long I dreamed of her; and when the east whitened, I sprang up, the thunder of the ocean in my ears, the strong sea-wind blowing into the open window.

"'She is asleep,' I thought, and I leaned from the window and peered out into the east.

"The sea called to me, tossing its thousand arms; the soaring gulls, dipping, rising, wheeling above the sandbar, screamed and clamored for a playmate. I slipped into my bathing-suit, dropped from the window upon the soft sand, and in a moment had plunged head foremost into the surf, swimming beneath the waves towards the open sea.

"Under the tossing ocean the voice of the waters was in my ears—a low, sweet voice, intimate, mysterious. Through singing foam and broad, green, glassy depths, by whispering sandy channels atrail with sea-weed, and on, on, out into the vague, cool sea, I sped, rising to the top, sinking, gliding. Then at last I flung myself out of water, hands raised, and the clamor of the gulls filled my ears.

"As I lay, breathing fast, drifting on the sea, far out beyond the gulls I saw a flash of white, and an arm was lifted, signalling me.

"'Daisy!' I called.

"A clear hail came across the water, distinct on the sea-wind, and at the same instant we raised our hands and moved towards each other.

"How we laughed as we met in the sea! The white dawn came up out of the depths, the zenith turned to rose and ashes.

"And with the dawn came the wind—a great sea-wind, fresh, aromatic, that hurled our voices back into our throats and lifted the sheeted spray above our heads. Every wave, crowned with mist, caught us in a cool embrace, cradled us, and slipped away, only to leave us to another wave, higher, stronger, crested with opalescent glory, breathing incense.

"We turned together up the coast, swimming lightly side by side, but our words were caught up by the winds and whirled into the sky.

"We looked up at the driving clouds; we looked out upon the pallid waste of waters, but it was into each other's eyes we looked, wondering, wistful, questioning the reason of sky and sea. And there in each other's eyes we read the mystery, and we knew that earth and sky and sea were created for us alone.

"Drifting on by distant sands and dunes, her white fingers touching mine, we spoke, keying our tones to the wind's vast harmony. And we spoke of love.

"Gray and wide as the limitless span of the sky and the sea, the winds gathered from the world's ends to bear us on; but they were not familiar winds; for now, along the coast, the breakers curled and showed a million fangs, and the ocean stirred to its depths, uneasy, ominous, and the menace of its murmur drew us closer as we moved.

"Where the dull thunder and the tossing spray warned us from sunken reefs, we heard the harsh challenges of gulls; where the pallid surf twisted in yellow coils of spume above the bar, the singing sands murmured of treachery and secrets of lost souls agasp in the throes of silent undertows.

"But there was a little stretch of beach glimmering through the mountains of water, and towards this we turned, side by side. Around us the water grew warmer; the breath of the following waves moistened our cheeks; the water itself grew gray and strange about us.

"'We have come too far,' I said; but she only answered:

"'Faster, faster! I am afraid!' The water was almost hot now; its aromatic odor filled our lungs.

"'The Gulf loop!' I muttered. 'Daisy, shall I help you?'

"'No. Swim—close by me! Oh-h! Dick—'

"Her startled cry was echoed by another—a shrill scream, un-utterably horrible—and a great bird flapped from the beach, splashing and beating its pinions across the water with a thundering noise.

"Out across the waves it blundered, rising little by little from the water, and now, to my horror, I saw another monstrous bird swinging in the air above it, squealing as it turned on its vast wings. Before I could speak we touched the beach, and I half lifted her to the shore.

"'Quick!' I repeated. 'We must not wait.'

"Her eyes were dark with fear, but she rested a hand on my shoulder, and we crept up among the dune-grasses and sank down by the point of sand where the rough shelter stood, surrounded by the iron-ringed piles.

"She lay there, breathing fast and deep, dripping with spray. I had no power of speech left, but when I rose wearily to my knees and looked out upon the water my blood ran cold. Above the ocean, on the breast of the roaring wind, three enormous birds sailed, turning and wheeling among one another; and below, drifting with the gray stream of the Gulf loop, a colossal bulk lay half submerged—a gigantic lizard, floating belly upward.

"Then Daisy crept kneeling to my side and touched me, trembling from head to foot.

"'I know,' I muttered. 'I must run back for the rifle.'

"'And—and leave me?'

"I took her by the hand, and we dragged ourselves through the wire-grass to the open end of a boiler lying in the sand.

"She crept in on her hands and knees, and called to me to follow.

"'You are safe now,' I cried. 'I must go back for the rifle.'

"'The birds may—may attack you.'

"'If they do I can get into one of the other boilers,' I said. 'Daisy, you must not venture out until I come back. You won't, will you?'

"'No-o,' she whispered, doubtfully.

"'Then—good-bye.'

"'Good-bye,' she answered, but her voice was very small and still.

"'Good-bye,' I said again. I was kneeling at the mouth of the big iron tunnel; it was dark inside and I could not see her, but, before I was conscious of it, her arms were around my neck and we had kissed each other.

"I don't remember how I went away. When I came to my proper senses I was swimming along the coast at full speed, and over my head wheeled one of the birds, screaming at every turn.

"The intoxication of that innocent embrace, the close impress of her arms around my neck, gave me a strength and recklessness that neither fear nor fatigue could subdue. The bird above me did not even frighten me. I watched it over my shoulder, swimming strongly, with the tide now aiding me, now stemming my course; but I saw the shore passing quickly, and my strength increased, and I shouted when I came in sight of the house, and scrambled up on the sand, dripping and excited. There was nobody in sight, and I gave a last glance up into the air where the bird wheeled, still screeching, and hastened into the house. Freda stared at me in amazement as I seized the rifle and shouted for the professor.

"'He has just gone to town, with Captain McPeek in his wagon,' stammered Freda.

"'What!' I cried. 'Does he know where his daughter is?'

"'Miss Holroyd is asleep—not?' gasped Freda.

"'Where's Frisby?' I cried, impatiently.

"'Yimmie?' quavered Freda.

"'Yes, Jimmie; isn't there anybody here? Good Heavens! where's that man in the shop?'

"'He also iss gone,' said Freda, shedding tears, 'to buy papier-mache. Yimmie, he iss gone to post bills.'

"I waited to hear no more, but swung my rifle over my shoulder, and, hanging the cartridge-belt across my chest, hurried out and up the beach. The bird was not in sight.

"I had been running for perhaps a minute when, far up on the dunes, I saw a yellow dog rush madly through a clump of sweet-bay, and at the same moment a bird soared past, rose, and hung hovering just above the thicket. Suddenly the bird swooped; there was a shriek and a yelp from the cur, but the bird gripped it in one claw and beat its wings upon the sand, striving to rise. Then I saw

Frisby—paste, bucket, and brush raised—fall upon the bird, yelling lustily. The fierce creature relaxed its talons, and the dog
rushed on, squeaking with terror. The bird turned on Frisby and
sent him sprawling on his face, a sticky mass of paste and sand.
But this did not end the struggle. The bird, croaking horridly, flew
at the prostrate bill-poster, and the sand whirled into a pillar above
its terrible wings. Scarcely knowing what I was about, I raised my
rifle and fired twice. A scream echoed each shot, and the bird rose
heavily in a shower of sand; but two bullets were embedded in that
mass of foul feathers, and I saw the wires and scarlet tape uncoil-
ing on the sand at my feet. In an instant I seized them and passed
the ends around a cedar-tree, hooking the clasps tight. Then I cast
one swift glance upward, where the bird wheeled, screeching, anchored like a kite to the pallium wires; and I hurried on across the
dunes, the shells cutting my feet and the bushes tearing my wet
swimming-suit, until I dripped with blood from shoulder to ankle.
Out in the ocean the carcass of the thermosaurus floated, claws
outspread, belly glistening in the gray light, and over him circled
two birds. As I reached the shelter I knelt and fired into the mass
of scales, and at my first shot a horrible thing occurred—the lizard-
like head writhed, the slitted yellow eyes sliding open from the film
that covered them. A shudder passed across the undulating body,
the great scaled belly heaved, and one leg feebly clawed at the air.
    "The thing was still alive!
    "Crushing back the horror that almost paralyzed my hands, I
planted shot after shot into the quivering reptile, while it writhed
and clawed, striving to turn over and dive; and at each shot the
black blood spurted in long, slim jets across the water. And now
Daisy was at my side, pale and determined, swiftly clasping each
tape-marked wire to the iron rings in the circle around us. Twice I
filled the magazine from my belt, and twice I poured streams of
steel-tipped bullets into the scaled mass, twisting and shuddering
on the sea. Suddenly the birds steered towards us. I felt the wind
from their vast wings. I saw the feathers erect, vibrating. I saw the
spread claws outstretched, and I struck furiously at them, crying
to Daisy to run into the iron shelter. Backing, swinging my clubbed
rifle, I retreated, but I tripped across one of the taut pallium wires,

and in an instant the hideous birds were on me, and the bone in my forearm snapped like a pipe-stem at a blow from their wings. Twice I struggled to my knees, blinded with blood, confused, almost fainting; then I fell again, rolling into the mouth of the iron boiler.

"When I struggled back to consciousness Daisy knelt silently beside me, while Captain McPeek and Professor Holroyd bound up my shattered arm, talking excitedly. The pain made me faint and dizzy. I tried to speak and could not. At last they got me to my feet and into the wagon, and Daisy came, too, and crouched beside me, wrapped in oilskins to her eyes. Fatigue, lack of food, and excitement had combined with wounds and broken bones to extinguish the last atom of strength in my body; but my mind was clear enough to understand that the trouble was over and the thermosaurus safe.

"I heard McPeek say that one of the birds that I had anchored to a cedar-tree had torn loose from the bullets and had winged its way heavily out to sea. The professor answered: 'Yes, the ekaf-bird; the others were ool-ylliks. I'd have given my right arm to have secured them.' Then for a time I heard no more; but the jolting of the wagon over the dunes roused me to keenest pain, and I held out my right hand to Daisy. She clasped it in both of hers, and kissed it again and again.

"There is little more to add, I think. Professor Bruce Stoddard's scientific pamphlet will be published soon, to be followed by Professor Holroyd's sixteen volumes. In a few days the stuffed and mounted thermosaurus will be placed on free public exhibition in the arena of Madison Square Garden, the only building in the city large enough to contain the body of this immense winged reptile."

The young man hesitated, looking long and earnestly at Miss Barrison.

"Did you marry her?" she asked, softly.

"You wouldn't believe it," said the young man, earnestly— "you wouldn't believe it, after all that happened, if I should tell you that she married Professor Bruce Stoddard, of Columbia—would you?"

"Yes, I would," said Miss Barrison. "You never can tell what a girl will do."

"That story of yours," I said, "is to me the most wonderful and valuable contribution to nature study that it has ever been my fortune to listen to. You are fitted to write; it is your sacred mission to produce. Are you going to?"

"I am writing," said the young man, quietly, "a nature book. Sir Peter Grebe's magnificent monograph on the speckled titmouse inspired me. But nature study is not what I have chosen as my life's mission."

He looked dreamily across at Miss Barrison. "No, not natural phenomena," he repeated, "but unnatural phenomena. What Professor Hyssop has done for Columbia, I shall attempt to do for Harvard. In fact, I have already accepted the chair of Psychical Phenomena at Cambridge."

I gazed upon him with intense respect.

"A personal experience revealed to me my life's work," he went on, thoughtfully stroking his blond mustache. "If Miss Barrison would care to hear it—"

"Please tell it," she said, sweetly.

"I shall have to relate it clothed in that artificial garb known as literary style," he explained, deprecatingly.

"It doesn't matter," I said, "I never noticed any style at all in your story of the thermosaurus."

He smiled gratefully, and passed his hand over his face; a far-away expression came into his eyes, and he slowly began, hesitating, as though talking to himself:

I

"It was high noon in the city of Antwerp. From slender steeples floated the mellow music of the Flemish bells, and in the spire of the great cathedral across the square the cracked chimes clashed discords until my ears ached.

"When the fiend in the cathedral had jerked the last tuneless clang from the chimes, I removed my fingers from my ears and sat down at one of the iron tables in the court. A waiter, with his face shaved blue, brought me a bottle of Rhine wine, a tumbler of cracked ice, and a siphon.

"'Does monsieur desire anything else?' he inquired.

"'Yes—the head of the cathedral bell-ringer; bring it with vinegar and potatoes,' I said, bitterly. Then I began to ponder on my great-aunt and the Crimson Diamond.

"The white walls of the Hôtel St. Antoine rose in a rectangle around the sunny court, casting long shadows across the basin of the fountain. The strip of blue overhead was cloudless. Sparrows twittered under the eaves the yellow awnings fluttered, the flowers swayed in the summer breeze, and the jet of the fountain splashed among the water-plants.

"On the sunny side of the piazza the tables were vacant; on the shady side I was lazily aware that the tables behind me were occupied, but I was indifferent as to their occupants, partly because I shunned all tourists, partly because I was thinking of my great-aunt.

"Most old ladies are eccentric, but there is a limit, and my great-aunt had overstepped it. I had believed her to be wealthy—she died bankrupt. Still, I knew there was one thing she did possess, and

174

that was the famous Crimson Diamond. Now, of course, you know who my great-aunt was.

"Excepting the Koh-i-noor and the Regent, this enormous and unique stone was, as everybody knows, the most valuable gem in existence. Any ordinary person would have placed that diamond in a safe-deposit. My great-aunt did nothing of the kind. She kept it in a small velvet bag, which she carried about her neck. She never took it off, but wore it dangling openly on her heavy silk gown.

"In this same bag she also carried dried catnip-leaves, of which she was inordinately fond. Nobody but myself, her only living relative, knew that the Crimson Diamond lay among the sprigs of catnip in the little velvet bag.

"'Harold,' she would say, 'do you think I'm a fool? If I place the Crimson Diamond in any safe-deposit vault in New York, somebody will steal it, sooner or later.' Then she would nibble a sprig of catnip and peer cunningly at me. I loathed the odor of catnip and she knew it. I also loathed cats. This also she knew, and of course surrounded herself with a dozen. Poor old lady! One day she was found dead in her bed in her apartments at the Waldorf. The doctor said she died from natural causes. The only other occupant of her sleeping-room was a cat. The cat fled when we broke open the door, and I heard that she was received and cherished by some eccentric people in a neighboring apartment.

"Now, although my great-aunt's death was due to purely natural causes, there was one very startling and disagreeable feature of the case. The velvet bag containing the Crimson Diamond had disappeared. Every inch of the apartment was searched, the floors torn up, the walls dismantled, but the Crimson Diamond had vanished. Chief of Police Conlon detailed four of his best men on the case, and, as I had nothing better to do, I enrolled myself as a volunteer. I also offered $25,000 reward for the recovery of the gem. All New York was agog.

"The case seemed hopeless enough, although there were five of us after the thief. McFarlane was in London, and had been for a month, but Scotland Yard could give him no help, and the last I heard of him he was roaming through Surrey after a man with a white spot in his hair. Harrison had gone to Paris. He kept writing me that clews were plenty and the scent hot, but as Dennet, in Berlin, and Clancy, in Vienna, wrote me the same thing, I began to doubt these gentlemen's ability.

"'You say,' I answered Harrison, 'that the fellow is a Frenchman, and that he is now concealed in Paris; but Dennet writes me by the same mail that the thief is undoubtedly a German, and was seen yesterday in Berlin. To-day I received a letter from Clancy, assuring me that Vienna holds the culprit, and that he is an Austrian from Trieste. Now, for Heaven's sake,' I ended, 'let me alone and stop writing me letters until you have something to write about.'

"The night-clerk at the Waldorf had furnished us with our first clew. On the night of my aunt's death he had seen a tall, grave-faced man hurriedly leave the hotel. As the man passed the desk he removed his hat and mopped his forehead, and the night-clerk noticed that in the middle of his head there was a patch of hair as white as snow.

"We worked this clew for all it was worth, and, a month later, I received a cable despatch from Paris, saying that a man answering to the description of the Waldorf suspect had offered an enormous crimson diamond for sale to a jeweller in the Palais Royal. Unfortunately the fellow took fright and disappeared before the jeweller could send for the police, and since that time McFarlane in London, Harrison in Paris, Dennet in Berlin, and Clancy in Vienna had been chasing men with white patches on their hair until no gray-headed patriarch in Europe was free from suspicion. I myself had sleuthed it through England, France, Holland, and Belgium, and now I found myself in Antwerp at the Hôtel St. Antoine, without a clew that promised anything except another outrage on some respectable white-haired citizen. The case seemed hopeless enough, unless the thief tried again to sell the gem. Here was our only hope, for, unless he cut the stone into smaller ones, he had no more chance of selling it than he would have had if he had stolen the Venus of Milo and peddled her about the Rue de Seine. Even were he to cut up the stone, no respectable gem collector or jeweller would buy a crimson diamond without first notifying me; for although a few red stones are known to collectors, the color of the

Crimson Diamond was absolutely unique, and there was little probability of an honest mistake.

"Thinking of all these things, I sat sipping my Rhine wine in the shadow of the yellow awnings. A large white cat came sauntering by and stopped in front of me to perform her toilet, until I wished she would go away. After a while she sat up, licked her whiskers, yawned once or twice, and was about to stroll on, when, catching sight of me, she stopped short and looked me squarely in the face. I returned the attention with a scowl, because I wished to discourage any advances towards social intercourse which she might contemplate; but after a while her steady gaze disconcerted me, and I turned to my Rhine wine. A few minutes later I looked up again. The cat was still eying me.

"'Now what the devil is the matter with the animal,' I muttered; 'does she recognize in me a relative?'

"'Perhaps,' observed a man at the next table.

"'What do you mean by that?' I demanded.

"'What I say,' replied the man at the next table.

"I looked him full in the face. He was old and bald and appeared weak-minded. His age protected his impudence. I turned my back on him. Then my eyes fell on the cat again. She was still gazing earnestly at me.

"Disgusted that she should take such pointed public notice of me, I wondered whether other people saw it; I wondered whether there was anything peculiar in my own personal appearance. How hard the creature stared! It was most embarrassing.

"'What has got into that cat?' I thought. 'It's sheer impudence. It's an intrusion, and I won't stand it!' The cat did not move. I tried to stare her out of countenance. It was useless. There was aggressive inquiry in her yellow eyes. A sensation of uneasiness began to steal over me—a sensation of embarrassment not unmixed with awe. All cats looked alike to me, and yet there was something about this one that bothered me—something that I could not explain to myself, but which began to occupy me.

"She looked familiar—this Antwerp cat. An odd sense of having seen her before, of having been well acquainted with her in former years, slowly settled in my mind, and, although I could never remember the time when I had not detested cats, I was almost convinced that my relations with this Antwerp tabby had once been intimate if not cordial. I looked more closely at the animal. Then an idea struck me—an idea which persisted and took definite shape in spite of me. I strove to escape from it, to evade it, to stifle and smother it; an inward struggle ensued which brought the perspiration in beads upon my cheeks—a struggle short, sharp, decisive. It was useless—useless to try to put it from me—this idea so wretchedly bizarre, so grotesque and fantastic, so utterly inane— it was useless to deny that the cat bore a distinct resemblance to my great-aunt!

"I gazed at her in horror. What enormous eyes the creature had!

"'Blood is thicker than water,' said the man at the next table.

"'What does he mean by that?' I muttered, angrily, swallowing a tumbler of Rhine wine and seltzer. But I did not turn. What was the use?

"'Chattering old imbecile,' I added to myself, and struck a match, for my cigar was out; but, as I raised the match to relight it, I encountered the cat's eyes again. I could not enjoy my cigar with the animal staring at me, but I was justly indignant, and I did not intend to be routed. 'The idea! Forced to leave for a cat!' I sneered. 'We will see who will be the one to go!' I tried to give her a jet of seltzer from the siphon, but the bottle was too nearly empty to carry far. Then I attempted to lure her nearer, calling her in French, German, and English, but she did not stir. I did not know the Flemish for 'cat.'

"'She's got a name, and won't come,' I thought. 'Now, what under the sun can I call her?'

"'Aunty,' suggested the man at the next table.

"I sat perfectly still. Could that man have answered my thoughts?—for I had not spoken aloud. Of course not—it was a coincidence—but a very disgusting one.

"'Aunty,' I repeated, mechanically, 'aunty, aunty—good gracious, how horribly human that cat looks!' Then, somehow or other, Shakespeare's words crept into my head and I found myself repeating: 'The soul of my grandam might haply inhabit a bird; the soul of—nonsense!' I growled— 'it isn't printed correctly! One might possibly say, speaking in poetical metaphor, that the soul of a bird might haply inhabit one's grandam—' I stopped short, flushing painfully. 'What awful rot!' I murmured, and lighted another cigar. The cat was still staring; the cigar went out. I grew more and more nervous. 'What rot!' I repeated. 'Pythagoras must have been an ass, but I do believe there are plenty of asses alive to-day who swallow that sort of thing.'

"'Who knows ?' sighed the man at the next table, and I sprang to my feet and wheeled about. But I only caught a glimpse of a pair of frayed coat-tails and a bald head vanishing into the dining-room. I sat down again, thoroughly indignant. A moment later the cat got up and went away.

II

"Daylight was fading in the city of Antwerp. Down into the sea sank the sun, tinting the vast horizon with flakes of crimson, and touching with rich deep undertones the tossing waters of the Scheldt. Its glow fell like a rosy mantle over red-tiled roofs and meadows; and through the haze the spires of twenty churches pierced the air like sharp, gilded flames. To the west and south the green plains, over which the Spanish armies tramped so long ago, stretched away until they met the sky; the enchantment of the after-glow had turned old Antwerp into fairy-land; and sea and sky and plain were beautiful and vague as the night-mists floating in the moats below.

"Along the sea-wall from the Rubens Gate all Antwerp strolled, and chattered, and flirted, and sipped their Flemish wines from slender Flemish glasses, or gossiped over krugs of foaming beer.

"From the Scheldt came the cries of sailors, the creaking of cordage, and the puff! puff! of the ferry-boats. On the bastions of the fortress opposite, a bugler was standing. Twice the mellow notes of the bugle came faintly over the water, then a great gun thundered from the ramparts, and the Belgian flag fluttered along the lanyards to the ground.

"I leaned listlessly on the sea-wall and looked down at the Scheldt below. A battery of artillery was embarking for the fortress.

The tublike transport lay hissing and whistling in the slip, and the stamping of horses, the rumbling of gun and caisson, and the sharp cries of the officers came plainly to the ear.

"When the last caisson was aboard and stowed, and the last trooper had sprung jingling to the deck, the transport puffed out into the Scheldt, and I turned away through the throng of promenaders, and found a little table on the terrace, just outside of the pretty cafe. And as I sat down I became aware of a girl at the next table—a girl all in white—the most ravishingly and distractingly pretty girl that I had ever seen. In the agitation of the moment I forgot my name, my fortune, my aunt, and the Crimson Diamond—all these I forgot in a purely human impulse to see clearly; and to that end I removed my monocle from my left eye. Some moments later I came to myself and feebly replaced it. It was too late; the mischief was done. I was not aware at first of the exact state of my feelings—for I had never been in love more than three or four times in all my life—but I did know that at her request I would have been proud to stand on my head, or turn a flip-flap into the Scheldt.

"I did not stare at her, but I managed to see her most of the time when her eyes were in another direction. I found myself drinking something which a waiter brought, presumably upon an order which I did not remember having given. Later I noticed that it was a loathsome drink which the Belgians call 'American grog,' but I swallowed it and lighted a cigarette. As the fragrant cloud rose in the air, a voice, which I recognized with a chill, broke into my dream of enchantment.

"Could he have been there all the while—there sitting beside that vision in white? His hat was off, and the ocean-breezes whispered about his bald head. His frayed coat-tails were folded carefully over his knees, and between the thumb and forefinger of his left hand he balanced a bad cigar. He looked at me in a mildly cheerful way, and said, 'I know now.'

"'Know what?' I asked, thinking it better to humor him, for I was convinced that he was mad.

"'I know why cats bite.'

"This was startling. I hadn't an idea what to say.

"'I know why,' he repeated; 'can you guess why?' There was a covert tone of triumph in his voice and he smiled encouragement. 'Come, try and guess,' he urged.

"I told him that I was unequal to problems.

"'Listen, young man,' he continued, folding his coattails closely about his legs— 'try to reason it out: why should cats bite? Don't you know? I do.'

"He looked at me anxiously.

"'You take no interest in this problem?' he demanded.

"'Oh yes.'

"'Then why do you not ask me why?' he said, looking vaguely disappointed.

"'Well,' I said, in desperation, 'why do cats bite?—hang it all!' I thought, 'it's like a burned-cork show, and I'm Mr. Bones and he's Tambo!'

"Then he smiled gently. 'Young man,' he said, 'cats bite because they feed on catnip. I have reasoned it out.'

"I stared at him in blank astonishment. Was this benevolent-looking old party poking fun at me? Was he paying me up for the morning's snub? Was he a malignant and revengeful old party, or was he merely feeble-minded? Who might he be? What was he doing here in Antwerp—what was he doing now?—for the bald one had turned familiarly to the beautiful girl in white.

"'Wilhelmina,' he said, 'do you feel chilly?' The girl shook her head.

"'Not in the least, papa.'

"'Her father!' I thought— 'her father!' Thank God she did not say 'popper'!

"'I have been to the Zoo to-day,' announced the bald one, turning towards me.

"'Ah, indeed,' I observed; 'er—I trust you enjoyed it.'

"'I have been contemplating the apes,' he continued, dreamily. 'Yes, contemplating the apes.'

"I tried to look interested.

"'Yes, the apes,' he murmured, fixing his mild eyes on me. Then he leaned towards me confidentially and whispered, 'Can you tell me what a monkey thinks?'

"'I cannot—' I replied, sharply.

"'Ah,' he sighed, sinking back in his chair, and patting the slender hand of the girl beside him— 'ah, who can tell what a monkey thinks?' His gentle face lulled my suspicions, and I replied, very gravely:

"'Who can tell whether they think at all?'

"'True, true! Who can tell whether they think at all; and if they do think, all! who can tell what they think?'

"'But,' I began, 'if you can't tell whether they think at all, what's the use of trying to conjecture what they *would* think if they *did* think?'

"He raised his hand in deprecation. 'Ah, it is exactly that which is of such absorbing interest—exactly that! It is the abstruseness of the proposition which stimulates research—which stirs profoundly the brain of the thinking world. The question is of vital and instant importance. Possibly you have already formed an opinion.'

"I admitted that I had thought but little on the subject.

"'I doubt,' he continued, swathing his knees in his coat-tails—'I doubt whether you have given much attention to the subject lately discussed by the Boston Dodo Society of Pythagorean Research.'

"'I am not sure,' I said, politely, 'that I recall that particular discussion. May I ask what was the question brought up?'

"'The *Felis domestica* question.'

"'Ah, that must indeed be interesting! And—er— what may be the *Felis do—do—*'

"'*Domestica*—not dodo. *Felis domestica*, the common or garden cat.'

"'Indeed,' I murmured.

"'You are not listening,' he said.

"I only half heard him. I could not turn my eyes from his daughter's face.

"'Cat!' shouted the bald one, and I almost leaped from my chair. 'Are you deaf?' he inquired, sympathetically.

"'No—oh no!' I replied, coloring with confusion; 'you were— pardon me—you were—er—speaking of the dodo. Extraordinary bird that—'

"'I was not discussing the dodo,' he sighed. 'I was speaking of cats.'

"'Of course,' I said.

"'The question is,' he continued, twisting his frayed coat-tails into a sort of rope— 'the question is, how are we to ameliorate the present condition and social status of our domestic cats?'

"'Feed 'em,' I suggested.

"He raised both hands. They were eloquent with patient expostulation. 'I mean their spiritual condition,' he said.

"I nodded, but my eyes reverted to that exquisite face. She sat silent, her eyes fixed on the waning flecks of color in the western sky.

"'Yes,' repeated the bald one, 'the spiritual welfare of our domestic cats.'

"'Toms and tabbies?' I murmured.

"'Exactly,' he said, tying a large knot in his coat-tails.

"'You will ruin your coat,' I observed.

"'Papa!' exclaimed the girl, turning in dismay, as that gentleman gave a guilty start, 'stop it at once!'

"He smiled apologetically and made a feeble attempt to conceal his coat-tails.

"'My dear,' he said, with gentle deprecation, 'I am so absent-minded—I always do it in the heat of argument.'

"The girl rose, and, bending over her untidy parent, deftly untied the knot in his flapping coat. When he was disentangled, she sat down and said, with a ghost of a smile, 'He is so very absent-minded.'

"'Your father is evidently a great student,' I ventured, pleasantly. How I pitied her, tied to this old lunatic!

"'Yes, he is a great student,' she said, quietly.

"'I am,' he murmured; 'that's what makes me so absent-minded. I often go to bed and forget to sleep.' Then, looking at me, he asked me my name, adding, with a bow, that his name was P. Royal Wyeth, Professor of Pythagorean Research and Abstruse Paradox.

"'My first name is Penny—named after Professor Penny, of Harvard,' he said; 'but I seldom use my first name in connection with my second, as the combination suggests a household remedy of penetrating odor.'

"'My name is Kensett,' I said, 'Harold Kensett, of New York.'

"'Student?'

"'Er—a little.'

"'Student of diamonds?'

"I smiled. 'Oh, I see you know who my great-aunt was,' I said.

"'I know her,' he said.

"'Ah—perhaps you are unaware that my great-aunt is not now living.'

"'I know her,' he repeated, obstinately.

"I bowed. What a crank he was!

"'What do you study? You don't fiddle away all your time, do you?' he asked.

"Now that was just what I did, but I was not pleased to have Miss Wyeth know it. Although my time was chiefly spent in killing time, I had once, in a fit of energy, succeeded in writing some verses 'To a Tomtit,' so I evaded a humiliating confession by saying that I had done a little work in ornithology.

"'Good!' cried the professor, beaming all over. 'I knew you were a fellow-scientist. Possibly you are a brother-member of the Boston Dodo Society of Pythagorean Research. Are you a dodo?'

"I shook my head. 'No, I am not a dodo.'

"'Only a jay?'

"'A—what?' I said, angrily.

"'A jay. We call the members of the Junior Ornithological Jay Society of New York, jays, just as we refer to ourselves as dodos. Are you not even a jay?'

"'I am not,' I said, watching him suspiciously.

"'I must convert you, I see,' said the professor, smiling.

"'I'm afraid I do not approve of Pythagorean research,' I began, but the beautiful Miss Wyeth turned to me very seriously, and, looking me frankly in the eyes, said:

"'I trust you will be open to conviction.'

"'Good Lord!' I thought. 'Can she be another lunatic?' I looked at her steadily. What a little beauty she was! She also, then, belonged to the Pythagoreans—a sect I despised. Everybody knows all about the Pythagorean craze, its rise in Boston, its rapid spread, and its subsequent consolidation with mental and Christian science, theosophy, hypnotism, the Salvation Army, the Shakers, the Dunkards, and the mind-cure cult, upon a business basis. I had hitherto regarded all Pythagoreans with the same scornful indifference which I accorded to the faith-curists; being a member of no particular church, I was scarcely prepared to take any of them seriously. Least of all did I approve of the 'business basis,' and I looked very much askance indeed at the 'Scientific and Religious Trust Company,' duly incorporated and generally known as the Pythagorean Trust, which, consolidating with mind-curists, faith-curists, and other flourishing salvation syndicates, actually claimed a place among ordinary trusts, and at the same time pretended to a control over man's future life. No, I could never listen—I was ashamed of even entertaining the notion, and I shook my head.

"'No, Miss Wyeth, I am afraid I do not care to listen to any reasoning on this subject.'

"'Don't you believe in Pythagoras?' demanded the professor, subduing his excitement with difficulty, and adding another knot to his coat-tails.

"'No,' I said, 'I do not.'

"'How do you know you don't?' inquired the professor.

"'Because,' I said, firmly, 'it is nonsense to say that the soul of a human being can inhabit a hen!'

"'Put it in a more simplified form!' insisted the professor. 'Do you believe that the soul of a hen can inhabit a human being?'

"'No, I don't!'

"'Did you ever hear of a hen-pecked man?' cried the professor, his voice ending in a shout.

"I nodded, intensely annoyed.

"'Will you listen to reason, then?' he continued, eagerly.

"'No,' I began, but I caught Miss Wyeth's blue eyes fixed on mine with an expression so sad, so sweetly appealing, that I faltered.

"'Yes, I will listen,' I said, faintly.

"'Will you become my pupil?' insisted the professor.

"I was shocked to find myself wavering, but my eyes were looking into hers, and I could not disobey what I read there. The longer I looked the greater inclination I felt to waver. I saw that I was going to give in, and, strangest of all, my conscience did not trouble me. I felt it coming—a sort of mild exhilaration took possession of me. For the first time in my life I became reckless—I even gloried in my recklessness.

"'Yes, yes,' I cried, leaning eagerly across the table, 'I shall be glad—delighted! Will you take me as your pupil?' My single eye-glass fell from its position unheeded. 'Take me! Oh, will you take me?' I cried. Instead of answering, the professor blinked rapidly at me for a moment. I imagined his eyes had grown bigger, and were assuming a greenish tinge. The corners of his mouth began to quiver, emitting queer, caressing little noises, and he rapidly added knot after knot to his twitching coat-tails. Suddenly he bent forward across the table until his nose almost touched mine. The pupils of his eyes expanded, the iris assuming a beautiful, changing, golden-green tinge, and his coat-tails switched violently. Then he began to mew.

"I strove to rouse myself from my paralysis—I tried to shrink back, for I felt the end of his cold nose touch mine. I could not move. The cry of terror died in my straining throat, my hands tightened convulsively; I was incapable of speech or motion. At the same time my brain became wonderfully clear. I began to remember everything that had ever happened to me— everything that I had ever done or said. I even remembered things that I had neither done nor said; I recalled distinctly much that had never happened. How fresh and strong my memory! The past was like a mirror, crystal clear, and there, in glorious tints and hues, the scenes of my childhood grew and glowed and faded, and gave place to newer and more splendid scenes. For a moment the episode of the cat at the Hôtel St. Antoine flashed across my mind. When it vanished a chilly stupor slowly clouded my brain; the scenes, the memories, the brilliant colors, faded, leaving me enveloped in a gray vapor, through which the two great eyes of the professor twinkled with a murky light. A peculiar longing stirred me—a strange yearning for something, I knew not what—but, oh! how I longed and yearned for it! Slowly this indefinite, incomprehensible longing became a living pain. Ah, how I suffered, and how the vapors seemed to crowd around me! Then, as at a great distance, I heard her voice, sweet, imperative:

"'Mew!' she said.

"For a moment I seemed to see the interior of my own skull, lighted as by a flash of fire; the rolling eyeballs, veined in scarlet, the glistening muscles quivering along the jaw, the humid masses of the convoluted brain; then awful darkness—a darkness almost tangible—an utter blackness, through which now seemed to creep a thin, silver thread, like a river crawling across a world—like a thought gliding to the brain—like a song, a thin, sharp song which some distant voice was singing— which I was singing.

"And I knew that I was mewing!

"I threw myself back in my chair and mewed with all my heart. Oh, that heavy load which was lifted from my breast! How good, how satisfying it was to mew! And how I did miaul and yowl!

"I gave myself up to it, heart and soul; my whole being thrilled with the passionate outpourings of a spirit freed. My voice trembled in the upper bars of a feline love-song, quavered, descended, swelling again into an intimation that I brooked no rival, and ended with a magnificent crescendo.

"I finished, somewhat abashed, and glanced askance at the professor and his daughter, but the one sat nonchalantly disentangling his coat-tails, and the other was apparently absorbed in the distant landscape. Evidently they did not consider me ridiculous. Flushing painfully, I turned in my chair to see how my grewsome solo had affected the people on the terrace. Nobody even looked at me. This, however, gave me little comfort, for, as I began to realize what I had done, my mortification and rage knew no bounds. I was ready to die of shame. What on earth had induced me to mew? I looked wildly about for escape—I would leap up—rush home to bury my burning face in my pillows, and, later, in the friendly cabin of a homeward-bound steamer. I would fly—fly at once! Woe to the man who blocked my way! I started to my feet, but at that moment I caught Miss Wyeth's eyes fixed on mine.

"'Don't go,' she said.

"What in Heaven's name lay in those blue eyes? I slowly sank back into my chair.

"Then the professor spoke: 'Wilhelmina, I have just received a despatch.'

"'Where from, papa?'

"'From India. I'm going at once.'

"She nodded her head, without turning her eyes from the sea. 'Is it important, papa?'

"'I should say so. The cashier of the local trust has compromised an astral body, and has squandered on her all our funds, including a lot of first mortgages on Nirvana. I suppose he's been dabbling in futures and is short in his accounts. I sha'n't be gone long.'

"'Then, good-night, papa,' she said, kissing him; 'try to be back by eleven.' I sat stupidly staring at them.

"'Oh, it's only to Bombay—I sha'n't go to Thibet to-night—good-night, my dear,' said the professor.

"Then a singular thing occurred. The professor had at last succeeded in disentangling his coat-tails, and now, jamming his hat over his ears, and waving his arms with a batlike motion, he climbed upon the seat of his chair and ejaculated the word 'Presto!' Then I found my voice.

"'Stop him!' I cried, in terror.

"'Presto! Presto!' shouted the professor, balancing himself on the edge of his chair and waving his arms majestically, as if preparing for a sudden flight across the Scheldt; and, firmly convinced that he not only meditated it, but was perfectly capable of attempting it, I covered my eyes with my hands.

"'Are you ill, Mr. Kensett?' asked the girl, quietly.

"I raised my head indignantly. 'Not at all, Miss Wyeth, only I'll bid you good-evening, for this is the nineteenth century, and I'm a Christian.'

"'So am I,' she said. 'So is my father.'

"'The devil he is,' I thought.

"Her next words made me jump.

"'Please do not be profane, Mr. Kensett.'

"How did she know I was profane? I had not spoken a word! Could it be possible she was able to read my thoughts? This was too much, and I rose.

"'I have the honor to bid you good-evening,' I began, and reluctantly turned to include the professor, expecting to see that gentleman balancing himself on his chair. The professor's chair was empty.

"'Oh,' said the girl, smiling, 'my father has gone.'

"'Gone! Where?'

"'To—to India, I believe.'

"I sank helplessly into my own chair.

"'I do not think he will stay very long—he promised to return by eleven,' she said, timidly.

"I tried to realize the purport of it all. 'Gone to India? Gone! How? On a broomstick? Good Heavens,' I murmured, 'am I insane?'

"'Perfectly,' she said, 'and I am tired; you may take me back to the hotel.'

"I scarcely heard her; I was feebly attempting to gather up my numbed wits. Slowly I began to comprehend the situation, to review the startling and humiliating events of the day. At noon, in the court of the Hôtel St. Antoine, I had been annoyed by a man and a cat. I had retired to my own room and had slept until dinner. In the evening I met two tourists on the sea-wall promenade. I had been beguiled into conversation—yes, into intimacy with these two tourists! I had had the intention of embracing the faith of Pythagoras! Then I had mewed like a cat with all the strength of my lungs. Now the male tourist vanishes—and leaves me in charge of the female tourist, alone and at night in a strange city! And now the female tourist proposes that I take her home!

"With a remnant of self-possession I groped for my eye-glass, seized it, screwed it firmly into my eye, and looked long and earnestly at the girl. As I looked, my eyes softened, my monacle dropped, and I forgot everything in the beauty and purity of the face before me. My heart began to beat against my stiff, white waistcoat. Had I dared—yes, dared to think of this wondrous little beauty as a female tourist? Her pale, sweet face, turned towards the sea, seemed to cast a spell upon the night. How loud my heart was beating! The yellow moon floated, half dipping in the sea, flooding land and water with enchanted lights. Wind and wave seemed to feel the spell of her eyes, for the breeze died away, the heaving Scheldt tossed noiselessly, and the dark Dutch luggers swung idly on the tide with every sail adroop.

"A sudden hush fell over land and water, the voices on the promenade were stilled; little by little the shadowy throng, the terrace, the sea itself vanished, and I only saw her face, shadowed against the moon.

"It seemed as if I had drifted miles above the earth, through all space and eternity, and there was naught between me and high heaven but that white face. Ah, how I loved her! I knew it—I never doubted it. Could years of passionate adoration touch her heart— her little heart, now beating so calmly with no thought of love to startle it from its quiet and send it fluttering against the gentle breast? In her lap her clasped hands tightened—her eyelids drooped as though some pleasant thought was passing. I saw the color dye her temples, I saw the blue eyes turn, half frightened, to my own, I saw—and I knew she had read my thoughts. Then we both rose, side by side, and she was weeping softly, yet for my life I dared not speak. She turned away, touching her eyes with a bit of lace, and I sprang to her side and offered her my arm.

"'You cannot go back alone,' I said.

"She did not take my arm.

"'Do you hate me, Miss Wyeth?'

"'I am very tired,' she said; 'I must go home.'

"'You cannot go alone.'

"'I do not care to accept your escort.'

"'Then—you send me away?'

"'No,' she said, in a hard voice. 'You can come if you like.' So I humbly attended her to the Hôtel St. Antoine.

III

As we reached the Place Verte and turned into the court of the hotel, the sound of the midnight bells swept over the city, and a horse-car jingled slowly by on its last trip to the railroad station.

"We passed the fountain, bubbling and splashing in the moon-lit court, and, crossing the square, entered the southern wing of the hotel. At the foot of the stairway she leaned for an instant against the banisters.

"'I am afraid we have walked too fast,' I said.

"She turned to me coldly. 'No—conventionalities must be observed. You were quite right in escaping as soon as possible.'

"'But,' I protested, 'I assure you—'

"She gave a little movement of impatience. 'Don't,' she said, 'you tire me—conventionalities tire me. Be satisfied—nobody has seen you.'

"'You are cruel,' I said, in a low voice— 'what do you think I care for conventionalities?'

"'You care everything—you care what people think, and you try to do what they say is good form. You never did such an original thing in your life as you have just done.'

"'You read my thoughts,' I exclaimed, bitterly. 'It is not fair—'

"'Fair or not, I know what you consider me—ill-bred, common, pleased with any sort of attention. Oh! why should I waste one word—one thought on you?'

"'Miss Wyeth—' I began, but she interrupted me.

"'Would you dare tell me what you think of me?—Would you dare tell me what you think of my father?'

"I was silent. She turned and mounted two steps of the stairway, then faced me again.

"'Do you think it was for my own pleasure that I permitted myself to be left alone with you? Do you imagine that I am flattered by your attention?—do you venture to think I ever could be? How dared you think what you did think there on the sea-wall?'

"'I cannot help my thoughts!' I replied.

"'You turned on me like a tiger when you awoke from your trance. Do you really suppose that you mewed? Are you not aware that my father hypnotized you?'

"'No—I did not know it,' I said. The hot blood tingled in my finger-tips, and I looked angrily at her.

"'Why do you imagine that I waste my time on you?' she said. 'Your vanity has answered that question—now let your intelligence answer it. I am a Pythagorean; I have been chosen to bring in a convert, and you were the convert selected for me by the Mahatmas of the Consolidated Trust Company. I have followed you from New York to Antwerp, as I was bidden, but now my courage fails, and I shrink from fulfilling my mission, knowing you to be the type of man you are. If I could give it up—if I could only go away—never, never again to see you! Ah, I fear they will not permit it!—until my mission is accomplished. Why was I chosen—I, with a woman's heart and a woman's pride. I—I hate you!'

"'I love you,' I said, slowly.

"She paled and looked away.

"'Answer me,' I said.

"Her wide, blue eyes turned back again, and I held them with mine. At last she slowly drew a long-stemmed rose from the bunch at her belt, turned, and mounted the shadowy staircase. For a moment I thought I saw her pause on the landing above, but the moonlight was uncertain. After waiting for a long time in vain, I moved away, and in going raised my hand to my face, but I stopped short, and my heart stopped too, for a moment. In my hand I held a long-stemmed rose.

"With my brain in a whirl I crept across the court and mounted the stairs to my room. Hour after hour I walked the floor, slowly at first, then more rapidly, but it brought no calm to the fierce tumult of my thoughts, and at last I dropped into a chair before the empty fireplace, burying my head in my hands.

"Uncertain, shocked, and deadly weary, I tried to think—I strove to bring order out of the chaos in my brain, but I only sat staring at the long-stemmed rose. Slowly I began to take a vague pleasure in its heavy perfume, and once I crushed a leaf between my palms, and, bending over, drank in the fragrance.

"Twice my lamp flickered and went out, and twice, treading softly, I crossed the room to relight it. Twice I threw open the door, thinking that I heard some sound without. How close the air was!—how heavy and hot! And what was that strange, subtle odor which had insensibly filled the room? It grew stronger and more penetrating, and I began to dislike it, and to escape it I buried my nose in the half-opened rose. Horror! The odor came from the rose—and the rose itself was no longer a rose—not even a flower now—it was only a bunch of catnip; and I dashed it to the floor and ground it under my heel.

"'Mountebank!' I cried, in a rage. My anger grew cold—and I shivered, drawn perforce to the curtained window. Something was there, outside. I could not hear it, for it made no sound, but I knew it was there, watching me. What was it? The damp hair stirred on my head. I touched the heavy curtains. Whatever was outside them sprang up, tore at the window, and then rushed away.

"Feeling very shaky, I crept to the window, opened it, and leaned out. The night was calm. I heard the fountain splashing in the moonlight and the sea-winds soughing through the palms. Then I closed the window and turned back into the room; and as I stood there a sudden breeze, which could not have come from without, blew sharply in my face, extinguishing the candle and sending the long curtains bellying out into the room. The lamp on the table flashed and smoked and sputtered; the room was littered with fly-ing papers and catnip leaves. Then the strange wind died away, and somewhere in the night a cat snarled.

"I turned desperately to my trunk and flung it open. Into it I threw everything I owned, pell-mell, closed the lid, locked it, and, seizing my mackintosh and travelling-bag, ran down the stairs, crossed the court, and entered the night-office of the hotel. There I called up the sleepy clerk, settled my reckoning, and sent a por-ter for a cab.

"'Now,' I said, 'what time does the next train leave?'

"'The next train for where?'

"'Anywhere!'

"The clerk locked the safe, and, carefully keeping the desk be-tween himself and me, motioned the office-boy to look at the time-tables.

"'Next train, 2.10. Brussels—Paris,' read the boy.

"At that moment the cab rattled up by the curbstone, and I sprang in while the porter tossed my traps on top. Away we bumped over the stony pavement, past street after street lighted dimly by tall gas-lamps, and alley after alley brilliant with the glare of villanous all-night café-concerts, and then, turning, we rumbled past the Circus and the Eldorado, and at last stopped with a jolt before the Brussels station.

"I had not a moment to lose. 'Paris!' I cried— 'first-class!' and, pocketing the book of coupons, hurried across the platform to where the Brussels train lay. A guard came running up, flung open the door of a first-class carriage, slammed and locked it after I had jumped in, and the long train glided from the arched station out into the starlit morning.

"I was all alone in the compartment. The wretched lamp in the roof flickered dimly, scarcely lighting the stuffy box. I could not see to read my time-table, so I wrapped my legs in the travelling-rug and lay back, staring out into the misty morning. Trees, walls, telegraph-poles flashed past, and the cinders drove in showers against the rattling windows. I slept at times, fitfully, and once, springing up, peered sharply at the opposite seat, possessed with the idea that somebody was there.

"When the train reached Brussels I was sound asleep, and the guard awoke me with difficulty.

"'Breakfast, sir?' he asked.

"'Anything,' I sighed, and stepped out to the platform, rubbing my legs and shivering. The other passengers were already break-fasting in the station cafe, and I joined them and managed to swallow a cup of coffee and a roll.

"The morning broke gray and cloudy, and I bundled myself into my mackintosh for a tramp along the platform. Up and down I stamped, puffing a cigar, and digging my hands deep in my pockets, while the other passengers huddled into the warmer compartments of the train or stood watching the luggage being lifted into the forward mail-carriage. The wait was very long; the hands of the great clock pointed to six, and still the train lay motionless along the platform. I approached a guard and asked him whether anything was wrong.

"'Accident on the line,' he replied; 'monsieur had better go to his compartment and try to sleep, for we may be delayed until noon.'

"I followed the guard's advice, and, crawling into my corner, wrapped myself in the rug and lay back watching the rain-drops spattering along the window-sill. At noon the train had not moved, and I lunched in the compartment. At four o'clock in the afternoon the station-master came hurrying along the platform, crying, 'Montez! montez! messieurs, s'il vous plait'—and the train steamed out of the station and whirled away through the flat, tree-less Belgian plains. At times I dozed, but the shaking of the car always awoke me, and I would sit blinking out at the endless stretch of plain, until a sudden flurry of rain blotted the landscape from my eyes. At last a long, shrill whistle from the engine, a jolt, a series of bumps, and an apparition of red trousers and bayonets warned me that we had arrived at the French frontier. I turned out with the others, and opened my valise for inspection, but the customs officials merely chalked it, without examination, and I hurried back to my compartment amid the shouting of guards and the clanging of station bells. Again I found that I was alone in the compartment, so I smoked a cigarette, thanked Heaven, and fell into a dreamless sleep.

"How long I slept I do not know, but when I awoke the train was roaring through a tunnel. When again it flashed out into the open country I peered through the grimy, rain-stained window and saw that the storm had ceased and stars were twinkling in the sky. I stretched my legs, yawned, pushed my travelling-cap back from my forehead, and, stumbling to my, feet, walked up and down the compartment until my cramped muscles were relieved. Then I sat down again, and, lighting a cigar, puffed great rings and clouds of fragrant smoke across the aisle.

"The train was flying; the cars lurched and shook, and the windows rattled accompaniment to the creaking panels. The smoke from my cigar dimmed the lamp in the ceiling and hid the opposite seat from view. How it curled and writhed in the corners, now eddying upward, now floating across the aisle like a veil! I lounged back in my cushioned seat, watching it with interest. What queer shapes it took! How thick it was becoming!—how strangely luminous! Now it had filled the whole compartment, puff after puff crowding upward, waving, wavering, clouding the windows, and blotting the lamp from sight. It was most interesting. I had never before smoked such a cigar. What an extraordinary brand! I examined the end, flicking the ashes away. The cigar was out. Fumbling for a match to relight it, my eyes fell on the drifting smoke-curtain which swayed across the corner opposite. It seemed almost tangible. How like a real curtain it hung, gray, impenetrable! A man might hide behind it. Then an idea came into my head, and it persisted until my uneasiness amounted to a vague terror. I tried to fight it off—I strove to resist—but the conviction slowly settled upon me that something was behind that smoke-veil—something which had entered the compartment while I slept.

"'It can't be,' I muttered, my eyes fixed on the misty drapery; 'the train has not stopped.'

"The car creaked and trembled. I sprang to my feet and swept my arm through the veil of smoke. Then my hair rose on my head. For my hand touched another hand, and my eyes had met two other eyes.

"I heard a voice in the gloom, low and sweet, calling me by name; I saw the eyes again, tender and blue; soft fingers touched my own.

"'Are you afraid?' she said.

"My heart began to beat again, and my face warmed with returning blood.

"'It is only I,' she said, gently.

"I seemed to hear my own voice speaking as if at a great distance, 'You here—alone?'

"'How cruel of you!' she faltered; 'I am not alone.' At the same instant my eyes fell upon the professor, calmly seated by the farther window. His hands were thrust into the folds of a corded and tasselled dressing-gown, from beneath which peeped two enormous feet encased in carpet slippers. Upon his head towered a yellow night-cap. He did not pay the slightest attention to either me or his daughter, and, except for the lighted cigar which he kept shifting between his lips, he might have been taken for a wax dummy.

"Then I began to speak, feebly, hesitating like a child.

"'How did you come into this compartment? You—you do not possess wings, I suppose? You could not have been here all the time. Will you explain—explain to me? See, I ask you very humbly, for I do not understand. This is the nineteenth century, and these things don't fit in. I'm wearing a Dunlap hat—I've got a copy of the New York *Herald* in my bag—President Roosevelt is alive, and everything is so very unromantic in the world! Is this real magic? Perhaps I'm filled with hallucinations. Perhaps I'm asleep and dreaming. Perhaps you are not really here—nor I—nor anybody, nor anything!'

"The train plunged into a tunnel, and when again it dashed out from the other end the cold wind blew furiously in my face from the farther window. It was wide open; the professor was gone.

"'Papa has changed to another compartment,' she said, quietly. 'I think perhaps you were beginning to bore him.'

"Her eyes met mine and she smiled.

"'Are you very much bewildered?'

"I looked at her in silence. She sat very quietly, her hands clasped above her knee, her curly hair glittering to her girdle. A long robe, almost silvery in the twilight, clung to her young figure; her bare feet were thrust deep into a pair of shimmering Eastern slippers.

"'When you fled,' she sighed, 'I was asleep and there was no time to lose. I barely had a moment to go to Bombay, to find papa, and return in time to join you. This is an East-Indian costume.'

"Still I was silent.

"'Are you shocked?' she asked, simply.

"'No,' I replied, in a dull voice, 'I'm past that.'

"'You are very rude,' she said, with the tears starting to her eyes.

"'I do not mean to be. I only wish to go away—away somewhere and find out what my name is.'

"'Your name is Harold Kensett.'

"'Are you sure?' I asked, eagerly.

"'Yes—what troubles you?'

"'Is everything plain to you? Are you a sort of prophet and second-sight medium? Is nothing hidden from you?' I asked.

"'Nothing,' she faltered. My head ached and I clasped it in my hand.

"A sudden change came over her. 'I am human— believe me!' she said, with piteous eagerness. 'Indeed, I do not seem strange to those who understand. You wonder, because you left me at midnight in Antwerp and you wake to find me here. If, because I find myself reincarnated, endowed with senses and capabilities which few at present possess—if I am so made, why should it seem strange? It is all so natural to me. If I appear to you—'

"'Appear?'

"'Yes—'

"'Wilhelmina!' I cried, 'can you vanish?'

"'Yes,' she murmured; 'does it seem to you unmaidenly?'

"'Great Heaven!' I groaned.

"'Don't!' she cried, with tears in her voice— 'oh, please don't! Help me to bear it! If you only knew how awful it is to be different from other girls—how mortifying it is to me to be able to vanish— oh; how I hate and detest it all!'

"'Don't cry,' I said, looking at her pityingly.

"'Oh, dear me!' she sobbed. 'You shudder at the sight of me because I can vanish.'

"'I don't!' I cried.

"'Yes, you do! You abhor me—you shrink away! Oh, why did I ever see you?—why did you ever come into my life?—what have I done in ages past, that now, reborn, I suffer cruelly—cruelly?'

"'What do you mean?' I whispered. My voice trembled with happiness.

"'I?—nothing; but you think me a fabled monster.'

"'Wilhelmina—my sweet Wilhelmina,' I said, 'I don't think you a fabled monster. I love you; see—see—I am at your feet; listen to me, my darling—'

"She turned her blue eyes to mine. I saw tears sparkling on the curved lashes.

"'Wilhelmina, I love you,' I said again.

"Slowly she raised her hands to my head and held it a moment, looking at me strangely. Then her face grew nearer to my own, her glittering hair fell over my shoulders, her lips rested on mine.

"In that long, sweet kiss the beating of her heart answered mine, and I learned a thousand truths, wonderful, mysterious, splendid; but when our lips fell apart, the memory of what I learned departed also.

"'It was so very simple and beautiful,' she sighed, 'and I—I never saw it. But the Mahatmas knew—ah, they knew that my mission could only be accomplished through love.'

"'And it is,' I whispered, 'for you shall teach me—me, your husband.'

"'And—and you will not be impatient? You will try to believe?'

"'I will believe what you tell me, my sweetheart.'

"'Even about—cats?'

"Before I could reply the farther window opened and a yellow night-cap, followed by the professor, entered from somewhere without. Wilhelmina sank back on her sofa, but the professor needed not to be told, and we both knew he was already busily reading our thoughts.

"For a moment there was dead silence—long enough for the professor to grasp the full significance of what had passed. Then he uttered a single exclamation, 'Oh!'

"After a while, however, he looked at me for the first time that evening, saying, 'Congratulate you, Mr. Kensett, I'm sure,' tied several knots in the cord of his dressing-gown, lighted a cigar, and paid no further attention to either of us. Some moments later he opened the window again and disappeared. I looked across the aisle at Wilhelmina.

"'You may come over beside me,' she said, shyly.

IV

"It was nearly ten o'clock and our train was rapidly approaching Paris. We passed village after village wrapped in mist, station after station hung with twinkling red and blue and yellow lanterns, then sped on again with the echo of the switch-bells ringing in our ears:

"When at length the train slowed up and stopped, I opened the window and looked out upon a long, wet platform, shining under the electric lights.

"A guard came running by, throwing open the doors of each compartment, and crying, 'Paris next! Tickets, if you please.'

"I handed him my book of coupons, from which he tore several and handed it back. Then he lifted his lantern and peered into the compartment, saying, 'Is monsieur alone?'

"I turned to Wilhelmina.

"'He wants your ticket—give it to me.'

"'What's that?' demanded the guard.

"I looked anxiously at Wilhelmina.

"'If your father has the tickets—' I began, but was interrupted by the guard, who snapped:

"'Monsieur will give himself the trouble to remember that I do not understand English.'

"'Keep quiet!' I said, sharply, in French. 'I am not speaking to you.'

"The guard stared stupidly at me, then at my luggage, and finally, entering the car, knelt down and peered under the seats. Presently he got up, very red in the face, and went out slamming the door. He had not paid the slightest attention to Wilhelmina, but I distinctly heard him say, 'Only Englishmen and idiots talk to themselves!'

"'Wilhelmina,' I faltered, 'do you mean to say that that guard could not see you?'

"She began to look so serious again that I merely added, 'Never mind, I don't care whether you are invisible or not, dearest.'

"'I am not invisible to you,' she said; 'why should you care?'

"A great noise of bells and whistles drowned our voices, and, amid the whirring of switch-bells, the hissing of steam, and the cries of 'Paris! All out!' our train glided into the station.

"It was the professor who opened the door of our carriage. There he stood, calmly adjusting his yellow night-cap and drawing his dressing-gown closer with the corded tassels.

"'Where have you been?' I asked.

"'On the engine.'

"'In the engine, I suppose you mean,' I said.

"'No, I don't; I mean on the engine—on the pilot. It was very refreshing. Where are we going now?'

"'Do you know Paris?' asked Wilhelmina, turning to me.

"'Yes. I think your father had better take you to the Hôtel Normandie on the Rue de l'Echelle—'

"'But you must stay there, too!'

"'Of course—if you wish—'

She laughed nervously.

"'Don't you see that my father and I could not take rooms—now? You must engage three rooms for yourself. "

"'Why ?' I asked, stupidly.

"'Oh, dear—why, because we are invisible.'

"I tried to repress a shudder. The professor gave Wilhelmina his arm, and, as I studied his ensemble, I thanked Heaven that he was invisible.

"At the gate of the station I hailed a four-seated cab, and we rattled away through the stony streets, brilliant with gas-jets, and in a few moments rolled smoothly across the Avenue de l'Opéra, turned into the Rue de l'Echelle, and stopped. A bright little page, all over buttons, came out, took my luggage, and preceded us into the hallway.

"I, with Wilhelmina on my arm and the professor shuffling along beside me, walked over to the desk.

"'Room?' said the clerk. 'We have a very desirable room on the second, fronting the Rue St. Honoré—'

"'But we—that is, I want three rooms—three separate rooms!' I said.

"The clerk scratched his chin. 'Monsieur is expecting friends?'

"'Say yes,' whispered Wilhelmina, with a suspicion of laughter in her voice.

"'Yes,' I repeated, feebly.

"'Gentlemen, of course?' said the clerk, looking at me narrowly.

"'One lady.'

"'Married, of course?'

"'What's that to you?' I said, sharply. 'What do you mean by speaking to us—'

"'Us!'

"'I mean to me,' I said, badly rattled; 'give me the rooms and let me get to bed, will you?'

"'Monsieur will remember,' said the clerk, coldly, 'that this is an old and respectable hotel.'

"'I know it,' I said, smothering my rage.

"The clerk eyed me suspiciously.

"'Front!' he called, with irritating deliberation. 'Show this gentleman to apartment ten.'

"'How many rooms are there!' I demanded.

"'Three sleeping-rooms and a parlor.'

"'I will take it,' I said, with composure.

"'On probation,' muttered the clerk, insolently.

"Swallowing the insult, I followed the bell-boy up the stairs, keeping between him and Wilhelmina, for I dreaded to see him walk through her as if she were thin air. A trim maid rose to meet us and conducted us through a hallway into a large apartment. She threw open all the bedroom-doors and said, 'Will monsieur have the goodness to choose?'

"'Which will you take,' I began, turning to Wilhelmina.

"'I? Monsieur!' cried the startled maid.

"That completely upset me. 'Here,' I muttered, slipping some silver into her hand; 'now, for the love of Heaven, run away!'

"When she had vanished with a doubtful 'Merci, monsieur!' I handed the professor the keys and asked him to settle the thing with Wilhelmina.

"Wilhelmina took the corner room, the professor rambled into the next one, and I said good-night and crept wearily into my own chamber. I sat down and tried to think. A great feeling of fatigue weighted my spirits.

"'I can think better with my clothes off,' I said, and slipped the coat from my shoulders. How tired I was! 'I can think better in bed,' I muttered, flinging my cravat on the dresser and tossing my shirt-studs after it. I was certainly very tired. 'Now,' I yawned, grasping the pillow and drawing it under my head— 'now I can think a bit.' But before my head fell on the pillow sleep closed my eyes.

"I began to dream at once. It seemed as though my eyes were wide open and the professor was standing beside my bed.

"'Young man,' he said, 'you've won my daughter and you must pay the piper!'

"'What piper?' I said.

"'The Pied Piper of Hamelin, I don't think,' replied the professor, vulgarly, and before I could realize what he was doing he had drawn a reed pipe from his dressing-gown and was playing a strangely annoying air. Then an awful thing occurred. Cats began to troop into the room, cats by the hundred—toms and tabbies, gray, yellow, Maltese, Persian, Manx—all purring and all marching round and round, rubbing against the furniture, the professor, and even against me. I struggled with the nightmare.

"'Take them away!' I tried to gasp.

"'Nonsense!' he said; 'here is an old friend.'

"I saw the white tabby cat of the Hôtel St. Antoine.

"'An old friend,' he repeated, and played a dismal melody on his reed.

"I saw Wilhelmina enter the room, lift the white tabby in her arms, and bring her to my side.

"'Shake hands with him,' she commanded.

"To my horror the tabby deliberately extended a paw and tapped me on the knuckles.

"'Oh!' I cried, in agony; 'this is a horrible dream! Why, oh, why can't I wake!'

"'Yes,' she said, dropping the cat, 'it is partly a dream, but some of it is real. Remember what I say, my darling; you are to go to-morrow morning and meet the twelve-o'clock train from Antwerp at the Gare du Nord. Papa and I are coming to Paris on that train. Don't you know that we are not really here now, you silly boy? Good-night, then. I shall be very glad to see you.'

"I saw her glide from the room, followed by the professor, playing a gay quick-step, to which the cats danced two and two.

"'Good-night, sir,' said each cat as it passed my bed; and I dreamed no more.

"When I awoke, the room, the bed had vanished; I was in the street, walking rapidly; the sun shone down on the broad, white pavements of Paris, and the streams of busy life flowed past me on either side. How swiftly I was walking! Where the devil was I going? Surely I had business somewhere that needed immediate attention. I tried to remember when I had awakened, but I could not. I wondered where I had dressed myself; I had apparently taken great pains with my toilet, for I was immaculate, monocle and all, even down to a long-stemmed rose nestling in my button-hole. I knew Paris and recognized the streets through which I was hurrying. Where could I be going? What was my hurry? I glanced at my watch and found I had not a moment to lose. Then, as the bells of the city rang out mid-day, I hastened into the railroad station on the Rue Lafayette and walked out to the platform. And as I looked down the glittering track, around the distant curve shot a locomotive followed by a long line of cars. Nearer and nearer it came, while the station-gongs sounded and the switch-bells began ringing all along the track.

"'Antwerp express!' cried the sous-chef de gare, and as the train slipped along the tiled platform I sprang upon the steps of a first-class carriage and threw open the door.

"'How do you do, Mr. Kensett?' said Wilhelmina Wyeth, springing lightly to the platform. 'Really it is very nice of you to come to the train.' At the same moment a bald, mild-eyed gentleman emerged from the depths of the same compartment, carrying a large, covered basket.

"'How are you, Kensett?' he said. 'Glad to see you again. Rather warm in that compartment—no, I will not trust this basket to an expressman; give Wilhelmina your arm and I'll follow. We go to the Normandie, I believe?'

"All the morning I had Wilhelmina to myself, and at dinner I sat beside her, with the professor opposite. The latter was cheerful enough, but he nearly ruined my appetite, for he smelled strongly of catnip. After dinner he became restless and fidgeted about in his chair until coffee was brought, and we went up to the parlor of our apartment. Here his restlessness increased to such an extent that I ventured to ask him if he was in good health.

"'It's that basket—the covered basket which I have in the next room,' he said.

"'What's the trouble with the basket?' I asked.

"'The basket's all right—but the contents worry me.'

"'May I inquire what the contents are?' I ventured.

"The professor rose.

"'Yes,' he said, 'you may inquire of my daughter.' He left the room, but reappeared shortly, carrying a saucer of milk.

"I watched him enter the next room, which was mine.

"'What on earth is he taking that into my room for?' I asked Wilhelmina. 'I don't keep cats.'

"'But you will,' she said.

"'I? Never!'

"'You will if I ask you to.'

"'But—but you won't ask me.'

"'But I do.'

"'Wilhelmina!'

"'Harold!'

"'I detest cats.'

"'You must not.'

"'I can't help it.'

"'You will when I ask it. Have I not given myself to you? Will you not make a little sacrifice for me?'

"'I don't understand—'

"'Would you refuse my first request?'

"'No,' I said, miserably, 'I will keep dozens of cats—'

"'I do not ask that; I only wish you to keep one,'

"'Was that what your father had in that basket?' I asked, suspiciously.

"'Yes, the basket came from Antwerp.'

"'What! The white Antwerp cat!' I cried.

"'Yes.'

"'And you ask me to keep that cat? Oh, Wilhelmina!'

"'Listen!' she said. 'I have a long story to tell you; come nearer, close to me. You say you love me?'

"I bent and kissed her.

"'Then I shall put you to the proof,' she murmured.

"'Prove me!'

"'Listen. That cat is the same cat that ran out of the apartment in the Waldorf when your great-aunt ceased to exist—in human shape. My father and myself, having received word from the Mahatmas of the Trust Company, sheltered and cherished the cat. We were ordered by the Mahatmas to convert you. The task was appalling—but there is no such thing as refusing a command, and we laid our plans. That man with a white spot in his hair was my father—'

"'What! Your father is bald.'

"'He wore a wig then. The white spot came from dropping chemicals on the wig while experimenting with a substance which you could not comprehend.'

"'Then—then that clew was useless; but who could have taken the Crimson Diamond? And who was the man with the white spot on his head who tried to sell the stone in Paris?'

"'That was my father.'

"'He—he—st—took the Crimson Diamond!' I cried, aghast.

"'Yes and no. That was only a paste stone that he had in Paris. It was to draw you over here. He had the real Crimson Diamond also.'

"'Your father?'

"'Yes. He has it in the next room now. Can you not see how it disappeared, Harold? Why, the cat swallowed it!'

"'Do you mean to say that the white tabby swallowed the Crimson Diamond?'

"'By mistake. She tried to get it out of the velvet bag, and, as the bag was also full of catnip, she could not resist a mouthful, and unfortunately just then you broke in the door and so startled the cat that she swallowed the Crimson Diamond.'

"There was a painful pause. At last I said:

"'Wilhelmina, as you are able to vanish, I suppose you also are able to converse with cats.'

"'I am,' she replied, trying to keep back the tears of mortification.

"'And that cat told you this?'

"'She did.'

"'And my Crimson Diamond is inside that cat?'

"'It is.'

"'Then,' said I, firmly, 'I am going to chloroform the cat.'

"'Harold!' she cried, in terror, 'that cat is your great-aunt!'

"I don't know to this day how I stood the shock of that announcement, or how I managed to listen while Wilhelmina tried to explain the transmigration theory, but it was all Chinese to me. I only knew that I was a blood relation of a cat, and the thought nearly drove me mad.

"'Try, my darling, try to love her,' whispered Wilhelmina; 'she must be very precious to you—'

"'Yes, with my diamond inside her,' I replied, faintly.

"'You must not neglect her,' said Wilhelmina.

"'Oh no, I'll always have my eye on her—I mean I will surround her with luxury—er, milk and bones and catnip and books—er—does she read?'

"'Not the books that human beings read. Now, go and speak to your aunt, Harold.'

"'Eh! How the deuce—'

"'Go; for my sake try to be cordial.'

"She rose and led me unresistingly to the door of my room.

"'Good Heavens!' I groaned; 'this is awful.'

"'Courage, my darling!' she whispered. 'Be brave for love of me.'

"I drew her to me and kissed her. Beads of cold perspiration started in the roots of my hair, but I clenched my teeth and entered the room alone. The room was dark and I stood silent, not knowing where to turn, fearful lest I step on my aunt! Then, through the dreary silence, I called, 'Aunty!'

"A faint noise broke upon my ear, and my heart grew sick, but I strode into the darkness, calling, hoarsely:

"'Aunt Tabby! It is your nephew!'

"Again the faint sound. Something was stirring there among the shadows—a shape moving softly along the wall, a shade which glided by me, paused, wavered, and darted under the bed. Then I threw myself on the floor, profoundly moved, begging, imploring my aunt to come to me.

"'Aunty! Aunty!' I murmured. 'Your nephew is waiting to take you to his heart!'

"At last I saw my great-aunt's eyes shining in the dark."

The young man's voice grew hushed and solemn, and he lifted his hand in silence:

"Close the door. That meeting is not for the eyes of the world! Close the door upon that sacred scene where great-aunt and nephew are united at last."

A long pause followed; deep emotion was visible in Miss Barrison's sensitive face. She said:

"Then—you are married?"

"No," replied Mr. Kensett, in a mortified voice.

"Why not?" I asked, amazed.

"Because," he said, "although my fiancée was prepared to accept a cat as her great-aunt, she could not endure the complications that followed."

"What complications?" inquired Miss Barrison.

The young man sighed profoundly, shaking his head.

"My great-aunt had kittens," he said, softly.

The tremendous scientific importance of these experiences excited me beyond measure. The simplicity of the narrative, the elaborate attention to corroborative detail, all bore irresistible testimony to the truth of these accounts of phenomena vitally important to the entire world of science.

We all dined together that night—a little earnest company of knowledge-seekers in the vast wilderness of the unexplored; and we lingered long in the dining-car, propounding questions, advancing theories, speculating upon possibilities of most intense interest. Never before had I known a man whose relatives were cats and kittens, but he did not appear to share my enthusiasm in the matter.

"You see," he said, looking at Miss Barrison, "it may be interesting from a purely scientific point of view, but it has already proved a bar to my marrying."

"Were the kittens black?" I inquired.

"No," he said, "my aunt drew the color-line, I am proud to say."

"I don't see," said Miss Barrison, "why the fact that your great-aunt is a cat should prevent you from marrying."

"It wouldn't prevent *me!*" said the young man, quickly.

"Nor me," mused Miss Barrison— "if I were really in love."

Meanwhile I had been very busy thinking about Professor Farrago, and, coming to an interesting theory, advanced it.

"If," I began, "he marries one of those transparent ladies, what about the children?"

"Some would be, no doubt, transparent," said Kensett.

"They might be only translucent," suggested Miss Barrison.

"Or partially opaque," I ventured. "But it's a risky marriage—not to be able to see what one's wife is about—"

"That is a silly reflection on women," said Miss Barrison, quietly. "Besides, a girl need not be transparent to conceal what she's doing."

This observation seemed to end our postprandial and tripartite conference; Miss Barrison retired to her stateroom presently;

after a last cigar, smoked almost in silence, the young man and I bade each other a civil good-night and retired to our respective berths.

I think it was at Richmond, Virginia, that I was awakened by the negro porter shaking me very gently and repeating, in a pleasant, monotonous voice: "Teleg'am foh you, suh! Teleg'am foh Mistuh Gilland, suh. 'Done call you 'lev'm times sense breakfass, suh! Las' call foh luncheon, suh. Teleg'am foh—"

"Heavens!" I muttered, sitting up in my bunk, "is it as late as that! Where are we?" I slid up the window-shade and sat blinking at a flood of sunshine.

"Telegram?" I said, yawning and rubbing my eyes. "Let me have it. All right, I'll be out presently. Shut that curtain! I don't want the entire car to criticise my pink pajamas!"

"Ain' nobody in de cyar, 'scusin yo'se'f, suh," grinned the porter, retiring.

I heard him, but did not comprehend, sitting there sleepily unfolding the scrawled telegram. Suddenly my eyes flew wide open; I scanned the despatch with stunned incredulity:

Atlanta, Georgia.
"We couldn't help it. Love at first sight. Married this morning in Atlanta. Wildly happy. Forgive. Wire blessing.
"(Signed) Harold Kensett,
"Helen Barrison Kensett."

"Porter!" I shouted. "Porter! Help!"

There was no response.

"Oh, Lord!" I groaned, and rolled over, burying my head in the blankets; for I understood at last that Science, the most jealous, most exacting of mistresses, could never brook a rival.

THE THIRD EYE

Although the man's back was turned toward me, I was uncomfortably conscious that he was watching me. How he could possibly be watching me while I stood directly behind him, I did not ask myself; yet, nevertheless, instinct warned me that I was being inspected; that somehow or other the man was staring at me as steadily as though he and I had been face to face and his faded, sea-green eyes were focussed upon me.

It was an odd sensation which persisted in spite of logic, and of which I could not rid myself. Yet the little waitress did not seem to share it. Perhaps she was not under his glassy inspection. But then, of course, I could not be either.

No doubt the nervous tension incident to the expedition was making me supersensitive and even morbid.

Our sail-boat rode the shallow torquoise-tinted waters at anchor, rocking gently just off the snowy coral reef on which we were now camping. The youthful waitress who, for economy's sake, wore her cap, apron, collar and cuffs over her dainty print dress, was seated by the signal fire writing in her diary. Sometimes she thoughtfully touched her pencil point with the tip of her tongue; sometimes she replenished the fire from a pile of dead mangrove branches heaped up on the coral reef beside her. Whatever she did she accomplished gracefully.

As for the man, Grue, his back remained turned toward us both and he continued, apparently, to scan the horizon for the sail which we all expected. And all the time I could not rid myself of the unpleasant idea that somehow or other he was looking at me, watching attentively the expression of my features and noting my every movement.

210

The smoke of our fire blew wide across leagues of shallow, spar-kling water, or, when the wind veered, whirled back into our faces across the reef, curling and eddying among the standing mangroves like fog drifting.

Seated there near the fire, from time to time I swept the hori-zon with my marine glasses; but there was no sign of Kemper; no sail broke the far sweep of sky and water; nothing moved out there save when a wild duck took wing amid the dark raft of its compan-ions to circle low above the ocean and settle at random, invisible again except when, at intervals, its white breast flashed in the sun-shine.

Meanwhile the waitress had ceased to write in her diary and now sat with the closed book on her knees and her pencil resting against her lips, gazing thoughtfuly at the back of Grue's head!

It was a ratty head of straight black hair, and looked greasy. The rest of him struck me as equally unkempt and dingy—a youngish man, lean, deeply bitten by the sun of the semi-tropics to a mahogany hue, and unusually hairy.

I don't mind a brawny, hairy man, but the hair on Grue's arms and chest was a rusty red, and like a chimpanzee's in texture, and sometimes a wildly absurd idea possessed me that the man needed it when he went about in the palm forests without his clothes.

But he was only a "poor white"—a "cracker" recruited from one of the reefs near Pelican Light, where he lived alone by fishing and selling his fish to the hotels at Heliatrope City. The sail-boat was his; he figured as our official guide on this expedition—an expedi-tion which already had begun to worry me a great deal.

For it was, perhaps, the wildest goose chase and the most ab-surdly hopeless enterprise ever undertaken in the interest of sci-ence by the Bronx Park authorities.

Nothing is more dreaded by scientists than ridicule; and it was in spite of this terror of ridicule that I summoned sufficient cour-age to organize an exploring party and start out in search of some-thing so extraordinary, so hitherto unheard of, that I had not dared reveal to Kemper by letter the object of my quest.

No, I did not care to commit myself to writing just yet; I had merely sent Kemper a letter to join me on Sting-ray Key.

He telegraphed me from Tampa that he would join me at the rendezvous; and I started directly from Bronx Park for Heliatrope City; arrived there in three days; found the waitress all ready to start with me; inquired about a guide and discovered the man Grue in his hut off Pelican Light; made my bargain with him; and set sail for Sting-ray Key, the most excited and the most nervous young man who ever had dared disaster in the sacred cause of science.

Everything was now at stake, my honour, reputation, career, fortune. For, as chief of the Anthropological Field Survey Department of the great Bronx Park Zoölogical Society, I was perfectly aware that no scientific reputation can survive ridicule.

Nevertheless, the die had been cast, the Rubicon crossed in a sail-boat containing one beachcombing cracker, one hotel waitress, a pile of camping kit and special utensils, and myself!

How was I going to tell Kemper? How was I going to confess to him that I was staking my reputation as an anthropologist upon a letter or two and a personal interview with a young girl—a waitress at the Hotel Gardenia in Heliatrope City?

I lowered my sea-glasses and glanced sideways at the waitress. She was still chewing the end of her pencil, reflectively.

She was a pretty girl, one Evelyn Grey, and had been a country school-teacher in Massachusetts until her health broke.

Florida was what she required; but that healing climate was possible to her only if she could find there a self-supporting position.

Also she had nourished an ambition for a postgraduate education, with further aspirations to a Government appointment in the Smithsonian Institute.

All very worthy, no doubt—in fact, particularly commendable because the wages she saved as waitress in a Florida hotel during the winter were her only means of support while studying for college examinations during the summer in Boston, where she lived.

Yet, although she was an inmate of Massachusetts, her face and figure would have ornamented any light-opera stage. I never looked at her but I thought so; and her cuffs and apron merely accentuated the delusion. Such ankles are seldom seen when the curtain rises after the overture. Odd that frivolous thoughts could flit through an intellect dedicated only to science!

The man, Grue, had not stirred from his survey of the Atlantic Ocean. He had a somewhat disturbing capacity for remaining motionless—like a stealthy and predatory bird which depends on immobility for agressive and defensive existence.

The sea-wind fluttered his cotton shirt and trousers and the tattered brim of his straw hat. And always I felt as though he were watching me out of the back of his ratty head, through the ravelled straw brim that sagged over his neck.

The pretty waitress had now chewed the end of her pencil to a satisfactory pulp, and she was writing again in her diary, very intently, so that my cautious touch on her arm seemed to startle her.

Meeting her inquiring eyes I said in a low voice:

"I am not sure why, but I don't seem to care very much for that man, Grue. Do you?"

She glanced at the water's edge, where Grue stood, immovable, his back still turned to us.

"I never liked him," she said under her breath.

"Why?" I asked cautiously.

She merely shrugged her shoulders. She did it gracefully.

I said:

"Have you any particular reason for disliking him?"

"He's dirty."

"He *looks* dirty, yet every day he goes into the sea and swims about. He ought to be clean enough."

She thought for a moment, then:

"He seems, somehow, to be fundamentally unclean—I don't mean that he doesn't wash himself. But there are certain sorts of animals and birds and other creatures from which one instinctively shrinks—not, perhaps, because they are materially unclean—"

"I understand," I said. After a silence I added: "Well, there's no chance now of sending him back, even if I were inclined to do so. He appears to be familiar with these latitudes. I don't suppose we could find a better man for our purpose. Do you?"

"No. He was a sponge fisher once, I believe."

"Did he tell you so?"

"No. But yesterday, when you took the boat and cruised to the south, I sat writing here and keeping up the fire. And I saw Grue climbing about among the mangroves over the water in a most uncanny way; and two snake-birds sat watching him, and they never moved. He didn't seem to see them; his back was toward them. And then, all at once, he leaped backward at them where they sat on a mangrove, and he got one of them by the neck—"

"What!"

The girl nodded.

"By the neck," she repeated, "and down they went into the water. And what do you suppose happened?"

"I can't imagine," said I with a grimace.

"Well, Grue went under, still clutching the squirming, flapping bird; and he *stayed* under."

"Stayed under the *water?*"

"Yes, longer than any sponge diver I ever heard of. And I was becoming frightened when the bloody bubbles and feathers began to come up—"

"*What* was he doing under water?"

"He must have been tearing the bird to pieces. Oh, it was quite unpleasant, I assure you, Mr. Smith. And when he came up and looked at me out of those very vitreous eyes he resembled something horridly amphibious... And I felt rather sick and dizzy."

"He's got to stop that sort of thing!" I said angrily. "Snake-birds are harmless and I won't have him killing them in that barbarous fashion. I've warned him already to let birds alone. I don't know how he catches them or why he kills them. But he seems to have a mania for doing it—"

I was interrupted by Grue's soft and rather pleasant voice from the water's edge, announcing a sail on the horizon. He did not turn when speaking. The next moment I made out the sail and focussed my glasses on it.

"It's Professor Kemper," I announced presently.

"I'm so glad," remarked Evelyn Grey.

I don't know why it should have suddenly occurred to me, apropos of nothing, that Billy Kemper was unusually handsome. Or why I should have turned and looked at the pretty waitress—except that she was, perhaps, worth gazing upon from a purely non-scientific point of view. In fact, to a man not entirely absorbed in scientific research and not passionately and irrevocably wedded to his profession, her violet-blue eyes and rather sweet mouth might have proved disturbing.

As I was thinking about this she looked up at me and smiled.

"It's a good thing," I thought to myself, "that I am irrevocably wedded to my profession." And I gazed fixedly across the Atlantic Ocean.

There was scarcely sufficient breeze of a steady character to bring Kemper to Sting-ray Key; but he got out his sweeps when I hailed him and came in at a lively clip, anchoring alongside of our boat and leaping ashore with that unnecessary dash and abandon which women find pleasing.

Glancing sideways at my waitress through my spectacles, I found her looking into a small hand mirror and patting her hair with one slim and suntanned hand.

When Professor Kemper landed on the coral he shot a curious look at Grue, and then came striding across the reef to me.

"Hello, Smithy!" he said, holding out his hand. "Here I am, you see! Now what's up—"

Just then Evelyn Grey got up from her seat beside the fire; and Kemper turned and gazed at her with every symptom of unfeigned approbation.

I introduced him. Evelyn Grey seemed a trifle indifferent. A good-looking man doesn't last long with a clever woman. I smiled to myself, polishing my spectacles gleefully. Yet, I had no idea why I was smiling.

We three people turned and walked toward the comb of the reef. A solitary palm represented the island's vegetation, except, of course, for the water-growing mangroves.

I asked Miss Grey to precede us and wait for us under the palm; and she went forward in that light-footed way of hers which, to any non-scientific man, might have been a trifle disturbing. It had no effect upon me. Besides, I was looking at Grue, who had gone to the fire and was evidently preparing to fry our evening meal of fish and rice. I didn't like to have him cook, but I wasn't going to do it myself; and my pretty waitress didn't know how to cook anything more complicated than beans. We had no beans.

Kemper said to me:

"Why on earth did you bring a waitress?"

"Not to wait on table," I replied, amused. "I'll explain her later. Meanwhile, I merely want to say that you need not remain with this expedition if you don't want to. It's optional with you."

"That's a funny thing to say!"

"No, not funny; sad. The truth is that if I fail I'll be driven into obscurity by the ridicule of my brother scientists the world over. I had to tell them at the Bronx what I was going after. Every man connected with the society attempted to dissuade me, saying that the whole thing was absurd and that my reputation would suffer if I engaged in such a ridiculous quest. So when you hear what that girl and I are after out here in the semitropics, and when you are in possession of the only evidence I have to justify my credulity, if you want to go home, go. Because I don't wish to risk your reputation as a scientist unless you choose to risk it yourself."

He regarded me curiously, then his eyes strayed toward the palm-tree which Evelyn Grey was now approaching.

"All right," he said briefly, "let's hear what's up."

So we moved forward to rejoin the girl, who had already seated herself under the tree.

She looked very attractive in her neat cuffs, tiny cap, and pink print gown, as we approached her.

"Why does she dress that way?" asked Kemper, uneasily.

"Economy. She desires to use up the habiliments of a service which there will be no necessity for her to reënter if this expedition proves succesful."

"Oh. But Smithy—"

"What?"

"Was it—moral—to bring a waitress?"

"Perfectly," I replied sharply. "Science knows no sex!"

"I don't understand how a waitress can be scientific," he muttered, "and there seems to be no question about her possessing plenty of sex—"

"If that girl's conclusions are warranted," I interrupted coldly, "she is a most intelligent and clever person. *I* think they are warranted. If you don't, you may go home as soon as you like."

I glanced at him; he was smiling at her with that strained politeness which alters the natural expression of men in the imminence of a conversation with a new and pretty woman.

I often wonder what particular combination of facial muscles are brought into play when that politely receptive expression transforms the normal and masculine features into a fixed simper.

When Kemper and I had seated ourselves, I calmly cut short the small talk in which he was already indulging, and to which, I am sorry to say, my pretty waitress was beginning to respond. I had scarcely thought it of her—but that's neither here nor there—and I invited her to recapitulate the circumstances which had resulted in our present foregathering here on this strip of coral in the Atlantic Ocean. She did so very modestly and without embarrassment, stating the case and reviewing the evidence so clearly and so simply that I could see how every word she uttered was not only amazing but also convincing Kemper.

When she had ended he asked a few questions very seriously:

"Granted," he said, "that the pituitary gland represents what we assume it represents, how much faith is to be placed in the testimony of a Seminole Indian?"

"A Seminole Indian," she replied, "has seldom or never been known to lie. And where a whole tribe testify alike the truth of what they assert can not be questioned."

"How did you make them talk? They are a sullen, suspicious people, haughty, uncommunicative, seldom even replying to an ordinary question from a white man."

"They consider me one of them."

"Why?" he asked in surprise.

"I'll tell you why. It came about through a mere accident. I was waitress at the hotel; it happened to be my afternoon off; so I went down to the coquina dock to study. I study in my leisure moments, because I wish to fit myself for a college examination."

Her charming face became serious; she picked up the hem of her apron and continued to pleat it slowly and with precision as she talked:

"There was a Seminole named Tiger-tail sitting there, his feet dangling above his moored canoe, evidently waiting for the tide to turn before he went out to spear crayfish. I merely noticed he was sitting there in the sunshine, that's all. And then I opened my mythology book and turned to the story of Argus, on which I was reading up.

"And this is what happened: there was a picture of the death of Argus, facing the printed page which I was reading—the well-known picture where Juno is holding the head of the decapitated monster—and I had-read scarcely a dozen words in the book before the Seminole beside me leaned over and placed his forefinger squarely upon the head of Argus.

"'Who?' he demanded.

"I looked around good-humoredly and was surprised at the evident excitement of the Indian. They're not excitable, you know.

"'That,' said I, 'is a Greek gentleman named Argus.' I suppose he thought I meant a Minorcan, for he nodded. Then, without further comment, he placed his finger on Juno.

"'*Who?*' he inquired emphatically.

"I said flippantly: 'Oh, that's only my aunt, Juno.'

"'Aunty of you?'

"'Yes.'

"'She kill 'um Three-eye?'

"Argus had been depicted with three eyes.

"'Yes,' I said, 'my Aunt Juno had Argus killed.'

"'Why kill 'um?'

"'Well, Aunty needed his eyes to set in the tails of the peacocks which drew her automobile. So when they cut off the head of Argus my aunt had the eyes taken out; and that's a picture of how she set them into the peacock.'

"'Aunty of *you?*' he repeated.

"'Certainly,' I said gravely; 'I am a direct descendant of the Goddess of Wisdom. That's why I'm always studying when you see me down on the dock here.'

"'*You Seminole!*' he said emphatically.

"'Seminole,' I repeated, puzzled.

"'You Seminole! Aunty Seminole—*you* Seminole!'

"'Why, Tiger-tail?'

"'Seminole hunt Three-eye long time—hundred, hundred year—hunt 'um Three-eye, kill 'um Three-eye.'

"'You say that for hundreds of years the Seminoles have hunted a creature with three eyes?'

"'Sure! Hunt 'um now!'

"'*Now?*'

"'Sure!'

"'But, Tiger-tail, if the legends of your people tell you that the Seminoles hunted a creature with three eyes hundreds of years ago, certainly no such three-eyed creatures remain today?'

"'Some.'

"'What! Where?'

"'Black Bayou.'

"'Do you mean to tell me that a living creature with three eyes still inhabits the forests of Black Bayou ?'

"'Sure. Me see 'um. Me kill 'um three-eye man.'

"'You have killed a man who had *three eyes?*'

"'Sure!'

"'A man? *With three eyes?*'

"'Sure.'"

The pretty waitress, excitedly engrossed in her story, was unconsciously acting out the thrilling scene of her dialogue with the Indian, even imitating his voice and gestures. And Kemper and I listened and watched her breathlessly, fascinated by her lithe and supple grace as well as by the astounding story she was so frankly unfolding with the consummate artlessness of a natural actress.

She turned her flushed face to us:

"I made up my mind," she said, "that Tiger-tail's story was worth investigating. It was perfectly easy for me to secure corroboration, because that Seminole went back to his Everglade camp and told every one of his people that I was a white Seminole because my ancestors also hunted the three-eyed man and nobody except a Seminole could know that such a thing as a three-eyed man existed.

"So, the next afternoon off, I embarked in Tiger-tail's canoe and he took me to his camp. And there I talked to his people, men and women, questioning, listening, putting this and that together, trying to discover some foundation for their persistent statements concerning men, still living in the jungles of Black Bayou, who had three eyes instead of two.

"All told the same story; all asserted that since the time their records ran the Seminoles had hunted and slain every three-eyed man they could catch; and that as long as the Seminoles had lived in the Everglades the three-eyed men had lived in the forests beyond Black Bayou."

She paused, dramatically, cooling her cheeks in her palms and looking from Kemper to me with eyes made starry by excitement.

"And *what* do you think!" she continued, under her breath. "To prove what they said they brought for my inspection a skull. And then two more skulls like the first one.

"Every skull had been painted with Spanish red; the coarse black hair still stuck to the scalps. And, behind, just over where the pituitary gland is situated, was a hollow, bony orbit—unmistakaby the socket of a *third eye!*"

"W-where are those skulls?" demanded Kemper, in a voice not entirely under control.

"They wouldn't part with one of them. I tried every possible persuasion. On my own responsibility, and even before I communicated with Mr. Smith—" turning toward me, "—I offered them twenty thousand dollars for a single skull, staking my word of honour that the Bronx Museum would pay that sum.

"It was useless. Not only do the Seminoles refuse to part with one of those skulls, but I have also learned that I am the first person with a white skin who has ever even heard of their existence—so profoundly have these red men of the Everglades guarded their secret through centuries."

After a silence Kemper, rather pale, remarked:

"This is a most astonishing business, Miss Grey."

"What do you think about it?" I demanded. "Is it not worth while for us to explore Black Bayou?"

He nodded in a dazed sort of way, but his gaze remained riveted on the girl. Presently he said:

"Why does Miss Grey go?"

She turned in surprise:

"Why am I going? But it is *my* discovery—*my* contribution to science, isn't it?"

"Certainly!" we exclaimed warmly and in unison. And Kemper added: "I was only thinking of the dangers and hardships. Smith and I could do the actual work—"

"Oh!" she cried in quick protest, "I wouldn't miss one moment of the excitement, one pain, one pang! I *love* it! It would simply break my heart not to share every chance, hazard, danger of this expedition—every atom of hope, excitement, despair, uncertainty—and the ultimate success—the unsurpassable thrill of exultation in the final instant of triumph!"

She sprang to her feet in a flash of uncontrollable enthusiasm, and stood there, aglow with courage and resolution, making a highly agreeable picture in her apron and cuffs, the sea wind fluttering the bright tendrils of her hair under her dainty cap.

We got to our feet much impressed; and now absolutely convinced that there did exist, somewhere, descendants of prehistoric men in whom the third eye placed in the back of the head for purposes of defensive observation—had not become obsolete and reduced to the traces which we know only as the pituitary body or pituitary gland.

Kemper and I were, of course, aware that in the insect world the ocelli served the same purpose that the degenerate pituitary body once served in the occiput of man.

As we three walked slowly back to the campfire, where our evening meal was now ready, Evelyn Grey, who walked between us, told us what she knew about the hunting of these three-eyed men by the Seminoles—how intense was the hatred of the Indians for these people, how murderously they behaved toward any one of them whom they could track down and catch.

"Tiger-tail told me," she went on, "that in all probability the strange race was nearing extinction, but that all had not yet been exterminated because now and then, when hunting along Black Bayou, traces of living three-eyed men were still found by him and his people.

"No later than last week Tiger-tail himself had startled one of these strange denizens of Black Bayou from a meal of fish; and had heard him leap through the bushes and plunge into the water. It appears that centuries of persecution have made these three-eyed men partly amphibious—that is, capable of filling their lungs with air and remaining under water almost as long as a turtle."

"That's impossible!" said Kemper bluntly.

"I thought so myself," she said with a smile, "until Tiger-tail told me a little more about them. He says that they can breathe through the pores of their skins; that their bodies are covered with a thick, silky hair, and that when they dive they carry down with them enough air to form a sort of skin over them, so that under water their bodies appear to be silver-plated."

"Good Lord!" faltered Kemper. "That is a little too much!"

"Yet," said I, "that is exactly what air-breathing water beetles do. The globules of air, clinging to the body-hairs, appear to silver-plate them; and they can remain below indefinitely, breathing through spiracles. Doubtless the skin pores of these men have taken on the character of spiracles."

"You know," he said in a curious, flat voice, which sounded like the tones of a partly stupified man, "this whole business is so grotesque—apparently so wildly absurd—that it's having a sort of nightmare effect on me." And, dropping his voice to a whisper close to my ear: "Good heavens!" he said. "Can you reconcile such a creature as we are starting out to hunt, with anything living known to science?"

"No," I replied in guarded tones. "And there are moments, Kemper, since I have come into possession of Miss Grey's story, when I find myself seriously doubting my own sanity."

"I'm doubting mine, now," he whispered, "only that girl is so fresh and wholesome and human and sane—"

"She is a very clever girl," I said.

"And really beautiful!"

"She is intelligent," I remarked. There was a chill in my tone which doubtless discouraged Kemper, for he ventured nothing further concerning her superficially personal attractions.

After all, if any questions of priority were to arise, the pretty waitress was *my* discovery. And in the scientific world it is an inflexible rule that he who first discovers any particular specimen of any species whatever is first entitled to describe and comment upon that specimen without interference or unsolicited advice from anybody.

Maybe there was in my eye something that expressed as much. For when Kemper caught my cold gaze fixed upon him he winced and looked away like a reproved setter dog who knew better. Which also, for the moment, put an end to the rather gay and frivolous line of small talk which he had again begun with the pretty waitress.

I was exceedingly surprised at Professor William Henry Kemper, D. F.

As we approached the campfire the loathsome odour of frying mullet saluted my nostrils.

Kemper, glancing at Grue, said aside to me:

"That's an odd-looking fellow. What is he? Minorcan?"

"Oh, just a beachcomber. I don't know what he is. He strikes me as dirty—though he can't be so, physically. I don't like him and I don't know why. And I wish we'd engaged somebody else to guide us."

Toward dawn something awoke me and I sat up in my blanket under the moon. But my leg had not been pulled.

Kemper snored at my side. In her little dog-tent the pretty waitress probably was fast asleep. I knew it because the string she had tied to one of her ornamental ankles still lay across the ground convenient to my hand. In any emergency I had only to pull it to awake her.

A similar string, tied to my ankle, ran parallel to hers and disappeared under the flap of her tent. This was for her to pull if she liked. She had never yet pulled it. Nor I the other. Nevertheless I truly felt that these humble strings were, in a subtler sense, ties that bound us together. No wonder Kemper's behaviour had slightly irritated me.

I looked up at the silver moon; I glanced at Kemper's unlovely bulk, swathed in a blanket; I contemplated the dog-tent with, perhaps, that slight trace of sentiment which a semi-tropical moon is likely to inspire even in a jellyfish. And suddenly I remembered Grue and looked for him.

He was accustomed to sleep in his boat, but I did not see him in either of the boats. Here and there were a few lumpy shadows in the moonlight, but none of them was Grue lying prone on the ground. Where the devil had he gone?

Cautiously I untied my ankle string, rose in my pajamas, stepped into my slippers, and walked out through the moonlight.

There was nothing to hide Grue, no rocks or vegetation except the solitary palm on the backbone of the reef.

I walked as far as the tree and looked up into the arching fronds. Nobody was up there. I could see the moonlit sky through the fronds. Nor was Grue lying asleep anywhere on the other side of the coral ridge.

And suddenly I became aware of all my latent distrust and dislike for the man. And the vigour of my sentiments surprised me because I really had not understood how deep and thorough my dislike had been.

Also, his utter disappearance struck me as uncanny. Both boats were there; and there were many leagues of sea to the nearest coast.

Troubled and puzzled I turned and walked back to the dead embers of the fire. Kemper had merely changed the timbre of his snore to a whistling aria, which at any other time would have enraged me. Now, somehow, it almost comforted me.

Seated on the shore I looked out to sea, racking my brains for an explanation of Grue's disappearance. And while I sat there racking them, far out on the water a little flock of ducks suddenly scattered and rose with frightened quackings and furiously beating wings.

For a moment I thought I saw a round, dark object on the waves where the flock had been.

And while I sat there watching, up out of the sea along the reef to my right crawled a naked, dripping figure holding a dead duck in his mouth.

Fascinated, I watched it, recognising Grue with his ratty black hair all plastered over his face.

Whether he caught sight of me or not, I don't know; but he suddenly dropped the dead duck from his mouth, turned, and dived under water.

It was a grim and horrid species of sport or pastime, this amphibious business of his, catching wild birds and dragging them about as though he were an animal.

Evidently he was ashamed of himself, for he had dropped the duck. I watched it floating by on the waves, its head under water. Suddenly something jerked it under, a fish perhaps, for it did not come up and float again, as far as I could see.

When I went back to camp Grue lay apparently asleep on the north side of the fire. I glanced at him in disgust and crawled into my tent.

The next day Evelyn Grey awoke with a headache and kept her tent. I had all I could do to prevent Kemper from prescribing for her. I did that myself, sitting beside her and testing her pulse for hours at a time, while Kemper took one of Grue's grains and went off into the mangroves and speared grunt and eels for a chowder which he said he knew how to concoct.

Toward afternoon the pretty waitress felt much better, and I warned Kemper and Grue that we should sail for Black Bayou after dinner.

Dinner was a mess, as usual, consisting of fried mullet and rice, and a sort of chowder in which the only ingredients I recognised were sections of crayfish.

After we had finished and had withdrawn from the fire, Grue scraped every remaining shred of food into a kettle and went for it. To see him feed made me sick, so I rejoined Miss Grey and Kemper, who had found a green cocoanut and were alternately deriving nourishment from the milk inside it.

Somehow or other there seemed to me a certain levity about that performance, and it made me uncomfortable; but I managed to smile a rather sickly smile when they offered me a draught, and I took a pull at the milk—I don't exactly know why, because I don't like it. But the moon was up over the sea, now, and the dusk was languorously balmy, and I didn't care to leave those two drinking milk out of the same cocoanut under a tropic moon.

Not that my interest in Evelyn Grey was other than scientific. But after all it was I who had discovered her.

We sailed as soon as Grue, gobbling and snuffling, had cleaned up the last crumb of food. Kemper blandly offered to take Miss Grey into his boat, saying that he feared my boat was overcrowded, what with the paraphernalia, the folding cages, Grue, Miss Grey, and myself.

I sat on that suggestion, but offered to take my own tiller and lend him Grue. He couldn't wriggle out of it, seeing that his alleged motive had been the overcrowding of my boat, but he looked rather sick when Grue went aboard his boat.

As for me, I hoisted sail with something so near a chuckle that it surprised me; and I looked at Evelyn Grey to see whether she had noticed the unseemly symptom.

Apparently she had not. She sat forward, her eyes fixed soulfully upon the moon. Had I been dedicated to any profession except a scientific one—but let that pass.

Grue in Kemper's sail-boat led, and my boat followed out into the silvery and purple dusk, now all sparkling under the high lustre of the moon.

Dimly I saw vast rafts of wild duck part and swim leisurely away to port and starboard, leaving a glittering lane of water for us to sail through; into the scintillant night from the sea sprang mullet, silvery, quivering, falling back into the wash with a splash.

Here and there in the moonlight steered ominous black triangles, circling us, leading us, sheering across bow and flashing wake, all phosphorescent with lambent sea-fire—the fins of great sharks.

"You need have no fear," said I to the pretty waitress.

She said nothing.

"Of course if you *are* afraid," I added, "perhaps you might care to change your seat."

There was room in the stern where I sat.

"Do you think there is any danger?" she asked.

"From sharks?"

"Yes."

"Reaching up and biting you?"

"Yes."

"Oh, I don't really suppose there is," I said, managing to convey the idea, I am ashamed to say, that the catastrophe was a possibility.

She came over and seated herself beside me. I was very much ashamed of myself, but I could not repress a triumphant glance ahead at the other boat, where Kemper sat huddled forward, evidently bored to extinction.

Every now and then I could see him turn and crane his neck as though in an effort to distinguish what was going on in our boat.

There was nothing going on, absolutely nothing. The moon was magnificent; and I think the pretty waitress must have been a little tired, for her head drooped and nodded at moments, even while I was talking to her about a specimen of *Euplectilla speciosa* on which I had written a monograph. So she must have been really tired, for the subject was interesting.

"You won't incommode my operations with sheet and tiller," I said to her kindly, "if you care to rest your head against my shoulder."

Evidently she was very tired, for she did so, and closed her eyes.

After a while, fearing that she might fall over backward into the sea—but let that pass... I don't know whether or not Kemper could distinguish anything aboard our boat. He craned his head enough to twist it off his neck.

To be so utterly, so blindly devoted to science is a great safeguard for a man. Single-mindedness, however, need not induce atrophy of every humane impulse. I drew the pretty waitress closer—not that the night was cold, but it might become so. Changes in the tropics come swiftly. It is well to be prepared.

Her cheek felt very soft against my shoulder. There seemed to be a faint perfume about her hair. It really was odd how subtly fragrant she seemed to be—almost, perhaps, a matter of scientific interest.

Her hands did not seem to be chilled; they did seem unusually smooth and soft.

I said to her: "When at home, I suppose your mother tucks you in; doesn't she?"

"Yes," she nodded sleepily.

"And what does she do then?" said I, with something of that ponderous playfulness with which I make scientific jokes at a meeting of the Bronx Anthropological Association, when I preside.

"She kisses me and turns out the light," said Evelyn Grey, innocently.

I don't know how much Kemper could distinguish. He kept dodging about and twisting his head until I really thought it would come off, unless it had been screwed on like the top of a piano stool.

A few minutes later he fired his pistol twice; and Evelyn sat up. I never knew why he fired; he never offered any explanation.

Toward midnight I could hear the roar of breakers on our starboard bow. Evelyn heard them, too, and sat up inquiringly.

"Grue has found the inlet to Black Bayou, I suppose," said I.

And it proved to be the case, for, with the surf thundering on either hand, we sailed into a smoothly flowing inlet through which the flood tide was running between high dunes all sparkling in the moonlight and crowned with shadowy palms.

Occasionally I heard noises ahead of us from the other boat, as though Kemper was trying to converse with us, but as his apropos was as unintelligible as it was inopportune, I pretended not to hear him. Besides, I had all I could do to manoeuvre the tiller and prevent Evelyn Grey from falling off backward into the bayou. Besides, it is not customary to converse with the man at the helm.

After a while—during which I seemed to distinguish in Kemper's voice a quality that rhymes with his name—his tones varied through phases all the way from irony to exasperation. After a while he gave it up and took to singing.

There was a moon, and I suppose he thought he had a voice. It didn't strike me so. After several somewhat melancholy songs, he let off his pistol two or three times and then subsided into silence.

I didn't care; neither his songs nor his shots interrupted—but let that pass, also.

We were now sailing into the forest through pool after pool of interminable lagoons, startling into unseen and clattering flight hundreds of waterfowl. I could feel the wind from their whistling wings in the darkness, as they drove by us out to sea. It seemed to startle the pretty waitress. It is a solemn thing to be responsible for a pretty girl's peace of mind. I reassured her continually, perhaps a trifle nervously. But there were no more pistol shots. Perhaps Kemper had used up his cartridges.

We were still drifting along under drooping sails, borne inland almost entirely by the tide, when the first pale, watery, gray light streaked the east. When it grew a little lighter, Evelyn sat up; all danger of sharks being over. Also, I could begin to see what was going on in the other boat. Which was nothing remarkable; Kemper slumped against the mast, his head turned in our direction; Grue sat at the helm, motionless, his tattered straw hat sagging on his neck.

When the sun rose, I called out cheerily to Kemper, asking him how he had passed the night. Evelyn also raised her head, pausing while bringing her disordered hair under discipline, to listen to his reply.

But he merely mumbled something. Perhaps he was still sleepy.

As for me, I felt exceedingly well; and when Grue turned his craft in shore, I did so, too; and when, under the overhanging foliage of the forest, the nose of my boat grated on the sand, I rose and crossed the deck with a step distinctly frolicsome.

Kemper seemed distant and glum; Evelyn Grey spoke to him shyly now and then, and I noticed she looked at him only when he was gazing elsewhere than at her. She had a funny, conciliatory air with him, half ashamed, partly humorous and amused, as though something about Kemper's sulky ill-humour was continually making tiny inroads on her gravity.

Some mullet had jumped into the two boats—half a dozen during our moonlight voyage—and these were now being fried with rice for us by Grue. Lord! How I hated to eat them!

After we had finished breakfast, Grue, as usual, did everything to the remainder except to get into the fry-pan with both feet; and as usual he sickened me.

When he'd cleaned up everything, I sent him off into the forest to find a dry shell-mound for camping purposes; then I made fast both boats, and Kemper and I carried ashore our paraphernalia, spare batterie-de-cuisine, firearms, fishing tackle, spears, harpoons, grains, oars, sails, spars, folding cage—everything with which a strictly scientific expedition is usually burdened.

Evelyn was washing her face in the crystal waters of a branch that flowed into the lagoon from under the live-oaks. She looked very pretty doing it, like a naiad or dryad scrubbing away at her forest toilet.

It was, in fact, such a pretty spectacle that I was going over to sit beside her while she did it, but Kemper started just when I was going to, and I turned away. Some men invariably do the wrong thing. But a handsome man doesn't last long with a pretty girl.

I was thinking of this as I stood contemplating an alligator slide, when Grue came back saying that the shore on which we had landed was the termination of a shell-mound, and that it was the only dry place he had found.

So I bade him pitch our tents a few feet back from the shore; and stood watching him while he did so, one eye reverting occasionally to Evelyn Grey and Kemper. They both were seated crosslegged beside the branch, and they seemed to be talking a great deal and rather earnestly. I couldn't quite understand what they found to talk about so earnestly and volubly all of a sudden, inasmuch as they had heretofore exchanged very few observations during a most brief and formal acquaintance, dating only from sundown the day before.

Grue set up our three tents, carried the luggage inland, and then hung about for a while until the vast shadow of a vulture swept across the trees.

I never saw such an indescribable expression on a human face as I saw on Grue's as he looked up at the huge, unclean bird. His vitreous eyes fairly glittered; the corners of his mouth quivered and grew wet; and to my astonishment he seemed to emit a low, mewing noise.

"What the devil are you doing?" I said impulsively, in my amazement and disgust.

He looked at me, his eyes still glittering, the corners of his mouth still wet; but the curious sounds had ceased.

"What?" he asked.

"Nothing. I thought you spoke." I didn't know what else to say.

He made no reply. Once, when I had partly turned my head, I was aware that he was warily turning his to look at the vulture, which had alighted heavily on the ground near the entrails and heads of the mullet, where he had cast them on the dead leaves.

I walked over to where Evelyn Grey and Kemper sat so busily conversing; and their volubility ceased as they glanced up and saw me approaching. Which phenomenon both perplexed and displeased me. I said:

"This is the Black Bayou forest, and we have the most serious business of our lives before us. Suppose you and I start out, Kemper, and see if there are any traces of what we are after in the neighborhood of our camp."

"Do you think it safe to leave Miss Grey alone in camp?" he asked gravely.

I hadn't thought of that:

"No, of course not," I said. "Grue can stay."

"I don't need anybody," she said quickly. "Anyway, I'm rather afraid of Grue."

"Afraid of Grue?" I repeated.

"Not exactly afraid. But he's—unpleasant."

"I'll remain with Miss Grey," said Kemper politely.

"Oh," she exclaimed, "I couldn't ask that. It is true that I feel a little tired and nervous, but I can go with you and Mr. Smith and Grue—"

I surveyed Kemper in cold perplexity. As chief of the expedition, I couldn't very well offer to remain with Evelyn Grey, but I didn't propose that Kemper should, either.

"Take Grue," he suggested, "and look about the woods for a while. Perhaps after dinner Miss Grey may feel sufficiently rested to join us."

"I am sure," she said, "that a few hours' rest in camp will set me on my feet. All I need is rest. I didn't sleep very soundly last night."

I felt myself growing red, and I looked away from them both.

"Oh," said Kemper, in apparent surprise, "I thought you had slept soundly all night long."

"Nobody," said I, "could have slept very pleasantly during that musical performance of yours."

"Were you singing?" she asked innocently of Kemper.

"He was singing when he wasn't firing off his pistol," I remarked. "No wonder you couldn't sleep with any satisfaction to yourself."

Grue had disappeared into the forest; I stood watching for him to come out again. After a few minutes I heard a furious but distant noise of flapping; the others also heard it; and we listened in silence, wondering what it was.

"It's Grue killing something," faltered Evelyn Grey, turning a trifle pale.

"Confound it!" I exclaimed. "I'm going to stop that right now."

Kemper rose and followed me as I started for the woods; but as we passed the beached boats Grue appeared from among the trees.

"Where have you been?" I demanded.

"In the woods."

"Doing what?"

"Nothing."

There was a bit of down here and there clinging to his cotton shirt and trousers, and one had caught and stuck at the corner of his mouth.

"See here, Grue," I said, "I don't want you to kill any birds except for camp purposes. Why do you try to catch and kill birds?"

"I don't."

I stared at the man and he stared back at me out of his glassy eyes.

"You mean to say that you don't, somehow or other, manage to catch and kill birds?"

"No, I don't."

There was nothing further for me to say unless I gave him the lie. I didn't care to do that, needing his services.

Evelyn Grey had come up to join us; there was a brief silence; we all stood looking at Grue; and he looked back at us out of his pale, washed-out, and unblinking eyes.

"Grue," I said, "I haven't yet explained to you the object of this expedition to Black Bayou. Now, I'll tell you what I want. But first let me ask you a question or two. You know the Black Bayou forests, don't you?"

"Yes."

"Did you ever see anything unusual in these forests?"

"No."

"Are you sure?"

The man stared at us, one after another. Then he said:

"What are you looking for in Black Bayou?"

"Something very curious, very strange, very unusual. So strange and unusual, in fact, that the great Zoölogical Society of the Bronx in New York has sent me down here at the head of this expedition to search the forests of Black Bayou."

"For what?" he demanded, in a dull, accentless voice.

"For a totally new species of human being, Grue. I wish to catch one and take it back to New York in that folding cage."

His green eyes had grown narrow as though sun-dazzled. Kemper had stepped behind us into the woods and was now busy setting up the folding cage. Grue remained motionless.

"I am going to offer you," I said, "the sum of one thousand dollars in gold if you can guide us to a spot where we may see this hitherto unknown species—a creature which is apparently a man but which has, in the back of his head, *a third eye*—"

I paused in amazement: Grue's cheeks had suddenly puffed out and were quivering; and from the corners of his slitted mouth he was emitting a whimpering sound like the noise made by a low-circling pigeon.

"Grue!" I cried. "What's the matter with you?"

"What is *he* doing?" screamed Grue, quivering from head to foot, but not turning around.

"Who?" I cried.

"The man behind me!"

"Professor Kemper? He's setting up the folding cage—"

With a screech that raised my hair, Grue whipped out his murderous knife and *hurled himself backward* at Kemper, but the latter shrank aside behind the partly erected cage, and Grue whirled around, snarling, hacking, and even biting at the wood frame and steel bars.

And then occurred a thing so horrid that it sickened me to the pit of my stomach; for the man's sagging straw hat had fallen off, and there, in the back of his head, through the coarse, black, ratty hair, I saw a glassy eye glaring at me.

"Kemper!" I shouted. "He's got a third eye! He's one of them! Knock him flat with your rifle-stock!" And I seized a shot-gun from the top of the baggage bundle on the ground beside me, and leaped at Grue, aiming a terrific blow at him.

But the glassy eye in the back of his head was watching me between the clotted strands of hair, and he dodged both Kemper and me, swinging his heavy knife in circles and glaring at us both out of the front and back of his head.

Kemper seized him by his arm, but Grue's shirt came off, and I saw his entire body was as furry as an ape's. And all the while he was snapping at us and leaping hither and thither to avoid our blows; and from the corners of his puffed cheeks he whined and whimpered and mewed through the saliva foam.

"Keep him from the water!" I panted, following him with clubbed shot-gun; and as I advanced I almost stepped on a soiled heap of foulness—the dead buzzard which he had caught and worried to death with his teeth.

Suddenly he threw his knife at my head, hurling it backward; dodged, screeched, and bounded by me toward the shore of the lagoon, where the pretty waitress was standing, petrified.

For one moment I thought he had her, but she picked up her skirts, ran for the nearest boat, and seized a harpoon; and in his fierce eagerness to catch her he leaped clear over the boat and fell with a splash into the lagoon.

As Kemper and I sprang aboard and looked over into the water, we could see him going down out of reach of a harpoon; and his body seemed to be silver-plated, flashing and glittering like a burnished eel, so completely did the skin of air envelope him, held there by the fur that covered him.

And, as he rested for a moment on the bottom, deep down through the clear waters of the lagoon where he lay prone, I could see, as the current stirred his long, black hair, the third eye looking up at us, glassy, unwinking, horrible.

A bubble or two, like globules of quicksilver, were detached from the burnished skin of air that clothed him, and came glittering upward.

Suddenly there was a flash; a flurrying cloud of blue mud; and Grue was gone.

After a long while I turned around in the muteness of my despair. And slowly froze.

For the pretty waitress, becomingly pale, was gathered in Kemper's arms, her cheek against his shoulder. Neither seemed to be aware of me.

"Darling," he said, in the imbecile voice of a man in love, "why do you tremble so when I am here to protect you? Don't you love and trust me?"

"Oo—h—yes," she sighed, pressing her cheek closer to his shoulder.

I shoved my hands into my pockets, passed them without noticing them, and stepped ashore.

And there I sat down under a tree, with my back toward them, all alone and face to face with the greatest grief of my life.

But which it was—the loss of her or the loss of Grue, I had not yet made up my mind.

THE IMMORTAL

I

As everybody knows, the great majority of Americans, upon reaching the age of natural selection, are elected to the American Institute of Arts and Ethics, which is, so to speak, the Ellis Island of the Academy.

Occasionally a general mobilization of the Academy is ordered and, from the teeming population of the Institute, a new Immortal is selected for the American Academy of Moral Endeavor by the simple process of blindfolded selection from *Who's Which*.

The motto of this most stately of earthly institutions is a peculiarly modest, truthful, and unintentional epigram by Tupper: "Unknown, I became Famous; Famous, I remain Unknown."

And so I found it to be the case; for, when at last I was privileged to write my name, "Smith, Academician," I discovered to my surprise that I knew none of my brother Immortals, and, more amazing still, none of them had ever heard of me.

This latter fact became the more astonishing to me as I learned the identity of the other Immortals.

Even the President of our great republic was numbered among these Olympians. I had every right to suppose that he had heard of me. I had happened to hear of him, because his Secretary of State once mentioned him at Chautauqua.

It was a wonderfully meaningless sensation to know nobody and to discover myself equally unknown amid that matchless companionship. We were like a mixed bunch of gods, Greek, Norse, Hindu, Hottentot—all gathered on Olympus, having never heard of each other but taking it for granted that we were all gods together and all members of this club.

My initiation into the Academy had been fixed for April first, and I was much worried concerning the address which I was of course expected to deliver on that occasion before my fellow members.

It had to be an exciting address because slumber was not an infrequent phenomenon among the Immortals on such solemn occasions. Like dozens of dozing Joves a dull discourse always set them nodding.

But always under such circumstances the pretty ushers from Barnard College passed around refreshments; a suffragette orchestra struck up; the ushers uprooted the seated Immortals and foxtrotted them into comparative consciousness.

But I didn't wish to have my inaugural address interrupted, therefore I was at my wits' ends to discover a subject of such exciting scientific interest that my august audience could not choose but listen as attentively as they would listen from the front row to some deathless stunt in vaudeville.

That morning I had left the Bronx rather early, hoping that a long walk might compose my thoughts and enable me to think of some sufficiently entertaining and unusual subject for my inaugural address.

I walked as far as Columbia University, gazed with rapture upon its magnificent architecture until I was as satiated as though I had arisen from a banquet at Childs'.

To aid mental digestion I strolled over to the noble home of the Academy and Institute adjoining Mr. Huntington's Hispano-Moresque Museum.

It was a fine, sunny morning, and the Immortals were being exercised by a number of pretty ushers from Barnard.

I gazed upon the impressive procession with pride unutterable; very soon I also should walk two and two in the sunshine, my dome crowned with figurative laurels, cracking scientific witticisms with my fellow inmates, or, perhaps, squeezing the pretty fingers of some— But let that pass.

I was, as I say, gazing upon this inspiring scene on a beautiful morning in February, when I became aware of a short and visibly vulgar person beside me, plucking persistently at my elbow.

"Are you the great Academician, Perfessor Smith?" he asked, tipping his pearl-coloured and somewhat soiled bowler.

"Yes," I said condescendingly. "Your description of me precludes further doubt. What can I do for you, my good man?"

"Are you this here Perfessor Smith of the Department of Anthropology in the Bronx Park Zoölogical Society?" he persisted.

"What do you desire of me?" I repeated, taking another look at him. He was exceedingly ordinary.

"Prof, old sport," he said cordially, "I took a slant at the papers yesterday, an' I seen all about the big time these guys had when you rode the goat—"

"Rode—*what?*"

"When you was elected. Get me?"

I stared at him. He grinned in a friendly way.

"The privacy of those solemn proceedings should remain sacred. It were unfit to discuss such matters with the world at large," I said coldly.

"I get you," he rejoined cheerfully.

"What do you desire of me?" I repeated. "Why this unseemly apropos?"

"I was comin' to it. Perfessor, I'll be frank. I need money—"

"You need brains!"

"No," he said good-humouredly, "I've got 'em; plenty of 'em; I'm overstocked with idees. What I want to do is to sell *you* a few—"

"Do you know you are impudent!"

"Listen, friend. I seen a piece in the papers as how you was to make the speech of your life when you ride the goat for these here guys on April first—"

"'I decline to listen—"

"*One* minute, friend! I want to ask you one thing! *What* are you going to talk about?"

I was already moving away but I stopped and stared at him.

"That's the question," he nodded with unimpaired cheerfulness, "*what* are you going to talk about on April the first? Remember it's the hot-air party of your life. *Ree*-member that each an' every paper in the United States will print what you say. Now, how about it, friend? Are you up in your lines?"

Swallowing my repulsion for him I said: "Why are you concerned as to what may be the subject of my approaching address?"

"There you are, Prof!" he exclaimed delightedly; "I want to do business with you. That's me! I'm frank about it. Say, there ought to be a wad of the joyful in it for us both—"

"What?"

"Sure. We can work it any old way. Take Tyng, Tyng and Company, the typewriter people. I'd be ashamed to tell you what I can get out o' them if you'll mention the Tyng-Tyng typewriter in your speech—"

"What you suggest is infamous!" I said haughtily.

"Believe *me* there's enough in it to make it a financial coup, and I ask you, Prof, isn't a financial coup respectable?"

"You seem to be morally unfitted to comprehend—"

"Pardon *me!* I'm fitted up regardless with all kinds of fixtures. I'm fixed to undertake anything. Now if you'd prefer the Bunsen Baby Biscuit bunch—why old man Bunsen would come across—"

"I won't do such things!" I said angrily.

"Very well, very well. Dont get riled, sir. That's only one way to build on Fifth Avenoo. I've got one hundred thousand other ways—"

"I don't want to talk to you—"

"They're honest—some of them. Say, if you want a stric'ly honest deal I've got the goods. Only it ain't as easy and the money ain't as big—"

"I don't want to talk to you—"

"Yes you do. You don't reelize it but you do. Why you're fixin' to make the holler of your life, ain't you? What are you goin' to say? Hey? What you aimin' to say to make those guys set up? What's the use of up-stagin'? Ain't you willin' to pay me a few plunks if I *dy*-vulge to you the most startlin' phenomena that has ever electrified civilization sense the era of P. T. Barnum!"

I was already hurrying away when the mention of that great scientist's name halted me once more.

The little flashy man had been tagging along at my heels, talking cheerfully and volubly all the while; and now, as I halted again, he struck an attitude, legs apart, thumbs hooked in his arm-pits, and his head cocked knowingly on one side.

"Prof," he said, "if you'd work in the Tyng-Tyng Company, or fix it up with Bunsen to mention his Baby Biscuits as the most nootritious of condeements, there'd be more in it for you an' me. But it's up to you."

"Well I won't!" I retorted.

"Very well, ve-ry well," he said soothingly. "Then look over another line o' samples. No trouble to show 'em—none at all, sir! Now if P. T. Barnum was alive—"

I said very seriously: "The name of that great discoverer falling from your illiterate lips has halted me a second time. His name alone invests your somewhat suspicious conversation with a dignity and authority heretofore conspicuously absent. If, as you hint, you have any scientific information for sale which P. T. Barnum might have considered worth purchasing, you may possibly find in me a client. Proceed, young sir."

"Say, listen, Bo—I mean, Prof. I've got the goods. Don't worry. I've got information in my think-box that would make your kick-in speech the event of the century. The question remains, do I get mine?"

"What is this scientific information?"

We had now walked as far as Riverside Drive. There were plenty of unoccupied benches. I sat down and he seated himself beside me.

For a few moments I gazed upon the magnificent view. Even he seemed awed by the proportions of the superb iron gas tank dominating the prospect.

I gazed at the colossal advertisements across the Hudson, at the freight trains below; I gazed upon the lordly Hudson itself, that majestic sewer which drains the Empire State, bearing within its resistless flood millions of tons of insoluble matter from that magic fairyland which we call "up-state," to the sea. And, thinking of disposal plants, I thought of that sublime paraphrase— "From the Mohawk to the Hudson, and from the Hudson to the Sea."

"Bo," he said, "I gotta hand it to you. Them guys might have got wise if you had worked in the Tyng-Tyng Company or the Bunsen stuff. There was big money into it, but it might not have went."

I waited curiously.

"But this here dope I'm startin' in to cook for you is a straight, reelible, an' hones' pill. P. T. Barnum he would have went a million miles to see what I seen last Janooary down in the Coquina country—"

"Where is that?"

"Say; that's what costs money to know. When I put you wise I'm due to retire from actyve business. Get me?"

"Go on."

"Sure. I was down to the Coquina country, adoin'—well, I was doin' rubes. I gotta be hones' with *you*, Prof. That's what I was a-doin' of—sellin' farms under water to suckers. Bee-u-tiful Florida! Own your own orange grove. Seven crops o' strawberries every winter in Gawd's own country—get me?"

He bestowed upon me a loathsome wink.

"Well, it went big till I made a break and got in Dutch with the Navy Department what was surveyin' the Everglades for a safe and sane harbor of refuge for the navy in time o' war.

"Sir, they was a-dredgin' up the farms I was sellin', an' the suckers heard of it an' squealed somethin' fierce, an' I had to hustle! Yes, sir, I had to git up an' mosey cross-lots. And what with the Federal Gov'ment chasin' me one way an' them rubes an' the sheriff of Pickalocka County racin' me t'other, I got lost for fair—yes, sir."

He smiled reminiscently, produced from his pockets the cold and offensive remains of a partly consumed cigar, and examined it critically. Then he requested a match.

"I shall now pass over lightly or in subdood silence the painful events of my flight," he remarked, waving his cigar and expelling a long squirt of smoke from his unshaven lips. "Surfice it to say that I got everythin' that was comin' to me, an' then some, what with snakes and murskeeters, an' briers an' mud, an' hunger an' thirst an' heat. Wasn't there a wop named Pizarro or somethin' what got lost down in Florida? Well, he's got nothin' on me. I never want to see the dam' state again. But I'll go back if *you* say so!"

His small rat eyes rested musingly upon the river; he sucked thoughtfully at his cigar, hooked one soiled thumb into the arm-hole of his fancy vest and crossed his legs.

"To resoom," he said cheerily; "I come out one day, half nood, onto the banks of the Miami River. The rest was a pipe after what I had went through.

"I trimmed a guy at Miami, got clothes and railroad fare, an' ducked.

"Now the valyble portion of my discourse is this here partial information concernin' what I seen—or rather what I run onto durin' my crool flight from my ree-lentless persecutors.

"An' these here is the facts: There is, contrary to maps, Coast Survey guys, an' general opinion, a range of hills in Florida, made entirely of coquina.

"It's a good big range, too, fifty miles long an' anywhere from one to five miles acrost.

"An' what I've got to say is this: Into them there Coquina hills there still lives the expirin' remains of the cave-men—"

"What!" I exclaimed incredulously.

"Or," he continued calmly, "to speak more stric'ly, the few individools of that there expirin' race is now totally reduced to a few women."

"Your statement is wild—"

"No; but *they're* wild. I seen 'em. Bein' extreemly bee-utiful I approached nearer, but they hove rocks at me, they did, an' they run into the rocks like squir'ls, they did, an' I was too much on the blink to stick around whistlin' for dearie.

"But I seen 'em; they was all dolled up in the skins of wild annermals. When I see the first one she was eatin' onto a ear of corn, an' I nearly ketched her, but she run like hellnall—yes, sir. Just like that.

"So next I looked for some cave guy to waltz up an' paste me, but no. An' after I had went through them dam' Coquina mountains I reelized that there was nary a guy left in this here expirin' race, only women, an' only about a dozen o' them."

He ceased, meditatively expelled a cloud of pungent smoke, and folded his arms.

"Of course," said I with a sneer, "you have proofs to back your pleasant tale?"

"Sure. I made a map."

"'I see," said I sarcastically. "You propose to have me pay you for that map?"

"Sure."

"How much, my confiding friend?"

"Ten thousand plunks."

I began to laugh. He laughed, too: "You'll pay 'em if you take my map an' go to the Coquina hills," he said.

I stopped laughing: "Do you mean that I am to go there and investigate before I pay you for this information?"

"Sure. If the goods ain't up to sample the deal is off."

"Sample? What sample?" I demanded derisively.

He made a gesture with one soiled hand as though quieting a balky horse.

"I took a snapshot, friend. You wanta take a slant at it?"

"You took a photograph of one of these alleged cave-dwellers?"

"I took ten but when these here cave-ladies hove rocks at me the fillums was put on the blink—all excep' this one which I dee-veloped an' printed."

He drew from his inner coat pocket a photograph and handed it to me the most amazing photograph I ever gazed upon. As-tounded, almost convinced I sat looking at this irrefutable evidence in silence. The smoke of his cigar drifting into my face aroused me from a sort of dazed inertia.

"Listen," I said, half strangled, "are you willing to wait for pay-ment until I personally have verified the existence of these—er—creatures?"

"You betcher! When you have went there an' have saw the goods, just let me have mine if they're up to sample. Is that right?"

"It seems perfectly fair."

"It is fair. I wouldn't try to do a scientific guy—no, sir. Me with-out no eddycation, only brains? Fat chance I'd have to put one over on a Academy sport what's chuck-a-block with Latin an' Greek an' scientific stuff an' all like that!"

I admitted to myself that he'd stand no chance.

"Is it a go?" he asked.

"Where is the map?" I inquired, trembling internally with ex-citement.

"Ha—ha!" he said. "Listen to my mirth! The map is inside here, old sport!" and he tapped his retreating forehead with one nicotine-stained finger.

"I see," said I, trying to speak carelessly; "you desire to pilot me."

"I don't desire to but I gotta go with you."

"An accurate map—"

"Can it, old sport! A accurate map is all right when it's pasted over the front of your head for a face. But I wear the other kind of map *inside* me conk. Get me?"

"I confess that I do not."

"Well, get *this*, then. It's a cash deal. If the goods is up to sample you hand me mine then an' there. I don't deliver no goods f.o.b. I shows 'em to you. After you have saw them it's up to you to round 'em up. That's all, as they say when our great President pulls a gun. There ain't goin' to be no shootin'; walk out quietly, ladies!"

After I had sat there for fully ten minutes staring at him I came to the only logical conclusion possible to a scientific mind.

I said: "You are, admittedly, unlettered; you are confessedly a chevalier of industry; personally you are exceedingly distasteful to me. But it is useless to deny that you are the most extraordinary man I ever saw... How soon can you take me to these Coquina hills?"

"Gimme twenty-four hours to—fix things," he said gaily.

"Is that all?"

"It's plenty, I guess. An'—say!"

"What?"

"It's a stric'ly cash deal. Get me?"

"I shall have with me a certified check for ten thousand dollars. Also a pair of automatics."

He laughed: "Huh!" he said, "I could loco your cabbage-palm soup if I was *that* kind! I'm on the level, Perfessor. If I wasn't I could get you in about a hundred styles while you was blinkin' at what you was a-thinkin' about. But I ain't no gun-man. You hadn't oughta pull that stuff on me. I've give you your chanst; take it or leave it."

I pondered profoundly for another ten minutes. And at last my decision was irrevocably reached.

"It's a bargain," I said firmly. "What is your name?"

"Sam Mink. Write it Samuel onto that there certyfied check—if you can spare the extra seconds from your valooble time."

II

On Monday, the first day of March, 1915, about 10:30 A. M., we came in sight of something which, until I had met Mink, I never had dreamed existed in southern Florida—a high range of hills.

It had been an eventless journey from New York to Miami, from Miami to Fort Coquina; but from there through an absolutely pathless wilderness as far as I could make out, the journey had been exasperating.

Where we went I do not know even now: sawgrass and water, hammock and shell mound, palm forests, swamps, wildernesses of water-oak and live-oak, vast stretches of pine, lagoons, sloughs, branches, muddy creeks, reedy reaches from which wild fowl rose in clouds where alligators lurked or lumbered about after stranded fish, horrible mangrove thickets full of moccasins and water-turkeys, heronry more horrible still, out of which the heat from a vertical sun distilled the last atom of nauseating effluvia—all these choice spots we visited under the guidance of the wretched Mink. I seemed to be missing nothing that might discourage or disgust me.

He appeared to know the way, somehow, although my compass became mysteriously lost the first day out from Fort Coquina.

Again and again I felt instinctively that we were travelling in a vast circle, but Mink always denied it, and I had no scientific instruments to verify my deepening suspicions.

Another thing bothered me: Mink did not seem to suffer from insects or heat; in fact, to my intense annoyance, he appeared to be having a comfortable time of it, eating and drinking with gusto, sleeping snugly under a mosquito bar, permitting me to do all camp work, the paddling as long as we used a canoe, and all the cooking, too, claiming, on his part, a complete ignorance of culinary art.

Sometimes he condescended to catch a few fish for the common pan; sometimes he bestirred himself to shoot a duck or two. But usually he played on his concertina during his leisure moments which were plentiful.

I began to detest Samuel Mink.

At first I was murderously suspicious of him, and I walked about with my automatic arsenal ostentatiously displayed. But he looked like such a miserable little shrimp that I became ashamed of my precautions. Besides, as he cheerfully pointed out, a little koonti soaked in my drinking water, would have done my business for me if he had meant me any physical harm. Also he had a horrid habit of noosing moccasins for sport; and it would have been easy for him to introduce one to me while I slept.

Really what most worried me was the feeling which I could not throw off that somehow or other we were making very little progress in any particular direction.

He even admitted that there was reason for my doubts, but he confided to me that to find these Coquina hills, was like traversing a maze. Doubling to and fro among forests and swamps, he insisted, was the only possible path of access to the undiscovered Coquina hills of Florida. Otherwise; he argued, these Coquina hills would long ago have been discovered.

And it seemed to me that he had been right when at last we came out on the edge of a palm forest and beheld that astounding blue outline of hills in a country which has always been supposed to lie as flat as a flabby flap-jack.

A desert of saw-palmetto stretched away before us to the base of the hills; game trails ran through it in every direction like sheep paths; a few moth-eaten Florida deer trotted away as we appeared.

Into one of these trails stepped Samuel Mink, burdened only with his concertina and a box of cigars. I, loaded with seventy pounds of impedimenta including a moving-picture apparatus, reeled after him.

He walked on jauntily toward the hills, his pearl-coloured bowler hat at an angle. Occasionally he played upon his concertina as he advanced; now and then he cut a pigeon wing. I hated him. At every toilsome step I hated him more deeply. He played "Tipperary" on his concertina.

"See 'em, old top?" he inquired, nodding toward the hills. "I'm a man of my word, I am. Look at 'em! Take 'em in, old sport! An' reemember, each an' every hill is guaranteed to contain one bony

fidy cave-lady what is the last vanishin' traces of a extinc' an'
dissappeerin' race!"

We toiled on—that is, I did, bowed under my sweating load of
paraphernalia. He skipped in advance like some degenerate twen-
tieth century faun, playing on his pipes the unmitigated melodies
of George Cohan.

"Watch your step!" he cried, nimbly avoiding the attentions of
a ground-rattler which tried to caress his ankle from under a saw-
palmetto.

With a shudder I gave the deadly little reptile room and floundered forward a prey to exhaustion, melancholy, and red-bugs. A
few buzzards kept pace with me, their broad, black shadows gliding ominously over the sun-drenched earth; blue-tail lizards went
rustling and leaping away on every side; floppy soft-winged butterflies escorted me; a strange bird which seemed to be dressed in
a union suit of checked gingham, flew from tree to tree as I plodded on, and squealed at me persistently.

At last I felt the hard coquina under foot; the cool blue shadow
of the hills enveloped me; I slipped off my pack, dumped it beside
a little rill of crystal water which ran sparkling from the hills, and
sat down on a soft and fragrant carpet of hound's-tongue.

After a while I drank my fill at the rill, bathed head, neck, face
and arms, and, feeling delightfully refreshed, leaned back against
the fern-covered slab of coquina.

"What are you doing?" I demanded of Mink who was unpack-
ing the kit and disengaging the moving-picture machine.

"Gettin' ready," he replied, fussing busily with the camera.

"You don't expect to see any cave people here, do you?" I asked
with a thrill of reviving excitement.

"Why not?"

"*Here?*"

"Cert'nly. Why the first one I seen was adrinkin' into this
brook."

"Here! Where I'm sitting?" I asked incredulously.

"Yes, sir, right there. It was this way; I was lyin' down, tryin' to
figure the shortes' way to Fort Coquina, an' wishin' I was nearer
Broadway than I was to the Equator, when I heard a voice say,

'Blub-blub, muck-a-muck!' an' then I seen two cave-ladies come sof'ly stealin' along."

"W-where?"

"Right there where you are a-sittin'. Say, they was lookers! An' they come along quiet like two big-eyed deer, kinder nosin' the air and listenin'.

"'Gee whiz,' thinks I, 'Longacre ain't got so much on them dames!' An' at that one o' them wore a wild-cat's skin an' that's all—an' a wild-cat ain't big. And t'other she sported pa'm-leaf pyjamas.

"So when they don't see nothin' around to hinder, they just lays down flat and takes a drink into that pool, lookin' up every swallow like little birds listenin' and kinder thankin' God for a good square drink.

"I knowed they was wild girls soon as I seen 'em. Also they sez to one another, 'Blub-blub!' Kinder sof'ly. All the same I've seen wilder ladies on Broadway so I took a chanst where I was squattin' behind a rock.

"So sez I, 'Ah there, sweetie Blub-blub! Have a taxi on me!' An' with that they is on their feet, quiverin' all over an' nosin' the wind. So first I took some snapshots at 'em with my Bijoo camera.

"I guess they scented me all right for I seen their eyes grow bigger, an' then they give a bound an' was off over the rocks; an' me after 'em. Say, that was some steeple-chase until a few more cave-ladies come out on them rocks above us an' hove chunks of coquina at me.

"An' with all that dodgin' an' duckin' of them there rocks the cave-girls got away; an' I seen 'em an' the other cave-ladies scurryin' into little caves—one whisked into this hole, another scuttled into that—bing! all over!

"All I could think of was to light a cigar an' blow the smoke in after the best-lookin' cave-girl. But I couldn't smoke her out, an' I hadn't time to starve her out. So that's all I know about this here pree-historic an' extinc' race o' vanishin' cave-ladies."

As his simple and illiterate narrative advanced I became proportionally excited; and, when he ended, I sprang to my feet in an uncontrollable access of scientific enthusiasm:

"Was she really pretty?" I asked.

"Listen, she was that peachy—"

"Enough!" I cried. "Science expects every man to do his duty! Are your films ready to record a scene without precedent in the scientific annals of creation?"

"They sure is!"

"Then place your camera and your person in a strategic position. This is a magnificent spot for an ambush! Come over beside me!"

He came across to where I had taken cover among the ferns behind the parapet of coquina, and with a thrill of pardonable joy I watched him unlimber his photographic artillery and place it in battery where my every posture and action would be recorded for posterity if a cave-lady came down to the water-hole to drink.

"It were futile," I explained to him in a guarded voice, "for me to attempt to cajole her as you attempted it. Neither playful nor moral suasion could avail, for it is certain that no cave-lady understands English."

"I thought o' that, too," he remarked. "I said, 'Blub-blub! muck-a-muck!' to 'em when they started to run, but it didn't do no good."

I smiled: "Doubtless," said I, "the spoken language of the cave-dweller is made up of similarly primitive exclamations, and you were quite right in attempting to communicate with the cave-ladies and establish a cordial entente. Professor Garner has done so among the Simian population of Gaboon. Your attempt is most creditable and I shall make it part of my record.

"But the main idea is to capture a living specimen of cave-lady, and corroborate every detail of that pursuit and capture upon the films.

"And believe me, Mr. Mink," I added, my voice trembling with emotion, "no Academician is likely to go to sleep when I illustrate my address with such pictures as you are now about to take!"

"The police might pull the show," he suggested.

"No," said I, "Science is already immune; art is becoming so. Only nature need fear the violence of prejudice; and doubtless she will continue to wear pantalettes and common-sense nighties as long as our great republic endures."

I unslung my field-glasses, adjusted them and took a penetrating squint at the hillside above.

Nothing stirred up there except a buzzard or two wheeling on tip-curled pinions above the palms.

Presently Mink inquired whether I had "lamped" anything, and I replied that I had not.

"They may be snoozin' in their caves," he suggested. "But don't you fret, old top; you'll get what's comin' to you and I'll get mine."

"About that check—" I began and hesitated.

"Sure. What about it?"

"I suppose I'm to give it to you when the first cave-woman appears."

"That's what!"

I pondered the matter for a while in silence. I could see no risk in paying him this draft on sight.

"All right," I said. "Bring on your cave-dwellers."

Hour succeeded hour, but no cave-dwellers came down to the pool to drink. We ate luncheon—a bit of cold duck, some koonti-bread, and a dish of palm-cabbage. I smoked an inexpensive cigar; Mink lit a more pretentious one. Afterward he played on his concertina at my suggestion on the chance that the music might lure a cave-girl down the hill. Nymphs were sometimes caught that way, and modern science seems to be reverting more and more closely to the simpler truths of the classics which, in our ignorance and arrogance, we once dismissed as fables unworthy of scientific notice.

However this Broadway faun piped in vain: no white-footed dryad came stealing through the ferns to gaze, perhaps to dance to the concertina's plaintive melodies.

So after a while he put his concertina into his pocket, cocked his derby hat on one side, gathered his little bandy legs under his person, and squatted there in silence, chewing the wet and bitter end of his extinct cigar.

Toward mid-afternoon I unslung my field-glasses again and surveyed the hill.

At first I noticed nothing, not even a buzzard; then, of a sudden, my attention was attracted to something moving among the fern-covered slabs of coquina just above where we lay concealed— a slim, graceful shape half shadowed under a veil of lustrous hair which glittered like gold in the sun.

"Mink!" I whispered hoarsely. "One of them is coming! This— this indeed is the stupendous and crowning climax of my scientific career!"

His comment was incredibly coarse: "Gimme the dough," he said without a tremor of surprise. Indeed there was a metallic ring of menace in his low and entirely cold tones as he laid one hand on my arm. "No welchin'," he said, "or I put the whole show on the bum!"

The overwhelming excitement of the approaching crisis neutralized my disgust; I fished out the certified check from my pocket and flung the miserable scrap of paper at him. "Get your machine ready!" I hissed. "Do you understand what these moments mean to the civilized world!"

"I sure do," he said.

Nearer and nearer came the lithe white figure under its glorious crown of hair, moving warily and gracefully amid the great coquina slabs—nearer, nearer, until I no longer required my glasses.

She was a slender red-lipped thing, blue-eyed, dainty of hand and foot.

The spotted pelt of a wild-cat covered her, or attempted to.

I unfolded a large canvas sack as she approached the pool. For a moment or two she stood gazing around her and her close-set ears seemed to be listening. Then, apparently satisfied, she threw back her beautiful young head and sent a sweet wild call floating back to the sunny hillside.

"Blub-blub!" rang her silvery voice; "blub-blub! Muck-a-muck!" And from the fern-covered hollows above other voices replied joyously to her reassuring call, "Blub-blub-blub!"

The whole bunch was coming down to drink-the entire remnant of a prehistoric and almost extinct race of human creatures was coming to quench its thirst at this water-hole. How I wished for James Barnes at the camera's crank! He alone could do justice to this golden girl before me.

One by one, clad in their simple yet modest gowns of pelts and garlands, five exquisitively superb specimens of cave-girl came gracefully down to the water-hole to drink.

Almost swooning with scientific excitement I whispered to the unspeakable Mink: "Begin to crank as soon as I move!" And, gathering up my big canvas sack I rose, and, still crouching, stole through the ferns on tip-toe.

They had already begun to drink when they heard me; I must have made some slight sound in the ferns, for their keen ears detected it and they sprang to their feet.

It was a magnificent sight to see them there by the pool, tense, motionless, at gaze, their dainty noses to the wind, their beautiful eyes wide and alert.

For a moment, enchanted, I remained spellbound in the presence of this prehistoric spectacle, then, waving my sack, I sprang out from behind the rock and cantered toward them.

Instead of scattering and flying up the hillside they seemed paralyzed, huddling together as though to get into the picture. Delighted I turned and glanced at Mink; he was cranking furiously.

With an uncontrollable shout of triumph and delight I pranced toward the huddling cave-girls, arms outspread as though heading a horse or concentrating chickens. And, totally forgetting the uselessness of urbanity and civilized speech as I danced around that lovely but terrified group, "Ladies!" I cried, "do not be alarmed, because I mean only kindness and proper respect. Civilization calls you from the wilds! Sentiment, pity, piety propel my legs, not the ruthless desire to injure or enslave you! Ladies! You are under the wing of science. An anthropologist is speaking to you! Fear nothing! Rather rejoice! Your wonderful race shall be rescued from extinction—even if I have to do it myself! Ladies, don't run!" They had suddenly scattered and were now beginning to dodge me. "I come among you bearing the precious promises of education, of religion, of equal franchise, of fashion!"

"Blub-blub!" they whimpered continuing to dodge me.

"Yes!" I cried in an excess of transcendental enthusiasm. "Blub-blub! And though I do not comprehend the exquisite simplicity of your primeval speech, I answer with all my heart, 'Blub-blub!'"

Meanwhile, they were dodging and eluding me as I chased first one, then another, one hand outstretched, the other invitingly clutching the sack.

A hasty glance at Mink now and then revealed him industriously cranking away.

Once I fell into the pool. That section of the film should never be released, I determined, as I blew the water out of my mouth, gasped, and started after a lovely, ruddy-haired cave-girl whose curiosity had led her to linger beside the pool in which I was floundering.

But run as fast as I could and skip hither and thither with all the agility I could muster I did not seem to be able to seize a single cave-girl.

Every few minutes, baffled and breathless, I rested; and they always clustered together uttering their plaintively musical "blub-blub," not apparently very much afraid of me, and even exhibiting curiosity. Now and then they cast glances toward Mink who was grinding away steadily, and I could scarcely retain a shout of joy as I realized what wonderful pictures he was taking. Indeed luck seemed to be with me, so far, for never once did these beautiful prehistoric creatures retire out of photographic range.

But otherwise the problem was becoming serious. I could not catch one of them; they eluded me with maddening swiftness and grace, my pauses to recover my breath became more frequent.

At last, dead beat, I sat down on a slab of coquina. And when I was able to articulate I turned around toward Mink.

"You'll have to drop your camera and come over and help me," I panted. "I'm all in!"

"Not quite," he said.

For a moment I did not understand him; then under my outraged eyes, and within the hearing of my horrified ear's a terrible thing occurred.

"Now, ladies!" yelled Mink, "all on for the fine-ally! Up-stage there, you red-headed little spot-crabber! Mabel! Take the call! Now smile the whole bloomin' bunch of you!"

What was he saying? I did not comprehend. I stared dully at the six cave-girls as they grouped themselves in a semi-circle behind me.

254   Robert W. Chambers

Then, as one of them came up and unfolded a white strip of cloth behind my head, the others drew from concealed pockets in their kilts of cat-fur, little silk flags of all nations and began to wave them.

Paralyzed I turned my head. On the strip of white cloth, which the tallest cave-girl was holding directly behind my head, was printed in large black letters:

Sunset Soap

For one cataclysmic instant I gazed upon this hideous spectacle, then with an unearthly cry I collapsed into the arms of the nicest looking one.

There is little more to say. Contrary to my fears the release of this outrageous film did not injure my scientific standing. Modern science, accustomed to proprietary testimonials, has become reconciled to such things.

My appearance upon the films in the movies in behalf of Sunset Soap, oddly enough, seemed to enhance my scientific reputation. Even such austere purists as Guilford, the Cubist poet, congratulated me upon my fearless independence of ethical tradition.

And I had lived to learn a gentler truth than that, for, the pretty girl who had been cast for Cave-girl No. 3—But let that pass. *Adhibenda est in jocando moderatio.*

Sweet are the uses of advertisement.

I

At the suggestion of several hundred thousand ladies desiring to revel and possibly riot in the saturnalia of equal franchise, the unnamed lakes in that vast and little known region in Alaska bounded by the Ylanqui River and the Thunder Mountains were now being inexorably named after women.

It was a beautiful thought. Already several exquisite, lonely bits of water, gem-set among the eternal peaks, mirrors for cloud and soaring eagle, a glass for the moon as keystone to the towering arch of stars, had been irrevocably labelled.

Already there was Lake Amelia Jones, Lake Sadie Dingleheimer, Lake Maggie McFadden, and Lake Mrs. Gladys Doolittle Batt.

I longed to see these lakes under the glamour of their newly added beauty.

Imagine, therefore, my surprise and happiness when I received the following communication from my revered and beloved chief, Professor Farrago, dated from the Smithsonian Institute, Washington, whither he had been summoned in haste to examine and pronounce upon the identity of a very small bird supposed to be a specimen of that rare and almost extinct creature, the two-toed titmouse, *Mustitta duototus*, to be scientifically exact, as I invariably strive to be.

The important letter in question was as follows:

To Percy Smith, B. S., D. F., etc., etc.,
Curator, Department of Anthropology,
Administration Building,
Bronx Park, N. Y.

My Dear Mr. Smith:

Several very important and determined ladies, recently honoured by the Government in having a number of lakes in Alaska named after them, have decided to make a pilgrimage to that region, inspired by a characteristic desire to gaze upon the lakes named after them individually.

They request information upon the following points:

1st. Are the waters of the lakes in that locality sufficiently clear for a lady to do her hair by? In that event, the expedition will not burden itself with looking-glasses.

2nd. Are there any hotels? (You need merely say, no. I have tried to explain to them that it is, for the most part, an unexplored wilderness, but they insist upon further information from you.)

3rd. If there are hotels, is there also running water to be had? (You may tell them that there is plenty of running water.)

4th. What are the summer outdoor amusements? (You may inform them that there is plenty of bathing, boating, fishing, and an abundance of shade trees. Also, excellent mountain-climbing to be had in the vicinity. You need not mention the pastimes of "Hunt the Flea" or "Dodge the Skeeter.")

I am not by nature cruel, Mr. Smith, but when these ladies informed me that they had decided to penetrate that howling and unexplored wilderness without being burdened or interfered with by any member of my sex, for one horrid and criminal moment I hoped they would. Because in that event none of them would ever come back.

However, in my heart milder and more humane sentiments prevailed. I pointed out to them the peril of their undertaking, the dangers of an unexplored region, the necessity of masculine guidance and support.

My earnestness and solicitude were, I admit, prompted partly by a desire to utilize this expensively projected expedition as a vehicle for the accumulation of scientific data. As soon as I heard of it I conceived the plan of attaching two members of our Bronx Park scientific staff to the expedition—you, and Mr. Brown.

But no sooner did these determined ladies hear of it than they repelled the suggestion with indignation.

Now, the matter stands as follows: These ladies don't want any man in the expedition; but they have at last realized that they've got to take a guide or two. And there are no feminine guides in Alaska.

Therefore, considering the immense and vital importance of such an opportunity to explore and report upon this unknown region at somebody else's expence, I suggest that you and Brown meet these ladies at Lake Mrs. Susan W. Pillsbury, which lies on the edge of the region to be explored: that you, without actually perjuring yourselves too horribly, convey to them the misleading impression that you are the promised guides provided for them by a cowed and avuncular Government; and that you take these fearsome ladies about and let them gaze at their reflections in the various lakes named after them; and that, while the expedition lasts, you secretly make such observations, notes, reports, and collections of the flora and fauna of the region as your opportunities may permit.

No time is to be lost. If, at Lake Susan W. Pillsbury, you find regular guides awaiting these ladies, you will bribe these guides to go away and you yourselves will then impersonate the guides.

I know of no other way for you to explore this region, as all our available resources at Bronx Park have already been spent in painting appropriate scenery to line the cages of the mammalia, and also in the present exceedingly expensive expedition in search of the polka-dotted boom-bock, which is supposed to inhabit the jungle beyond Lake Niggerplug.

My most solemn and sincere wishes accompany you. Bless you!

                                        Farrago.

II

This, then, is how it came about that "Kitten" Brown and I were seated, one midgeful morning in July, by the pellucid waters of Lake Susan W. Pillsbury, gnawing sections from a greasily fried trout, upon which I had attempted culinary operations.

Brown's baptismal name was William; but the unfortunate young man was once discovered indiscreetly embracing a pretty assistant in the Administration Building at Bronx, and, furthermore, was overheard to address her as "Kitten."

So Kitten Brown it was for him in future. After he had fought all the younger members of the scientific staff in turn, he gradually became resigned to this annoying *nom d'amour*.

Lightly but thoroughly equipped for scientific field research, we had arrived at the rendezvous in time to bribe the two guides engaged by the Government to go back to their own firesides.

A week later the formidable expedition of representative ladies arrived; and now they were sitting on the shore of Lake Susan W. Pillsbury, at a little distance from us, trying to keep the midges from their features and attempting to eat the fare provided for them by me. I myself couldn't eat it. No wonder they murmured. But hunger goaded them, to attack the greasy mess of trout and fried cornmeal.

Kitten was saying to me:

"Our medicine chest isn't very extensive. I hope they brought their own. If they didn't, some among us will never again see New York."

I stole a furtive glance at the unfortunate women. There was *one* among them—but let me first enumerate their heavy artillery:

There was the Reverend Dr. Amelia Jones, blond, adipose, and close to the four-score mark. She stepped high in the Equal Franchise ranks. Nobody had ever had the temerity to answer her back.

There was Miss Sadie Dingleheimer, fifty, emaciated, anemic, and gauntly glittering with thick-lensed eye-glasses. She was the President of the National Prophylactic Club, whatever that may be.

There was Miss Margaret McFadden, a Titian, profusely toothed, muscular, and President of the Hair Dressers' Union of the United States.

There was Mrs. Gladys Doolittle Batt, a grass one—Batt being represented as a vanishing point—President of the National Eugenic and Purity League; tall, gnarled, sinuously powerful, and prone to emotional attacks. The attacks were directed toward others.

These, then, composed the heavy artillery. The artillery of the light brigade consisted only of a single piece. Her name was Angelica White, a delegate from the Trained Nurses' Association of America. The nurses had been too busy with their business to attend such picnics, so one had been selected by lot to represent the busy Association on this expedition.

Angelica White was a tall, fair, yellow-haired girl of twenty-two or three, with violet-blue eyes and red lips, and a way of smiling a little when spoken to—but let that pass. I mean only to be scientifically minute. A passion for fact has ever obsessed me. I have little literary ability and less desire to sully my pen with that degraded form of letters known as fiction. Once in my life my mania for accuracy involved me lyrically. It was a short poem, but an earnest one:

> Truth is mighty and must prevail,
> Otherwise it were inadvisable to tell the tale.

I bestowed it upon the New York *Evening Post*, but declined remuneration. My message belonged to the world. I don't mean the newspaper.

Her eyes, then, were tinted with that indefinable and agreeable nuance which modifies blue to a lilac or violet hue.

Watching her askance, I was deeply sorry that my cooking seemed to pain her.

"Guide!" said Mrs. Doolittle Batt, in that remarkable, booming voice of hers.

"Ma'am!" said Kitten Brown and I with spontaneous alacrity, leaping from the ground as though shot at.

"This cooking," she said, with an ominous stare at us, "is atrocious. Don't you know how to cook?"

I said with a smiling attempt at ease:

"There are various ways of cooking food for the several species of mammalia which an all-wise Providence—"

"Do you think you're cooking for wild-cats?" she demanded.

Our smiles faded.

"It's my opinion that you're incompetent," remarked the Reverend Dr. Jones, slapping at midges with a hand that might have rocked all the cradles of the nation, but had not rocked any.

"We're not getting our money's worth," said Miss Dingleheimer, "even if the Government does pay your salaries."

I looked appealingly from one stony face to another. In Miss McFadden's eye there was the sombre glint of battle. She said:

"If you can guide us no better than you cook, God save us all this day week!" And she hurled the contents of her tin plate into Lake Susan W. Pillsbury.

Mrs. Doolittle Batt arose:

"Come," she said; "it is time we started. What is the name of the first lake we may hope to encounter?"

We knew no more than did they, but we said that Lake Gladys Doolittle Batt was the first, hoping to placate that fearsome woman.

"Come on, then!" she cried, picking up her carved and varnished mountain staff.

Miss Dingleheimer had brought one, too, from the Catskills.

So Kitten Brown and I loaded our mule, set him in motion, and drove him forward into the unknown.

Where we were going we had not the slightest idea; the margin of the lake was easy travelling, so easy that we never noticed that we had already gone around the lake three times, until Mrs. Batt recognized the fact and turned on us furiously.

I didn't know how to explain it, except to say feebly that I was doing it as a sort of preliminary canter to harden and inure the ladies.

"We don't need hardening!" she snarled. "Do you understand that!"

I comprehended that at once. But I forced a sickly smile and skipped forward in the wake of my mule, with something of the same abandon which characterizes the flight of an unwelcome dog.

In the terrified ear of Kitten I voiced my doubts concerning the prospects of a pleasant journey.

We marched in the following order: Arthur, the heavily laden mule, led; then came Kitten Brown and myself, all hung over with stew-pans, shotguns, rifles, cartridge-belts, ponchos, and the toilet reticules of the ladies; then marched the Reverend Dr. Jones, and, in order, filing behind her, Miss Dingleheimer, Mrs. Batt, Miss McFadden, and Miss White—the latter in her trained nurse's costume and wearing a red cross on her sleeve—an idea of Mrs. Batt, who believed in emergency methods.

Mrs. Batt also bore a banner, much interfered with by the foliage, bearing the inscription:

EQUAL RIGHTS!
EUGENICS OR EXTERMINATION!

After a while she shouted:

"Guide! Here, you may carry this banner for a while! I'm tired."

Kitten and I took turns with it after that. It was hard work, particularly as one by one in turn they came up and hung their parasols and shopping reticules all over us. We plodded forward like a pair of moving department stores, not daring to shift our burdens to Arthur, because we had already stuffed into the panniers of that simple and dignified animal all our collecting boxes, cyanide jars, butterfly nets, note-books, reels of piano wire, thermometers, barometers, hydrometers, stereometers, aeronoids, adnoids—everything, in fact, that guides are not supposed to pack into the woods, but which we had smuggled unbeknown to those misguided ones we guided.

And, to make room for our scientific paraphernalia, we had been obliged to do a thing so mean, so inexpressibly low, that I blush to relate it. But facts are facts; we discarded nearly a ton of feminine impedimenta. There was fancy work of all sorts in the making or in the raw—materials for knitting, embroidering, tatting, sewing, hemming, stitching, drawn-work, lace-making, crocheting.

Also we disposed of almost half a ton of toilet necessities—powder, perfumery, cosmetics, hot-water bags, slippers, negligees, novels, magazines, bon-bons, chewing-gum, hat-boxes, gloves, stockings, underwear.

We left enough apparel for each lady to change once. They'd have to do some scrubbing now. Science can not be halted by hatpins; cosmos can not be side-tracked by cosmetics.

Toward sunset we came upon a small, crystal clear pond, set between the bases of several lofty mountains. I was ready to drop with fatigue, but I nerved myself, drew a deep, exultant breath, and with one of those fine, sweeping gestures, I cried:

"Lake Mrs. Gladys Doolittle Batt! Eureka! At last! Excelsior!"

There was a profound silence behind me. I turned, striving to mask my apprehension with a smile. The ladies were regarding the pond in surprise. I admit that it was a pond, not a lake.

Injecting into my voice the last remnants of glee which I could summon, I shouted, "Eureka!" and began to caper about as though the size and beauty of the pond had affected me with irrepressible enthusiasm, hoping by my emotion to stampede the convention.

The cold voice of Mrs. Doolittle Batt checked my transports:

"Is that puddle named after *me?*" she demanded.

"M-ma'am?" I stammered.

"If that wretched frog-pond has been christened with my name, somebody is going to get into trouble," she said ominously.

A profound silence ensued. Arthur patiently switched at flies. As for me, I looked up at the majestic pines, gazed upon the lofty and eternal hills, then ventured a sneaking glance all around me. But I could discover no avenue of escape in case Mrs. Batt should charge me. "I had been informed," she began dangerously, "that the majestic body of water, which I understood had been honoured with my name, was twelve miles long and three miles wide. *This* appears to be a puddle!"

'B-b-but it's very p-pretty," I protested feebly. "It's quite round and clear, and it's nearly a quarter of a mile in d-diameter—"

"Mind your business!" retorted Mrs. Doolittle Batt. "I've been swindled!"

Kitten Brown knew more about women than did I. He said in a fairly steady voice:

"Madame, it is an outrage! The women of this mighty nation should make the Government answerable for its duplicity! Your lake should have been at least twenty miles long!"

Everybody turned and looked at Kitten. He was a handsome dog.

"This young man appears to have some trace of common-sense," said Mrs. Batt. "I shall see to it that the Government is held responsible for this odious act of insulting duplicity. I—I won't have my name given to this—this wallow!—" She advanced toward me, her small eyes blazing: I retreated to leeward of Arthur.

"Guide!" she said in a voice still trembling with passion. "Are you certain that you have made no mistake? You appear to be unusually ignorant."

"I am afraid there can be no room for doubt," I said, almost scared out of my senses.

"And on top of this outrage, am I to eat your cooking?" she demanded passionately. "Did I come here to look at this frog-pond and choke on your cooking? *Did* I?"

"*I* can cook," said a clear, pleasant voice at my elbow. And Miss White came forward, cool, clean, fresh as a posy in her uniform and cap. I immediately got behind her.

"I can cook very nicely," she said smilingly. "It is part of my profession, you know. So if you two guides will be kind enough to build the fire and help me—" She let her violet eyes linger on me for an instant, then on Brown. A moment later he and I were jostling each other in our eagerness to obey her slightest suggestion. It is that way with men.

So we built her a fire and unpacked our provisions, and we waited very politely on the ladies when dinner was ready.

It was a fine dinner—coffee, bacon, flap-jacks, soup, ash-bread, stewed chicken.

The heavy artillery, made ravenous by their journey, required vast quantities of ammunition. They banqueted largely. I gazed in amazement at Mrs. Doolittle Batt as she swallowed one flap-jack after another, while her eyes bulged larger and larger.

Nor was the capacity of Miss Dingleheimer and the Reverend Dr. Jones to be mocked at by pachyderms.

Brown and I left them eating while we erected the row of little tents. Every lady had demanded a separate tent.

So we cut saplings, set up the silk, drove pegs, and brought armfuls of balsam boughs.

I was afraid they'd demand their knitting and other utensils, but they had eaten to repletion, and were sleepy; and as each toilet case or reticule contained also a nightgown, they drew the flaps of their several tents without insisting that we unpack Arthur's panniers.

They all had disappeared within their tents except Miss White, who insisted on cooking something for us, although we protested that the scraps of the banquet were all right for mere guides.

She stood beside us for a few minutes, watching us busy with our delicious dinner.

"You poor fellows," she said gently. "You are nearly starved."

It is agreeable to be sympathized with by a tall, fair, fresh young girl. We looked up, simpering gratefully.

"This is really a most lovely little lake," she said, gazing out across the still, crystalline water which was all rose and gold in the sunset, save where the sombre shapes of the towering mountains were mirrored in glassy depths.

"It's odd," I said, "that no trout are jumping. There ought to be lots of them there, and this is their jumping hour."

We all looked at the quiet, oval bit of water. Not a circle, not the slightest ripple disturbed it.

"It must be deep," remarked Brown.

We gazed up at the three lofty peaks, the bases of which were the shores of this tiny gem among lakes. Deep, deep, plunging down into dusky profundity, the rocks fell away sheer into limpid depths.

"That little lake may be a thousand feet deep," I said. "In 1903 Professor Farrago, of Bronx Park, measured a lake in the Thunder Mountains, which was two thousand seven hundred and sixty-nine feet deep."

Miss White looked at me curiously.

Into a patch of late sunshine flitted a small butterfly—one of the *Grapta* species. It settled on a chip of wood, uncoiled its delicate proboscis, and spread its fulvous and deeply indented wings.

"*Grapta california*," remarked Brown to me.

"*Vanessa asteriska*," I corrected him. "Note the anal angle of the secondaries and the argentiferous discal area bordering the subcostal nervule."

"The characteristic stripes on the primaries are wanting," he demurred.

"It is double brooded. The summer form lacks the three darker bands."

A few moments' silence was broken by the voice of Miss White.

"I had no idea," she remarked, "that Alaskan guides were so familiar with entomological terms and nomenclature."

We both turned very red.

Brown mumbled something about having picked up a smattering. I added that Brown had taught me.

Perhaps she believed us; her blue eyes rested on us curiously, musingly. Also, at moments, I fancied there was the faintest glint of amusement in them.

She said:

"Two scientific gentlemen from New York requested permission to join this expedition, but Mrs. Batt refused them." She gazed thoughtfully upon the waters of Lake Gladys Doolittle Batt. "I wonder," she murmured, "what became of those two gentlemen."

It was evident that we had betrayed ourselves to this young girl.

She glanced at us again, and perhaps she noticed in our fascinated gaze an expression akin to terror, for suddenly she laughed— such a clear, sweet, silvery little laugh!

"For my part," she said, "I wish they had come with us. I like— men."

With that she bade us goodnight very politely and went off to her tent, leaving us with our hats pressed against our stomachs, attempting by the profundity of our bows to indicate the depth of our gratitude.

"*There's* a girl!" exclaimed Brown, as soon as she had disappeared behind her tent flaps. "She'll never let on to Medusa, Xantippe, Cassandra and Company. I *like* that girl, Smith."

"You're not the only one imbued by such sentiments," said I.

He smiled a fatuous and reminiscent smile. He certainly was good-looking. Presently he said:

"She has the most delightful way of gazing at a man—"

"I've noticed," I said pleasantly.

"Oh. Did she happen to glance at *you* that way?" he inquired.

I wanted to beat him.

All I said was:

"She's certainly some kitten." Which bottled that young man for a while.

We lay on the bank of the tiny lake, our backs against a huge pine-tree, watching the last traces of colour fading from peak and tree-top.

"'Isn't it queer," I said, "that not a trout has splashed? It can't be that there are no fish in the lake."

"There *are* such lakes."

"Yes, very deep ones. I wonder how deep this is."

"We'll be out at sunrise with our reel of piano wire and take soundings," he said. "The heavy artillery won't wake until they're ready to be loaded with flap-jacks."

I shuddered:

"They're fearsome creatures, Brown. Somehow, that resolute and bony one has inspired me with a terror unutterable."

"Mrs. Batt?"

"Yes."

He said seriously:

"She'll make a horrid outcry when she asks for her knitting. What are you going to tell her?"

"I shall say that Indians ambuscaded us while she was asleep, and carried off all those things."

"You lie very nicely, don't you?" he remarked admiringly.

"*In vitium ducit culpæ fuga*," said I. "Besides, they don't really need those articles."

He laughed. He didn't seem to be very much afraid of Mrs. Batt.

It had grown deliciously dusky, and myriads of stars were coming out. Little by little the lake lost its shape in the darkness, until only an irregular, star-set area of quiet water indicated that there was any lake there at all. I remember that Brown and I, reclining at the foot of the tree, were looking at the still and starry surface of the lake, over which numbers of bats were darting after insects; and I recollect that I was just about to speak, when, of a sudden, the silent and luminous surface of the water was shattered as with a subterranean explosion; a geyser of scintillating spray shot upward flashing, foaming, towering a hundred feet into the air. And through it I seemed to catch a glimpse of a vast, quivering, twisting mass of silver falling back with a crash into the lake, while the huge fountain rained spray on every side and the little lake rocked and heaved from shore to shore, sending great sheets of surf up over the rocks so high that the very tree-tops dripped.

Petrified, dumb, our senses almost paralyzed by the shock, our ears still deafened by the watery crash of that gigantic something that had fallen into the lake, and our eyes starting from their sockets, we stared at the darkness.

Slap—slash—slush went the waves, hitting the shore with a clashing sound almost metallic. Vision and hearing told us that the water in the lake was rocking like the contents of a bath-tub.

"G-g-good Lord!" whispered Brown. "Is there a v-volcano under that lake?"

"Did you see that huge, glittering shape that seemed to fall into the water?" I gasped.

"Yes. What was it? A meteor?"

"No. It was something that first came out of the lake and fell back—the way a trout leaps. Heavens! It couldn't have been alive, could it?"

"W-wh-what do you mean?" stammered Brown.

"It couldn't have been a f-f-fish, could it?" I asked with chattering teeth.

"No! *No!* It was as big as a Pullman car! It must have been a falling star. Did you ever hear of a fish as big as a sleeping car?"

I was too thoroughly unnerved to reply. The roaring of the surf had subsided somewhat, enough for another sound to reach our ears—a raucous, gallinacious, squawking sound.

I sprang up and looked at the row of tents. White-robed figures loomed in front of them. The heavy artillery was evidently frightened.

We went over to them, and when we got nearer they chastely scuttled into their tents and thrust out a row of heads—heads hideous with curl-papers.

"What was that awful noise? An earthquake?" shrilled the Reverend Dr. Jones. "I think I'll go home."

"Was it an avalanche?" demanded Mrs. Batt, in a deep and shaky voice. "Are we in any immediate danger, young man?"

I said that it was probably a flying-star which had happened to strike the lake and explode.

"What an awful region!" wailed Miss Dingleheimer. "I've had my money's worth. I wish to go back to New York at once. I'll begin to dress immediately—"

"It might be a million years before another meteor falls in this latitude," I said, soothingly.

"Or it might be ten minutes," sobbed Miss Dingleheimer. "What do *you* know about it, anyway! I want to go home. I'm putting on my stockings now. I'm getting dressed as fast as I can—"

Her voice was blotted out in a mighty crash from the lake. Appalled, I whirled on my heel, just in time to see another huge jet of water rise high in the starlight, another, another, until the entire lake was but a cluster of gigantic geysers exploding a hundred feet in the air, while through them, falling back into the smother of furious foam, great silvery bulks dropped crashing, one after another.

I don't know how long the incredible vision lasted; the woods roared with the infernal pandemonium, echoed and re-echoed from mountain to mountain; the tree-tops fairly stormed spray, driving it in sheets through the leaves; and the shores of the lake spouted surf long after the last vast, silvery shape had fallen back again into the water.

As my senses gradually recovered, I found myself supporting Mrs. Batt on one arm and the Reverend Dr. Jones upon my bosom. Both had fainted. I released them with a shudder and turned to look for Brown.

Somebody had swooned in his arms, too.

He was not noticing me, and as I approached him I heard him say something resembling the word "kitten."

In spite of my demoralization, another fear seized me, and I drew nearer and peered closely at what he was holding so nobly in his arms. It was, as I supposed, Angelica White.

I don't know whether my arrival occultly revived her, for as I stumbled over a tent-peg she opened her blue eyes, and then disengaged herself from Brown's arms.

"Oh, I am *so* frightened," she murmured. She looked at me sideways when she said it.

"Come," said I coldly to Brown, "let Miss White retire and lie down. This meteoric shower is over and so is the danger."

He evinced a desire to further soothe and minister to Miss White, but she said, with considerable composure, that she was feeling better; and Brown came unwillingly with me to inspect the heavy artillery lines.

That formidable battery was wrecked, the pieces dismounted and lying tumbled about in their emplacements.

But a vigorous course of cold water in dippers revived them, and we herded them into one tent and quieted them with some soothing prevarication, the details of which I have forgotten; but it was something about a flock of meteors which hit the earth every twelve billion years, and that it was now all over for another such interim, and everybody could sleep soundly with the consciousness of having assisted at a spectacle never before beheld except by a primordial protoplasmic cell.

Which flattered them, I think, for, seated once more at the base of our tree, presently we heard weird noises from the reconcentrados, like the moaning of the harbour bar.

They slept, the heavy guns, like unawakened engines of destruction all a-row in battery. But Brown and I, fearfully excited, still dazed and bewildered, sat with our fascinated eyes fixed on the lake, asking each other what in the name of miracles it was that we had witnessed and heard.

On one thing we were agreed. A scientific discovery of the most enormous importance awaited our investigation.

This was no time for temporising, for deception, for any species of polite shilly-shallying. We must, on the morrow, tear off our masks and appear before these misguided and feminine victims of our duplicity in our own characters as scientists. We must boldly avow our identities and flatly refuse to stir from this spot until the mystery of this astounding lake had been thoroughly investigated.

And so, discussing our policy, our plans for the morrow, and mutually reassuring each other concerning our common ability to successfully defy the heavy artillery, we finally fell asleep.

III

Dawn awoke me, and I sat up in my blanket and aroused Brown.

No birds were singing. It seemed unusual, and I spoke of it to Brown. Never have I witnessed such a still, strange daybreak. Mountains, woods, and water were curiously silent. There was not a sound to be heard, nothing stirred except the thin veil of vapour over the water, shreds of which were now parting from the shore and steaming slowly upward.

There was, it seemed to me, something slightly uncanny about this lake, even in repose. The water seemed as translucent as a dark crystal, and as motionless as the surface of a mirror. Nothing stirred its placid surface, not a ripple, not an insect, not a leaf floating.

Brown had lugged the pneumatic raft down to the shore where he was now pumping it full: I followed with the paddles, pole, and hydroscope. When the raft had been pumped up and was afloat, we carried the reel of gossamer piano-wire aboard, followed it pushed off, and paddled quietly through the level cobwebs of mist toward the centre of the lake. From the shore I heard a gruesome noise. It originated under one of the row of tents of the heavy artillery. Medusa, snoring, was an awesome sound in that wilderness and solitude of dawn.

I was unscrewing the centre-plug from the raft and screwing into the empty socket the lens of the hydroscope and attaching the battery, while Brown started his sounding; and I was still busy when an exclamation from my companion started me:

"We're breaking some records! Do you know it, Smith?"

"Where is the lead?"

"Three hundred fathoms and still running!"

"Nonsense!"

"Look at it yourself! It goes on unreeling: I've put the drag on. Hurry and adjust the hydroscope!"

I sighted the powerful instrument for two thousand feet, altering it from minute to minute as Brown excitedly announced the amazing depth of the lake. When he called out four thousand feet, I stared at him.

"There's something wrong—" I began.

"There's *nothing* wrong!" he interrupted. "Four thousand five hundred! Five thousand! Five thousand five hundred—"

"Are you squatting there and trying to tell me that this lake is over a mile deep!"

"Look for yourself !" he said in an unsteady voice. "Here is the tape! You can read, can't you? Six thousand feet—and running evenly. Six thousand five hundred!... Seven thousand! Seven thousand five—"

"It *can't* be!" I protested.

But it was true. Astounded, I continued to adjust the hydroscope to a range incredible, turning the screw to focus at a mile and a half, at two miles, at two and a quarter, a half, three-quarters, three miles, three miles and a quarter—click!

"Good Heavens!" he whispered. "This lake is three miles and a quarter deep!"

Mechanically I set the lachet, screwed the hood firm, drew out the black eye-mask, locked it, then, kneeling on the raft I rested my face in the mask, felt for the lever, and switched on the electric light.

Quicker than thought the solid lance of dazzling light plunged down through profundity, and the vast abyss of water was revealed along its pathway.

Nothing moved in those tremendous depths except, nearly two miles below, a few spots of tinsel glittered and drifted like flakes of mica.

At first I scarcely noticed them, supposing them to be vast beds of silvery bottom sand glittering under the electric pencil of the hydroscope. But presently it occurred to me that these brilliant specks in motion were not on the bottom—were a little less than two miles deep, and therefore suspended.

To be seen at all, at two miles' depth, whatever they were they must have considerable bulk.

"Do you see anything?" demanded Brown.

"Some silvery specks at a depth of two miles."

"What do they look like?"

"Specks."

"Are they in motion?"

"They seem to be."

"Do they come any nearer?"

After a while I answered:

"One of the specks seems to be growing larger.... I believe it is in motion and is floating slowly upward... It's certainly getting bigger... It's getting longer."

"Is it a fish?"

"It can't be."

"Why not?"

"It's impossible. Fish don't attain the size of whales in mountain ponds."

There was a silence. After an interval I said:

"Brown, I don't know what to make of that thing."

"Is it coming any nearer?"

"Yes."

"What does it look like now?"

"It *looks* like a fish. But it can't be. It looks like a tiny, silver minnow. But it can't be. Why, if it resembles a minnow in size at this distance—what can be its actual dimensions?"

"Let me look," he said.

Unwillingly I raised my head from the mask and yielded him my place.

A long silence followed. The western mountain-tops reddened under the rising sun; the sky grew faintly bluer. Yet, there was not a bird-note in that still place, not a flash of wings, nothing stirring.

Here and there along the lake shore I noticed unusual-looking trees—very odd-looking trees indeed, for their trunks seemed bleached and dead, and as though no bark covered them, yet every stark limb was covered with foliage—a thick foliage so dark in colour that it seemed black to me.

I glanced at my motionless companion where he knelt with his face in the mask, then I unslung my field-glasses and focussed them on the nearest of the curious trees.

At first I could not quite make out what I was looking at; then, to my astonishment, I saw that these stark, gray trees were indeed lifeless, and that what I had mistaken for dark foliage were velvety clusters of bats hanging there asleep—thousands of them thickly infesting and clotting the dead branches with a sombre and horrid effect of foliage.

I don't mind bats in ordinary numbers. But in such soft, motionless masses they slightly sickened me. There must have been literally tons of them hanging to the dead trees.

"This is pleasant," I said. "Look at those bats, Brown."

When Brown spoke without lifting his head, his voice was so shaken, so altered, that the mere sound of it scared me:

"Smith," he said, "there is a fish in here, shaped exactly like a brook minnow. And I should judge, by the depth it is swimming in, that it is about as long as an ordinary Pullman car."

His voice shook, but his words were calm to the point of commonplace. Which made the effect of his statement all the more terrific.

"A—a *minnow*—as big as a Pullman car?" I repeated, dazed.

"Larger, I think.... It looks to me through the hydroscope, at this distance, exactly like a tiny, silvery minnow. It's half a mile down... Swimming about... I can see its eyes; they must be about ten feet in diameter. I can see its fins moving. And there are about a dozen others, much deeper, swimming around.... This is easily the most overwhelming contribution made to science since the discovery of the purple-spotted dingle-bock, *Bukkus dinglii*... We've got to catch one of those gigantic fish!"

"How?" I gasped. "How are we going to catch a minnow as large as a sleeping car?"

"I don't know, but we've got to do it. We've got to manage it, somehow."

"It would require a steel cable to hold such a fish and a donkey engine to reel him in! And what about a hook? And if we had hook, line, steamwinch, and everything else, *what* about bait?"

He knelt for some time longer, watching the fish, before he resigned the hydroscope to me. Then I watched it; but it came no nearer, seeming contented to swim about at the depth of a little more than half a mile. Deep under this fish I could see others glittering as they sailed or darted to and fro.

Presently I raised my head and sat thinking. The sun now gilded the water; a little breeze ruffled it here and there where dainty cat's-paws played over the surface.

"What on earth do you suppose those gigantic fish feed on?" asked Brown under his breath.

I thought a moment longer, then it came to me in a flash of understanding, and I pointed at the dead trees.

"Bats!" I muttered. "They feed on bats as other fish feed on the little, ganzy-winged flies which dance over ponds! You saw those bats flying over the pond last night, didn't you? That explains the whole thing! Don't you understand? Why, what we saw were these gigantic fish leaping like trout after the bats. It was their feeding time!"

I do not imagine that two more excited scientists ever existed than Brown and I. The joy of discovery transfigured us. Here we had discovered a lake in the Thunder Mountains which was the deepest lake in the world; and it was inhabited by a few gigantic fish of the minnow species, the existence of which, hitherto, had never even been dreamed of by science.

"Kitten," I said, my voice broken by emotion, "which will you have named after you, the lake or the fish? Shall it be Lake Kitten Brown, or shall it be *Minnius kittenii?* Speak!"

"What about that old party whose name you said had already been given to the lake?" he asked piteously.

"Who? Mrs. Batt? Do you think I'd name such an important lake after *her?* Anyway, she has declined the honour."

"Very well," he said, "I'll accept it. And the fish shall be known as *Minnius Smithii!*"

Too deeply moved to speak, we bent over and shook hands with each other. In that solemn and holy moment, surcharged with ecstatic emotion, a deep, distant reverberation came across the water to our ears. It was the heavy artillery, snoring.

Never can I forget that scene; sunshine glittering on the pond, the silent forests and towering peaks, the blue sky overhead, the dead trees where thousands of bats hung in nauseating clusters, thicker than the leaves in Valembrosa—and Kitten Brown and I, cross-legged upon our pneumatic raft, hands clasped in pledge of deathless devotion to science and a fraternity unending.

"And how about that girl?" he asked.

"What girl?"

"Angelica White?"

"Well," said I, "*what* about her?"

"Does she go with the lake or with the fish?"

"What do you mean?" I asked coldly, withdrawing my hand from his clasp.

"I mean, which of us gets the first chance to win her?" he said, blushing. "There's no use denying that we both have been bowled over by her; is there?"

I pondered for several moments.

"She is an extremely intelligent girl," I said, stalling.

"Yes, and then some."

After a few minutes' further thought, I said:

"Possibly I am in error, but at moments it has seemed to me that my marked attentions to Miss White are not wholly displeasing to her. I may be mistaken—"

"I think you are, Smith."

"Why?"

"Because—well, because I seem to think so."

I said coldly:

"Because she happened to faint away in your arms last night is no symptom that she prefers you. Is it?"

"No."

"Then why do you seem to think that tactful, delicate, and assiduous attentions on my part may prove not entirely unwelcome to this unusually intelligent—"

"Smith!"

"What?"

"Miss White is not only a trained nurse, but she also is about to receive her diploma as a physician."

"How do you know?"

"She told me."

"When?"

"When you were building the fire last night. Also, she informed me that she had relentlessly dedicated herself to a eugenic marriage."

"When did she tell you *that?*"

"While you were bringing in a bucket of water from the lake last night. And furthermore, she told me that *I* was perfectly suited for a eugenic marriage."

"*When* did she tell you *that?*" I demanded.

"When she had—fainted—in my arms."

"How the devil did she come to say a thing like that?"

He became conspicuously red about the ears:

"Well, I had just told her that I had fallen in love with her—"

"Damn!" I said. And that's all I said; and seizing a paddle I made furiously for shore.

Behind me I heard the whirr of the piano wire as Brown started the electric reel. Later I heard him clamping the hood on the hydroscope; but I was too disgusted for any further words, and I dug away at the water with my paddle.

In various and weird stages of morning déshabillé the heavy artillery came down to the shore for morning ablutions, all a-row like a file of ducks.

They glared at me as I leaped ashore:

"I want my breakfast!" snapped Mrs. Batt. "Do you hear what I say, guide? And I don't wish to be kept waiting for it either! I desire to get out of this place as soon as possible."

"I'm sorry," I said, "but I intend to stay here for some time."

"What!" bawled the heavy artillery in booming unison.

But my temper had been sorely tried, and I was in a mood to tell the truth and make short work of it, too.

"Ladies," I said, "I'll not mince matters. Mr. Brown and I are not guides; we are scientists from Bronx Park, and we don't know a bally thing about this wilderness we're in!"

"Swindler!" shouted Mrs. Batt, in an enraged voice. "I knew very well that the United States Government would never have named that puddle of water after *me!*"

"Don't worry, madam! I've named it after Mr. Brown. And the new species of gigantic fish which I discovered in this lake I have named after myself. As for leaving this spot until I have concluded my scientific study of these fish, I simply won't. I intend to observe their habits and to capture one of them if it requires the remainder of my natural life to do so. I shall be sorry to detain you here during such a period, but it can't be helped. And now you know what the situation is, and you are at liberty to think it over after you have washed your countenances in Lake Kitten Brown."

Rage possessed the heavy artillery, and a fury indescribable seized them when they discovered that Indians had raided their half ton of feminine perquisites. I went up a tree.

When the tumult had calmed sufficiently for them to distinguish what I said, I made a speech to them. From the higher branches of a neighboring tree Kitten Brown applauded and cried, "Hear! Hear!"

"Ladies," I said, "you know the worst, now. If you keep me up this tree and starve me to death it will be murder. Also, you don't know enough to get out of these forests, but I can guide you back the way you came. I'll do it if you cease your dangerous demonstrations and permit Mr. Brown and myself to remain here and study these giant fish for a week or two."

They now seemed disposed to consider the idea. There was nothing else for them to do. So after an hour or two, Brown and I ventured to descend from our trees, and we went among them to placate them and ingratiate ourselves as best we might.

"Think," I argued, "what a matchless opportunity for you to be among the first discoverers of a totally new and undescribed species of giant fish! Think what a legacy it will be to leave such a record to posterity! Think how proud and happy your descendants will be to know that their ancestors assisted at the discovery of *Minnius Smithii!*"

"Why can't they be named after *me?*" demanded Mrs. Batt.

"Because," I explained patiently, "they have already been named after *me!*"

"Couldn't *something* be named after me?" inquired that fearsome lady.

"The bats," suggested Brown politely, "we could name a bat after you with pleasure—"

I thought for a moment she meant to swing on him. He thought so, too, and ducked.

"A bat!" she shouted. "Name a *bat* after *me!*"

"Many a celebrated scientist has been honoured by having his name conferred upon humbler fauna," I explained.

But she remained dangerous, so I went and built the fire, and squatted there, frying bacon, while on the other side of the fire, sitting side by side, Kitten Brown and Angelica White gazed upon each other with enraptured eyes. It was slightly sickening—but let that pass. I was beginning to understand that science is a jealous mistress and that any contemplated infidelity of mine stood every chance of being squelched. No; evidently I had not been fashioned for the joys of legal domesticity.

Science, the wanton jade, had not yet finished her dance with me. Apparently my maxixe with her was to be external. *Fides servanda est.*

That afternoon the heavy artillery held a council of war, and evidently came to a conclusion to make the best of the situation, for toward sundown they accosted me with a request for the raft, explaining that they desired to picnic aboard and afterward row about the lake and indulge in song.

So Brown and I put aboard the craft a substantial cold supper; and the heavy artillery embarked, taking aboard a guitar to be worked by Miss Dingleheimer, and knitting for the others.

It was a lovely evening. Brown and I had been discussing a plan to dynamite the lake and stun the fish, that method appealing to us as the only possible way to secure a specimen of the stupendous minnows which inhabited the depths. In fact, it was our only hope of possessing one of these creatures—fishing with a donkey engine, steel cable, and a hook baited with a bat being too uncertain and far more laborious and expensive.

I was still smoking my pipe, seated at the foot of the big pine-tree, watching the water turn from gold to pink: Brown sat higher up the slope, his arm around Angelica White. I carefully kept my back toward them.

On the lake the heavy artillery were revelling loudly, banqueting, singing, strumming the guitar, and trailing their hands overboard across the sunset-tinted water.

I was thinking of nothing in particular as I now remember, except that I noticed the bats beginning to flit over the lake; when Brown called to me from the slope above, asking whether it was perfectly safe for the heavy artillery to remain out so late.

"Why?" I demanded.

"Suppose," he shouted, "that those fish should begin to jump and feed on the bats again?"

I had never thought of that.

I rose and hurried nervously down to the shore, and, making a megaphone of my hands, I shouted:

"Come in! It isn't safe to remain out any longer!"

Scornful laughter from the artillery answered my appeal.

"You'd better come in!" I called. "You can't tell what might happen if any of those fish should jump—"

"Mind your business!" retorted Mrs. Batt. "We've had enough of your prevarications—"

Then, suddenly, without the faintest shadow of warning, from the centre of the lake a vast geyser of water towered a hundred feet in the air.

For one dreadful second I saw the raft hurled skyward, balanced on the crest of the stupendous fountain, spilling ladies, supper, guitars, and knitting in every direction.

Then a horrible thing occurred; fish after fish shot up out of the storm of water and foam, seizing, as they fell, ladies, luncheon, and knitting in mid-air, falling back with a crashing shock which seemed to rock the very mountains.

"Help!" I screamed. And fainted dead away.

Is it necessary to proceed? Literature nods; Science shakes her head. No, nothing but literature lies beyond the ripples which splashed musically upon the shore, terminating forever the last vibration from that immeasurable catstrophe.

Why should I go on? The newspapers of the nation have recorded the last scenes of the tragedy.

We know that tons of dynamite are being forwarded to that solitary lake. We know that it is the determination of the Government to rid the world of those gigantic minnows.

And yet, somehow, it seems to me as I sit writing here in my office, amid the verdure of Bronx Park, that the destruction of these enormous fish is a mistake.

What more splendid sarcophagus could the ladies of the lake desire than these huge, silvery, itinerant and living tombs?

What reward more sumptuous could anybody wish for than to rest at last within the interior dimness of an absolutely new species of anything?

For me, such a final repose as this would represent the highest pinnacle of sublimity, the uttermost zenith of mortal dignity.

So what more is there for me to say?

As for Angelica—but no matter. I hope she may be comparatively happy with Kitten Brown. Yet, as I have said before, handsome men never last. But she should have thought of that in time.

I absolve myself of all responsibility. She had her chance.

ONE OVER

I

Professor Farrago had remarked to me that morning:

"The city of New York always reminds me of a slovenly, fat woman with her dress unbuttoned behind."

I nodded.

"New York's architecture," said I, "—or what popularly passes for it—is all in front. The minute you get to the rear a pitiable condition is exposed."

He said: "Professor Jane Bottomly is all facade; the remainder of her is merely an occiputal backyard full of theoretical tin cans and broken bottles. I think we all had better resign."

It was a fearsome description. I trembled as I lighted an inexpensive cigar.

The sentimental feminist movement in America was clearly at the bottom of the Bottomly affair.

Long ago, in a reactionary burst of hysteria, the North enfranchised the Ethiopian. In a similar sentimental explosion of dementia, some sixty years later, the United States wept violently over the immemorial wrongs perpetrated upon the restless sex, opened the front and back doors of opportunity, and sobbed out, "Go to it, ladies!"

They are still going.

Professor Jane Bottomly was wished on us out of a pleasant April sky. She fell like a meteoric mass of molten metal upon the Bronx Park Zoölogical Society splashing her excoriating personality over everybody until everybody writhed.

I had not yet seen the lady. I did not care to. Sooner or later I'd be obliged to meet her but I was not impatient.

Now the Field Expeditionary Force of the Bronx Park Zoölogical Society is, perhaps, the most important arm of the service. Professor Bottomly had just been appointed official head of all field work. Why? Nobody knew. It is true that she had written several combination nature and love romances. In these popular volumes trees, flowers, butterflies, birds, animals, dialect, sobs, and sun-bonnets were stirred up together into a saccharine mess eagerly gulped down by a provincial reading public, which immediately protruded its tongue for more.

The news of her impending arrival among us was an awful blow to everybody at the Bronx. Professor Farrago fainted in the arms of his pretty stenographer; Professor Cornelius Lezard of the Batrachian Department ran around his desk all day long in narrowing circles and was discovered on his stomach still feebly squirming like an expiring top; Dr. Hans Fooss, our beloved Professor of Pachydermatology sat for hours weeping into his noodle soup. As for me, I was both furious and frightened, for, within the hearing of several people, Professor Bottomly had remarked in a very clear voice to her new assistant, Dr. Daisy Delmour, that she intended to get rid of me for the good of the Bronx because of my reputation for indiscreet gallantry among the feminine employees of the Bronx Society.

Professor Lezard overhead that outrageous remark and he hastened to repeat it to me.

I was lunching at the time in my private office in the Administration Building with Dr. Hans Fooss—he and I being too busy dissecting an unusually fine specimen of Dingue to go to the Rolling Stone Inn for luncheon—when Professor Lezard rushed in with the scandalous libel still sizzling in his ears.

"Everybody heard her say it!" he went on, wringing his hands. "It was a most unfortunate thing for anybody to say about you before all those young ladies. Every stenographer and typewriter there turned pale and then red."

"What!" I exclaimed, conscious that my own ears were growing large and hot. "Did that outrageous woman have the bad taste to say such a thing before all those sensitive girls!"

"She did. She glared at them when she said it. Several blondes and one brunette began to cry."

"I hope," said I, a trifle tremulously, "that no typewriter so far forgot herself as to admit noticing playfulness on my part."

"They all were tearfully unanimous in declaring you to be a perfect gentleman!"

"I am," I said. "I am also a married man—irrevocably wedded to science. I desire no other spouse. I am ineligible; and everybody knows it. If at times a purely scientific curiosity leads me into a detached and impersonally psychological investigation of certain—ah—feminine idiosyncrasies—"

"Certainly," said Lezard. "To investigate the feminine is more than a science; it is a duty!"

"Of a surety!" nodded Dr. Fooss.

I looked proudly upon my two loyal friends and bit into my cheese sandwich. Only men know men. A jury of my peers had exonerated me. What did I care for Professor Bottomly!

"All the same," added Lezard, "you'd better be careful or Professor Bottomly will put one over on you yet."

"I am always careful," I said with dignity.

"All men should be. It is the only protection of a defenseless coast line," nodded Lezard.

"Und neffer, neffer commid nodding to paper," added Dr. Fooss. "Don'd neffer write it, 'I lofe you like I was going to blow up alretty!' Ach, nein! Don'd you write down somedings. Effery man he iss entitled to protection; und so iss it he iss protected."

Stein in hand he beamed upon us benevolently over his knifeful of sauerfisch, then he fed himself and rammed it down with a hearty draught of Pilsner. We gazed with reverence upon Kultur as embodied in this great Teuton.

"That woman," remarked Lezard to me, "certainly means to get rid of you. It seems to me that there are only two possible ways for you to hold down your job at the Bronx. You know it, don't you?"

I nodded. "Yes," I said; "either I must pay marked masculine attention to Professor Bottomly: or I must manage to put one over on her."

"Of course," said Lezard, "the first method is the easier for *you*—"

"Not for a minute!" I said, hastily; "I simply couldn't become frolicsome with her. You say she's got a voice like a drill-sergeant and she goose-steps when she walks; and I don't mind admitting she has me badly scared already. No; she must be scientifically ruined. It is the only method which makes her elimination certain."

"But if her popular nature books didn't ruin her scientifically, how can we hope to lead her astray?" inquired Lezard.

"There is," I said, thoughtfully, "only one thing that can really ruin a scientist. Ridicule! I have braved it many a time, taking my scientific life in my hands in pursuit of unknown specimens which might have proved only imaginary. Public ridicule would have ended my scientific career in such an event. I know of no better way to end Professor Bottomly's scientific career and capability for mischief than to start her out after something which doesn't exist, inform the newspapers, and let her suffer the agonising consequences."

Dr. Fooss began to shout:

"The idea iss schön! colossal! prachtvol! ausgezeichnet! wunderbar! wunderschön! gemütlich—" A large, tough noodle checked him. While he labored with Teutonic imperturbability to master it Lezard and I exchanged suggestions regarding the proposed annihilation of this fearsome woman who had come ravening among us amid the peaceful and soporific environment of Bronx Park.

It was a dreadful thing for us to have our balmy Lotus-eaters' paradise so startlingly invaded by a large, loquacious, loud-voiced lady who had already stirred us all out of our agreeable, traditional and leisurely inertia. Inertia begets cogitation, and cogitation begets ideas, and ideas beget reflexion, and profound reflexion is the fundamental cornerstone of that immortal temple in which the goddess Science sits asleep between her dozing sisters, Custom and Religion.

This thought seemed to me so unusually beautiful that I wrote it with a pencil upon my cuff.

While I was writing it, quietly happy in the deep pleasure that my intellectual allegory afforded me, Dr. Fooss swabbed the last morsel of nourishment from his plate with a wad of rye bread, then bolting the bread and wiping his beard with his fingers and his fingers on his waistcoat, he made several guttural observations too profoundly German to be immediately intelligible, and lighted his porcelain pipe.

"Ach wass!" he remarked in ruminative fashion. "Dot Frauen-zimmer she iss to raise hell alretty determined. Von Pachyderma-tology she knows nodding. Maybe she leaves me alone, maybe it is to be 'raus mit me. I' weis' ni'! It iss aber besser one over on dat lady to put, yess?"

"It certainly is advisable," replied Lezard.

"Let us try to think of something sufficiently disastrous to ter-minate her scientific career," said I. And I bowed my rather strik-ing head and rested the point of my forefinger upon my forehead. Thought crystallises more quickly for me when I assume this atti-tude.

Out of the corner of my eye I saw Lezard fold his arms and sit frowning at infinity.

Dr. Fooss lay back in a big, deeply padded armchair and closed his prominent eyes. His pipe went out presently, and now and then he made long-drawn nasal remarks, in German, too complicated for either Lezard or for me to entirely comprehend. "We must try to get her as far away from here as possible," mused Lezard. "Is Oyster Bay *too* far and too cruel?"

I pondered darkly upon the suggestion. But it seemed unpleas-antly like murder.

"Lezard," said I, "come, let us reason together. Now *what* is woman's besetting emotion?"

"Curiosity?"

"Very well; assuming that to be true, what—ah—quality par-ticularly characterizes woman when so beset."

"Ruthless determination."

"Then," said I, "we ought to begin my exciting the curiosity of Professor Bottomly; and her ruthless determination to satisfy that curiosity should logically follow."

"How," he asked, "are we to arouse her curiosity?"

"By pretending that we have knowledge of something hitherto undiscovered, the discovery of which would redound to our scien-tific glory."

"I see. She'd want the glory for herself. She'd swipe it."

"She would," said I.

"Tee—hee!" he giggled; "Wouldn't it be funny to plant something phony on her—"

I waved my arms rather gracefully in my excitement:

"That is the germ of an idea!" I said. "If we could plant something—something—far away from here—very far away—if we could bury something—like the Cardiff Giant—"

"Hundreds and hundreds of miles away!"

"Thousands!" I insisted, enthusiastically.

"Tee-hee! In Tasmania, for example! Maybe a Tasmanian Devil might acquire her!"

"There exists a gnat," said I, "in Borneo—*Gnatus soporificus*—and when this tiny gnat stings people they never entirely wake up. It's really rather a pleasurable catastrophe, I understand. Life becomes one endless cat-nap—one delightful siesta, with intervals for light nourishment... She—ah—could sit very comfortably in some pleasant retreat and rock in a rocking-chair and doze quite happily through the years to come... And from your description of her I should say that the Soldiers' Home might receive her."

"It won't do," he said, gloomily.

"Why? Is it too much like crime?"

"Oh not at all. Only if she went to Borneo she'd be sure to take a mosquito-bar with her."

In the depressed silence which ensued Dr. Fooss suddenly made several Futurist observations through his nose with monotonous but authoritative regularity. I tried to catch his meaning and his eye. The one remained cryptic, the other shut.

Lezard sat thinking very hard. And as I fidgetted in my chair, fiddling nervously with various objects lying on my desk I chanced to pick up a letter from the pile of still unopened mail at my elbow.

Still pondering on Professor Bottomly's proposed destruction, I turned the letter over idly and my preoccupied gaze rested on the postmark. After a moment I leaned forward and examined it more attentively. The letter directed to me was postmarked Fort Carcajou, Cook's Peninsula, Baffin Land; and now I recalled the handwriting, having already seen it three or four times within the last month or so.

"Lezard," I said, "that lunatic trapper from Baffin Land has written to me again. What do you suppose is the matter with him? Is he just plain crazy or does he think he can be funny with me?"

Lezard gazed at me absently. Then, all at once a gleam of savage interest lighted his somewhat solemn features.

"Read the letter to me," he said, with an evil smile which instantly animated my own latent imagination. And immediately it occurred to me that perhaps, in the humble letter from the wilds of Baffin Land, which I was now opening with eager and unsteady fingers, might lie concealed the professional undoing of Professor Jane Bottomly, and the only hope of my own ultimate and scientific salvation.

The room became hideously still as I unfolded the pencil-scrawled sheets of cheap, ruled letter paper.

Dr. Fooss opened his eyes, looked at me, made porcine sounds indicative of personal well-being, relighted his pipe, and disposed himself to listen. But just as I was about to begin, Lezard suddenly laid his forefinger across his lips conjuring us to densest silence.

For a moment or two I heard nothing except the buzzing of flies. Then I stole a startled glance at my door. It was opening slowly, almost imperceptibly.

But it did not open very far—just a crack remained. Then, listening with all our might, we heard the cautiously suppressed breathing of somebody in the hallway just outside of my door.

Lezard turned and cast at me a glance of horrified intelligence. In dumb pantomime he outlined in the air, with one hand, the large and feminine amplification of his own person, conveying to us the certainty of his suspicions concerning the unseen eavesdropper.

We nodded. We understood perfectly that she was out there prepared to listen to every word we uttered.

A flicker of ferocious joy disturbed Lezard's otherwise innocuous features; he winked horribly at Dr. Fooss and at me, and uttered a faint click with his teeth and tongue like the snap of a closing trap.

"Gentlemen," he said, in the guarded yet excited voice of a man who is confident of not being overheard, "the matter under discussion admits of only one interpretation: a discovery—perhaps

the most vitally important discovery of all the centuries—is imminent.

"Secrecy is imperative; the scientific glory is to be shared by us
alone, and there is enough of glory to go around.

"Mr. Chairman, I move that epoch-making letter be read aloud!"

"I second dot motion!" said Dr. Fooss, winking so violently at
me that his glasses wabbled.

"Gentlemen," said I, "it has been moved and seconded that this
epoch-making letter be read aloud. All those in favor will kindly
say 'aye.'"

"Aye! Aye!" they exclaimed, fairly wriggling in their furtive joy.

"The contrary-minded will kindly emit the usual negation," I
went on... "It seems to be carried ... It *is* carried. The chairman
will proceed to the reading of the epoch-making letter."

I quietly lighted a five-cent cigar, unfolded the letter and read
aloud:

> "Joneses Shack,
> Golden Glacier,
> Cook's Peninsula, Baffin Land,
> March 15, 1915.

"Professor, Dear Sir:

"I already wrote you three times no answer having been
rec'd perhaps you think I'm kiddin' you're a dam' liar I ain't.

"Hoping to tempt you to come I will hereby tell you
more'n I told you in my other letters, the terminal moraine
of this here Golden Glacier finishes into a marsh, nothing
to see for miles excep' frozen tussock and mud and all flat
as hell for fifty miles which is where I am trappin' it for
mink and otter and now ready to go back to Fort Carcajou.
i told you what I seen stickin' in under this here marsh,
where anything sticks out the wolves have eat it, but most
of them there ellerphants is in under the ice and mud too
far for the wolves to git 'em.

"i ain't kiddin' you, there is a whole herd of furry
ellerphants in the marsh like as they were stuck there and
all lay down and was drownded like. Some has tusks and

some hasn't. Two ellerphants stuck out of the ice, I eat onto one, the meat was good and sweet and joosy, the damn wolves eat it up that night, I had cut stakes and rost for three months though and am eating off it yet.

"Thinking as how ellerphants and all like that is your graft, I being a keeper in the Mouse House once in the Bronx and seein' you nosin' around like you was full of scientific thinks, it comes to me to write you and put you next.

"If you say so I'll wait here and help you with them ellerphants. Livin' wages is all I ask also eleven thousand dollars for tippin' you wise. I won't tell nobody till I hear from you. I'm hones' you can trus' me. Write me to Fort Carcajou if you mean bizness. So no more respectfully,
                                    James Skaw."

When I finished reading I cautiously glanced at the door, and, finding it still on the crack, turned and smiled subtly upon Lezard and Fooss.

In their slowly spreading grins I saw they agreed with me that somebody, signing himself James Skaw, was still trying to hoax the Great Zoölogical Society of Bronx Park.

"Gentlemen," I said aloud, injecting innocent enthusiasm into my voice, "this secret expedition to Baffin Land which we three are about to organise is destined to be without doubt the most scientifically prolific field expedition ever organised by man.

"Imagine an entire herd of mammoths preserved in mud and ice through all these thousands of years!

"Gentlemen, no discovery ever made has even remotely approached in importance the discovery made by this simple, illiterate trapper, James Skaw."

"I thought," protested Lezard, "that *we* are to be announced as the discoverers."

"We are," said I, "the discoverers of James Skaw, which makes us technically the finders of the ice-preserved herd of mammoths—*technically*, you understand. A few thousand dollars," I added, carelessly, "ought to satiate James Skaw."

"We could name dot glacier after him," suggested Dr. Fooss.

"Certainly—the Skaw Glacier. That ought to be enough glory for him. It ought to satisfy him and prevent any indiscreet remarks," nodded Lezard.

"Gentlemen," said I, "there is only one detail that really troubles me. Ought we to notify our honoured and respected Chief of Division concerning this discovery?"

"Do you mean, should we tell that accomplished and fascinating lady, Professor Bottomly, about this herd of mammoths?" I asked in a loud, clear voice. And immediately answered my own question: "No," I said, "no, dear friends. Professor Bottomly already has too much responsibility weighing upon her distinguished mind. No, dear brothers in science, we should steal away unobserved as though setting out upon an ordinary field expedition. And when we return with fresh and immortal laurels such as no man before has ever worn, no doubt that our generous-minded Chief of Division will weave for us further wreaths to crown our brows—the priceless garlands of professional approval!" And I made a horrible face at my co-conspirators.

Before I finished Lezard had taken his own face in his hands for the purpose of stifling raucous and untimely mirth. As for Dr. Fooss, his small, porcine eyes snapped and twinkled madly behind his spectacles, but he seemed rather inclined to approve my flowers of rhetoric.

"Ja," said he, "so iss it besser oursellufs dot gefrozenss herd von elephanten to discover, und, by and by, die elephanten bei der Pronx Bark home yet again once more to bring. We shall therefore much praise thereby bekommen. Ach wass!"

"Gentlemen," said I, distinctly, "it is decided, then, that we shall say nothing concerning the true object of this expedition to Professor Bottomly."

Lezard and Fooss nodded assent.

Then, in the silence, we all strained our ears to listen. And presently we detected the scarcely heard sound of cautiously retreating footsteps down the corridor.

When it was safe to do so I arose and closed my door.

"I think," said I, with a sort of infernal cheerfulness in my tones, "that we are about to do something jocose to Jane Bottomly."

"A few," said Professor Lezard. He rose and silently executed a complicated ballet-step.

"I shall laff," said Dr. Fooss, earnestly, "und I shall laff, und I shall laff—ach Gott how I shall laff my pally head off!"

I folded my arms and turned romanesquely toward the direction in which Professor Bottomly had retreated.

"Viper!" I said. "The Bronx shall nourish you in its bosom no more! Fade away, Ophidian!"

The sentiment was applauded by all. There chanced to be in my desk a bottle marked: "That's all!" On the label somebody had written: "Do it now!" We did.

II

It was given out at the Bronx that our field expedition to Baffin Land was to be undertaken solely for the purpose of bringing back living specimens of the five-spotted Arctic woodcock—*Philohela quinquemaculata*—in order to add to our onomatology and our glossary of onomatopœia an ontogenesis of this important but hitherto unstudied sub-species.

I trust I make myself clear. Scientific statements should be as clear as the Spuyten Duyvil. *Sola in stagno salus!*

But two things immediately occurred which worried us; Professor Bottomly sent us official notification that she approved our expedition to Baffin Land, designated the steamer we were to take, and enclosed tickets. That scared us.

Then to add to our perplexity Professor Bottomly disappeared, leaving Dr. Daisy Delmour in charge of her department during what she announced might be "a somewhat prolonged absence on business."

And during the four feverish weeks of our pretended preparations for Baffin Land not one word did we hear from Jane Bottomly, which caused us painful inquietude as the hour approached for our departure.

Was this formidable woman actually intending to let us depart alone for the Golden Glacier? Was she too lazy to rob us of the secretly contemplated glory which we had pretended awaited us?

We had been so absolutely convinced that she would forbid our expedition, pack us off elsewhere, and take charge herself of an exploring party to Baffin Land, that, as the time for our leaving drew near we became first uneasy, and then really alarmed.

It would be a dreadful jest on us if she made us swallow our own concoction; if she revealed to our colleagues our pretended knowledge of the Golden Glacier and James Skaw and the supposedly ice-imbedded herd of mammoths, and then publicly forced us to investigate this hoax.

More horrible still would it be if she informed the newspapers and gave them a hint to make merry over the three wise men of the Bronx who went to Baffin Land in a boat.

"*What* do you suppose that devious and secretive female is up to?" inquired Lezard who, within the last few days, had grown thin with worry. "Is it possible that she is sufficiently degraded to suspect us of trying to put one over on her? Is that what she is now doing to us?"

"*Terminus est*—it is the limit!" said I.

He turned a morbid eye upon me. "She is making a monkey of us. That's what!"

"*Suspendenda omnia naso*," I nodded; "*tarde sed tute.*" When I think aloud in Latin it means that I am deeply troubled. "*Suum quemque scelus agitat.* Do you get me, Professor? I'm sorry I attempted to be sportive with this terrible woman. The curse of my scientific career has been periodical excesses of frivolity. See where this frolicsome impulse has landed me!—*super abyssum ambulans. Trahit sua quemque voluptas; transeat in exemplum!* She means to let us go to our destruction on this mammoth frappé affair."

But Dr. Fooss was optimistic:

"I tink she iss alretty herselluf by dot Baffin Land ge-gone," he said. "I tink she has der bait ge-swallowed. Ve vait; ve see; und so iss it ve know."

"But why hasn't she stopped our preparations?" I demanded. "If she wants all the glory herself why does she permit us to incur this expense in getting ready?"

"No mans can to know der vorkings of der mental brocess by a Frauenzimmer," said Dr. Fooss, wagging his head.

The suspense became nerve-racking; we were obliged to pack our camping kits; and it began to look as though we would have either to sail the next morning or to resign from the Bronx Park Zoölogical Society, because all the evening papers had the story in big type—the details and objects of the expedition, the discovery of the herd of mammoths in cold storage, the prompt organization of an expedition to secure this unparalleled deposit of prehistoric mammalia—everything was there staring at us in violent print, excepting only the name of the discoverer and the names of those composing the field expedition.

"She means to betray us after we have sailed," said Lezard, greatly depressed. "We might just as well resign now before this hoax explodes and bespatters us. We can take our chances in vaudeville or as lecturing professors with the movies." I thought so, too, in point of fact we all had gathered in my study to write out our resignations, when there came a knock at the door and Dr. Daisy Delmour walked in.

Oddly enough I had not before met Dr. Delmour personally; only formal written communications had hitherto passed between us. My idea of her had doubtless been inspired by the physical and intellectual aberrations of her chief; I naturally supposed her to be either impossible and corporeally redundant, or intellectually and otherwise as weazened as last year's Li-che nut.

I was criminally mistaken. And why Lezard, who knew her, had never set me right I could not then understand. I comprehended later.

For the feminine assistant of Professor Jane Bottomly, who sauntered into my study and announced herself, had the features of Athene, the smile of Aphrodite, and the figure of Psyche. I believe I do not exaggerate these scientific details, although it has been said of me that any pretty girl distorts my vision and my intellectual balance to the detriment of my calmer reason and my differentiating ability.

"Gentlemen," said Dr. Delmour, while we stood in a respectful semi-circle before her, modestly conscious of our worth, our toes turned out, and each man's features wreathed with that politely unnatural smirk which masculine features assume when confronted by feminine beauty. "Gentlemen, on the eve of your proposed departure for Baffin Land in quest of living specimens of the five-spotted *Philohela quinquemaculata*, I have been instructed by Professor Bottomly to announce to you a great good fortune for her, for you, for the Bronx, for America, for the entire civilized world.

"It has come to Professor Bottomly's knowledge, recently I believe, that an entire herd of mammoths lie encased in the mud and ice of the vast flat marshes which lie south of the terminal moraine of the Golden Glacier in that part of Baffin Land known as Dr. Cook's Peninsula.

"The credit of this epoch-making discovery is Professor Bottomly's entirely. How it happened, she did not inform me. One month ago today she sailed in great haste for Baffin Land. At this very hour she is doubtless standing all alone upon the frozen surface of that wondrous marsh, contemplating with reverence and awe and similar holy emotions the fruits of her own unsurpassed discovery!" Dr. Delmour's lovely features became delicately suffused and transfigured as she spoke; her exquisite voice thrilled with generous emotion; she clasped her snowy hands and gazed, enraptured, at the picture of Dr. Bottomly which her mind was so charmingly evoking.

"Perhaps," she whispered, "perhaps at this very instant, in the midst of that vast and flat and solemn desolation the only protuberance visible for miles and miles is Professor Bottomly. Perhaps the pallid Arctic sun is setting behind the majestic figure of Professor Bottomly, radiating a blinding glory to the zenith, illuminating the crowning act of her career with its unearthly aura!"

She gazed at us out of dimmed and violet eyes. "Gentlemen," she said, "I am ordered to take command of this expedition of yours; I am ordered to sail with you tomorrow morning on the Labrador and Baffin Line steamer *Dr. Cook*.

"The object of your expedition, therefore, is not to be the quest of *Philohela quinquemaculata*; your duty now is to corroborate the almost miraculous discovery of Professor Bottomly, and to disinter for her the vast herd of frozen mammoths, pack and pickle them, and get them to the Bronx.

"Tomorrow's morning papers will have the entire story: the credit and responsibility for the discovery and the expedition belong to Professor Bottomly, and will be given to her by the press and the populace of our great republic.

"It is her wish that no other names be mentioned. Which is right. To the discoverer belongs the glory. Therefore, the marsh is to be named Bottomly's Marsh, and the Glacier, Bottomly's Glacier.

"Yours and mine is to be the glory of laboring incognito under the direction of the towering scientific intellect of the age, Professor Bottomly.

"And the most precious legacy you can leave your children—if you get married and have any—is that you once wielded the humble pick and shovel for Jane Bottomly on the bottomless marsh which bears her name!"

After a moment's silence we three men ventured to look sideways at each other. We had certainly killed Professor Bottomly, scientifically speaking.

The lady was practically dead. The morning papers would consummate the murder. We didn't know whether we wanted to laugh or not.

She was now virtually done for; that seemed certain. So greedily had this egotistical female swallowed the silly bait we offered, so arrogantly had she planned to eliminate everybody excepting herself from the credit of the discovery, that there seemed now nothing left for us to do except to watch her hurdling deliriously toward destruction. *Should* we burst into hellish laughter?

We looked hard at Dr. Delmour and we decided not to—yet.

Said I: "To assist at the final apotheosis of Professor Bottomly makes us very, very happy. We are happy to remain incognito, mere ciphers blotted out by the fierce white light which is about to beat upon Professor Bottomly, fore and aft. We are happy that our participation in this astonishing affair shall never be known to science.

"But, happiest of all are we, dear Dr. Delmour, in the knowledge that *you* are to be with us and of us, incognito on this voyage now imminent; that you are to be our revered and beloved leader.

"And I, for one, promise you personally the undivided devotion of a man whose entire and austere career has been dedicated to science—in *all* its branches."

I stepped forward rather gracefully and raised her little hand to my lips to let her see that even the science of gallantry had not been neglected by me.

Dr. Daisy Delmour blushed.

"Therefore," said I, "considering the fact that our names are not to figure in this expedition; and, furthermore, in consideration of the fact that you are going, we shall be very, very happy to accompany you, Dr. Delmour." I again saluted her hand, and again Dr. Delmour blushed and looked sideways at Professor Lezard.

III

It was, to be accurate, exactly twenty-three days later that our voyage by sea and land ended one Monday morning upon the gigantic terminal moraine of the Golden Glacier, Cook's Peninsula, Baffin Land.

Four pack-mules carried our luggage, four more bore our persons; an arctic dicky-bird sat on a bowlder and said, "Pilly-willy-willy! Tweet! Tweet!"

As we rode out to the bowlder-strewn edge of the moraine the rising sun greeted us cordially, illuminating below us the flat surface of the marsh which stretched away to the east and south as far as the eye could see.

So flat was it that we immediately made out the silhouettes of two mules tethered below us a quarter of a mile away.

Something about the attitude of these mules arrested our attention, and, gazing upon them through our field-glasses we beheld Professor Bottomly.

That resourceful lady had mounted a pneumatic hammock upon the two mules, their saddles had sockets to fit the legs of the galvanized iron tripod.

No matter in which way the mules turned, sliding swivels on the hollow steel frames regulated the hammock slung between them. It was an infernal invention.

There lay Jane Bottomly asleep, her back hair drying over the hammock's edge, gilded to a peroxide lustre by the rays of the rising sun.

I gazed upon her with a sort of ferocious pity. Her professional days were numbered. *I* also had her number!

"How majestically she slumbers," whispered Dr. Delmour to me, "dreaming, doubtless, of her approaching triumph."

Dr. Fooss and Professor Lezard, driving the pack-mules ahead of them, were already riding out across the marsh.

"Daisy," I said, leaning from my saddle and taking one of her gloved hands into mine, "the time has come for me to disillusion you. There are no mammoths in that mud down there."

She looked at me in blue-eyed amazement.

"You are mistaken," she said; "Professor Bottomly is celebrated for the absolute and painstaking accuracy of her deductions and the boldness and the imagination of her scientific investigations. She is the most cautious scientist in America; she would never announce such a discovery to the newspapers unless she were perfectly certain of its truth."

I was sorry for this young girl. I pressed her hand because I was sorry for her. After a few moments of deepest thought I felt so sorry for her that I kissed her.

"You mustn't," said Dr. Delmour, blushing.

The things we mustn't do are so many that I can't always remember all of them.

"Daisy," I said, "shall we pledge ourselves to each other for eternity—here in the presence of this immemorial glacier which moves a thousand inches a year—I mean an inch every thousand years—here in these awful solitudes where incalculable calculations could not enlighten us concerning the number of cubic tons of mud in that marsh—here in the presence of these innocent mules—"

"Oh, look!" exclaimed Dr. Delmour, lifting her flushed cheek from my shoulder. "There is a man in the hammock with Professor Bottomly!"

I levelled my field-glasses incredulously. Good Heavens! There *was* a man there. He was sitting on the edge of the hammock in a dejected attitude, his booted legs dangling.

And, as I gazed, I saw the arm of Professor Bottomly raised as though groping instinctively for something in her slumber—saw her fingers close upon the blue-flannel shirt of her companion, saw his timid futile attempts to elude her, saw him inexorably hauled back and his head forcibly pillowed upon her ample chest.

"Daisy!" I faltered, "what does yonder scene of presumable domesticity mean?"

"I—I haven't the faintest idea!" she stammered.

"Is that lady married! Or is this revelry?" I asked, sternly.

"She wasn't married when she sailed from N-New-York," faltered Dr. Delmour.

We rode forward in pained silence, spurring on until we caught up with Lezard and Fooss and the pack-mules; then we all pressed ahead, a prey, now, to the deepest moral anxiety and agitation.

The splashing of our mule's feet on the partly melted surface of the mud aroused the man as we rode up and he scrambled madly to get out of the hammock as soon as he saw us.

A detaining feminine hand reached mechanically for his collar, groped aimlessly for a moment, and fell across the hammock's edge. Evidently its owner was too sleepy for effort.

Meanwhile the man who had floundered free from the hammock, leaped overboard and came hopping stiffly over the slush toward us like a badly-winged snipe.

"Who are you?" I demanded, drawing bridle so suddenly that I found myself astride of my mule's ears. Sliding back into the saddle, I repeated the challenge haughtily, inwardly cursing my horsemanship.

He stood balancing his lank six feet six of bony altitude for a few moments without replying. His large gentle eyes of baby blue were fixed on me.

"Speak!" I said. "The reputation of a lady is at stake! Who are you? We ask, before we shoot you, for purpose of future identification."

He gazed at me wildly. "I dunno who I be," he replied. "My name *was* James Skaw before that there lady went an' changed it on me. She says she has changed my name to hers. I dunno. All I know is I'm married."

"*Married!*" echoed Dr. Delmour.

He looked dully at the girl, then fixed his large mild eyes on me.

"A mission priest done it for her a month ago when we was hikin' towards Fort Carcajou. Hoonhel are you?" he added.

I informed him with dignity; he blinked at me, at the others, at the mules. Then he said with infinite bitterness:

"You're a fine guy, ain't you, a-wishin' this here lady onto a pore pelt-hunter what ain't never done nothin' to you!"

"Who did you say I wished on you?" I demanded, bewildered.

"That there lady a-sleepin' into the nuptool hammick! You wished her onto me—yaas you did! Whatnhel have I done to you, hey?"

We were dumb. He shoved his hand into his pocket, produced a slug of twist, slowly gnawed off a portion, and buried the remains in his vast jaw.

"All I done to you," he said, "was to write you them letters sayin's as how I found a lot of ellerphants into the mud.

"What you done to me was to send that there lady here. Was that gratitood? Man to man I ask you?"

A loud snore from the hammock startled us all. James Skaw twisted his neck turkey-like, and looked warily at the hammock, then turning toward me; "Aw," he said, "she don't never wake up till I have breakfast ready."

"James Skaw," I said, "tell me what has happened. On my word of honor I don't know."

He regarded me with lack-lustre eyes.

"I was a-settin' onto a bowlder," said he, "a-figurin' out whether you was a-comin' or not, when that there lady rides up with her led-mule a trail-in'.

"Sez she: 'Are you James Skaw?'

"Yes, marm,' sez I, kinder scared an' puzzled.

"'Where is them ellerphants?' sez she, reachin' down from her saddle an' takin' me by the shirt collar, an' beatin' me with her umbrella.

"Sez I, 'I have wrote to a certain gent that I would show him them ellerphants for a price. Bein' strictly hones' I can't show 'em to no one else until I hear from him.'

"With that she continood to argoo the case with her umbrella, never lettin' go of my shirt collar. Sir, she argood until dinner time, an' then she resoomed the debate until I fell asleep. The last I knowed she was still conversin'.

"An' so it went next day, all day long, an' the next day. I couldn't stand it no longer so I started for Fort Carcajau. But she bein' onto a mule, run me down easy, an' kep' beside me conversin' volooble.

"Sir, do you know what it is to listen to umbrella argooment every day, all day long, from sun up to night-fall? An' then some more?

"I was loony, I tell you, when we met the mission priest. 'Marry me,' sez she, 'or I'll talk you to death!" I didn't realise what she was sayin' an' what I answered. But them words I uttered done the job, it seems.

"We camped there an' slep' for two days without wakin.' When I waked up I was convalescent.

"She was good to me. She made soup an' she wrapped blankets onto me an' she didn't talk no more until I was well enough to endoor it.

"An' by'm'by she brooke the nooze to me that we was married an' that she had went as far as to marry me in the sacred cause of science because man an' wife is one, an' what I knowed about them ellerphants she now had a right to know.

"Sir, she had put one over on me. So bein, strickly hones' I had to show her where them ellerphants lay froze up under the marsh."

IV

Where the ambition of this infatuated woman had led her appalled us all. The personal sacrifice she had made in the name of science awed us.

Still when I remembered that detaining arm sleepily lifted from the nuptual hammock, I was not so certain concerning her continued martyrdom.

I cast an involuntary glance of critical appraisal upon James Skaw. He had the golden hair and beard of the early Christian martyr. His features were classically regular; he stood six feet six; he was lean because fit, sound as a hound's tooth, and really a superb specimen of masculine health.

Curry him and trim him and clothe him in evening dress and his physical appearance would make a sensation at the Court of St. James. Only his English required manicuring.

The longer I looked at him the better I comprehended that detaining hand from the hammock. *Fabas indulcet fames.*

Then, with a shock, it rushed over me that there evidently had been some ground for this man's letters to me concerning a herd of frozen mammoths.

Professor Bottomly had not only married him to obtain the information but here she was still camping on the marsh!

"James Skaw," I said, tremulously, "where are those mammoths?"

He looked at me, then made a vague gesture:

"Under the mud—everywhere—all around us."

"Has *she* seen them?"

"Yes, I showed her about a hundred. There's one under you. Look! you can see him through the slush."

"Ach Gott!" burst from Dr. Fooss, and he tottered in his saddle. Lezard, frightfully pale, passed a shaking hand over his brow. As for me my hair became dank with misery, for there directly under my feet, the vast hairy bulk of a mammoth lay dimly visible through the muddy ice.

What I had done to myself when I was planning to do Professor Bottomly suddenly burst upon me in all its hideous proportions. Fame, the plaudits of the world, the highest scientific honours— all these in my effort to annihilate her, I had deliberately thrust upon this woman to my own everlasting detriment and disgrace.

A sort of howl escaped from Dr. Fooss, who had dismounted and who had been scratching in the slush with his feet like a hen. For already this slight gallinaceous effort of his had laid bare a hairy section of frozen mammoth.

Lezard, weeping bitterly, squatted beside him clawing at the thin skin of ice with a pick-axe.

It seemed more than I could bear and I flung myself from my mule and seizing a spade, fell violently to work, the tears of rage and mortification coursing down my cheeks.

"Hurrah!" cried Dr. Delmour, excitedly, scrambling down from her mule and lifting a box of dynamite from her saddle-bags.

Transfigured with enthusiasm she seized a crowbar, traced in the slush the huge outlines of the buried beast, then, measuring with practiced eye the irregular zone of cleavage, she marked out a vast oval, dug holes along it with her bar, dropped into each hole a stick of dynamite, got out the batteries and wires, attached the fuses, covered each charge, and retired on a run toward the moraine, unreeling wire as she sped upward among the bowlders.

Half frantic with grief and half mad with the excitement of the moment we still had sense enough to shoulder our tools and drive our mules back across the moraine.

Only the mule-hammock in which reposed Professor Bottomly remained on the marsh. For one horrid instant temptation assailed me to press the button before James Skaw could lead the hammock-mules up to the moraine. It was my closest approach to crime.

With a shudder I viewed the approach of the mules. James Skaw led them by the head; the hammock on its bar and swivels swung gently between them; Professor Bottomly slept, lulled, no doubt, to deeper slumber by the gently swaying hammock.

When the hammock came up, one by one we gazed upon its unconscious occupant.

And, even amid dark and revengeful thoughts, amid a mental chaos of grief and fury and frantic self-reproach, I had to admit to myself that Jane Bottomly was a fine figure of a woman, and good-looking, too, and that her hair was all her own and almost magnificent at that.

With a modiste to advise her, a maid to dress her, I myself might have—but let that pass. Only as I gazed upon her fresh complexion and the softly parted red lips of Professor Bottomly, and as I noted the beautiful white throat and prettily shaped hands, a newer, bitterer, and more overwhelming despair seized me; and I realized now that perhaps I had thrown away more than fame, honours, applause; I had perhaps thrown away love!

At that moment Professor Bottomly awoke. For a moment her lilac-tinted eyes had a dazed expression, then they widened, and she lay very quietly looking from one to another of us, cradled in the golden glory of her hair, perfectly mistress of herself, and her mind as clear as a bell.

"Well," she said, "so you have arrived at last." And to Dr. Delmour she smilingly extended a cool, fresh hand.

"Have you met my husband?" she inquired.

We admitted that we had.

"James!" she called.

At the sound of her voice James Skaw hopped nimbly to do her bidding. A tender smile came into her face as she gazed upon her husband. She made no explanation concerning him, no apology for him. And, watching her, it slowly filtered into my mind that she liked him.

With one hand in her husband's and one on Dr. Delmour's arm she listened to Daisy's account of what we were about to do to the imbedded mammoth, and nodded approval.

James Skaw turned the mules so that she might watch the explosion. She twisted up her hair, then sat up in her hammock; Daisy Delmour pressed the electric button; there came a deep jarring sound, a vast upheaval, and up out of the mud rose *five or six dozen mammoths* and toppled gently over upon the surface of the ice.

Miserable as we were at such an astonishing spectacle we raised a tragic cheer as Professor Bottomly sprang out of her hammock and, telling Dr. Delmour to get a camera, seized her husband and sped down to where one of the great, hairy frozen beasts lay on the ice in full sunshine.

And then we tasted the last drop of gall which our over-slopping cup of bitterness held for us; Professor Bottomly climbed up the sides of the frozen mammoth, dragging her husband with her, and stood there waving a little American flag while Dr. Delmour used up every film in the camera to record the scientific triumph of the ages.

Almost idiotic with the shock of my great grief I reeled and tottered away among the bowlders. Fooss came to find me; and when he found me he kicked me violently for some time. "Esel dumkopf!" he said.

When he was tired Lezard came and fell upon me, showering me with kicks and anathema.

When he went away I beat my head with my fists for a while. Every little helped.

After a time I smelled cooking, and presently Dr. Delmour came to where I sat huddled up miserably in the sun behind the bowlder.

"Luncheon is ready," she said.

I groaned.

"Don't you feel well?"

I said that I did not.

She lingered apparently with the idea of cheering me up. "It's been such fun," she said. "Professor Lezard and I have already located over a hundred and fifty mammoths within a short distance of here, and apparently there are hundreds, if not thousands, more in the vicinity. The ivory alone is worth over a million dollars. Isn't it wonderful!"

She laughed excitedly and danced away to join the others. Then, out of the black depth of my misery a feeble gleam illuminated the Stygian obscurity. There was one way left to stay my approaching downfall—only one. Professor Bottomly meant to get rid of me, "for the good of the Bronx," but there remained a way to ward off impending disaster. And though I had lost the opportunity of my life by disbelieving the simple honesty of James Skaw,—and though the honors and emoluments and applause which ought to have been mine were destined for this determined woman, still, if I kept my head, I should be able to hold my job at the Bronx.

Dr. Delmour was immovable in the good graces of Professor Bottomly; and the only way for me to retain my position was to marry her.

The thought comforted me. After a while I felt well enough to arise and partake of some luncheon.

They were all seated around the campfire when I approached. I was welcomed politely, inquiries concerning my health were offered; but the coldly malevolent glare of Dr. Fooss and the calm contempt in Lezard's gaze chilled me; and I squatted down by Daisy Delmour and accepted a dish of soup from her in mortified silence.

Professor Bottomly and James Skaw were feasting connubially side by side, and she was selecting titbits for him which he dutifully swallowed, his large mild eyes gazing at vacancy in a gentle, surprised sort of way as he gulped down what she offered him.

Neither of them paid any attention to anybody else.

Fooss gobbled his lunch in a sort of raging silence; Lezard, on the other side of Dr. Delmour, conversed with her continually in undertones.

After a while his persistent murmuring began to make me uneasy, even suspicious, and I glared at him sideways.

Daisy Delmour, catching my eye, blushed, hesitated, then leaning over toward me with delightful confusion she whispered:

"I know that you will he glad to hear that I have just promised to marry your closest friend, Professor Lezard—"

"What!" I shouted with all my might, "have *you* put one over on me, too?"

Lezard and Fooss seized me, for I had risen and was jumping up and down and splashing them with soup.

"Everybody has put one over on me!" I shrieked. "Everybody! Now I'm going to put one over on myself !"

And I lifted my plate of soup and reversed it on my head.

They told me later that I screamed for half an hour before I swooned.

Afterward, my intellect being impaired, instead of being dismissed from my department, I was promoted to the position which I now hold as President Emeritus of the Consolidated Art Museums and Zoölogical Gardens of the City of New York.

I have easy hours, little to do, and twenty ornamental stenographers and typewriters engaged upon my memoirs which I dictate when I feel like it, steeped in the aroma of the most inexpensive cigar I can buy at the Rolling Stone Inn.

There is one typist in particular—but let that pass.

Vir sapit qui pauca loquitor.

When I returned to the plateau from my investigation of the crater, I realized that I had descended the grassy pit as far as any human being could descend. No living creature could pass that barrier of flame and vapour. Of that I was convinced.

Now, not only the crater but its steaming effluvia was utterly unlike anything I had ever before beheld. There was no trace of lava to be seen, or of pumice, ashes, or of volcanic rejecta in any form whatever. There were no sulphuric odours, no pungent fumes, nothing to teach the olfactory nerves what might be the nature of the silvery steam rising from the crater incessantly in a vast circle, ringing its circumference halfway down the slope.

Under this thin curtain of steam a ring of pale yellow flames played and sparkled, completely encircling the slope.

The crater was about half a mile deep; the sides sloped gently to the bottom.

But the odd feature of the entire phenomenon was this: the bottom of the crater seemed to be entirely free from fire and vapour. It was disk-shaped, sandy, and flat, about a quarter of a mile in diameter. Through my field-glasses I could see patches of grass and wild flowers growing in the sand here and there, and the sparkle of water, and a crow or two, feeding and walking about.

I looked at the girl who was standing beside me, then cast a glance around at the very unusual landscape. We were standing on the summit of a mountain some two thousand feet high, looking into a cup-shaped depression or crater, on the edges of which we stood.

This low, flat-topped mountain, as I say, was grassy and quite treeless, although it rose like a truncated sugar-cone out of a wilderness of trees which stretched for miles below us, north, south,

east, and west, bordered on the horizon by towering blue mountains, their distant ranges enclosing the forests as in a vast
amphitheatre.

From the centre of this enormous green floor of foliage rose
our grassy hill, and it appeared to be the only irregularity which
broke the level wilderness as far as the base of the dim blue ranges
encircling the horizon.

Except for the log bungalow of Mr. Blythe on the eastern edge of
this grassy plateau, there was not a human habitation in sight, nor
a trace of man's devastating presence in the wilderness around us.

Again I looked questioningly at the girl beside me and she
looked back at me rather seriously.

"Shall we seat ourselves here in the sun?" she asked.

I nodded.

Very gravely we settled down side by side on the thick green
grass.

"Now," she said, "I shall tell you why I wrote you to come out
here. Shall I?"

"By all means, Miss Blythe."

Sitting cross-legged, she gathered her ankles into her hands,
settling herself as snugly on the grass as a bird settles on its nest.

"The phenomena of nature," she said, "have always interested
me intensely, not only from the artistic angle but from the scientific point of view.

"It is different with father. He is a painter; he cares only for
the artistic aspects of nature. Phenomena of a scientific nature bore
him. Also, you may have noticed that he is of a—a slightly impatient disposition."

I had noticed it. He had been anything but civil to me when I
arrived the night before, after a five-hundred mile trip on a mule,
from the nearest railroad—a journey performed entirely alone and
by compass, there being no trail after the first fifty miles.

To characterize Blythe as slightly impatient was letting him
down easy. He was a selfish, bad-tempered old pig.

"Yes," I said, answering her, "I did notice a negligible trace of
impatience about your father."

She flushed.

"You see I did not inform my father that I had written to you. He doesn't like strangers; he doesn't like scientists. I did not dare tell him that I had asked you to come out here. It was entirely my own idea. I felt that I *must* write you because I am positive that what is happening in this wilderness is of vital scientific importance."

"How did you get a letter out of this distant and desolate place?" I asked.

"Every two months the storekeeper at Windflower Station sends in a man and a string of mules with staples for us. The man takes our further orders and our letters back to civilization."

I nodded.

"He took my letter to you—among one or two others I sent—"

A charming colour came into her cheeks. She was really extremely pretty. I liked that girl. When a girl blushes when she speaks to a man he immediately accepts her heightened colour as a personal tribute. This is not vanity: it is merely a proper sense of personal worthiness.

She said thoughtfully:

"The mail bag which that man brought to us last week contained a letter which, had I received it earlier, would have made my invitation to you unnecessary. I'm sorry I disturbed you."

"*I* am not," said I, looking into her beautiful eyes.

I twisted my mustache into two attractive points, shot my cuffs, and glanced at her again, receptively.

She had a far-away expression in her eyes. I straightened my necktie. A man, without being vain, ought to be conscious of his own worth.

"And now," she continued, "I am going to tell you the various reasons why I asked so celebrated a scientist as yourself to come here."

I thanked her for her encomium.

"Ever since my father retired from Boston to purchase this hill and the wilderness surrounding it," she went on, "ever since he came here to live a hermit's life—a life devoted solely to painting landscapes—I also have lived here all alone with him. That is three years, now. And from the very beginning—from the very first day of our arrival, somehow or other I was conscious that there was something abnormal about this corner of the world."

She bent forward, lowering her voice a trifle:

"Have you noticed," she asked, "that so many things seem to be *circular* out here?"

"Circular?" I repeated, surprised.

"Yes. That crater is circular; so is the bottom of it; so is this plateau, and the hill; and the forests surrounding us; and the mountain ranges on the horizon."

"But all this is natural."

"Perhaps. But in those woods, down there, there are, here and there, great circles of crumbling soil—*perfect* circles a mile in diameter."

"Mounds built by prehistoric man, no doubt."

She shook her head:

"These are not prehistoric mounds."

"Why not?"

"Because they have been freshly made."

"How do you know?"

"The earth is freshly upheaved; great trees, partly uprooted, slant at every angle from the sides of the enormous piles of newly upturned earth; sand and stones are still sliding from the raw ridges."

She leaned nearer and dropped her voice still lower:

"More than that," she said, "my father and I both have seen one of these huge circles *in the making!*"

"What!" I exclaimed, incredulously.

"It is true. We have seen several. And it enrages father."

"Enrages?"

"Yes, because it upsets the trees where he is painting landscapes, and tilts them in every direction. Which, of course, ruins his picture; and he is obliged to start another, which vexes him dreadfully."

I think I must have gaped at her in sheer astonishment.

"But there is something more singular than that for you to investigate," she said calmly. "Look down at that circle of steam which makes a perfect ring around the bowl of the crater, halfway down. Do you see the flicker of fire under the vapour?"

"Yes."

She leaned so near and spoke in such a low voice that her fragrant breath fell upon my cheek:

"In the fire, under the vapours, there are little animals."

"What!!"

"Little beasts live in the fire—slim, furry creatures, smaller than a weasel. I've seen them peep out of the fire and scurry back into it... *Now* are you sorry that I wrote you to come? And will you forgive me for bringing you out here?"

An indescribable excitement seized me, endowing me with a fluency and eloquence unusual:

"I thank you from the bottom of my heart!" I cried; "—from the depths of a heart the emotions of which are entirely and exclusively of scientific origin!"

In the impulse of the moment I held out my hand; she laid hers in it with charming diffidence.

"Yours is the discovery," I said. "Yours shall be the glory. Fame shall crown you; and perhaps if there remains any reflected light in the form of a by-product, some modest and negligible little ray may chance to illuminate me."

Surprised and deeply moved by my eloquence, I bent over her hand and saluted it with my lips.

She thanked me. Her pretty face was rosy.

It appeared that she had three cows to milk, new-laid eggs to gather, and the construction of some fresh butter to be accomplished.

At the bars of the grassy pasture slope she dropped me a curtsey, declining very shyly to let me carry her lacteal paraphernalia.

So I continued on to the bungalow garden, where Blythe sat on a camp stool under a green umbrella, painting a picture of something or other.

"Mr. Blythe!" I cried, striving to subdue my enthusiasm. "The eyes of the scientific world are now open upon this house! The searchlight of Fame is about to be turned upon you—"

"I prefer privacy," he interrupted. "That's why I came here. I'll be obliged if you'll turn off that searchlight."

"But, my dear Mr. Blythe—"

"I want to be let alone," he repeated irritably. "I came out here to paint and to enjoy privately my own paintings."

If what stood on his easel was a sample of his pictures, nobody was likely to share his enjoyment.

"Your work," said I, politely, "is—is—"

"Is what!" he snapped. "*What* is it—if you think you know?"

"It is entirely, so to speak, *per se*—by itself "

"What the devil do you mean by that?"

I looked at his picture, appalled. The entire canvas was one monotonous vermillion conflagration. I examined it with my head on one side, then on the other side; I made a funnel with both hands and peered intently through it at the picture. A menacing murmuring sound came from him.

"Satisfying—exquisitely satisfying," I concluded. "I have often seen such sunsets—"

"What!"

"I mean such prairie fires—"

"Damnation!" he exclaimed. "I'm painting a bowl of nasturtiums!"

"I was speaking purely in metaphor," said I with a sickly smile. "To me a nasturtium by the river brink is more than a simple flower. It is a broader, grander, more magnificent, more stupendous symbol. It may mean anything, everything—such as sunsets and conflagrations and Götterdämmerungs! Or—" and my voice was subtly modulated to an appealing and persuasive softness— "it may mean nothing at all—chaos, void, vacuum, negation, the exquisite annihilation of what has never even existed."

He glared at me over his shoulder. If he was infected by Cubist tendencies he evidently had not understood what I said.

"If you won't talk about my pictures I don't mind your investigating this district," he grunted, dabbing at his palette and plastering a wad of vermilion upon his canvas; "but I object to any public invasion of my artistic privacy until I am ready for it."

"When will that be?"

He pointed with one vermilion-soaked brush toward a long, low, log building.

"In that structure," he said, "are packed one thousand and ninety-five paintings—all signed by me. I have executed one or two every day since I came here. When I have painted exactly ten thousand pictures, no more, no less, I shall erect here a gallery large enough to contain them all.

"Only real lovers of art will ever come here to study them. It is five hundred miles from the railroad. Therefore, I shall never have to endure the praises of the dilettante, the patronage of the idler, the vapid rhapsodies of the vulgar. Only those who understand will care to make the pilgrimage."

He waved his brushes at me:

"The conservation of national resources is all well enough—the setting aside of timber reserves, game preserves, bird refuges, all these projects are very good in a way. But I have dedicated this wilderness as a last and only refuge in all the world for true Art! Because true Art, except for my pictures, is, I believe, now practically extinct!... You're in my way. Would you mind getting out?"

I had sidled around between him and his bowl of nasturtiums, and I hastily stepped aside. He squinted at the flowers, mixed up a flamboyant mess of colour on his palette, and daubed away with unfeigned satisfaction, no longer noticing me until I started to go. Then:

"What is it you're here for, anyway?" he demanded abruptly. I said with dignity:

"I am here to investigate those huge rings of earth thrown up in the forest as by a gigantic mole." He continued to paint for a few moments:

"Well, go and investigate 'em," he snapped. "I'm not infatuated with your society."

"What do you think they are?" I asked, mildly ignoring his wretched manners.

"I don't know and I don't care, except, that sometimes when I begin to paint several trees, the very trees I'm painting are suddenly heaved up and tilted in every direction, and all my work goes for nothing. *That* makes me mad! Otherwise, the matter has no interest for me."

"But what in the world could cause—"

"I don't know and I don't care!" he shouted, waving palette and brushes angrily. "Maybe it's an army of moles working all together under the ground; maybe it's some species of circular earthquake. I don't know! I don't care! But it annoys me. And if you can devise any scientific means to stop it, I'll be much obliged to you. Otherwise, to be perfectly frank, you bore me."

"The mission of Science," said I solemnly, "is to alleviate the inconveniences of mundane existence. Science, therefore, shall extend a helping hand to her frailer sister, Art—"

"Science can't patronize Art while I'm around!" he retorted. "I won't have it!"

"But, my dear Mr. Blythe—"

"I won't dispute with you, either! I don't like to dispute!" he shouted. "Don't try to make me. Don't attempt to inveigle me into discussion! I know all I want to know. I don't want to know anything you want me to know, either!"

I looked at the old pig in haughty silence, nauseated by his conceit. After he had plastered a few more tubes of vermilion over his canvas he quieted down, and presently gave me an oblique glance over his shoulder.

"Well," he said, "what else are you intending to investigate?"

"Those little animals that live in the crater fires," I said bluntly.

"Yes," he nodded, indifferently, "there are creatures which live somewhere in the fires of that crater."

"Do you realize what an astounding statement you are making?" I asked.

"It doesn't astound *me*. What do I care whether it astounds you or anybody else? Nothing interests me except Art."

"But—"

"I tell you nothing interests me except Art!" he yelled. "Don't dispute it! Don't answer me! Don't irritate me! I don't care whether anything lives in the fire or not! Let it live there!"

"But have you actually seen live creatures in the flames ?"

"Plenty! *Plenty!* What of it? What about it? Let 'em live there, for all I care. I've painted pictures of 'em, too. That's all that interests me."

"What do they look like, Mr. Blythe?"

"Look like? *I* don't know! They look like weasels or rats or bats or cats or—stop asking me questions! It irritates me! It depresses me! Don't ask any more! Why don't you go in to lunch? And—tell my daughter to bring me a bowl of salad out here. *I've* no time to stuff myself. Some people have. *I* haven't. You'd better go in to lunch... And tell my daughter to bring me seven tubes of Chinese vermilion with my salad!"

"You don't mean to mix—" I began, then checked myself before his fury.

"I'd rather eat vermilion paint on my salad than sit here talking to you!" he shouted.

I cast a pitying glance at this impossible man, and went into the house. After all, he was *her* father. I *had* to endure him.

After Miss Blythe had carried to her father a large bucket of lettuce leaves, she returned to the veranda of the bungalow.

A delightful luncheon awaited us; I seated her, then took the chair opposite.

A delicious omelette, fresh biscuit, salad, and strawberry preserves, and a tall tumbler of iced tea imbued me with a sort of mild exhilaration.

Out of the corner of my eye I could see Blythe down in the garden, munching his lettuce leaves like an ill-tempered rabbit, and daubing away at his picture while he munched.

"Your father," said I politely, "is something of a genius."

"I am so glad you think so," she said gratefully. "But don't tell him so. He has been surfeited with praise in Boston. That is why we came out here."

"Art," said I, "is like science, or tobacco, or tooth-wash. Every man to his own brand. Personally, I don't care for his kind. But who can say which is the best kind of anything? Only the consumer. Your father is his own consumer. He is the best judge of what he likes. And that is the only true test of art, or anything else."

"How delightfully you reason!" she said. "How logically, how generously!"

"Reason is the handmaid of Science, Miss Blythe."

She seemed to understand me. Her quick intelligence surprised me, because I myself was not perfectly sure whether I had emitted piffle or an epigram.

As we ate our strawberry preserves we discussed ways and means of capturing a specimen of the little fire creatures which, as she explained, so frequently peeped out at her from the crater fires, and, at her slightest movement, scurried back again into the flames. Of course I believed that this was only her imagination. Yet, for years I had entertained a theory that fire supported certain unknown forms of life.

"I have long believed," said I, "that fire is inhabited by living organisms which require the elements and temperature of active combustion for their existence—microorganisms, but not," I added smilingly, "any higher type of life."

"In the fireplace," she ventured diffidently, "I sometimes see curious things—dragons and snakes and creatures of grotesque and peculiar shapes."

I smiled indulgently, charmed by this innocently offered contribution to science. Then she rose, and I rose and took her hand in mine, and we wandered over the grass toward the crater, while I explained to her the difference between what we imagine we see in the glowing coals of a grate fire and my own theory that fire is the abode of living animalculae. On the grassy edge of the crater we paused and looked down the slope, where the circle of steam rose, partly veiling the pale flash of fire underneath.

"How near can we go?" I inquired.

"Quite near. Come; I'll guide you."

Leading me by the hand, she stepped over the brink and we began to descend the easy grass slope together.

There was no difficulty about it at all. Down we went, nearer and nearer to the wall of steam, until at last, when but fifteen feet away from it, I felt the heat from the flames which sparkled below the wall of vapour. Here we seated ourselves upon the grass, and I knitted my brows and fixed my eyes upon this curious phenomenon, striving to discover some reason for it.

Except for the vapour and the fires, there was nothing whatever volcanic about this spectacle, or in the surroundings.

From where I sat I could see that the bed of fire which encircled the crater, and the wall of vapour which crowned the flames, were about three hundred feet wide. Of course this barrier was absolutely impassable. There was no way of getting through it into the bottom of the crater.

A slight pressure from Miss Blythe's fingers engaged my attention; I turned toward her, and she said:

"There is one more thing about which I have not told you. I feel a little guilty, because *that* is the real reason I asked you to come here."

"What is it?"

"I think there are emeralds on the floor of that crater."

"Emeralds!"

"I *think* so." She felt in the ruffled pocket of her apron, drew out a fragment of mineral, and passed it to me.

I screwed a jeweler's glass into my eye and examined it in astonished silence. It was an emerald; a fine, large, immensely valuable stone, if my experience counted for anything. One side of it was thickly coated with vermilion paint.

"Where did this come from?" I asked in an agitated voice.

"From the floor of the crater. Is it really an emerald?"

I lifted my head and stared at the girl incredulously.

"It happened this way," she said excitedly. "Father was painting a picture up there by the edge of the crater. He left his palette on the grass to go to the bungalow for some more tubes of colour. While he was in the house, hunting for the colours which he wanted, I stepped out on the veranda, and I saw some crows alight near the palette and begin to stalk about in the grass. One bird walked right over his wet palette; I stepped out and waved my sun-bonnet to frighten him off, but he had both feet in a sticky mass of Chinese vermilion, and for a moment was unable to free himself.

"I almost caught him, but he flapped away over the edge of the crater, high above the wall of vapour, sailed down onto the crater floor, and alighted.

"But his feet bothered him; he kept hopping about on the bottom of the crater, half running, half flying; and finally he took wing and rose up over the hill.

"As he flew above me, and while I was looking up at his vermilion feet, something dropped from his claws and nearly struck me. It was that emerald."

When I had recovered sufficient composure to speak steadily, I took her beautiful little hand in mine.

"This," said I, "is the most exciting locality I have ever visited for purposes of scientific research. Within this crater may lie millions of value in emeralds. You are probably, today, the wealthiest heiress upon the face of the globe!"

I gave her a winning glance. She smiled, shyly, and blushingly withdrew her hand. For several exquisite minutes I sat there beside her in a sort of heavenly trance. How beautiful she was! How engaging—how sweet—how modestly appreciative of the man beside her, who had little beside his scientific learning, his fame, and a kind heart to appeal to such youth and loveliness as hers!

There was something about her that delicately appealed to me. Sometimes I pondered what this might be; sometimes I wondered how many emeralds lay on that floor of sandy gravel below us.

Yes, I loved her. I realised it now. I could even endure her father for her sake. I should make a good husband. I was quite certain of that.

I turned and gazed upon her, meltingly. But I did not wish to startle her, so I remained silent, permitting the chaste language of my eyes to interpret for her what my lips had not yet murmured. It was a brief but beautiful moment in my life.

"The way to do," said I, "is to trap several dozen crows, smear their feet with glue, tie a ball of Indian twine to the ankle of every bird, then liberate them. Some are certain to fly into the crater and try to scrape the glue off in the sand. Then," I added, triumphantly, "all we have to do is to haul in our birds and detach the wealth of Midas from their sticky claws!"

"That is an excellent suggestion," she said gratefully, "but I can do that after you have gone. All I wanted you to tell me was whether the stone is a genuine emerald."

I gazed at her blankly.

"You are here for purposes of scientific investigation," she added, sweetly. "I should not think of taking your time for the mere sake of accumulating wealth for my father and me."

There didn't seem to be anything for me to say at that moment. Chilled, I gazed at the flashing ring of fire.

And, as I gazed, suddenly I became aware of a little, pointed muzzle, two pricked-up ears, and two ruby-red eyes gazing intently out at me from the mass of flames.

The girl beside me saw it, too.

"Don't move!" she whispered. "That is one of the flame creatures. It may venture out if you keep perfectly still."

Rigid with amazement, I sat like a stone image, staring at the most astonishing sight I had ever beheld.

For several minutes the ferret-like creature never stirred from where it crouched in the crater fire; the alert head remained pointed toward us; I could even see that its thick fur must have possessed the qualities of asbestos, because here and there a hair or two glimmered incandescent; and its eyes, nose, and whiskers glowed and glowed as the flames pulsated around it.

After a long while it began to move out of the fire, slowly, cautiously, cunning eyes fixed on us—a small, slim, wiry, weasel-like creature on which the sunlight fell with a vitreous glitter as it crept forward into the grass.

Then, from the fire behind, another creature of the same sort appeared, another, others, then dozens of eager, lithe, little animals appeared everywhere from the flames and began to frisk and play and run about in the grass and nibble the fresh, green, succulent herbage with a snipping sound quite audible to us.

One came so near my feet that I could examine it minutely.

Its fur and whiskers seemed heavy and dense and like asbestos fibre, yet so fine as to appear silky. Its eyes, nose, and claws were scarlet, and seemed to possess a glassy surface.

I waited my opportunity, and when the little thing came nosing along within reach, I seized it.

Instantly it emitted a bewildering series of whistling shrieks, and twisted around to bite me. Its body was icy.

"Don't let it bite!" cried the girl. "Be careful, Mr. Smith!"

But its jaws were toothless; only soft, cold gums pinched me, and I held it twisting and writhing, while the icy temperature of its body began to benumb my fingers and creep up my wrist, paralyzing my arm; and its incessant and piercing shrieks deafened me. In vain I transferred it to the other hand, and then passed it from one hand to the other, as one shifts a lump of ice or a hot potato, in an attempt to endure the temperature: it shrieked and squirmed and doubled, and finally wriggled out of my stiffened and useless hands, and scuttled away into the fire.

It was an overwhelming disappointment. For a moment it seemed unendurable.

"Never mind," I said, huskily, "if I caught one in my hands, I can surely catch another in a trap."

"I am so sorry for your disappointment," she said, pitifully.

"Do *you* care, Miss Blythe?" I asked.

She blushed.

"Of course I care," she murmured.

My hands were too badly frost-nipped to become eloquent. I merely sighed and thrust them into my pockets. Even my arm was too stiff to encircle her shapeful waist. Devotion to Science had temporarily crippled me. Love must wait. But, as we ascended the grassy slope together, I promised myself that I would make her a good husband, and that I should spend at least part of every day of my life in trapping crows and smearing their claws with glue.

That evening I was seated on the veranda beside Wilna—Miss Blythe's name was Wilna—and what with gazing at her and fitting together some of the folding box-traps which I always carried with me—and what with trying to realise the pecuniary magnificence of our future existence together, I was exceedingly busy when Blythe came in to display, as I supposed, his most recent daub to me.

The canvas he carried presented a series of crimson speckles, out of which burst an eruption of green streaks—and it made me think of stepping on a caterpillar.

My instinct was to placate this impossible man. He was *her* father. I meant to honour him if I had to assault him to do it.

"Supremely satisfying!" I nodded, chary of naming the subject. "It is a stride beyond the art of the future: it is a flying leap out of the Not Yet into the Possibly Perhaps! I thank you for enlightening me, Mr. Blythe. I am your debtor."

He fairly snarled at me:

"What are *you* talking about!" he demanded.

I remained modestly mute.

To Wilna he said, pointing passionately at his canvas:

"The crows have been walking all over it again! I'm going to paint in the woods after this, earthquakes or no earthquakes. Have the trees been heaved up anywhere recently?"

"Not since last week," she said, soothingly. "It usually happens after a rain."

"I think I'll risk it then—although it did rain early this morning. I'll do a moonlight down there this evening." And, turning to me: "If you know as much about science as you do about art you won't have to remain here long—I trust."

"What?" said I, very red.

He laughed a highly disagreeable laugh, and marched into the house. Presently he bawled for dinner, and Wilna went away. For her sake I had remained calm and dignified, but presently I went out and kicked up the turf two or three times; and, having foozled my wrath, I went back to dinner, realising that I might as well begin to accustom myself to my future father-in-law.

It seemed that he had a mania for prunes, and that's all he permitted anybody to have for dinner. Disgusted, I attempted to swallow the loathly stewed fruit, watching Blythe askance as he hurriedly stuffed himself, using a tablespoon, with every symptom of relish.

"Now," he cried, shoving back his chair, "I'm going to paint a moonlight by moonlight. Wilna, if Billy arrives, make him comfortable, and tell him I'll return by midnight." And without taking the trouble to notice me at all, he strode away toward the veranda, chewing vigorously upon his last prune.

"Your father," said I, "is eccentric. Genius usually is. But he is a most interesting and estimable man. I revere him."

"It is kind of you to say so," said the girl, in a low voice.

I thought deeply for a few moments, then:

"Who is 'Billy?'" I inquired, casually.

I couldn't tell whether it was a sudden gleam of sunset light on her face, or whether she blushed.

"Billy," she said softly, "is a friend of father's. His name is William Green."

"Oh."

"He is coming out here to visit—father—I believe."

"Oh. An artist; and doubtless of mature years."

"He is a mineralogist by profession," she said, "—and somewhat young."

"Oh."

"Twenty-four years old," she added. Upon her pretty face was an absent expression, vaguely pleasant. Her blue eyes became dreamy and exquisitely remote.

I pondered deeply for a while:

"Wilna?" I said.

"Yes, Mr. Smith?" as though aroused from agreeable meditation.

But I didn't know exactly what to say, and I remained uneasily silent, thinking about that man Green and his twenty-four years, and his profession, and the bottom of the crater, and Wilna—and striving to satisfy myself that there was no logical connection between any of these.

"I think," said I, "that I'll take a bucket of salad to your father."

Why I should have so suddenly determined to ingratiate myself with the old grouch I scarcely understood: for the construction of a salad was my very best accomplishment.

Wilna looked at me in a peculiar manner, almost as though she were controlling a sudden and not unpleasant inward desire to laugh.

Evidently the finer and more delicate instincts of a woman were divining my motive and sympathizing with my mental and sentimental perplexity.

So when she said: "I don't think you had better go near my father," I was convinced of her gentle solicitude in my behalf.

"With a bucket of salad," I whispered softly, "much may be accomplished, Wilna." And I took her little hand and pressed it gently and respectfully. "Trust all to me," I murmured.

She stood with her head turned away from me, her slim hand resting limply in mine. From the slight tremor of her shoulders I became aware how deeply her emotion was now swaying her. Evidently she was nearly ready to become mine.

But I remained calm and alert. The time was not yet. Her father had had his prunes, in which he delighted. And when pleasantly approached with a bucket of salad he could not listen otherwise than politely to what I had to say to him. Quick action was necessary—quick but diplomatic action—in view of the imminence of this young man Green, who evidently was *persona grata* at the bungalow of this irritable old dodo.

Tenderly pressing the pretty hand which I held, and saluting the finger-tips with a gesture which was, perhaps, not wholly ungraceful, I stepped into the kitchen, washed out several heads of lettuce, deftly chopped up some youthful onions, constructed a seductive French dressing, and, stirring together the crisp ingredients, set the savoury masterpiece away in the ice-box, after tasting it. It was delicious enough to draw sobs from any pig.

When I went out to the veranda, Wilna had disappeared. So I unfolded and set up some more box-traps, determined to lose no time.

Sunset still lingered beyond the chain of western mountains as I went out across the grassy plateau to the cornfield.

Here I set and baited several dozen aluminium crow-traps, padding the jaws so that no injury could be done to the birds when the springs snapped on their legs.

Then I went over to the crater and descended its gentle, grassy slope. And there, all along the borders of the vapoury wall, I set box-traps for the lithe little denizens of the fire, baiting every trap with a handful of fresh, sweet clover which I had pulled up from the pasture beyond the cornfield.

My task ended, I ascended the slope again, and for a while stood there immersed in pleasurable premonitions.

Everything had been accomplished swiftly and methodically within the few hours in which I had first set eyes upon this extraordinary place—everything!—love at first sight, the delightfully lightning-like wooing and winning of an incomparable maiden and heiress; the discovery of the fire creatures; the solving of the emerald problem.

And now everything was ready, crow-traps, firetraps, a bucket of irresistible salad for Blythe, a modest and tremulous avowal for Wilna as soon as her father tasted the salad and I had pleasantly notified him of my intentions concerning his lovely offspring.

Daylight faded from rose to lilac; already the mountains were growing fairy-like under that vague, diffuse lustre which heralds the rise of the full moon. It rose, enormous, yellow, unreal, becoming imperceptibly silvery as it climbed the sky and hung aloft like a stupendous arc-light flooding the world with a radiance so white and clear that I could very easily have written verses by it, if I wrote verses.

Down on the edge of the forest I could see Blythe on his camp-stool, madly besmearing his moonlit canvas, but I could not see Wilna anywhere. Maybe she had shyly retired somewhere by herself to think of me.

So I went back to the house, filled a bucket with my salad, and started toward the edge of the woods, singing happily as I sped on feet so light and frolicsome that they seemed to skim the ground. How wonderful is the power of love!

When I approached Blythe he heard me coming and turned around.

"What the devil do *you* want?" he asked with characteristic civility.

"I have brought you," said I gaily, "a bucket of salad."

"I don't want any salad!"

"W-what?"

"I never eat it at night." said confidently:

"Mr. Blythe, if you will taste this salad I am sure you will not regret it." And with hideous cunning I set the bucket beside him on the grass and seated myself near it. The old dodo grunted and continued to daub the canvas; but presently, as though forgetfully, and from sheer instinct, he reached down into the bucket, pulled out a leaf of lettuce, and shoved it into his mouth.

My heart leaped exultantly. I had him!

"Mr. Blythe," I began in a winningly modulated voice, and, at the same instant, he sprang from his camp-chair, his face distorted.

"There are onions in this salad!" he yelled. "What the devil do you mean! Are you trying to poison me! What are you following me about for, anyway? Why are you running about under foot every minute!"

"My dear Mr. Blythe," I protested—but he barked at me, kicked over the bucket of salad, and began to dance with rage.

"What's the matter with you, anyway!" he bawled. "Why are you trying to feed me? What do you mean by trying to be attentive to me!"

"I—I admire and revere you—"

"No you don't!" he shouted. "I don't want you to admire me! I don't desire to be revered! I don't like attention and politeness! Do you hear! It's artificial—out of date—ridiculous! The only thing that recommends a man to me is his bad manners, bad temper, and violent habits. There's some meaning to such a man, none at all to men like you!"

He ran at the salad bucket and kicked it again.

"They all fawned on me in Boston!" he panted. "They ran about under foot! They bought my pictures! And they made me sick! I came out here to be rid of 'em!"

I rose from the grass, pale and determined.

"You listen to me, you old grouch!" I hissed. "I'll go. But before I go I'll tell you why I've been civil to you. There's only one reason in the world: I want to marry your daughter! And I'm going to do it!"

I stepped nearer him, menacing him with outstretched hand:

"As for you, you pitiable old dodo, with your bad manners and your worse pictures, and your degraded mania for prunes, you are a necessary evil that's all, and I haven't the slightest respect for either you or your art!"

"Is that true?" he said in an altered voice.

"True?" I laughed bitterly. "Of course it's true, you miserable dauber!"

"D-dauber !" he stammered.

"Certainly! I *said* 'dauber,' and I mean it. Why, your work would shame the pictures on a child's slate!"

"Smith," he said unsteadily, "I believe I have utterly misjudged you. I believe you are a good deal of a man, after all—"

"I'm man enough," said I, fiercely, "to go back, saddle my mule, kidnap your daughter, and start for home. And I'm going to do it!"

"Wait!" he cried. "I don't want you to go. If you'll remain I'll be very glad. I'll do anything you like. I'll quarrel with you, and you can insult my pictures. It will agreeably stimulate us both. Don't go, Smith—"

"If I stay, may I marry Wilna?"

"If you ask me I won't let you!"

"Very well!" I retorted, angrily. "Then I'll marry her anyway!"

"That's the way to talk! Don't go, Smith. I'm really beginning to like you. And when Billy Green arrives you and he will have a delightfully violent scene—"

"What!"

He rubbed his hands gleefully.

"He's in love with Wilna. You and he won't get on. It is going to be very stimulating for me—I can see that! You and he are going to behave most disagreeably to each other. And I shall be exceedingly unpleasant to you both! Come, Smith, promise me that you'll stay!"

Profoundly worried, I stood staring at him in the moonlight, gnawing my mustache.

"Very well," I said, "I'll remain if—"

Something checked me, I did not quite know what for a moment. Blythe, too, was staring at me in an odd, apprehensive way. Suddenly I realised that under my feet the ground was stirring.

"Look out!" I cried; but speech froze on my lips as beneath me the solid earth began to rock and crack and billow up into a high, crumbling ridge, moving continually, as the sod cracks, heaves up, and crumbles above the subterranean progress of a mole.

Up into the air we were slowly pushed on the evergrowing ridge; and with us were carried rocks and bushes and sod, and even forest trees.

I could hear their tap-roots part with pistol-like reports; see great pines and hemlocks and oaks moving, slanting, settling, tilting crazily in every direction as they were heaved upward in this gigantic disturbance.

Blythe caught me by the arm; we clutched each other, balancing on the crest of the steadily rising mound.

"W-what is it?" he stammered. "Look! It's circular. The woods are rising in a huge circle. What's happening? Do you know?"

Over me crept a horrible certainty that *something living* was moving under us through the depths of the earth—something that, as it progressed, was heaping up the surface of the world above its unseen and burrowing course—something dreadful, enormous, sinister, and *alive!*

"Look out!" screamed Blythe; and at the same instant the crumbling summit of the ridge opened under our feet and a fissure hundreds of yards long yawned ahead of us.

And along it, shining slimily in the moonlight, a vast, viscous, ringed surface was moving, retracting, undulating, elongating, writhing, squirming, shuddering.

"It's a worm!" shrieked Blythe. "Oh, God! It's a mile long!"

As in a nightmare we clutched each other, struggling frantically to avoid the fissure; but the soft earth slid and gave way under us, and we fell heavily upon that ghastly, living surface.

Instantly a violent convulsion hurled us upward; we fell on it again, rebounding from the rubbery thing, strove to regain our feet and scramble up the edges of the fissure, strove madly while the mammoth worm slid more rapidly through the rocking forests, carrying us forward with a speed increasing.

Through the forest we tore, reeling about on the slippery back of the thing, as though riding on a plowshare, while trees clashed and tilted and fell from the enormous furrow on every side; then, suddenly out of the woods into the moonlight, far ahead of us we could see the grassy upland heave up, cake, break, and crumble above the burrowing course of the monster.

"It's making for the crater!" gasped Blythe; and horror spurred us on, and we scrambled and slipped and clawed the billowing sides of the furrow until we gained the heaving top of it.

As one runs in a bad dream, heavily, half-paralyzed, so ran Blythe and I, toiling over the undulating, tumbling upheaval until, half-fainting, we fell and rolled down the shifting slope onto solid and unvexed sod on the very edges of the crater.

Below us we saw, with sickened eyes, the entire circumference of the crater agitated, saw it rise and fall as avalanches of rock and earth slid into it, tons and thousands of tons rushing down the slope, blotting from our sight the flickering ring of flame, and extinguishing the last filmy jet of vapour.

Suddenly the entire crater caved in and filled up under my anguished eyes, quenching for all eternity the vapour wall, the fire, and burying the little denizens of the flames, and perhaps a billion dollars' worth of emeralds under as many billion tons of earth.

Quieter and quieter grew the earth as the gigantic worm bored straight down into depths immeasurable. And at last the moon shone upon a world that lay without a tremor in its milky lustre.

"I shall name it *Verma gigantica*," said I, with a hysterical sob; "but nobody will ever believe me when I tell this story!"

Still terribly shaken, we turned toward the house. And, as we approached the lamplit veranda, I saw a horse standing there and a young man hastily dismounting.

And then a terrible thing occurred; for, before I could even shriek, Wilna had put both arms around that young man's neck, and both of his arms were clasping her waist.

Blythe was kind to me. He took me around the back way and put me to bed.

And there I lay through the most awful night I ever experienced, listening to the piano below, where Wilna and William Green were singing, "Un Peu d'Amour."

In the new white marble Administration Building at Bronx Park, my private office separated the offices of Dr. Silas Quint and Professor Boomly; and it had been arranged so on purpose, because of the increasingly frequent personal misunderstanding between these two celebrated entomologists. It was very plain to me that a crisis in this quarrel was rapidly approaching.

A bitter animosity had for some months existed on both sides, born of the most intense professional jealousy. They had been friends for years. No unseemly rivalry disturbed this friendship as long as it was merely a question of collecting, preparing, and mounting for exhibition the vast numbers of butterflies and moths which haunt this insectivorous earth. Even their zeal in the eternal hunt for new and undescribed species had not made them enemies.

I am afraid that my suggestion for the construction of a great glass flying-cage for *living* specimens of moths and butterflies started the trouble between these hitherto godly and middle-aged men. That, and the Carnegie Educational Medal were the causes which began this deplorable affair.

Various field collectors, employed by both Quint and Boomly, were always out all over the world foraging for specimens; also, they were constantly returning with spoils from every quarter of the globe.

Now, to secure rare and beautiful living specimens of butterflies and moths for the crystal flying-cage was a serious and delicate job. Such tropical insects could not survive the journey of several months from the wilds of Australia, India, Asia, Africa, or the jungles of South America—nor could semi-tropical species endure the captivity of a few weeks or even days, when captured in the West Indies, Mexico, or Florida. Only our duller-coloured, smaller, and hardier native species tolerated capture and exhibition.

Therefore, the mode of procedure which I suggested was for our field expeditions to obtain males and females of the same species of butterfly or moth, mate them, and, as soon as any female deposited her eggs, place the tiny pearl-like eggs in cold storage to retard their hatching, which normally occurs, in the majority of species, within ten days or two weeks.

This now was the usual mode of procedure followed by the field collectors employed by Dr. Quint and Professor Boomly. And not only were the eggs of various butterflies and moths so packed for transportation, but a sufficient store of their various native food-plants was also preserved, where such food-plants could not be procurred in the United States. So when the eggs arrived at Bronx Park, and were hatched there in due time, the young caterpillars had plenty of nourishment ready for them in cold storage.

Might I not, legitimately, have expected the Carnegie Educational Medal for all this? I have never received it. I say this without indignation—even without sorrow. I merely make the statement.

Yet, my system was really a very beautiful system; a tiny batch of eggs would arrive from Ceylon, or Sumatra, or Africa; when taken from cold storage and placed in the herbarium they would presently hatch; the caterpillars were fed with their accustomed food-plant—a few leaves being taken from cold storage every day for them—they would pass through their three or four moulting periods, cease feeding in due time, transform into the chrysalis stage, and finally appear in all the splendour and magnificence of butterfly or moth.

The great glass flying-cage was now alive with superb moths and butterflies, flitting, darting, fluttering among the flowering bushes or feeding along the sandy banks of the brook which flowed through the flying-cage, bordered by thickets of scented flowers. And it was like looking at a meteoric shower of winged jewels, where the huge metallic-blue *Morphos* from South America flapped and sailed, and; the orange and gold and green *Ornithoptera* from

Borneo pursued their majestic, bird-like flight—where big, glitter-ing *Papilios* flashed through the bushes or alighted nervously to feed for a few moments on jasmine and phlox, and where the slowly flopping *Heliconians* winged their way amid the denser tangles of tropical vegetation.

Nothing like this flying-cage had ever before been seen in New York; thousands and thousands of men, women, and children thronged the lawn about the flying-cage all day long.

By night, also, the effect was wonderful; the electric lights among the foliage broke out; the great downy-winged moths, which had been asleep all day while the butterflies flitted through the sunshine, now came out to display their crimson or peacock-spot-ted wings, and the butterflies folded their wings and went to bed for the night.

The public was enchanted, the authorities of the Bronx proud and delighted; all apparently was happiness and harmony. Except that nobody offered me the Carnegie medal.

I was sitting one morning in my office, which, as I have said, separated the offices of Dr. Quint and Professor Boomly, when there came a loud rapping on my door, and, at my invitation, Dr. Quint bustled in—a little, meagre, excitable, near-sighted man with pointed mustaches and a fleck of an imperial smudging his lower lip.

"Last week," he began angrily, "young Jones arrived from Singapore bringing me the eggs of *Erebia astarte*, the great Silver Moon butterfly. Attempts to destroy them have been made. Last night I left them in a breeding-cage on my desk. Has anybody been in there?"

"I don't know," I said. "What has happened?"

"I found an ichneumon fly in the cage yesterday!" he shouted; "and this morning the eggs have either shrunk to half their size or else the eggs of another species have been secretly substituted for them and the Silver Moon eggs stolen! Has *he* been in there?"

"Who?" I asked, pretending to misunderstand.

"*He!*" demanded Quint fiercely. "If he has I'll kill him some day."

He meant his one-time friend, Dr. Boomly. Alas!

"For heaven's sake, why are you two perpetually squabbling?" I asked wearily. "You used to be inseparable friends. Why can't you make up?"

"Because I've come to know him. That's why! I have unmasked this—this Borgia—this Machiavelli—this monster of duplicity! Matters are approaching a point where something has got to be done short of murder. I've stood all his envy and jealousy and cheap imputations and hints and contemptible innuendoes that I'm going to—"

He stopped short, glaring at the doorway, which had suddenly been darkened by the vast bulk of Professor Boomly—a figure largely abdominal but majestic—like the massive butt end of an elephant. For the rest, he had a rather insignificant and peevish face and a melancholy mustache that usually looked damp.

"Mr. Smith," he said to me, in his thin, high, sarcastic voice—a voice incongruously at variance with his bulk— "has anybody had the infernal impudence to enter my room and nose about my desk?"

"Yes, *I* have!" replied Quint excitedly. "I've been in your room. What of it? What about it?"

Boomly permitted his heavy-lidded eyes to rest on Quint for a moment, then, turning to me: "I want a patent lock put on my door. Will you speak to Professor Farrago?"

"I want one put on mine, too!" cried Quint. "I want a lock put on my door which will keep envious, dull-minded, mentally broken-down, impertiment, and fat people out of my office!"

Boomly flushed heavily.

"Fat?" he repeated, glaring at Quint. "Did you say 'fat?'"

"Yes, *fat*—intellectually and corporeally fat! I want that kind of individual kept out. I don't trust them. I'm afraid of them. Their minds are atrophied. They are unmoral, possibly even criminal! I don't want them in my room snooping about to see what I have and what I'm doing. I don't want them to sneak in, eaten up with jealousy and envy, and try to damage the eggs of the Silver Moon butterfly because the honour and glory of hatching them would probably procure for me the Carnegie Educational Medal—"

"Why, you little, dried-up, protoplasmic atom!" burst out Boomly, his face suffused with passion, "Are you insinuating that I have any designs on your batch of eggs?"

"It's my belief," shouted Quint, "that you want that medal your-self, and that you put an ichneumon fly in my breeding-cage in hopes it would sting the eggs of the Silver Moon."

"If you found an ichneumon fly there," retorted Boomly, "you probably hatched it in mistake for a butterfly!" And he burst into a peal of contemptuous laughter, but his little, pig-like eyes under the heavy lids were furious.

"I now believe," said Quint, trembling with rage, "that you have criminally substituted a batch of common *Plexippus* eggs for the Silver Moon eggs I had in my breeding-cage! I believe you are suf-ficiently abandoned to do it!"

"Ha! Ha!" retorted Boomly scornfully. "I don't believe you ever had anything in your breeding-cage except a few clothes moths and cockroaches!"

Quint began to dance: "You *did* take them!" he yelled; "and you left me a bunch of milkweed butterflies' eggs! Give me my eggs or I shall violently assault you!"

"Assault your grandmother!" remarked Boomly, with unscien-tific brevity. "What do you suppose I want of your ridiculous eggs? Haven't I enough eggs of *Heliconius salome* hatching to give me the Carnegie medal if I want it?"

"The Silver Moon eggs are unique!" cried Quint. "You know it! You know that if they hatch, pupate, and become perfect insects that I shall certainly be awarded—"

"You'll be awarded the Matteawan medal," remarked Boomly with venom.

Quint ran at him with a half-suppressed howl, his momentum carrying him halfway up Professor Boomly's person. Then, losing foothold, he fell to the floor and began to kick in the general direc-tion of Professor Boomly.

It was a sorrowful sight to see these two celebrated scientists panting, mauling, scuffling and punching each other around the room, tables and chairs and scrapbaskets flying in every direction, and I mounted on the window-sill horrified, speechless, trying to keep clear of the revolving storm centre.

"Where are my Silver Moon eggs!" screamed Dr. Quint. "Where are my eggs that Jones brought me from Singapore—you entomological robber! You've got 'em somewhere! If you don't give 'em up I'll find means to destroy you!"

"You insignificant pair of maxillary palpi!" bellowed Professor Boomly, galloping after Dr. Quint as he dodged around my desk. "I'll pull off those antennæ you call whiskers if I can get hold of 'em—"

Dr. Quint's threatened mustaches bristled as he fled before the elephantine charge of Professor Boomly—once again around my desk, then out into the hall, where I heard the door of his office slam, and Boomly, gasping, panting, breathing vengeance outside, and vowing to leave Quint quite whiskerless when he caught him.

It was a painful scene for scientists to figure in or to gaze upon. Profoundly shocked and upset, I locked up the anthropological department offices and went out into the Park, where the sun was shining and a gentle June wind stirred the trees.

Too completely upset to do any more work that day, I wandered about amid the gaily dressed crowds at hazard; sometimes I contemplated the monkeys; sometimes gazed sadly upon the seals. They dashed and splashed and raced round and round their tank, or crawled up on the rocks, craned their wet, sleek necks, and barked—houp! houp! houp!

For luncheon I went over to the Rolling Stone Restaurant. There was a very pretty girl there—an unusually pretty girl—or perhaps it was one of those days on which every girl looked unusually pretty to me. There are such days.

Her voice was exquisite when she spoke. She said:

"We have, today, corned beef hash, fried ham and eggs, liver and bacon—" but let that pass, too.

I took my tea very weak; by that time I learned that her name was Mildred Case; that she had been a private detective employed in a department store, and that her duties had been to nab wealthy ladies who forgot to pay for objects usually discovered in their reticules, bosoms, and sometimes in their stockings.

But the confinement of indoor work had been too much for Mildred Case, and the only out-door job she could find was the position of lady waitress in the rustic Rolling Stone Inn.

She was very, very beautiful, or perhaps it was one of those days—but let that pass, too.

"You are the great Mr. Percy Smith, Curator of the Anthropological Department, are you not?" she asked shyly.

"Yes," I said modestly; and, to slightly rebuke any superfluous
pride in me, I paraphrased with becoming humility, pointing upward: "but remember, Mildred, there is One greater than I."

"Mr. Carnegie?" she nodded innocently. That was true, too. I
let it go at that.

We chatted: she mentioned Professor Boomly and Dr. Quint,
gently deploring the rupture of their friendship. Both gentlemen,
in common with the majority of the administration personnel, were
daily customers at the Rolling Stone Inn. I usually took my lunch
from my boarding-house to my office, being too busy to go out for
mere nourishment. That is why I had hitherto missed Mildred Case.

"Mildred," I said, "I do not believe it can be wholesome for a
man to eat sandwiches while taking minute measurements of de-
funct monkeys. Also, it is not a fragrant pastime. Hereafter I shall
lunch here."

"It will be a pleasure to serve you," said that unusually—there
I go again! It was an unusually beautiful day in June. Which careful, exact, and scientific statement, I think ought to cover the subject under consideration.

After luncheon I sadly selected a five-cent cigar; and, as I hesitated, lingering over the glass case, undecided still whether to give
full rein to this contemplated extravagance, I looked up and found
her beautiful grey eyes gazing into mine.

"What gentle thoughts are yours, Mildred?" I said softly.

"The cigar you have selected," she murmured, "is fly-specked."

Deeply touched that this young girl should have cared—that she
should have expressed her solicitude so modestly, so sweetly, concerning the maculatory condition of my cigar, I thanked her and
purchased, for the same sum, a packet of cigarettes.

That was going somewhat far for me. I had never in all my life
even dreamed of smoking a cigarette. To a reserved, thoughtful,
and scientific mind there is, about a packet of cigarettes, something undignified, something vaguely frolicsome.

When I paid her for them I felt as though, for the first time in
my life, I had let myself go.

Oddly enough, in this uneasy feeling of gaiety and abandon, a curious sensation of exhilaration persisted.

We had quite a merry little contretemps when I tried to light my cigarette and the match went out, and then *she* struck another match, and we both laughed, and *that* match was extinguished by her breath.

Instantly I quoted: "'Her breath was like the new-mown hay—'"

"Mr. Smith!" she said, flushing slightly.

"'Her eyes,' I quoted, 'were like the stars at even!'"

"You don't mean *my* eyes, do you?"

I took a puff at my unlighted cigarette. It also smelled like recently mown hay. I felt that I was slipping my cables and heading toward an unknown and tempestuous sea.

"What time are you free, Mildred?" I asked, scarcely recognising my own voice in such reckless apropos.

She shyly informed me.

I struck a match, re-lighted my cigarette, and took one puff. That was sufficient: I was adrift. I realised it, trembled internally, took another puff.

"If," said I carelessly, "on your way home you should chance to stroll along the path beyond the path that leads to the path which—"

I paused, checked by her bewildered eyes. We both blushed.

"Which way do you usually go home?" I asked, my ears afire.

She told me. It was a suitably unfrequented path.

So presently I strolled thither; and seated myself under the trees in a bosky dell.

Now, there is a quality in boskiness not inappropriate to romantic thoughts. Boskiness, cigarettes, a soft afternoon in June, the hum of bees, and the distant barking of the seals, all these were delicately blending to inspire in me a bashful sentiment.

A specimen of *Papilio turnus*, di-morphic form, *Glaucus*, alighted near me; I marked its flight with scientific indifference. Yet it is a rare species in Bronx Park.

A mock-orange bush was in snowy bloom behind me; great bunches of wistaria hung over the rock beside me.

The combination of these two exquisite perfumes seemed to make the boskiness more bosky.

There was an unaccustomed and sportive lightness to my step when I rose to meet Mildred, where she came loitering along the shadow-dappled path.

She seemed surprised to see me.

She thought it rather late to sit down, but she seated herself. I talked to her enthusiastically about anthropology. She was so interested that after a while she could scarcely keep still, moving her slim little feet restlessly, biting her pretty lower lip, shifting her position—all certain symptoms of an interest in science which even approached excitement.

Warmed to the heart by her eager and sympathetic interest in the noble science so precious, so dear to me, I took her little hand to soothe and quiet her, realizing that she might become overexcited as I described the pituitary body and why its former functions had become atrophied until the gland itself was nearly obsolete.

So intense her interest had been that she seemed a little tired. I decided to give adequate material support to her spinal process. It seemed to rest and soothe her. I don't remember that she said anything except: "Mr. *Smith!*" I don't recollect what we were saying when she mentioned me by name rather abruptly.

The afternoon was wonderfully still and calm. The month was June.

After a while—quite a while—some little time in point of accurate fact—she detected the sound of approaching footsteps.

I remember that she was seated at the opposite end of the bench, rather feverishly occupied with her hat and her hair, when young Jones came hastily along the path, caught sight of us, halted, turned violently red—being a shy young man—but instead of taking himself off, he seemed to recover from a momentary paralysis.

"Mr. Smith!" he said sharply. "Professor Boomly has disappeared; there's a pool of blood on his desk; his coat, hat, and waistcoat are lying on the floor, the room is a wreck, and Dr. Quint is in there tearing up the carpet and behaving like a madman. We think he suddenly went insane and murdered Professor Boomly. What is to be done?"

Horrified, I had risen at his first word. And now, as I understood the full purport of his dreadful message, my hair stirred under my hat and I gazed at him, appalled.

"What is to be done?" he demanded. "Shall I telephone for the police?"

"Do you actually believe," I faltered, "that this unfortunate man has murdered Boomly?"

"I don't know. I looked over the transom, but I couldn't see Professor Boomly. Dr. Quint has locked the door."

"And he's tearing up the carpet?"

"Like a lunatic. I didn't want to call in the police until I'd asked you. Such a scandal in Bronx Park would be a frightful thing for us all—" He hesitated, looked around, coldly, it seemed to me, at Mildred Case. "A scandal," he repeated, "is scarcely what might be expected among a harmonious and earnest band of seekers after scientific knowledge. Is it, Mil—Miss Case?"

Now, I don't know why Mildred should have blushed. There was nothing that I could see in this young man's question to embarrass her.

Preoccupied, still confused by the shock of this terrible news, I looked at Jones and at Mildred; and they were staring rather oddly at each other. I said: "If this affair turns out to be as ghastly as it seems to promise, we'll have to call in a detective. I'll go back immediately."

"Why not take me, also?" asked Mildred Case, quietly.

"What?" I asked, looking at her.

"Why not, Mr. Smith? I was once a private detective."

Surprised at the suggestion, I hesitated.

"If you desire to keep this matter secret—if you wish to have it first investigated privately and quietly—would it not be a good idea to let me use my professional knowledge before you call in the police? Because as soon as the police are summoned all hope of avoiding publicity is at an end."

She spoke so sensibly, so quietly, so modestly, that her offer of assistance deeply impressed me.

As for young Jones, he looked at her steadily in that odd, chilling manner, which finally annoyed me. There was no need of his being snobbish because this very lovely and intelligent young girl happened to be a waitress at the Rolling Stone Inn.

"Come," I said unsteadily, again a prey to terrifying emotions; "let us go to the Administration Building and learn how matters

stand. If this affair is as terrible as I fear it to be, science has received the deadliest blow ever dealt it since Cagliostro perished."

As we three strode hastily along the path in the direction of the
Administration Building, I took that opportunity to read these two
youthful fellow beings a sermon on envy, jealousy, and covet-
eousness.

"See," said I, "to what a miserable condition the desire for no-
toriety and fame has brought two learned and enthusiastic delvers
in the vineyard of endeavor! The mad desire for the Carnegie medal
completely turned the hitherto perfectly balanced brains of these
devoted disciples of Science. Envy begat envy, jealousy begat jealousy, pride begat pride, hatred begat hatred—"

"It's like that book in the Bible where everybody begat everybody else," said Mildred seriously.

At first I thought she had made an apt and clever remark; but
on thinking it over I couldn't quite see its relevancy. I turned and
looked into her sweet face. Her eyes were dancing with brilliancy
and her sensitive lips quivered. I feared she was near to tears from
the reaction of the shock. Had Jones not been walking with us—
but let that go, too.

We were now entering the Administration Building, almost
running; and as soon as we came to the closed door of Dr. Quint's
room, I could hear a commotion inside—desk drawers being pulled
out and their contents dumped, curtains being jerked from their
rings, an unmistakable sound indicating the ripping up of a carpet—
and through all this din the agitated scuffle of footsteps.

I rapped on the door. No notice taken. I rapped and knocked
and called in a low, distinct voice.

Suddenly I recollected I had a general pass-key on my ring
which unlocked any door in the building. I nodded to Jones and to
Mildred to stand aside, then, gently fitting the key, I suddenly
pushed out the key which remained on the inside, turned the lock,
and flung open the door.

A terrible sight presented itself: Dr. Quint, hair on end, both
mustaches pulled out, shirt, cuffs, and white waistcoat smeared
with blood, knelt amid the general wreckage on the floor, in the
act of ripping up the carpet.

"Doctor!" I cried in a trembling voice. "What have you done to Professor Boomly?"

He paused in his carpet ripping and looked around at us with a terrifying laugh.

"I've settled *him!*" he said. "If you don't want to get all over dust you'd better keep out "

"Quint!" I cried. "Are you crazy?"

"Pretty nearly. Let me alone—"

"Where is Boomly!" I demanded in a tragic voice. "Where is your old friend, Billy Boomly? Where is he, Quint? And what does *that* mean—that pool of blood on the floor? Whose is it?"

"It's Bill's," said Quint, coolly ripping up another breadth of carpet and peering under it.

"What!" I exclaimed. "Do you admit that?"

"Certainly I admit it. I told him I'd terminate him if he meddled with my Silver Moon eggs."

"You mean to say that you shed blood—the blood of your old friend—merely because he meddled with a miserable batch of butterfly's eggs?" I asked, astounded.

"I certainly did shed his blood for just that particular thing! And listen; you're in my way—you're standing on a part of the carpet which I want to tear up. Do you mind moving?"

Such cold-blooded calmness infuriated me. I sprang at Quint, seized him, and shouted to Jones to tie his hands behind him with the blood-soaked handkerchief which lay on the floor.

At first, while Jones and I were engaged in the operation of securing the wretched man, Quint looked at us both as though surprised; then he grew angry and asked us what the devil we were about.

"Those who shed blood must answer for it!" I said solemnly.

"What? What's the matter with you?" he demanded in a rage. "Shed blood? What if I did? What's that to you? Untie this handkerchief, you unmentionable idiot!"

I looked at Jones:

"His mind totters," I said hoarsely.

"What's that!" cried Quint, struggling to get off the chair whither I had pushed him: but with my handkerchief we tied his ankles to the rung of the chair, heedless of his attempts to kick us, and sprang back out of range.

"Now," I said, "what have you done with the poor victim of your fury? Where is he? Where is all that remains of Professor Boomly?"

"Boomly? I don't know where he is. How the devil should I know?"

"Don't lie," I said solemnly.

"Lie! See here, Smith, when I get out of this chair I'll settle you, too—"

"Quint! There is another and more terrible chair which awaits such criminals as you!"

"You old fluff!" he shouted. "I'll knock your head off, too. Do you understand? I'll attend to you as I attended to Boomly—"

"Assassin!" I retorted calmly. "Only an alienist can save you now. In this awful moment—"

A light touch on my arm interrupted me, and, a trifle irritated, as any man might be when checked in the full flow of eloquence, I turned to find Mildred at my elbow.

"Let me talk to him," she said in a quiet voice. "Perhaps I may not irritate him as you seem to."

"Very well," I said. "Jones and I are here as witnesses." And I folded my arms in an attitude not, perhaps, unpicturesque.

"Dr. Quint," said Mildred in her soft, agreeable voice, and actually smiling slightly at the self-confessed murderer, "is it really true that you are guilty of shedding the blood of Professor Boomly?"

"It is," said Quint, coolly.

She seemed rather taken aback at that, but presently recovered her equanimity.

"Why?" she asked gently.

"Because he attempted a most hellish crime!" yelled Quint.

"W-what crime?" she asked faintly.

"I'll tell you. He wanted the Carnegie medal and he knew it would be given to me if I could incubate and hatch my batch of Silver Moon butterfly eggs. He realised well enough that his *Heliconian* eggs were not as valuable as my Silver Moon eggs. So first he sneaked in here and put an ichneumon fly in my breeding-cage. And next he stole the Silver Moon eggs and left in their place some common *Plexippus* eggs, thinking that because they were very similar I would not notice the substitution.

"I did notice it! I charged him with that cataclysmic outrage. He laughed. We came into personal collision. He chased me into my room."

Panting, breathless with rage at the memory of the morning's defeat which I had witnessed, Quint glared at me for a moment. Then he jerked his head toward Mildred:

"As soon as he went to luncheon—Boomly, I mean—I climbed over that transom and dropped into this room. I had been hunting for ten minutes before I found my Silver Moon eggs hidden under the carpet. So I pocketed them, climbed back over the transom, and went to my room."

He paused dramatically, staring from one to another of us:

"Boomly was there!" he said slowly.

"Where?" asked Mildred with a shudder.

"In my room. He had picked the lock. I told him to get out! He went. I shouted after him that I had recovered the Silver Moon eggs and that I should certainly be awarded the Carnegie medal.

"Then that monster in human form laughed a horrible laugh, avowing himself guilty of a crime still more hideous than the theft of the Silver Moon eggs! Do you know what he had done?"

"W-what?" faltered Mildred.

"He had stolen from cold storage and had concealed the leaves of the Bimba bush, brought from Singapore to feed the Silver Moon caterpillars! *That's* what Boomly had done!

"*And my Silver Moon eggs had already begun to hatch!!! And my caterpillars would starve!!!!*"

His voice ended in a yell; he struggled on his chair until it nearly upset.

"You lunatic!" I shouted. "Was that a reason for spilling the blood of a human being!"

"It was reason enough for me!"

"Madman!"

"Let me loose! He's hidden those leaves somewhere or other! I've torn this place to pieces looking for them. I've got to find them, I tell you—"

Mildred went to the infuriated entomologist and laid a firm hand on his shoulder:

"Listen," she said: "how do you know that Professor Boomly has not concealed these Bimba leaves on his own person?"

Quint ceased his contortions and gaped at her.

"I never thought of that," he said.

"What have you done with him?" she asked, very pale.

"I tell you, I don't know."

"You must know what you did with him," she insisted.

Quint shook his head impatiently, apparently preoccupied with other thoughts. We stood watching him in silence until he looked up and became conscious of our concentrated gaze.

"My caterpillars are starving," he began violently. "I haven't anything else they'll eat. They feed only on the Bimba leaf. They *won't* eat anything else. It's a well-known fact that they won't. Why, in Johore, where they came from, they'll travel miles over the ground to find a Bimba bush—"

"What!" exclaimed Mildred.

"Certainly—miles! They'd starve sooner than eat anything except Bimba leaves. If there's a bush within twenty miles they'll find it—"

"Wait," said Mildred quietly. "Where are these starving caterpillars?"

"In a glass jar in my pocket—here! What the devil are you doing!" For the girl had dexterously slipped the glass jar from his coat pocket and was holding it up to the light.

Inside it were several dozen tiny, dark caterpillars, some resting disconsolately on the sides of the glass, some hungrily travelling over the bottom in pitiful and hopeless quest of nourishment.

Heedless of the shouts and threats of Dr. Quint, the girl calmly uncorked the jar, took on her slender forefinger a single little caterpillar, replaced the cork, and, kneeling down, gently disengaged the caterpillar. It dropped upon the floor, remained motionless for a moment, then, turning, began to travel rapidly toward the doorway behind us.

"Now," she said, "if poor Professor Boomly really has concealed these Bimba leaves upon his own person, this little caterpillar, according to Dr. Quint, is certain to find those leaves."

Overcome with excitement and admiration for this intelligent and unusually beautiful girl, I seized her hands and congratulated her.

"Murder," said I to the miserable Quint, "will out! This infant caterpillar shall lead us to that dark and secret spot where you had hoped to conceal the horrid evidence of your guilt. Three things have undone you—a caterpillar replete with mysterious instinct, a humble bunch of Bimba leaves, and the marvellous intelligence of this young and lovely girl. Madman, your hour has struck!"

He looked at me in a dazed sort of way, as though astonishment had left him unable to articulate. But I had become tired of his violence and his shouts and yells; so I asked Jones for his handkerchief, and, before Quint knew what I was up to I had tied it over his mouth.

He became a brilliant purple, but all he could utter was a furious humming, buzzing noise.

Meanwhile, Jones had opened the door; the little caterpillar, followed by Mildred and myself, continued to hustle along as though he knew quite well where he was going.

Down the hallway he went in undulating haste, past my door, we all following in silent excitement as we discovered that, parallel to the caterpillar's course, ran a gruesome trail of blood drops.

And when the little creature turned and made straight for the door of Professor Farrago, our revered chief, the excitement among us was terrific.

The caterpillar halted; I gently tried the door; it was open.

Instantly the caterpillar crossed the threshold, wriggling forward at top speed. We followed, peering fearfully around us. Nobody was visible.

Could Quint have dragged his victim here?

By Heaven, he had! For the caterpillar was travelling straight under the lounge upon which Professor Farrago was accustomed to repose after luncheon, and, dropping on one knee, I saw a fat foot partly protruding from under the shirred edges of the fringed drapery.

"He's there!" I whispered, in an awed voice to the others. "Courage, Miss Case! Try not to faint."

Jones turned and looked at her with that same odd expression; then he went over to where she stood and coolly passed one arm around her waist. "Try not to faint, Mildred," he said. "It might muss your hair."

It was a strange thing to say, but I had no time then to analyze it, for I had seized the fat foot which partly protruded from under the sofa, clad in a low-cut congress gaiter and a white sock.

And then *I* nearly fainted, for instead of the dreadful, inert resistance of lifeless clay, the foot wriggled and tried to kick at me.

"Help!" came a thin but muffled voice. "Help! Help, in the name of Heaven!"

"Boomly!" I cried, scarcely believing my ears.

"Take that man away, Smith!" whimpered Boomly. "He's a devil! He'll murder me! He made my nose bleed all over everything!"

"Boomly! You're *not* dead!"

"Yes, I am!" he whined. "I'm dead enough to suit me. Keep that little lunatic off—that's all I ask. He can have his Carnegie medal for all I care, only tie him up somewhere—"

"Professor Boomly!" cried Mildred excitedly. "Have you any Bimba leaves concealed about your person?"

"Yes, I have," he said sulkily. There came a hitch of the fat foot, a heavy scuffling sound, heavy panting, and then, skittering out across the floor came a flat, sealed parcel.

"There you are," he said; "now, let me alone until that fiend has gone home."

"He won't attack you again," I said. "Come out."

But Professor Boomly flatly declined to stir.

I looked at the parcel: it was marked: "Bimba leaves; Johore."

With a sigh of unutterable relief, I picked up the ravenous little caterpillar, placed him on the packet, and turned to go. And didn't.

It is a very sickening fact I have now to record. But to a scientist all facts are sacred, sickening or otherwise.

For what I caught a glimpse of, just outside the door in the hallway, was Jones kissing Mildred Case. And being shyly indemnified for his trouble with a gentle return in kind. Both his arms were around her waist; both her hands rested upon his shoulders; and, as I looked—but let it pass!—let it pass.

Deliberately I fished in my pocket, found my packet of cigarettes, lighted one.

Tobacco diffugiunt mordaces curae et laetificat cor hominis!

Coachwhip Publications

CoachwhipBooks.com

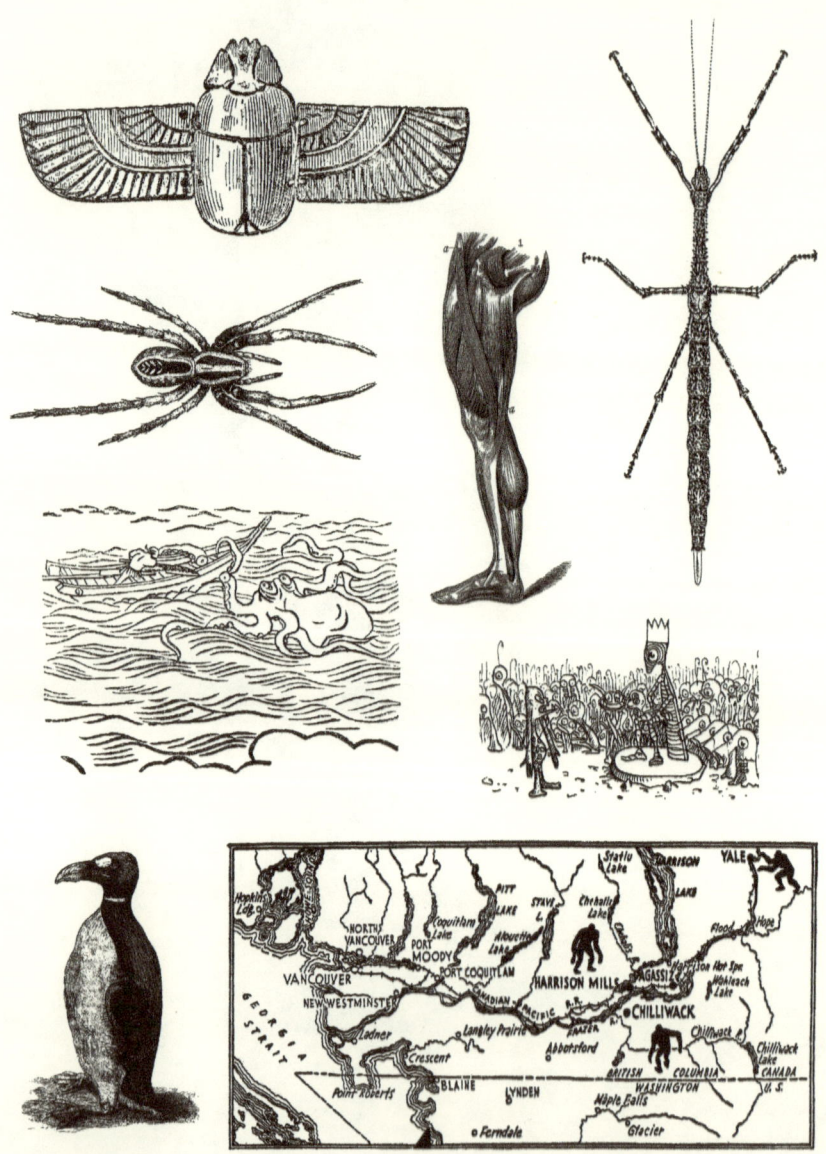

Coachwhip Books.com
Also Available

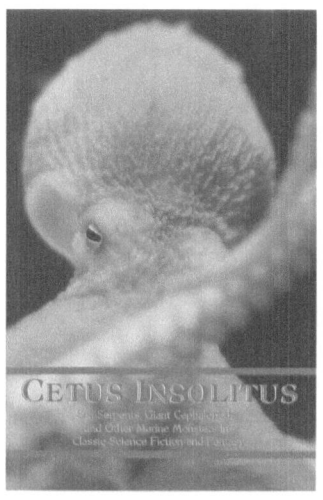

Sea Monsters

Killer Plants

Dinosaurs Amuck

Deadly Bugs